ACCLAIM FOR JANE LANGTON AND HER
DIVINE INSPIRATION

"Langton . . . gathers the various plot strands into as neat a bow as you'll find . . . [It's] perfect."
—*New York Daily News*

"Simply divine . . . Langton has emerged as one of the best of U.S. mystery writers, the American equivalent of Britain's Ruth Rendell and P. D. James."
—*San Diego Union-Tribune*

"A 'Laura'-like love story, a vivid cadre of organists and a much-beset minister are further pleasures in Langton's lively work."
—*Los Angeles Times Book Review*

"A satisfying and entertaining mystery . . . plenty of humor and suspense, [and] a wealth of eccentric characters . . . Highly recommended."
—*Booklist*

PENGUIN CRIME FICTION

DIVINE INSPIRATION

Jane Langton is the author of *God in Concord* and eight other Homer Kelly mysteries. She lives in Lincoln, Massachusetts.

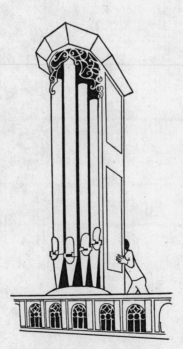

DIVINE
INSPIRATION

◆ ◆ ◆ ◆ ◆

A Homer Kelly Mystery

JANE LANGTON

PENGUIN BOOKS

PENGUIN BOOKS
Published by the Penguin Group
Penguin Books USA Inc., 375 Hudson Street, New York, New York 10014, U.S.A.
Penguin Books Ltd, 27 Wrights Lane, London W8 5TZ, England
Penguin Books Australia Ltd, Ringwood, Victoria, Australia
Penguin Books Canada Ltd, 10 Alcorn Avenue, Toronto, Ontario, Canada M4V 3B2
Penguin Books (N.Z.) Ltd, 182–190 Wairau Road, Auckland 10, New Zealand

Penguin Books Ltd, Registered Offices: Harmondsworth, Middlesex, England

First published in the United States of America by Viking Penguin,
a division of Penguin Books USA Inc., 1993
Published in Penguin Books 1994

1 3 5 7 9 10 8 6 4 2

Line drawings by the author

PUBLISHER'S NOTE
This is a work of fiction. Names, characters, places, and incidents either are the product of
the author's imagination or are used fictitiously, and any resemblance to actual persons,
living or dead, events, or locales is entirely coincidental.

ACKNOWLEDGMENTS
Martin Luther quotations on pages 50, 201, 219, 382, and 398 are from *Luther, His Life and
Times* by Richard Friedenthal and are used by permission of Weidenfeld and Nicolson,
Ltd. Other Luther quotations are from *The Table Talk of Martin Luther*, translated and edited
by William Hazlitt, H. G. Bohn, 1857; *Martin Luther, the Man and His Work*, by Arthur C.
McGiffert, Century, 1912; and *The Hymns of Martin Luther*, edited by Leonard Woolsey
Bacon and Nathan H. Allen, Scribner's, 1883. The words to Luther's hymn "A Mighty
Fortress" were translated by Frederick Hedge. Luther's hymn texts on pages 370, 384, and
391 were translated by Jane Langton, whose translation of one verse of a chorus from
Bach's *St. John Passion* appears on page 227. A few passages from Martin Luther and J. S.
Bach are from Albert Schweitzer's *J. S. Bach*, Breitkopf & Härtel, 1911.
    Five measures from J. S. Bach's "Magnificat" are used by permission of C. F. Peters
Corporation. The music for eight of Bach's chorales is from *371 Vierstimmige Choralgesänge
von Johann Sebastian Bach*, Breitkopf & Härtel, 1845. The two measures from the choral
prelude "In dir ist Freude" from Bach's *Little Organ Book* are used by permission of Edwin
F. Kalmus.

THE LIBRARY OF CONGRESS HAS CATALOGUED THE HARDCOVER AS FOLLOWS:
Langton, Jane.
Divine inspiration: a Homer Kelly mystery/Jane Langton.
p. cm.
ISBN 0-670-84709-7 (hc.)
ISBN 0 14 01.7376 5 (pbk.)
1. Kelly, Homer (Fictitious character)—Fiction.
2. Lawyers—Massachusetts—Fiction. I. Title.
PS3562.A515D5 1993
813´54—dc20   93–1693

Printed in the United States of America
Set in Postscript Bembo
Designed by Ann Gold

FOR AUDREY AND EDWIN BRIGGS
AND FOR LIBBY BLANK

PROLOGUE

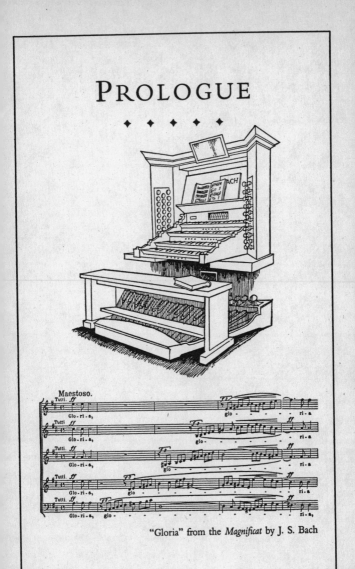

"Gloria" from the *Magnificat* by J. S. Bach

T wo introductions must be made at once.

The first is to the new pipe organ in the Church of the Commonwealth in Boston's Back Bay.

It is an American organ, made in Marblehead, trucked down to Boston and installed in the balcony of the church by the local representative of the maker, organist and organ builder Alan Starr. Eagerly hovering over Alan as he works is the music director of the Church of the Commonwealth, James Castle. It is Castle who chose the builder and the specifications. When the organ is ready, Castle will play it.

Starr has spent weeks setting it up, fastening in place the tall wooden cases and standing in their racks thirty-nine of the ranks of pipes above their wind chests, and settling the console into its niche at the front of the balcony. All the delicate tracker mechanisms have been assembled. Henceforth a pulled stop knob will withdraw the gag from a row of pipes and a struck key will activate a hinged rod, permitting a single pipe to sound its note.

There is still much work to be done. Alan will spend months adjusting the open mouths of the pipes with his delicate tuning and voicing tools, listening and changing, nicking and prying, until each reed and flue pipe speaks its note correctly in the reverberating chamber that is the sanctuary of the Church of the Commonwealth.

Not everyone is happy about the new organ. "There we were with the finest pipe organ in Boston," complains church treasurer Kenneth Possett. "Granted, it was half destroyed in the fire, but surely it could have been repaired. I must say, I blame

Reverend Kraeger. Oh, not just because it was his carelessness that started the fire. It's his whole attitude toward Castle. Whatever Castle wants, Castle gets. And damn the expense."

"You'd think Castle would have been satisfied with the biggest instrument in New England," grumbles old Dennis Partridge, a member of the Music Committee. "Five keyboards and fourteen thousand pipes!"

"Oh, the man's a musical snob. The old organ was out of style, that was the trouble. The rage right now is for this old-fashioned kind. Everybody wants to abandon their magnificent electropneumatic pipe organs and go back to mechanical action. It's as if the advancements of science had never happened."

"Maybe it was a conspiracy, the fire that destroyed the organ and killed that poor sexton. Maybe Kraeger and Castle set the fire together. I'm only joking, of course."

"Maybe it's no joke."

But there are supporters as well as detractors for Castle's new organ. Martin Kraeger himself, the minister, is its principal champion. On the day the first truckload arrived from Marblehead he was there on the sidewalk, eager to lend a hand. He carted in some of the pipe trays himself, supporting them on his belly with his powerful arms, shouting questions, wanting to know what the labels meant—*Nazard, Tierce, Prestant.*

Edith Frederick is another staunch defender. Mrs. Frederick is even more ignorant about pipe organs than Kraeger—she doesn't know Bourdon from Chimney Flute or Mixture from Diapason—but she is the sole trustee of the music endowment that has come down in her late husband's family. The endowment is enormous.

After the fire Mrs. Frederick came forward with her arms full of money. "The best," she said to James Castle. "Get the very best."

And he had. On the day the organ arrived, Castle astonished his student, Alan Starr, by saying something sentimental as they carried one of the sixteen-foot pipe trays into the church. Normally a wry and witty man, he said baldly, "Glory, that's what we're going to have here. Glory, nothing less."

"Well, sure," agreed Alan. "Glory it is. Hey, watch out for that corner."

The glory, of course, was bound up in the sensitive mechanisms of the tracker rods and in Castle's choice of stops. Any organist, reading the list of specifications, would recognize their possibilities.

GREAT DIVISION

Bourdon 16' (wood)

Prestant 8' (I–II)

Spitzflute 8'

Octave 4'

Chimney Flute 4'

Nazard 2⅔'

Fifteenth 2' (I–II)

Tierce 1⅗'

Cornet II–V

Mixture V–IX

Double Trumpet 16'

Trumpet en Chamade 8'

Clarion 4'

Zimbelstern

CHOIR DIVISION

Stopped Diapason 8'

Prestant 4'

Spire Flute 4'

Fifteenth 2'

Larigot 1⅓'

Mixture II–III

Glockenspiel ½'

Regal 8'

POSITIVE DIVISION

Violin Diapason 8'

Chimney Flute 8'

Italian Principal 4'

Nazard 2⅔'

Doublet 2'

Quarte de Nazard 2'

Tierce 1⅗'

Mixture IV

Cymbal III

Cremona 8'

English Horn 8'

SWELL DIVISION

Spindle Flute 8'

Viola da Gamba 8'

Voix Celeste 8'

Gemshorn 4'

Night Horn 2'

Clarion Mixture V–VI

Bärpfeiffe 16'

Trumpet 8'

PEDAL DIVISION

Prestant 16′	Mixture V
Bourdon 16′	Contra Bombarde 32′
Octave 8′	Trombone 16′
Rohrpipe 8′	Trumpet 8′
Superoctave 4′	Clarion 4′

COUPLERS

Great, Positive, Swell, Choir to Pedal	Swell to Positive
	Balanced Swell Pedal
Positive, Swell, Choir to Great	Balanced Crescendo Pedal

So much for the first introduction.

The second is to an occupant of the house next door to the church. The name of this resident of 115 Commonwealth Avenue is Charles Hall. Charley was born fourteen months ago in Brigham and Women's Hospital. At birth his specifications were as follows:

> *Weight: seven pounds, two ounces*
> *Length: 21 inches*
> *Hair: brown*
> *Eyes: blue*

Charley is a tractable child, although he does not yet walk or talk. His mother is sure he is not retarded, but sometimes she worries about him. Surely before long her child will say his first word?

But like the organ, which has yet to be voiced, Charley Hall is not ready to speak.

ADVENT

✦ ✦ ✦ ✦ ✦

"Puer natus in Bethlehem"
Chorale harmonized by J. S. Bach

A boy is born in Bethlehem,
Alleluia!
Rejoice, rejoice, Jerusalem,
Alleluia! Alleluia!

◆ ◆ ◆ ◆

CHAPTER 1

*When I lay sucking at my mother's breast, I had no notion
how I should afterwards eat, drink, or live.*

Martin Luther

The baby was wide awake, although it was after his
bedtime. His mother had dressed him in shoes and
warm socks and a woolly hooded zipsuit. He was
hot. He stood up in his crib and bounced, enjoying the
creak of the springs. The curtains were drawn and he could
see nothing in his little room but the dark shapes of the
dresser and the changing table, and a streak of light under
the door.

From the next room he could hear music, and his mother
talking to someone. Her voice was comforting, as always.
The music flowed around his head, his mother's words went
up and down.

The other voice was sharper. "The car's ready. Your stuff
is in the back seat. Let's go."

"I'm not coming. I've changed my mind."

"You've what?"

"I've got to tell them. I can't let him take the blame. I'm
not coming with you."

"Look, I told you, it isn't just *this* fire, it's all of them.
Not to mention manslaughter and murder. You're not just
in trouble, you're in prison."

"I don't care. I want to tell them. I've got to."

"My God, Rosie, Kraeger's all right. His congregation
has gorged itself on the pleasure of forgiving him. Forget
about Kraeger. Come on."

"No, no, I've changed my mind. I'm not coming. I can't

let him be blamed for what he didn't do. Let go of me, let go! *Let go!*"

The baby stopped bouncing and listened to the unfamiliar sound of a scuffle, and his mother's angry voice, shouting above the music. He began to cry.

◆ ◆ ◆ ◆

CHAPTER 2

. . . the great and perfect wisdom of God in His marvellous
work of music . . .   Martin Luther

Running up the dark steps of the Church of the
Commonwealth, Alan Starr didn't notice the baby
at first, crawling up the stairs ahead of him, all by
itself.

He was absorbed in the muffled sound of the organ leaking through the closed doors. There were awful irregulari-
ties within each rank. No one would be able to judge the
new instrument until he himself had voiced nearly three
thousand pipes, nicking apertures, adjusting tongues, tuning
wires and resonators.

Even so, even unvoiced, the organ responded brightly to
James Castle's catapulting counterpoint. The driving sixteenth notes fell on Alan's ears like rain in a dry land. He
had been born with a thirst for harmonious noise, for
"Rock-a-bye, Baby" and all that came after. The sound of
the new organ from Marblehead was piercingly clear. The
old organ had never sounded like this, in spite of its fourteen thousand pipes and its swarming electropneumatic im-
itation of all the instruments in the orchestra.

But perhaps only James Castle was good enough to coax
this sort of brilliance from the new organ. Castle was in a
class by himself. He was, after all, the most famous student
of the legendary Harold Oates. Since Alan in his turn was
Castle's pupil, he sometimes imagined himself a kind of musical grandson of the great Oates.

"Is it true?" he had once asked Castle. "Did he really play
like that? You know the way people talk." Alan rolled his

eyes comically upward. "They say he was divinely inspired by God."

Castle had guffawed. "Divinely inspired? Harold Oates?" But then he grinned at Alan. "Well, who knows? Perhaps in his own way he was."

Now, hurrying up the church steps in the dark, Alan almost stumbled over the baby. He stopped short and looked at it in surprise. It was crawling up the cold stone steps of the Church of the Commonwealth, slapping down a hand on the step above, hauling itself up on one knee, sitting down with a thump, reaching up to the next step.

The baby was alone. No one else was climbing the steps behind it, or watching it from the sidewalk. What was a baby doing on the street alone in the dark? "Look here," said Alan, "where's your mother?"

The baby paid no attention. It caught sight of a man walking a dog along the sidewalk. At once it turned around and started down the stairs again, making extraordinary speed. Transfixed, Alan watched it patter after the dog, which was tugging its owner across Clarendon Street toward the building excavation on the other side. The traffic slowed down, then charged forward.

"Hey," said Alan. He galloped after the baby and snatched it up just as it put a hand down into the gutter. The cars rushed by, oblivious, while Alan stood on the curb, looking down at the child in his arms, breathing hard.

In the light of the street lamp he could see that it was quite a nice-looking baby with alert blue eyes. Its cheeks were plump and dirty, with clean streaks where tears had run down. Its face had a kind of hilarious expression.

Whose baby was it? Alan looked along the row of town houses and up and down the tree-lined park dividing the two lanes of traffic on Commonwealth Avenue. A few kids were moving past the marble bust of a long-forgotten mayor of Boston, heading for the bars on Boylston Street, their shoulders hunched against the cold. The baby's mother was nowhere in sight.

Music flooded out of the church. Castle was trying the reed stops. Even through the closed doors the sound was thrilling—the brilliant clarion, the rampant trumpet.

Alan had an appointment with Castle. They were to spend the evening in a swift overview of all the ranks, and Castle was going to say exactly what tonal values he wanted, and Alan was going to write it down. He was late. What the hell should he do with the baby?

It occurred to him that its careless mother might be in the church, listening to the organ. Holding the baby with one arm, Alan walked quickly up the steps. He had never held an infant before, but there didn't seem to be much to it. The baby fitted comfortably against his shoulder and chuckled in his ear.

He pushed open the door with one elbow, walked across the vestry and entered the sanctuary.

At once he was surrounded by the atmosphere of American Protestant holiness, circa 1887. The church had been built in obedience to the architectural ideals of John Ruskin. Ruskin's lamps of *Obedience! Truth! Power! Beauty! Life! Memory! Sacrifice!* had shone upon the supporting pilings as they were driven into the damp silt and clay of the filled land of Boston's Back Bay. The lamps had glistened on the rising walls of Roxbury pudding stone, on the checkered sandstone and granite of the tower, on the elaborate decoration of the interior. The winds of architectural fashion had long since blown out most of those noble lamps, one by one, but the usefulness of the building had not changed. It was still a sturdy and handsome structure, dark within, glowing with stained glass, gleaming with polished wood.

Only the lamp of Truth still flared up now and then, flickering brightly enough to fill the pews on Sunday mornings and brim the collection plates with dollar bills.

The preaching, of course, had changed. The mild and respectable Protestant faith that had established the parish as a denomination unto itself in the middle of the nineteenth century had drifted farther from orthodoxy every year. The present pastor, Martin Kraeger, had started his ministerial life as a Lutheran, but he had grown farther and farther away from his background. Now what was he? A lapsed Lutheran, an occasional Transcendentalist, a moderate Unitarian, an unsilent Quaker and a wry Existentialist, with a few molecules of contemplative Buddhism thrown in. His congregation accepted the intellectual jumble. They seldom examined their pastor's tissue of beliefs, or attempted to unravel one piece of patchwork from another.

Alan walked up the center aisle, holding the baby, inhaling the scent of extinguished candles, the leathery smell of the old Bible on the pulpit, the stuffing in the pew cushions, the lingering fragrance of perfumed sopranos and clean-shaven tenors. There was still a hint of scorching in the air, a sharp recollection of the fire that had burned the balcony and destroyed the old organ and taken the life of the sexton, old Mr. Plummer.

Alan winced as he caught the acrid scent, remembering the anguished look on the face of Martin Kraeger the morning after the fire. Alan had been called in at once, to assess the damage to the organ. He had examined it in the presence of Kraeger, James Castle and Edith Frederick, church treasurer Kenneth Possett, and the chief from the local fire station on Boylston Street.

Kraeger's ugly face had been a study in wretchedness. He kept saying, "It was my fault." He had been smoking carelessly, he said, up there in the balcony, talking to Castle. And there had been lighted candles all over the place for the evening wedding. Had old Mr. Plummer extinguished them all? Were some of them still burning under the balcony when Kraeger left at midnight with Castle? Only a few hours later it had gone up in flames.

Kraeger had already confessed his fault to the firefighters as they dragged their hoses around the burning building. He had confessed it to the people watching the fire as they stood gaping behind a rope barrier. He had told the reporter from the *Globe* and the kids with the video camera from Channel 4. All New England had seen him the next morning on the local news. There he was in person, weeping over the burned body of Mr. Plummer. It was a gruesome and pitiful picture. "Entirely unfit for children," complained a committee of mothers in a letter of protest.

Alan had seen the episode on the morning news while he hauled on his clothes to go to the church. He had raced up Beacon Hill and down again from his room on Russell Street, and gasped his way across the Public Garden and arrived at the Church of the Commonwealth out of breath. Inside the sanctuary he found the others standing around the organ in the half-ruined balcony. As an organ student of James Castle's, Alan already knew Reverend Kraeger and Mrs. Frederick. Church treasurer Kenneth Possett was new to him, and the chief of the local fire department, and another stranger who came puffing up the balcony stairs, stumbling over the charred remains of chairs recently occupied by the choir.

It was a tall man in a rumpled shirt. "My God," said the man, "what a disaster. It's hard to believe a careless cigarette could have done all this."

"Oh, there you are, Homer." Kenneth Possett introduced Homer Kelly to Martin Kraeger, Mrs. Frederick, James Castle, the fire chief, and Alan Starr. "Homer's an old friend of mine. Right now he's teaching at that ancient institution of higher learning across the river, but he used to be a policeman. I thought he might be able to help us figure out what happened."

"It's not just a question of cigarettes," said the chief, turning to Homer. "It was candles too. That wedding, they had candles all over the place last night. It's a wonder there's any churchgoers left in the world, the way they go out of their way to burn themselves up with candles. Electricity, Jesus! You'd think Thomas Alva Edison never got born."

"It was all my fault," murmured Martin Kraeger. His exhausted face was still black with smoke. His hands were wrapped in bandages.

The fire chief looked at him grimly and said nothing, remembering the insane way Kraeger had rushed into the building at the height of the blaze to look for the missing sexton, endangering the lives of the firefighters who had to drag him out again—as if they didn't have enough to do, saving the rest of the building, watering down the blowing embers, watching the roofs of the neighboring town houses. The man was a maniac.

Ken Possett turned to Castle. "The point is, what are we going to do about the organ? Can anything be salvaged? Is it a total loss?"

And then Castle turned to Alan, the visiting expert. Alan had already made up his mind. He had glanced at the scorched façade pipes and opened the narrow door to the chamber where the others were massed in their thousands upon thousands. Everyone else looked at him too, and he shrugged his shoulders. "It's totaled, I'm afraid. Oh, you might salvage a few of the smallest metal flue pipes, but most of them are a dead loss. The wooden flues are wrecked, the solid-state control board is a mess, and the console"—Alan gestured helplessly at the blistered keyboards, the scorched rows of stop knobs—"well, you can see for yourselves, there's nothing left."

"All those pipes," whimpered Ken Possett, "fourteen thousand pipes, you're telling us they're all gone?"

"Well, say, thirteen thousand nine hundred of them. I'm sorry."

And then Mrs. Frederick stepped gallantly forward. "My mind is made up. The Church of the Commonwealth must have a magnificent pipe organ. Jim, I want you to pick the best in the world. It will be my gift to the church, in memory of Henry."

Afterward Alan tried to picture Jim's face—had there been a sly look of triumph? He couldn't remember. He had been too interested himself in the idea of the new organ. He had wanted to nudge Castle and say, "Marblehead, right?"

But Castle did not need to be told. Next day Alan accompanied him to Marblehead and showed him the organ that had been ordered and cancelled by a failing church in Sioux Falls, South Dakota. And then it had taken the people in Marblehead only a few months to adjust it to Castle's specifications.

And here it was, ready for tuning and voicing, Mrs. Frederick's magnificent new tracker organ, with casework of cherry and three thousand five hundred seventy new pipes rising in tiers beside the stained-glass window of Moses and the Burning Bush. For the next few months its destiny was up to Alan Starr.

The baby was beginning to squirm. Alan jiggled it up and down, and walked along the center aisle until he could look back up at the balcony and see Castle at the organ console. There he was, high above the rows of pews, his back to the pulpit, the pipes rising around him.

The fugue came to an end. Castle lifted his hands from the keyboard and held up one finger. Alan was silent, listening. The baby listened too. "Four seconds," said Alan.

Castle turned on the bench and looked down at him gleefully. "Four, right. Four seconds of reverberation. Pretty good. If we took out all the pew cushions we'd probably get five. Hey, what have you got there? Is that yours?"

"No." Alan bounced the baby in his arms. "I found it outside on the steps." He looked around. "I thought its mother might be in here someplace."

"The baby was on the steps? You mean all by itself?" Castle got up and leaned over the railing to take a look. "Babies shouldn't be left alone. Good Lord."

"I think it's going to sleep. Wait a minute. I'll be right up." Reaching into a pew he tumbled the cushion to the floor, then lowered the baby onto it and latched the pew door. "How's that?"

"Looks okay to me, but what do I know about babies? Hey, did you bring the extra stop knob?"

"Sure." Alan galloped up the steps to the balcony and took the blank stop knob out of his pocket. "What do you want it for?"

"Divine inspiration." Castle took the stop knob and tried it in the empty space above Spitzflute and Octave on the panel for the Great organ. "Put it right here."

"What do you mean, put it there? You want to add another rank? Good grief, you don't start with a stop knob, for Christ's sake."

"No, no, I don't want it connected to anything in particular. Just directly to God, that's all. It's for divine inspiration. I want you to paint DIV INSP on it. So I can give it a yank whenever I lose touch with whatever the hell's going on in the service. You know, whenever Kraeger mumbles in his beard or my page turner drops the music."

"Oh, right, good idea. Every organ should have a knob like that."

They got to work. Castle went through the ranks for the Great division, and went on to the Choir, the Positive, the Swell, the Pedal. Alan took notes.

"When are the thirty-two-footers coming?" said Castle, using both feet to send a deep Bourdon fifth shuddering through the building.

"Soon, I hope. Hey, what's that squeal?"

"God, it must be a cipher." Castle turned around on the bench. "Oh, no, it's not. It's your little friend. The baby's awake."

Alan raced down the balcony stairs and picked up the baby just as it flung one leg over the arm of the pew. In another moment it would have fallen into the aisle. At once it stopped crying and smiled at him.

"Cute little critter," said Castle, looking down from above. "Maybe it lives around here. Did you try the house next door?"

"No. Good idea." Alan bounced the baby gently. "Look, the job should take me three or four months, if the thirty-two-foot pipes get here soon. But I'll have the Great division done by the end of January. Mrs. Frederick wants to have a celebration. Can you find something to play on a single manual? Something really—what was the word—glorious?"

Castle turned away and shuffled his music. "Oh, that's right, the end of January. Yes, yes, she told me. Oh, sure, there'll be no problem finding the music. But I won't be here. It will have to be somebody else. I'm going away for a while."

"You won't be here?"

"My mother's ill. Very ill. I haven't seen much of her in the last few years, and it's high time I tried to be a dutiful son. Look, why don't you take over the performance for the celebration? You're the best student I ever had—next to Rosie, of course."

"Rosie? Oh, of course, Rosie. I keep hearing about the magnificent Rosie."

"You never met Rosie?" Castle laughed. "You sound envious. Well, you should be. She's damned good."

"Look, I'm sorry about your mother. Couldn't you come back just for a day or two, to play the concert yourself?"

Castle picked up his music and stood up. "I think not."

"Too bad. People aren't going to be happy when I show up instead of you." Alan shouldered the baby and began walking down the aisle.

"Oh, Alan," said Castle softly, looking down over the

balcony railing. "Goodbye. I probably won't see you again. Before I go, I mean."

"Oh, well, have a good trip. I hope your mother's better soon. So long."

Outdoors the December night was chill. Alan carried the baby past the church, and past the church office building next door. The next edifice in the block-long row of town houses was a five-story brownstone.

He stopped and stared at it in surprise. The front door was wide open.

◆ ◆ ◆ ◆

CHAPTER 3

Our Lord God is like a printer, who sets the letters backwards.
Martin Luther

The door was at street level. There were no steps. Alan put his head into the entry, then walked in, carrying the baby.

There was an inner door, but it too was open, and then a large hall with another open door and a staircase. A small blanket lay in the doorway.

It was like a moment in a dream—the open doors, the silence, the blanket glowing in the light from the street lamp outside.

Boldly Alan walked into the apartment, calling, "Is anyone here?"

There was no response, only a slight humming noise. Light streamed from an inner room. Shifting the baby in his arms, Alan shut the door behind him and walked into the living room. At once he found the source of the humming, a pair of old-fashioned audiocassette recorders lying on a shelf.

He switched them off. The humming stopped. Someone must have been recording from one to the other.

Turning, he looked around the room. "How about it?" he said to the baby. "Is this where you live?"

The baby looked at him solemnly. But it was surely the right place. There was a playpen in the middle of the spacious room, and when Alan went exploring he found a crib in a small bedroom at one side.

The baby's parents must have mysteriously gone away, leaving all the doors open. The baby had crawled out of the house to seek its fortune in the wide world.

It was squirming again and whimpering. What did it want? Babies had two famous physical needs. You put milk in at one end and changed a diaper at the other. Bravely he took on the diaper problem. In the baby's room he found a table covered with a flannel blanket. On the floor lay a big package of paper diapers.

Alan lowered the baby to the table and laid it on its back. It began to howl. For the next five minutes he wrestled with the task of disrobing, cleaning and diapering a small heaving animal. Fortunately the shape of the diaper corresponded more or less to the shape of the child, which was, he was interested to observe, a boy.

Next? Wash the boy's face. Alan took him to the bathroom and mopped at his grubby cheeks with a washcloth. The baby submitted to this indignity with hiccuping sighs, emerging clean and pink. Alan looked at him proudly. Now that he had an investment in this infant's care, he felt a sense of possessiveness. Bonding, it was called.

He felt possessive too about the empty apartment. For the moment it was Alan Starr's own pleasant Back Bay residence. It was many degrees finer than his own small place on the wrong side of Beacon Hill. There were dark high walls, a ceiling with a molded pattern in the plaster, and large windows looking out on a small brick-walled garden.

The furnishings too were handsomer than his own homely collection of castoffs from his mother's house in Brunswick, Maine. A harpsichord with a painted sounding board stood beside the playpen. There were bookcases all over one wall, a shining table with Hitchcock chairs, a desk piled high with papers, a yellow sofa beside the fireplace. On the mantel lay an enormous conch shell.

As a desirable dwelling Alan could imagine nothing better. The baby was lucky. His parents must be rich. Apartments on Commonwealth Avenue did not come cheap.

The baby was jiggling restlessly in Alan's arms, driving

down its fat legs, making small unhappy noises. He felt a rush of concern. The poor thing was probably hungry.

"All right, little guy." He carried the baby into the kitchen and flung open the refrigerator door with a proprietary flourish. On the top shelf he found a baby bottle full of milk, ready to his hand. He had known it would be there. It was almost as if he had put it there himself. He took out the bottle and started for the living room, intending to settle down on the sofa with baby and bottle and decide what to do next.

Only then did he see the stain on the kitchen floor. It was a long streak, as though something had been dragged across the white quarry tiles, leaking a reddish-brown fluid.

Holding the baby carefully, Alan bent down to look. Most of the stain had dried, but there was a puddled place that was still wet, and it was a bright purplish red.

It was blood, decided Alan with dismay. The streak was somebody's life blood.

"For Christ's sake, didn't you hear me kick the door? Where the hell have you been?"

"Asleep! I was asleep! Oh, my God, what's the matter with her? Here, put her down, put her down. Is she dead? My God, Sonny, what happened?"

"Christ, I don't know what happened. She fell. Quick, take her feet. Wait till I turn her on her side."

"Oh, my God, her head! We've got to call an ambulance!"

"You can't call a fucking ambulance. You've got to do something. It's up to you. Shock, right? She's in shock?"

"Oh, Sonny, I don't know. I don't remember. It's been years. Oh, my God, she looks bad."

◆ ◆ ◆ ◆

CHAPTER 4

Occasion salutes thee, and reaches out her forelock to thee, saying:
"Here I am, take hold of me."　　　　Martin Luther

I t was obvious to Alan what had happened. Someone
had been hurt. The father or the mother had been hurt,
and one of them had rushed the other to the hospital,
throwing open all the doors, hurrying out in a panic, leaving the baby behind.

Or perhaps the person who had been hurt had been
alone, and had staggered out into the street, looking for
help. Perhaps the mother or father was lying unconscious
on the sidewalk somewhere right now. Well, it wasn't Alan's
problem. It was a matter for the police.

His arms were sagging. He laid the heavy baby down on
his back in the playpen and handed him the bottle. Could
he hold it by himself? He could. He grasped it eagerly and
popped the nipple into his mouth. "Good for you, kid,"
said Alan, watching with admiration as the milk began to
disappear.

He found the telephone on the wall over the desk, next
to a bulletin board covered with snapshots. Alan put his
hand on the phone, and then paused, entranced.

The pictures were mostly of the baby. Was this the father,
this man in uniform holding the newborn child? Navy?
Coast Guard? Alan didn't know one uniform from another.
The most appealing picture was a single large photograph of
the infant with his mother. It was a black-and-white
closeup of their two faces, enlarged almost to life size.

Alan took his hand away from the phone and leaned on
the desk, studying the picture, feeling an impulse to climb
into its black-and-white world. He had already connected

himself to the baby and the apartment, and now he felt attached to the mother as well. Both baby and mother were looking soberly at the camera. Her hair was neither dark nor blond. It hung short and straight, as though cut around the rim of a bowl.

The real live baby in the playpen was whimpering again. Alan guessed what it needed. He had seen it in the movies. He picked up the baby, held it upright against his shoulder and patted its back. The baby belched politely, and Alan put it down again, aware of another surge of fatherly feeling.

He went back to the telephone and dialed 911.

The police officer at the other end of the line didn't quibble when Alan explained about the abandoned baby and the blood on the floor. He asked a few sharp questions, and then said, "We'll be right over."

Alan hung up, feeling like a good citizen who had acted properly in a crisis. He looked again at the picture of the baby's mother, and wondered what had happened to her. Then he began rummaging among the papers on the desk. Almost at once he found a sad one, a six-month-old newspaper clipping:

NAVY PILOT KILLED IN HELICOPTER ACCIDENT
U.S. Naval Reserve Ensign Theodore Hall, 27, of 115 Commonwealth Avenue, Boston, was killed yesterday when a high wind sent his craft against the roof of a hangar at the Naval Air Station in South Weymouth. Hall is survived by his wife Rosalind and infant son Charles.

Sad. The baby was fatherless, his mother a widow. Really sad.

The baby's name was Charles Hall. It was too formal a name for a baby. Alan looked again at the picture of the baby with his mother, and said their names aloud, "Charley and Rosalind Hall."

Rosalind Hall? The name had a familiar ring. Surely

Rosalind Hall was a member of the American Guild of Organists. He had seen her name over and over again, in one connection or another. He groaned. Oh, of course, Rosalind Hall was Rosie Hall, Castle's favorite pupil. *You sound envious,* Castle had said. *Well, you should be. She's damned good.* One couldn't help suspecting he was in love with the woman, although Alan wasn't sure Castle preferred women to men. Maybe he did, and maybe he didn't.

But it was worse than that. Rosie wasn't just a name on a list, she wasn't simply a student of Castle's. She was someone who was always being shoved down Alan's throat. She was a widow, and her friends were trying to marry her off. People were always telling him, "Oh, you've got to meet Rosie Hall." His sister Betsy was the worst. She had been to boarding school with Rosie, she was always talking about her. Once she had even arranged a date for the two of them, but at the last minute Rosie had called Betsy to say she was sick, and Alan had told Betsy the hell with it, and that had been that. He was sick of hearing the woman's name.

A siren sounded from the street. The high whine spiralled down and stopped. The police cruiser was pulling up outside.

Swiftly, his curiosity still unsatisfied, Alan opened the desk drawer and groped inside it. His fingers closed on a key. It had a tag, *#115 Rear.* Pulling the drawer farther open, he found a small notebook, and flipped the pages. It was full of musical scribblings.

The doorbell rang. Without thinking, Alan pocketed the key and deposited the notebook in one of the zippered compartments of his down jacket.

Then he went to the door and flung it open.

CHAPTER 5

*When two goats meet upon a narrow bridge over deep water,
how do they behave?*   Martin Luther

T here were two of them, a man and a woman, both
in uniform.

"Mr. Starr?" said the man. "My name's McCormack. This is Sergeant Steeple."

Alan glanced at McCormack's identification and stood
back to let them in. They looked at him curiously and followed him into Rosie Hall's living room, their eyes roving
left and right, taking in the harpsichord, the playpen, the
sleeping baby.

McCormack looked tired. He plopped himself down on
the sofa. "You say the door was open? Give me that again."

Alan explained again in more detail. McCormack's face
was mobile. His eyebrows went up and down, he smiled, he
frowned, he scribbled in a pocket notebook. Sergeant Steeple stood solemnly at one side, refusing to sit. Her face was
expressionless, her jaw large, her bosom massive.

McCormack put away his notebook. His eyebrows shot
up. "Isn't the church next door the one where they had that
fire last year?"

"Oh, that's right. That's why I'm here. I'm installing the
new organ. I was on my way in, and there was this baby on
the church steps."

Sergeant Steeple walked heavily to the playpen and
looked down at Charley. "This is the child?"

Well, naturally it's the child. Who did you think it was? Alan
watched as she bent over stiffly and picked up Charley. For
the first time it dawned on him that this formidable woman
would be in charge of the baby from now on. He felt a

pang of dismay. "Hey," he said impulsively, taking a step toward her, "wait a minute."

Sergeant Steeple straightened up with a creak of her corset and looked at him sternly, holding Charley at arm's length like a sack of flour. Charley woke up and burst into loud sobs. "Well?" said Sergeant Steeple, glaring at Alan.

He reached for the baby. "Let me take him."

Charley howled. Sergeant Steeple shouted above the racket, "What's it to you? I thought you were a stranger, right?"

"Well, sure, but maybe I can calm him down."

Reluctantly she dumped Charley into Alan's arms. The baby quieted at once, and began sucking his thumb. Sergeant Steeple looked resentful. "Where's all the kid's things?"

Alan led the way into the baby's room, feeling heartsick. Poor little Charley, what was going to happen to him now?

He left the policewoman to gather Charley's clothes, and went into the kitchen with the baby in his arms to find McCormack on his knees, using a pipette to get a blood sample from the floor. McCormack got to his feet with a wheeze. Alan watched as he emptied the sample into a small jar, screwed the cap on tightly and enclosed jar and pipette in a plastic bag.

"Will you be able to identify whose blood it is?" said Alan.

"Well, of course we can figure out the blood type. Then we'll try to get the mother's medical records. Maybe the baby was born in a local hospital." McCormack wagged his head wisely. "But even if it's the same type, it wouldn't prove it was hers."

Sergeant Steeple appeared, carrying a plastic bag bulging with Charley's possessions.

"Sergeant," said Alan, appealing to her, "what happens to the baby from now on?"

She glowered at him. "Relatives, we look for relatives. If he's got no relatives, he goes into foster care."

"You mean some stranger might be taking care of him?" Suddenly it seemed terrible to Alan that this marvelous child should be sent out into the bureaucratic world of Boston's social welfare system all by himself. "Hey, why don't you let me take care of him?"

The policewoman narrowed her eyes. "Who are you anyway, the father? Lotsa times it's the father kidnaps the child. How come you're so interested in this kid? Here, let me have him."

Alan held Charley tighter, and backed away. "Oh, for Christ's sake, I'm not his father. I told you, his father's dead. I never saw this baby before in my life. I never saw his mother. I've never been in this house before. I found the baby on the steps of the church, like I told you, and I only figured he came from here because the door was open."

"Well, okay," said Sergeant Steeple, "but I can't give this baby to nobody without they go through the Department of Social Services." Reaching for Charley, she tried to tug him away. Alan hung on. For a moment there was a tussle, with Charley whimpering in the middle.

Alan gave up. There was no point in arguing. "Well, look. Can I find out where he's going to be, so I can visit him?"

Primly the woman gathered Charley to her stiff bosom. At once he began to cry. She shouted above his sobs, "Social Services. You got to ask them."

"Jesus," said McCormack, holding his ears. "I get enough of this at home."

"What are you going to do about Rosie?" shouted Alan. They looked at him blankly. "His mother, Rosalind Hall. She's missing, remember?"

McCormack reached up and plucked something from the kitchen wall. It was a key, dangling from a board. "We'll send over a detective. Missing persons, we've got a department, they've got a system." He tried the key in the front door. It worked. Then McCormack wandered around the apartment, giving it a cursory examination.

Alan watched him try the bureau drawers in Rosie's bedroom and open the medicine cabinet in the bathroom and shuffle the papers on her desk. Pulling something out of the pile he held it up, a money clip of twenty-dollar bills. "No burglary, apparently. Okay, we're through for now. Come on, we'll turn out the lights and lock the place up."

Alan followed them out of the apartment to the sidewalk. Charley was still crying in Sergeant Steeple's embrace. Alan watched as they got into the cruiser. His heart ached for Charley, who was reaching out his arms over the sergeant's thick blue shoulder.

"Bye-bye, Charley," he said, trying to smile, waving his hand. He stood helplessly on the sidewalk as the cruiser drove away, Charley's screams fading as the car moved in the direction of Dartmouth Street.

Three hours earlier Alan had not known of the existence of young Charley Hall. How could such a short acquaintance with this little blob of human flesh leave him so bereft? His peace of mind was fractured. Turning away from Rosalind Hall's apartment, he walked to the church, climbed the steps and tried the door. It was locked. He fumbled in his pocket for the key.

Inside the vestibule there were only glimmers of light from the street lamps outside, superimposing the shadows of bare branches over the geometric patterns of the William Morris tiles on the floor. The sanctuary too was dark and silent. Castle had gone home.

Only the stained-glass windows were dimly visible— the Wise and Foolish Virgins over the pulpit to the east, the Three Kings to the south, Daniel in the Lions' Den to the north, and Moses and the Burning Bush at the west end of the balcony, in a forest of new organ pipes. The symbolism connecting the four windows was a mystery, but they were famous creations from the workshop of John La Farge.

Alan looked up at the Three Kings. The sky behind the three majestic figures was made of light-refracting blue glass knobs the size of Ping-Pong balls. In the kings' hands as they knelt before the child in the manger were pale objects of yellow glass, chalices gleaming like gold.

Charley Hall too was a baby, but nobody was bringing him presents of gold and frankincense and myrrh. In his case it was all misery, loneliness and abandonment—that was what the chalices of the Department of Social Services would be offering to Charley Hall.

♦ ♦ ♦ ♦

CHAPTER 6

*The world is full of such works of wonder, but we are blind,
and cannot see them.*   Martin Luther

Whh hen Martin Kraeger left his apartment on
Dartmouth Street and walked up Commonwealth to the church, he found the traffic on
Clarendon backed up behind an obstruction. A barrier had
been erected by a crew from the Water and Sewer Commission. A blue truck was parked on the sidewalk. Two lanes of
cars were edging into one, sounding resentful horns.

Kraeger had to jump across a river of water running
along the gutter. He leaned over and looked into the manhole. "Hello, down there, good morning. May I ask what
you're doing?"

A couple of men in hard hats looked up. "New construction," said one of them. "They got to drain the site."

"Oh, I see. You mean for the new hotel."

"Right. Buried sump pump, water comes up this pipe
here, we connect it to the sewer line. All done now." The
two men climbed out of the manhole, and the talkative one
gestured at the excavation. "Sump pump, see, it's to keep
the hole dry, right?"

"I see." Kraeger turned and stared down into the pit. It
was deep. Concrete pilings lay in a heap at one side. A crane
stood idle. He watched one of the men from the Water and
Sewer Commission bang the manhole cover down again
over the hole. "I wonder how long the construction will
take?" he said, thinking with dread of the noise of the pile
driver, the din of machine-driven tools.

"Jeez, I don't know. They say there's money problems. I
don't know what the hell." The two men removed the bar-

riers and the truck pulled away. As the traffic surged forward in two lanes, Kraeger ducked back across the street, walked around the corner and climbed the church steps.

There was fresh paint on the door frame, and the great Longmeadow stones above the heavy arch of the entry were rosy and clean, their scorched surfaces sandblasted away. At last Kraeger could walk into the building without a stab of anguish. He was grateful to Ken Possett's friend, that tall odd-looking man called Homer Kelly, who had found no reason to suspect arson. Kelly had persuaded the arson squad that the fire was an accident, and the arson squad had informed the insurance company, and the company had paid up. The organ had not been insured, unfortunately, but the financial settlement had rebuilt the balcony and replaced the cracked glass in the Moses window. Once again the burning bush blazed fiery red and Moses held up his pink hands in wonder.

"You can be grateful," said Ken Possett, "that the sexton didn't have a bunch of aggrieved relatives to sue us for ten million dollars."

This heartless remark had caused Martin Kraeger a good deal of suffering. In the middle of the night he turned uneasily in his bed, while out of the dark rose the image of the charred body of Mr. Plummer, his lips open in a silent scream, his fingers hooked in agony.

But Kraeger's Lutheran upbringing stood him in good stead. Since childhood he had grown away from strict Lutheran conformity, no longer believing human nature to be corrupt, no longer concerning himself with the remission of sins by grace, the hope of eternal bliss. To him Luther's devil was a metaphor for human weakness. But he kept alive his respect for Luther the man, for his pungent and violent wit, his powerful resolution, the forcefulness and courage with which he had tossed aside every obstacle. Most of all he admired Luther's faith, his total submission to the will of God.

Daily Kraeger hurled himself into whatever task lay before him, but he did so serenely, accepting his fate. He took to his heart his own guilt in the death of Mr. Plummer, and bowed down before it. But he went forward, hiding the scar that would never heal.

In the vestibule of the church he was confronted at once by his new building manager, Donald Woody. "Hey, Martin, we've got a problem with one of the windows. I think we've got to get those stained-glass people over here again to take a look."

"Which window is it, the Three Kings?"

"No, it's the one in the east wall. All those ladies with yellow hair."

"The Wise and Foolish Virgins." Kraeger smiled. "Amazing the way they ran to blondes in Biblical times." He followed Woody into the sanctuary and they stood below the window and looked up at it.

It was one of La Farge's miracles of light and dark. The lamps of the wise virgins glowed with a feverish brightness around the dazzling bridegroom, while the foolish virgins hovered in the darkness, their lamps extinguished.

"See there, on the left?" said Woody. "Those windows weigh sixty pounds a square foot. If they get out of line, they'll fall."

"Good Lord, it's buckled there at the bottom. Good for you, Woody. Of course, call them right away."

"I just thought I'd ask you first. I know you're concerned about the budget and all."

"When is a church not concerned about the budget?" Kraeger gave Woody a grim smile. "But we have to do what we have to do. This is obviously an emergency."

"You'll be getting some income pretty soon from that daycare center. I finally got those ground floor rooms in the basement cleared out. That woman Ruth Raymond, she's been calling me every day, wanting to know if it'll be ready in January. She's got half the kids in Boston signed up."

"That's wonderful, Woody. I'm so glad you saw the use-fulness of those basement rooms. A daycare center! It's a superb idea."

"Oh, and say, Martin, I found an old picture downcellar when I was clearing out, a portrait of somebody named Wigglesworth, that's what the label says."

"Wigglesworth! The Reverend Walter Ephraim Wigglesworth? But that's wonderful! Walter Wigglesworth was the presiding minister for this congregation, way back when they were meeting on Tremont Street. A tremendously inspiring preacher, that's what everybody said."

"No kidding. Well, that explains the book he's holding. It's got a title painted on the front in gold leaf, *Divine Inspiration*. I'll bring it up this afternoon."

Kraeger watched Woody walk purposefully away down the aisle, and congratulated himself on finding so perfect a new sexton. Donald Woody had come on the job last August during Kraeger's vacation, to replace the late Mr. Plummer. Martin had come back to the church to find the once-seedy sanctuary with its blackened balcony and ruined organ cleared of charred timbers and scorched pipes. The repairs to the balcony were half done, the pews had been refinished, the stained glass professionally cleaned, the floor tiles washed and waxed. Everything was running smoothly. Since then Woody had solved all the small housekeeping problems in the kitchen, the parish hall, the church school, the basement club room, the meeting rooms, the offices; he had identified major difficulties with the plumbing, the oil-fired furnaces, the steam radiators, the security system. He had worked out a schedule for annual repairs. In October he had planted a thousand spring bulbs in the garden with his own hands.

"We've certainly got a winner in that Donald Woody," said Kraeger to Loretta Fawcett, his executive secretary, walking through her small room on the way to his office.

"We certainly do," agreed Loretta, taking half the credit,

because she had welcomed Woody on his first day on the job, while her boss was camping in the Adirondacks with his little daughter Pansy.

But the truth was altogether different. On Woody's first day Loretta had made a serious mistake. She had failed to pass along to the new sexton Martin Kraeger's seven-page list of directions. Kraeger had written it by hand on the last day of July. Loretta was to type it up and deliver it to Donald Woody as soon as he arrived.

"It's very important," he told her, "especially the beginning."

"Well, of course," said Loretta.

But she hadn't done it. Loretta Fawcett was a kindly and cheerful woman with a passion for knitting, crocheting and needlework, but she was an abominable secretary. Kraeger had long since discovered that he must type up his letters and sermons himself rather than depend on Loretta, because she was always deep in some vast project—an entire crocheted bedspread, a giant needlepoint tapestry. When he handed her the list for the new sexton she had been knitting a colossal pair of orange overalls.

"You won't forget? He's got to understand this first part as soon as he arrives." Kraeger pointed it out to Loretta, the first paragraphs, over which he had taken special care:

First and foremost, you must know that this building and all the other buildings in the Back Bay, including Trinity Church and the Boston Public Library, rest on pilings. This area was once subject to the tidal flow of the Charles River. The river was dammed up and the Back Bay filled with gravel and sand in the nineteenth century. Most of the pilings are made of wood, just as they are in Venice. As long as they remain water-soaked, they are extremely strong. But if they are allowed to dry out by a lowering of the water table, they will rot and turn to powder. Cautionary example: part of the Boston Public Library caved in, back in 1930.

Therefore your first duty is to REMEMBER THE PIL-

INGS. You will find among the gear in your office a weighted tape measure. It is to be periodically lowered through the holes in the basement floor. If the space between floor and water exceeds four feet, water must be artificially supplied. These observation wells are to be found in the following places: in the northeast corner of your office, in the southeast corner of the boiler room, on the west side of the big storeroom.

Unfortunately Loretta promptly lost the sheaf of directions for Donald Woody. Well, she didn't exactly lose it. She rolled it into a ball in her workbasket with the orange overalls, and there it lay for six weeks while she ran up a sweater for her niece's new baby in coral pink (everybody was so pleased! A girl at last, after all those boys!).

When Donald Woody arrived on the job, he came to Kraeger's office at once, looking for orders.

"He's on vacation," explained Loretta, staring at her knitting, her fingers flying. (The baby was due any minute.)

"Oh. Well, I wonder if somebody could show me what I'm supposed to do around here."

"Well, I don't know. You could talk to Mr. Hyde, he's the substitute for August, but he doesn't know anything about anything."

"I see." Donald Woody was nonplussed. "Well, maybe there's some directions down in my office, like taped to the wall or something."

"Oh, wait a sec." Loretta suddenly remembered the notes she hadn't yet typed up, and she pulled open a drawer, knowing full well that it contained only a couple of knitting magazines. "Well, never mind. I'll bet there's directions down there in the basement, like you said."

But when Woody found his way to his basement office, he found no directions taped to the wall, and none on his desk. It didn't matter. Donald Woody was a take-charge kind of guy. Before long he had the place running smoothly. After all, he had already worked in a big urban church in Topeka. He made a schedule of daily, weekly and monthly tasks, he wrote up a budget, he ordered supplies for the next half year. He interviewed applicants for the job of night watchman, and hired a kid from Boston University. He was a superb manager. His job was a creative challenge every day. Never had the complex of buildings been so clean and shining. Never had the mechanical systems run so smoothly.

But no one ever pointed out to Woody the small metal lids in the basement floor, bolted flush with the concrete. No one ever told him what they were for.

And Martin Kraeger never mentioned the pilings when he came home from his vacation. It never occurred to him to repeat his written directions verbally, since his new employee had everything under such perfect control.

Loretta came across the directions one day in November, after the baby shower for her niece, after everyone had oohed and aahed over the tiny pink sweater, after she opened her workbasket again and took out the warmup suit she was making for her nephew Scott. When she unrolled the huge wad of orange yarn, the seven closely written sheets of directions for Donald Woody fell out on the floor.

Loretta picked them up. "Oh, well," she said to herself, "there's no point typing them up now. He knows all about everything anyway." And she tossed them in the wastebasket.

So Donald Woody never learned that the metal lids in the floor of his basement office were bolted over two-inch pipes leading down to the water table. He never understood the purpose of the weighted tape measure coiled in his desk drawer. Woody carried on his multitudinous tasks with superb efficiency, tramping over the metal disks a hundred times a day, while the water table under the church fell slowly, drawn down by a hundred sump pumps in the buildings left and right, and now by the new pump in the excavation across the street. Slowly, very slowly, the wa-

ter surrounding the three thousand buried pilings sank a
fraction of an inch every day.

Unfortunately the last decade had been one of the driest
in years. Snow had not accumulated on the Berkshire hills,
to melt and cascade down in little waterfalls and gush into
mountain streams that plunged into bigger streams and
emptied into the Connecticut River, the Merrimack, the
Sudbury, the Mystic, the Charles, and filled ponds and lakes
and potholes and puddles, and seeped into the ground everywhere to recharge the water table.

In the Back Bay there were underground rivers moving
mysteriously through the filled land, through the fine sand
and gravel brought from Needham on railway cars. Slowly
they sank from a level of five and a half feet above Boston
City Base to four, although there were strange hills of water
here and there, and mysterious hollows where it lay lower
than anywhere else.

Even the occasional rain pelting down on the vast roof of
Trinity Church in Copley Square failed to recharge the soil
around the building. The water sank below the tops of the
four thousand pilings supporting the vast tower of red granite that loomed over the square.

But Trinity was in no danger. When the water fell to a
certain significant point a buzzer sounded. At once the alert
building manager began pumping Boston water to recharge
the basin beneath the building and supply the loss. The water bill of Trinity Church rose astronomically, and the members of the vestry were dismayed.

The building manager was called in to explain the
problem. "I'm sorry," he said, "but what else can we do?
Surely you don't want the pilings to dry out?"

"No, indeed," said the rector, looking around the table
and raising a mollifying hand. "May I make a motion of
confidence in our manager's decision to continue drawing
water at the present rate? All in favor say aye."

Other building managers and superintendents and janitors throughout the Back Bay were similarly alarmed. They acted at once, summoning from the water mains of the city of Boston enough to supply their needs. The churches were quick to do the same—Emmanuel, Advent, Annunciation, Old South, First Baptist, First Lutheran, the Church of the Covenant, First and Second Unitarian-Universalist. The hotels too called for more—the Copley Plaza and the Ritz.

Sixty miles away the Quabbin Reservoir sank an inch or two, as millions of gallons of water poured through the tunnel every day, running downhill through dirt and rock, under field, farm and forest, all the way to Boston.

Only the filled land under the Church of the Commonwealth went unsupplied with fresh gushes of underground water. Below the parish office building and below the four great piers of the tower, the water table shared the moisture of the buildings west of it, but under the sanctuary it sloped steeply downward to the east. The throbbing pump in the excavation across the street drew down the water further.

The pump had been forgotten. Lawsuits were holding up construction. One day a car pulled up beside the excavation. A court hack jumped out, skidded down the slope and handed the job engineer an order to cease and desist. The engineer looked at the piece of paper, threw up his hands, bellowed at the crane operator and the guy working the power shovel to get the hell home, leaped into his car and careened away from the curb and the excavation and the whole job of building a five-story hotel with Georgian exterior and luxury interior fittings, raced home and burst in on his wife, fuming and steaming, to find her *in flagrante* with his best friend, and in the succeeding uproar and confusion the little matter of the necessity of turning off the sump pump under the excavation at the corner of Commonwealth and Clarendon utterly vanished from his mind.

The neglected pump had long since sucked the excavation dry. Now it was pumping groundwater, relentlessly draining the saturated soil at level four, sending the water pulsing into a pipe to be carried by way of the West Side Interceptor to a pumping station and a treatment plant and eventual discharge into Boston Harbor. It was gone for good.

✦ ✦ ✦ ✦

CHAPTER 7

How many sorts of deaths are in our bodies? Nothing is therein but death.   Martin Luther

James Castle was saying goodbye to one thing after another. He walked around the music room and looked for the last time at the pictures on the wall, the photographs of former choir directors and organists. His own teacher, the celebrated Harold Oates, had performed only once in the Church of the Commonwealth (once had been enough), but Castle had hung his picture on the wall with the others. It was a surprisingly respectable side view. The savage glitter of the eyes was not visible. The muttered obscenities had not been recorded.

Goodbye, Oates. Goodbye, all the rest of you. Castle walked out into the hall. At once he encountered Edith Frederick.

She was not someone to be dismissed with a passing nod. Edith was responsible for the new organ, for the paid soloists in his choir, for the fact that his income as director of church music was the largest east of the Rocky Mountains.

Her ignorance was the cross he had to bear. Edith's late husband had been the great appreciator, the lover of sacred music, but unfortunately he was dead and gone. He had left to his wife the distribution of the largesse from the Frederick Music Endowment. Edith was generous and openhanded. She was also tone-deaf and musically illiterate.

Today, as always, he bent the knee. "Good morning, Edith. You look like a rose this morning." It was a fawning remark, and Castle cursed his habit of speaking in this way to Mrs. Frederick. The truth was, the woman seemed particularly hollow-cheeked and old today, in spite of her smart pink jacket with its silver buttons.

Edith Frederick dismissed the compliment. She knew the cruel effect of the sunshine raking down on her wrinkled face from the skylight overhead. She was always intensely conscious of the direction of the light. *Thank you, dear hostess, but I won't sit on the sofa beside the lamp. I'd prefer this straight-backed chair facing the window.*

She looked at Castle reproachfully. "Oh, Jim, is it true you're taking a holiday? You're going off at once without warning, at a time like this? What about all the Christmas services we've planned?"

Feebly Castle flapped his hands. "I'm sorry, Edith. It isn't a holiday. My mother's ill. I don't know how long I'll be gone."

"I'm very sorry to hear it." Edith's sorrow was not the sympathetic kind but the disappointed-in-you kind.

"I wish I could help you find some interim people. There are plenty of good ones—some of my students, Alan Starr, Barbara Inch, Pip Tower. It's too bad Rosie Hall has disappeared. She was the best of all. But I can recommend all the rest. I leave it up to you." Castle pressed Edith's hand and hurried away down the hall to say goodbye to Martin Kraeger.

Edith's smile faded. It had once been famous for its charm—*I'm smiling because nothing terrible has ever happened to me, and I'm rich and I'm young and I've just bought a Jacobean table.* Now it was a muscular act of will—*I smile, although my husband died choking on a chicken bone and I suffer from angina pectoris and my old friends are disappearing one by one.*

Looking up at the skylight, Edith put her hands to her ravaged cheeks.

Martin Kraeger's study was a handsome chamber, adorned by the church architect of 1887 with oak panelling, an elaborate marble fireplace and a niche carved with a scallop shell. The niche had once contained a bust of Christ with his eyes rolled skyward. Now a computer was wedged into it, a lump of gray plastic below the shining cherry of the fluted shell. There had been no other place to put it because the massive furniture in Kraeger's study took such a lot of room—the immense sofa and six sanctimonious chairs crowned with ogee arches and finials. They had once graced the Tremont Street study of the blessed Wigglesworth, who was said to have arisen from naps on the sofa in a state of rapturous grace.

As a chamber for the present pastor of the Church of the Commonwealth, the room was certainly dignified enough. It would have been still more exalted if Loretta Fawcett had not dumped a lot of ecclesiastical desiderata here and there,

boxes of sermons and orders of service she ought to have filed away long ago.

And there were gifts from grateful parishioners—a pale watercolor by one of the deacons, said to represent the Church of the Commonwealth, and a wall-hanging made of string, weeds, and puffs of rabbit fur created by Joyce Pinwick, the director of the church school. Often the rabbit fur floated free and got up Kraeger's nose. The sofa was piled with homemade pillows, mostly the work of Loretta Fawcett, but one was a needlepoint masterpiece by Edith Frederick.

Another was an anomaly, a pink satin sacred heart, the work of an elderly confused parishioner who misunderstood the differences in the sacred articles of faith among the various orders of the Catholic Church and the doctrines of a multitude of Protestant denominations.

Perhaps the Church of the Commonwealth was confused in the same way. Newcomers would often inquire, "What kind of church *is* this anyway?" and then the old hands would say, "Well, it's sort of this and that." Before long the new people got used to it, and soon they too were saying to puzzled visitors, "It's this and that. It's kind of this and that."

Officially the church was nondenominational. Kraeger himself picked and chose from a broad spectrum, faithful to no single orthodoxy. He believed in a historical Jesus rather than a divine one. Even so, some of the more liberal members of his congregation were dissatisfied with his reverence for the moral genius of the man, and they were uncomfortable with the intensity of his feeling about the tragedy of the crucifixion. Whenever he brought it up, they nudged each other in their pews and whispered, "There he goes again."

Kraeger's personal view of humankind was dark. For him the crucifixion was not a single event but a paradigm of the fate forever awaiting the good and the brave. Perhaps there was something to be said after all for the doctrine of human depravity.

But his aspect was cheerful. In choosing one path over another, day after day, one moment to the next, he felt free of doubt. His faith permitted him to be careless and easy in all he said and did. His pessimism about humanity was not evident in his public person, which was loud, confident, hearty, affectionate and ironical. His pain over his part in the death of the sexton he now kept to himself, making a private penance by turning over a portion of his income to a shelter for homeless people on Kansas Street.

"There's no evidence it was your fault," Homer Kelly had said. It was true that Homer wasn't an official member of any police force; he wasn't even a private investigator. He was a professor of American Literature at Harvard. But he had once been a lieutenant detective in the office of the District Attorney of Middlesex County. Somehow he had awed the arson squad—with his colorful reputation and his extravagant way of speaking—into accepting his whimsical judgment. *Not your fault,* he had said. Kraeger did not feel absolved. The weight on his soul was permanent, one more proof of the failure of his personal life.

Kraeger's marriage had been his principal mistake. He had married impulsively, attaching himself to a foolish woman who sued him for divorce shortly after the birth of their daughter Pansy, who was now four years old. His confidence in his power to attract a woman more suitable than Kay Kraeger was zero.

In person Martin Kraeger was heavyset and homely, with jowls and small piglike eyes. But ugliness liberates. He could be friendly with women without causing hearts to beat, without arousing that flutter of feminine devotion so typical of congregations circulating around a single dominant male. He seldom went so far as to embrace members of his congregation in that ceremony of hugging that was now correct pastoral etiquette, and yet the intensity of his engulfing interest often gave his parishioners the sense of being wrapped in a mighty bearlike clasp, eaten up and swallowed whole.

When James Castle walked into Kraeger's study, he found him on his knees, going through the cardboard boxes on the floor of his closet. Somewhere in this swarm of shifting papers were the documents divorcing Martin Kraeger from his ex-wife. He had to find them because Kay was making silly demands that were surely not part of their legal agreement.

He sprang to his feet and shook Castle's hand. "Jim, I never thanked you for sticking up for me about the fire."

"I was just saying what I thought. Your cigarettes didn't have anything to do with it. When we left the church that night there wasn't any smoldering cigarette on the floor or anywhere else."

"The trouble is, I can't remember what I did with the stubs. Did I grind them out on the floor? I don't think I would have done that. I probably rubbed them out on the sole of my shoe, but I'm not absolutely positive. Filthy habit. Thank God I've given it up."

"Look, it's all over now. I just came in to say goodbye. I'm leaving this afternoon. My mother's condition keeps getting worse. Actually this is a good time for me to be gone, while Alan voices the pipes. It takes months."

"Do you mean the organ can't be used for months?"

"Oh, no, I don't mean that. Whenever he finishes one rank of pipes, it will be available. You'll have to hire a substitute for Sunday services. I don't know when I'll be back." Castle took a step forward, and put his hand on Kraeger's arm. His voice was constricted. "It's been a great thing in my life, Martin, making music to go with those good words of yours."

"For me too. You know that. And there's plenty more to come. Hurry back." Kraeger watched with surprise as Castle walked out, blowing his nose. Why was the man so worked up? Well, his mother was at death's door, why shouldn't he be worked up? Then Kraeger found himself thinking uncharitably that if Castle's mother was his own mother, he wouldn't be sorry she was ill, he'd be intensely relieved. On the one occasion when they had met, the woman had not impressed him favorably, to put it mildly.

It was just last fall. He had made the mistake of dropping in on Castle the day after Thanksgiving without warning. Castle lived at a classy address on Beacon Hill. Martin found it, and pressed the bell. At once he wished he hadn't. There were wild screams within. They stopped, and after a moment Castle opened the door, his face pale, his pinkish-gray hair standing up around his freckled bald head. Angry faces filled the background. Mumbling with embarrassment, Castle introduced his relatives—a brother, a couple of uncles, a mother, and a feeble-looking younger sister lying on a sofa under a blanket. They all stared blankly at Martin, and muttered something as he nodded amiably at each of them in turn. All except the mother, whose response to his extended hand was to turn around rudely and show her back.

It was some sort of ghastly Thanksgiving family reunion. "I'll come another time," Martin said lamely, and beat a hasty retreat. The screaming broke out again as soon as the door closed behind him. It was a woman's clamorous voice, the mother's obviously, since the sister didn't look capable of screaming.

Afterward Castle had said nothing about it to Martin, and therefore Kraeger hadn't brought it up either, having a delicate regard for his parishioners' privacy. If they came to him for help he gave it in generous measure, but not otherwise. Now he couldn't help wondering about the old witch whose last days Castle was attending so dutifully. Maybe she wasn't as bad as she had seemed.

Kraeger heaved himself out of his chair and put Castle's strange family out of his mind. It was time for lunch, and he had a hearty appetite. Martin Luther had provided the excuse: *If Our Lord is permitted to create nice, large pike and good Rhine wine, presumably I may be allowed to eat and drink.*

Opening his closet, he yanked his coat off its hanger, dislodging at the same time one of the black gowns he wore on Sunday mornings. He picked it up and looked at it, wondering if it was the one he had been wearing at the evening wedding on the night of the fire. He had never looked in the pockets for a cigarette stub. Groping, he found nothing but an old order of service for last Thanksgiving.

There was another gown in the closet somewhere, an old one missing most of its fastenings. Kraeger groped in the back of the closet and brought out a limp black garment. It was in a sorry condition. If he had been wearing it on the night of the wedding, the bride's mother would have been shocked. There were coffee stains all down one side. He found nothing in the left pocket but a safety pin, but in the right there were three cigarette stubs.

He took them out and held them in the palm of his hand. They looked pitiful and familiar. He could almost remember putting them into that very same pocket on the night in question. Was he imagining it?

Oh well, the hell with it. Who would believe him? And perhaps he had smoked four cigarettes, not just three, and left one of them smoldering on the floor.

Kraeger swung the closet door shut, but it wouldn't close because Loretta Fawcett had stored an easel among the coats and gowns. Martin couldn't avoid reading the words some idiot had inscribed on the big pad of newsprint, *Spirituality = Creativity.* Oh, God, churches had a lot to answer for.

On the way out he stumbled over more of Loretta's stuff. He had asked her months ago to sort all these papers and distribute them in the church archives. Everybody said he should fire the woman, but he couldn't bring himself to do it. Now he smiled at Loretta as he passed her desk. Walking heavily down the hall, he thumped down the stairs and hurried out-of-doors.

A cold rain had begun to fall.

Martin pulled his coat collar up around his chin and walked quickly in the direction of Copley Square. Across Clarendon Street the excavation looked like a hole in hell.

CHRISTMAS

✦ ✦ ✦ ✦ ✦

"Ermuntre dich, mein schwacher Geist"
Chorale harmonized by J. S. Bach

Break forth, O beauteous heavenly Light,
And usher in the morning;
Ye shepherds, shrink not with affright,
But hear the angel's warning.
This child, now weak in infancy,
Our confidence and joy shall be,
The power of Satan breaking,
Our peace eternal making.

✦ ✦ ✦ ✦

CHAPTER 8

When natural music is heightened and polished by art . . .
one man sings a simple tune . . . together with which three,
four or five voices also sing . . . performing as it were a
heavenly dance.   Martin Luther

Alan Starr sat at the keyboard of a small portable organ in Emmanuel Church on Newbury Street, feeling ridiculous in a green tam-o'-shanter and tunic.
The tunic was itchy. In agony, Alan adjusted the gold rope
around his waist and reached up a furtive thumb to scratch.

Christmas was a hectic season for organists, even for an
organ builder and repairman like Alan, because he hired
himself out to play here and there. His colleagues in the
American Guild of Organists were busy too, even the ones
without steady church jobs, like Pip Tower and Gilda
Honeycutt and Jack Newcomb and Peggy Throstle.

At this festive time of year all the churches in the Back
Bay vied with one another in pageantry. Only at the
Church of the Commonwealth were the celebrations sub-
dued, because the new organ wasn't ready and James Castle
was away on leave. Pip Tower was filling in for the two can-
dlelight services and the one on Christmas day. Alan hurried through the voicing of four ranks of pipes, so that Pip
would have something to work with. Only forty-six more
to go. "You've got Bourdon sixteen on the Pedal," he told
Pip, "and Prestant eight, Octave four and Spitzflute eight on
the Great, and that's all."

Pip wasn't satisfied. "What, no mixture? How can I turn
on the congregation without a mixture? Where's the ecstasy,
where's the rapture?"

Alan felt sorry for Pip. He was a good-looking guy with
very white skin and thinning blond hair, getting on for
thirty. Like Alan, he was a student of Castle's, but although

he was a fine performer he seemed unable to land a regular church job. For years now he had been cadging Sunday morning substitutions and taking anything else he could get. Of course the job market for organists was impossible. The only regular positions were in churches and temples, and openings were scarce. There was no other employment but the occasional wedding or funeral, and unfortunately nobody seemed to be getting married any more and the old folks were healthier all the time. "Well, okay," said Alan, "I'll see what I can do. I can't promise."

But by working at odd hours he managed to finish the Mixture rank on the Great division, and Pip had his moment of rapture.

At Emmanuel Episcopal it was all rapture. They were doing a Bach cantata and a medieval miracle play. There were long-haired women in velvet gowns with lutes and men in tights with dulcimers. *Christ our blessed Savior,* sang the women, *now in the manger lay.* Alan couldn't help thinking again about young Charley Hall. What sort of manger was poor Charley lying in right now? It had been two weeks since he had been carried off in the police cruiser, clutched to the hard blue bosom of Sergeant Steeple. Alan's efforts to discover his whereabouts had been fruitless.

He had been tossed from one telephone extension to another. When at last he reached Mrs. Marilynne Barker, a mighty general in the Department of Social Services, she held him at arm's length.

"Are you the child's father? A relative? A friend of the family? No? Then what exactly is your interest in Charles Hall?"

"It's just that I'm concerned about him. I was the one who found him on the street after his mother disappeared."

"Is that all? You have no other connection with the child? Then I'm sorry, Mr. Starr, I can give you no information."

Alan continued to feel a pang of anxiety. What would

happen to the poor little kid if his mother never came back? And where in the hell was she?

Rosalind Hall's disappearance was now common knowledge among the community of organists in Boston. The dramatic details of Alan's rescue of her child, his entry into the open door of her apartment, his discovery of the blood on the floor—the whole story had been printed in the *Boston Globe,* along with Rosie's picture.

Her friends were upset. "Where can she be?" said Barbara Inch, who had been closest to Rosie. "What could possibly have happened?"

Jack Newcomb didn't hide his glee. "All the more opportunities for us," he said ruthlessly. "Rosie always got the plums. She was everybody's first choice. After Castle, of course. Now they're both gone. Less competition, right?"

Peggy Throstle was shocked by Rosie's disappearance. "How could she abandon her little boy? I think it's terrible."

Barbara was outraged. "How can you talk like that? She may have been badly hurt. She would never have left that baby if she'd been all right. Somebody should be trying to find her."

Alan Starr agreed with Barbara. Were the police doing anything at all? He cut Rosie's picture out of the paper and taped it over the sink in his room on Russell Street. The picture kept nudging him, it wouldn't leave him alone.

But neither did the demands of the Christmas season. At this time of year there was a regimented jollification in all the churches of the Back Bay, a tinseled charm that somehow outbalanced the reality of the surrounding city of metal and cement, the bland grind of traffic on the streets, the flashing windshields, the multitudinous offices with their data-processing machines, their ten thousand printouts folding over and over.

In the sanctified spaces of the churches of Copley Square and Newbury Street and Commonwealth Avenue the gray truths of daily life were swagged with garlands of laurel and wreaths of balsam. The scent of the north woods filled lofty interiors rich with timbered ceilings and acres of stained glass. Chancels were crowded with chirping children, pews thronged with churchgoers drugged with holy revelry. There was an infectious aura about the week before Christmas that seemed for the moment something more than a Dickensian mass hallucination. For a few days the illusion of peace on earth prevailed in the Back Bay.

There was no peace for Alan Starr. He had agreed to help with too many special services. After the miracle play at Emmanuel he had barely time to tear off his itchy shirt, pull on his jacket and pants and race down Berkeley Street to the Church of the Annunciation, slipping and sliding on the icy sidewalk.

Annunciation was another high-church Episcopal establishment. In the late nineteenth century there had been a demand along the broad new avenues of the Back Bay for the liturgical splendor of Anglican services, a hunger for red brocade and flickering candles and images of saints. Pale Brahmin noses had twitched gratefully, inhaling the fragrance of swinging censers, weak eyes had blinked in the dim light of the Middle Ages, educated ears had taken pleasure in the sonorities of *The Book of Common Prayer*. It was all very British, and everything British was good.

Alan slipped onto the organ bench at Annunciation and played a brisk prelude while the choir waited to process down the center aisle. Processions were important in the Church of the Annunciation. It was the highest of the high churches in the Back Bay. It was as close to Catholic as a Protestant church could come without falling into the arms of the pope.

You wouldn't want to get any closer. Catholicism had been the religion of the immigrants who had swarmed into the North End and South Boston, Irishmen who by the raw strength of their arms built the railroads in which the Yankees of the Back Bay invested. It was the religion of the men who laid the sleepers and pounded the spikes, who roamed the countryside looking for work, plowing for Yankee farmers, felling trees in Yankee woodlots, caring for Yankee beasts of burden. It was the faith of the Irish women who tended the deafening machines in Yankee textile factories, who lived in the attics of Yankee town houses and cooked in the basement and did the laundry.

There were no Catholic churches in the Back Bay. If the Irish servants wanted to attend Mass, let them walk to St. Cecilia's across the tracks, and be back in time to serve dinner.

Now in the Episcopal Church of the Annunciation the processional advanced. Alan pulled out a couple more stops and launched into "O Come, All Ye Faithful." Pacing in front of the choir, Barbara Inch was close enough to wink at him. Normally Barbara was the organist at Annunciation as well as the choir director, but this week her duties were so taxing, she had called on Alan to help out. Hastily now he pulled out a mixture as the congregation rose to sing.

Joyful and triumphant. Alan glanced at Barbara, and saw her lean toward the verger marching beside her. She was saying something, and at once the verger stopped singing, convulsed with laughter. As the rector ascended the chancel steps in front of them he turned his head and glowered.

Alan grinned and added a couple of brilliant reeds as he swung into the last verse, *Yea, Lord, we greet thee, born this happy morning.* There was only one trouble with Barbara, she was too funny for her own good.

"They've warned me," she had told Alan. "I may lose my job."

She had not turned over a new leaf.

"How is she?"
"She keeps drifting off. Her pulse, God, it's so slow."
"Has she said anything yet?"
"Just 'Charley.' She keeps mumbling 'Charley.' "

"Oh, Jesus, her kid. Christ, it's not my fault. I couldn't take the kid too."

"Forget it, Sonny. He's okay. Social Services, they've got him, that's what the paper said."

"How's Helen?"

"Helen? Oh, my God, Sonny, she won't speak to me. She won't speak to her own mother. She's worse than ever. God! What about the other one?"

"The other one?"

"You know. You saw the X ray."

"Oh, that one. Horrible outlook. Surgery next week. I keep track. Every now and then I—adjust things slightly."

"You adjust things slightly! Oh, good for you, Sonny. Oh, that's rich. My clever boy."

THE NEW YEAR

"Das alte Jahr vergangen ist"
Chorale harmonized by J. S. Bach

With this new year we raise new songs,
To praise the Lord with hearts and tongues.
For His support in troubles past,
Wherewith our life was overcast.

CHAPTER 9

*The dream I had lately, will be made true; 'twas that I was
dead, and stood by my grave, covered with rags. . . .*
                                                            Martin Luther

Edith Frederick lived on Beacon Street. Her house
had been in her husband's family since its construction by Blaikie and Blaikie in 1888. The façade was
elaborate with wrought iron. A heavy stone bow front rose
beside the sumptuous entry.

But the house was not a fortress. It had been broken into
by a merciless thief, a burglar with no interest in snatching
up the silver. Instead he had attacked Edith herself, he had
battered her, yanked out handfuls of hair and flattened her
breasts, knocked out her teeth and tugged loose the fresh
skin of her face so that it sagged beneath her chin. The thief
was still lurking in the house, in closets, in the pantry, in the
cellar, reaching out to dim her sight, to drive knives into
her ears and a sword down her throat.

Edith fought back as well as she could. This morning her
weapon was a new wardrobe for the new year.

The proprietor of the dress shop on Newbury Street
knew her tastes exactly. She trotted out the little boiled
jackets that Edith loved, the angora turtlenecks, the pleated
woolen skirts. Cleverly she had saved them for Mrs. Frederick from last year, guessing they were going out of style.

Edith was delighted. She chose six pretty jackets in wine,
forest green, black, gray, navy and winter white.

"Edge-stitched," said the proprietor softly, displaying a selection of pleated skirts.

"Oh, good," said Edith, knowing how gaily the pleats
would twinkle as she walked, how the panels of light and
shadow would swish to left and right. She chose them in

five colors to go with the jackets—gray, black, navy, Dress Gordon and Black Watch.

Edith wore the gray combination out of the shop. The new gray sweater of softest angora rose warmly above her coat collar, hiding the stringy skin of her neck. Walking quickly along Clarendon Street, she looked into the faces of the young people as they thrust past her, plump girls with masses of disordered hair and weedy-looking boys, their noses red with cold. Did they notice her? No, they gave her not a glance.

How old were they? They had been babies only a few years ago. It made Edith tremble, the way the young were forever rushing into life, surging into adulthood around her, each mini-generation thrusting her further into old age. To each new batch she must seem still more doddering and superannuated.

Edith stared at the boy veering toward her now across the sidewalk—surely he was less than fourteen. If she were to say to him, "I was born in 1915," it would seem fantastically remote, as though she had started life during the Civil War. She gave him a challenging look, commanding him to see her, to recognize that a woman of stature was walking toward him, but the boy only turned his head to the street and spat. A ball of white foam fell toward the pavement, translucent in the morning light.

Edith recoiled and hurried past him—but the boy wasn't spitting at Edith. He was spitting at his father, he was spitting at school.

At least in the Church of the Commonwealth she would find the esteem she deserved. Edith had been coming here since childhood. It was like another home. She had met Henry in the church when it had been part of a whole Back Bay neighborhood of familiar places, a community of friends and relations.

In Edith's youth there had been a lovely shape to her life—Friday afternoons at the Symphony, dancing classes at the Somerset under the tyranny of Miss Blanding, rounds of parties, musicales and concerts. Edith smiled, remembering the morning after her coming-out party when all her best friends had refused to go home to bed. They had shocked the cook by making their own breakfasts in the basement kitchen, then scandalized her mother by running off to the Sunday morning service at the Church of the Commonwealth in ball gowns and tuxedoes.

Edith and Henry, Ginny and Abby and Nick and Richard and Edgar, they had been full of high spirits in those days, but their good manners were the result of gentle rearing in pleasant homes on Marlborough Street or Newbury or Beacon or Commonwealth Avenue, houses with sumptuous reception halls and monumental staircases. Their country places were more modest, big wooden houses where everyone took pride in living simply, with only a cook and a couple of maids and a gardener.

It was all gone now. The Great Depression had scattered her friends. Luckily Henry's family had survived intact, its wealth secure, soundly invested in government bonds. The others had not been so fortunate. Their houses had been sold and broken up into flats.

And therefore it was all young professional couples now along Commonwealth Avenue, and dentists and doctors. Marlborough and Beacon were brimming with students from Boston University and Northeastern, careless young people with hideous styles of dress and frightening haircuts, totally ignorant of the history of the houses they occupied, unfamiliar with the fine old families who had lived in them once upon a time—Sturgises, Dwights, Welds, Wheelwrights, Osgoods, Brewsters, Coffins, Searses, Abbotts. The good old names meant nothing. The new ones were so outlandish! But of course it was a good thing, Edith could see that. *Give me your tired, your poor, etc.,* you couldn't argue with it.

Still, there was something sad about the change. No

longer could she walk down the street to take tea with a family of cousins. No longer was she pillowed on a sturdy support system in the basement, where the laundress plunged red arms in hot water to scrub the shirts and soaked the collars in starch and pressed the sheets with a smoothing iron and billowed them over the beds and tucked them in. No longer did coal rattle down the chute into the bin, no longer did the grate clatter as it was shaken down, no longer were the ashes lugged up to the alley. Gone were the invitations on the hall table—gone, all gone away—along with the musicales and the dinner dances and the balls.

With tenderness Edith remembered her mother's dressing table, with the hand mirror of heavy silver and the matching brush, comb, shoehorn and buttonhook. Flown to the winds of heaven were the lacy dresser scarf, the eiderdown puff and the fragrant spills of powder, gone with the other lovely things—gone too with dreadful forgotten wars, with doughboys marching too fast on the scratched film, lying swollen and dead on the barbed wire. Edith shuddered.

But the Church of the Commonwealth was still there, occupying the same corner as always. The church was a monument to the unity of Edith's life, to lasting values in an era of terrifying change. On the first shopping day of the new year she stood on the cold grass of the narrow park running down the center of the avenue and looked up at the tower, feeling a strong sense of possession, as if the sixty-two courses of Roxbury pudding stone belonged to her, and the decorative stripes of Longmeadow freestone, and the medieval interior. The sanctuary was something to be especially proud of, Edith knew, because the stone vaults were the first in the United States.

The new organ of course was truly her own. The organ was the direct result of Henry's investment in South African diamond cartels in the decade before his death. All the profits, every single dollar, had gone to form the new trust for the church, the Frederick Music Endowment.

Edith knew nothing about its source. The other day, listening to the voicing of the Spire Flute, she had not given a thought to the thousands of black laborers somewhere in South Africa, hacking at the soil with pickaxes. The pressurized air blown into the pipe from the windchest of the organ bore no relation to the gasping breath of a black man with tubercular lungs in a Kimberley diamond mine. If the blowing air whispered anything to the Spire Flute, it was the story of Henry's cleverness and generosity, and that was all.

Here and now, on this second day of January, Edith waited for the green light, then walked across the street to the arched entry of the church, copied, she knew, from some medieval cathedral in southern France. As usual the aura of the building reached out to enclose her. It gave her a sense of expansion to enter the church, to feel herself part of so majestic a thing. Within these walls her timid life was founded on solid stone, uplifted by luminous panels of stained glass. Here for the moment it had weight and sublimity, it was not simply a succession of fragile pearls on a raveling string.

"Good morning, Loretta," she said brightly, walking into the secretary's office. "Is Mr. Kraeger in?"

"Martin? Oh, sure, he's in."

"Do you think he'd mind if I took a few minutes of his time?"

Loretta leaned forward and yelled "MARTIN," then flopped her knitting over and started back on the next row.

Edith turned away in sorrow, remembering secretaries from the past—Millicent Marchbanks with her Remington typewriter, Amelia Parsons with her mimeograph machine, Nedda Mistletoe with her splendid new filing system, and even Dorothy Keene with her newfangled word processor. Loretta Fawcett was a pitiful comedown.

"I'm sorry to disturb you, Martin, but Alan tells me the

organ is sufficiently voiced so that it can be played regularly from now on."

"Oh, yes, he told me. He's finished half a dozen ranks. Doesn't it sound great?"

Mrs. Frederick hastened to the business at hand. "I'm arranging with the music committee to audition candidates for the job of substitute while Jim Castle is away."

"Good for you." Kraeger waved at the sofa and moved aside a stuffed animal belonging to his daughter Pansy, and a crystal ball, the gift of a comedian in the congregation. Picking up a fallen pillow, he said, "Do sit down."

The pillow was the one Edith had made for him herself. She pretended not to notice the grubby condition of her fine stitches, although it gave her a pang, remembering all the loving hours she had spent with the bright strands of wool. It distressed her that Kraeger made such a bear's den of his fine mock-Tudor study. Disorder bothered Edith.

She talked about the substitute organist, the arrangements for tryouts, the importance of the temporary position, the salary, which would be the same as that paid to James Castle. "It's such a prestigious appointment. It will be a great boost to someone's career."

"That's very generous of you, Edith." Kraeger admired the fragile woman sitting so upright on the monstrous sofa. Edith Frederick was stiff and prudish and often irritatingly old-fashioned and conventional, but she was also affectionate, vulnerable, easily wounded, and truly generous. Tin ear and all, she had devoted herself to the musical life of the church.

But she was old. How old? Kraeger didn't know. Looking at the hollows in her cheeks, the withered dewlaps, the sad descending lines around her mouth, he thought of Holbein's woodcuts of the Dance of Death—all those agile skeletons arm in arm with emperors and bishops, plucking the sleeves of nuns and stout German burghers with their bony fingers, summoning them without warning, dragging them away. Now, looking at Edith Frederick, he could almost see the jolly skeleton hovering beside her, its arms hooked tenderly around her little jacket, its empty eye sockets snapping at the joke, its grin widening in silent laughter. Well, the bony fingers would be reaching for all of them before long—just as they had reached for Mr. Plummer. Death had taken him without warning in the same way.

Kraeger winced and suffered.

♦ ♦ ♦ ♦

CHAPTER 10

Take hold of time, while 'tis time, and now, while 'tis now.
Martin Luther

A lan spent the week after Christmas with his parents and his sister Betsy in Brunswick, Maine. During the day he did his best to be a cheerful son and brother, but at night he couldn't sleep for thinking about Rosie Hall.

He sounded out Betsy. "What was she like, I mean, really?"

"Rosie?" Betsy frowned, trying to explain. "She was smart, that's for sure. Let's see—she bit her fingernails."

"Well, where do you think she's gone?"

"How should I know? But it's terrible, really. The blood on the floor! And the baby being left behind like that. Ghastly, just incredibly ghastly."

Alan made up his mind. When he got back to Boston he would hire somebody, like that professor-policeman who had looked into the fire at Commonwealth, Homer Kelly. Kelly would know how to look for a missing person.

And Alan could afford to pay him, at least for a while. His parents had given him money for Christmas. He was supposed to spend it on a better place to live.

"Alan, dear," said his mother, "I want you to find a nicer apartment. You can't entertain your friends in that squalid hole on Russell Street."

Alan told her his friends lived in places just as bad if not worse, but that seemed to pain her even more. He went back to Boston with the check in his pocket and a guilty conscience. But when he walked into his rented room, it looked fine. There was nothing the matter with it. One of these days he'd hang up his clothes and put up some shelving. If he spent a weekend painting the place it would be almost respectable, even to his mother.

No time for that now. Alan lifted a bag of pipe-notching tools from a chair and sat down to call Homer Kelly.

"Mr. Kelly? My name's Alan Starr. We met on the day after the fire in the Church of the Commonwealth. I was there to look at the organ. But I'm calling about something else. I wonder if you remember the disappearance a month ago of Rosalind Hall? It was in the news for a while. Her baby was left behind, remember?"

"Oh, yes, of course, the abandoned baby."

"Well, I'm the one who found him and called the police."

"That's right, I remember your name. What can I do for you, Alan Starr?"

Alan explained. In his own ears his interest in the matter sounded feeble, just as it had seemed to Mrs. Barker in the Department of Social Services.

But Homer Kelly didn't boggle. "I've got a tutorial this morning. I could meet you afterward, say around noon?"

"A tutorial? That's right, you're a professor. What do you teach, Professor Kelly?"

"Oh, one thing and another. Thoreau and Emerson. Do you know Christopher Cranch? *Tell me, brother, what are we?/Spirits bathing in the sea/Of Deity!* I don't know if that sort of thing will come in handy. What do you think?"

There was a pause while Alan sorted it out. "Well, I guess it can't do any harm. Could you meet me at 115 Commonwealth Avenue? It's Rosie's apartment, near Clarendon Street."

Alan spent the morning at the Church of the Commonwealth, voicing the new organ. What should he work on next? More foundation stops on the Great? Or get started on the Choir?

Pip Tower was there to lend a hand, to sit at the console

depressing one key after another while Alan worked among the pipes, notching a languid, shaping a lip.

For a concert organist like Pip it was a comedown, but as usual he had to take whatever work he could get. He was only one of many Boston Conservatory graduates eking out a living with part-time jobs. They were a minor population of opera singers, flutists, string players and pianists, scraping along by giving lessons, filling in as temporary secretaries, working as hospital orderlies, bartenders, waiters, hoping for the big concert opportunity, the opening in a church somewhere, a symphony orchestra, the music department of a university.

Pip was darkly comic on the subject. "We were fools to choose church music in the first place. Who cares about sacred music in the United States? It's a crass vulgar country of atheists and unbelievers. I'm an atheist myself, so what the hell? Of course there are all those people on the religious right, but their music comes from Nashville."

He sat at the console of the new organ in the balcony of the Church of the Commonwealth and listened while Alan explained from within the massed rows of pipes. "You just play one key at a time, while I work my way up the rank. Degrees of glory, that's what you listen for. Jim Castle wants glory. Here, wait a minute." Alan used his voicing spoon on the lower lip of a Spindle Flute to make the flue a little narrower.

Pip played low C on the Swell keyboard. "It's still a little breathy."

Alan made the opening still narrower. "Try it now. What do you think?"

"Glorious. Absolutely glorious."

"Wait a sec. I'll make it more so. How is it now?"

"Even more glorious. Divinely, gloriously glorious. What about that old biddy who paid for it? Do you have to please her too?"

"What? I can't hear you very well."

Pip spoke louder. "That old crone with the moneybags, Mrs. Frederick. Why doesn't she subsidize good-looking young guys with talent? Maybe she needs a boyfriend. Only, God, imagine going to bed with an old hag like Edith Frederick."

"Try the D-natural."

They worked at it all morning, then called it quits. "I don't suppose you could pay me right now?" said Pip, looking embarrassed.

"Oh, sure." Alan counted out a bunch of bills and handed them over. Then he stopped in the office of the accountant, Jenny Franklin, hoping to be reimbursed.

Jenny tut-tutted. "Alan, you really ought to be more systematic. You should make out a request ahead of time, with the address and social security number, and then I'll send a check." But she reimbursed him. "Just this once."

On his way out, Alan met Mrs. Frederick in the vestibule beside the table of church bulletins and pious pamphlets— *Walter Wigglesworth and His Times, Stained Glass at Commonwealth, Our Ministry to Children and Youth, Sermons from a City Church.*

She held out her hand to Alan. Her face was gray. "Alan, tell me, who was that young man?"

"What young man?"

"He just went out. Thin, with fair hair."

Alan was in a hurry. He threw open the door and called back to Mrs. Frederick, "Tower, Philip Tower. Organist, old friend of mine." In the side garden of the church he passed Donald Woody and a man in a heavy overcoat. They were staring up at the window high overhead.

Alan stopped and looked too. The Wise and Foolish Virgins were only dark shapes of glass.

"Have to take the whole thing out," said the man in the overcoat. "Starts to buckle, you've got to reshape the whole outer edge. Building's probably settled, changed the outlines. We'll have to make a template."

"Well, you'll be putting something temporary in its place, right?" said Woody. "Something translucent? Most of the morning light comes in that east window."

"Well, you've got several alternatives—"

Alan stopped listening and hurried away, while behind him, unnoticed, Edith Frederick slipped out of the church and started home, eager for the comfort of a cup of Hu Kwa tea beside the fire in her own bedroom, with its apricot walls and silk comforter and the portrait sketch over the fireplace, Great-Aunt Amelia by John Singer Sargent. As she walked along Commonwealth Avenue, pulling her scarf close around her throat, she committed the name to memory. *Philip Tower.*

Edith had been meeting with the other members of the Music Committee, but before the meeting she had spent a few moments in the sanctuary. Sitting under the balcony during the voicing of the Spindle Flute, she had heard every cruel word—*old biddy, old crone, old hag.* Bitterly she vowed never to forget. The name of the brutal young man was *Philip Tower.*

"Department of Social Services, Mrs. Barker speaking."

"Oh, good, I've been trying to reach you. Your phone sure is busy. Mrs. Barker, my name is Arthur Victoria. I'm with the Boston Hygiene Inspectional Services Department."

"Never heard of it."

"Rodent control, vermin in public buildings, lead paint removal. We have a complaint about rats in one of your foster homes."

"Rats? What did you say your name was?"

"Victoria, Arthur Victoria."

Mrs. Barker wrote it down. "Rats, you say? Which foster home?"

"Well, that's just it. We've lost the complaint form. All we remember is the child's name, Charles Hall. Can you tell us where he is situated?"

Mrs. Barker sucked her pencil thoughtfully. A complaint about rats? She had an acute sense of smell, useful for sniffing out rats of an entirely different kind. Picking up the Boston phone book, she slammed it down on her desk and flipped the pages. "Wait a minute, let me find your department in the phone book, and I'll call you right back. What was that again? Hygiene Inspectional Services?"

Arthur Victoria hung up.

◆ ◆ ◆ ◆

CHAPTER 11

Great people and champions are special gifts of God.
                                    Martin Luther

When Alan arrived at Number 115 Commonwealth Avenue, he found Homer Kelly waiting for him. Homer's greeting was hearty. Alan guessed that other people's business was his meat and drink.

"Oh, shit," said Alan, when his stolen key failed to open the front door.

"Damn," said Homer, whose obscenities derived from an earlier age. "Do you suppose there's a back entrance?"

"The key says *Rear*. Let's try the alley."

They walked past the church and turned the corner on Clarendon. "What's going on over there?" said Homer, staring across the street at the excavation, where power shovel and crane still sat idly in the hole.

"Litigation, I think. Somebody's suing somebody. Everything's on hold."

In the alley it was easy to distinguish the first private house. A brick wall surrounded its small back yard, separating it from the parking places for MINISTER and BUILDING MANAGER. "This must be Number 115," said Alan. "You can see this wall from her living room."

"But there's a padlock on the gate. Your key won't open that."

Alan looked at him inquisitively. "How good are you at climbing?"

"Old hand," said Homer. Wedging the toe of one shoe on the edge of a brick, he grasped the top of the wall and tried to heave himself over. "Ugh, umph, whoops!" Alan gave him a boost, and Homer fell clumsily into a bush on the other side.

Alan vaulted nimbly after him, and helped him up. "Oh, no, I'm afraid you've torn that handsome jacket. Gee, I'm sorry. It looks expensive."

"Morgan Memorial," mumbled Homer, looking with horror at the ripped fabric. In truth the jacket was a Christmas present from his wife, and it had come from a fancy men's clothing store, probably Brooks Brothers. Mary had pasted a discount-store label on the box, because that was more Homer's style.

Rosie Hall's garden was handsome, even in winter, with its ivy-ringed circle of grass. The back door of the house projected at one side.

The key worked. Homer grinned at Alan, and said, "Sshh."

"Don't we need a search warrant or something?"

"And you with a stolen key in your hand? What a question."

They pressed forward into the small entry, which contained only a couple of plastic trash barrels. When Homer tried the knob of one of the inner doors, it turned freely in his hand, and they entered the living room of Rosalind Hall's apartment.

In a moment they were looking at the snapshots on the wall above Rosie's desk. Homer had seen the big picture of Rosie and Charley on the front page of the *Boston Globe*. Looking at it again he was unprepared for the sense of pathos. "The baby's safe enough, I suppose, but where the hell is his mother?"

Alan grimaced, and turned away to the shelf of cassette recorders beside the desk. Their black plastic surfaces were dusty. "I told you about these. They were switched on when I came in. She must have been recording from one to the other. Yes, look, they've both got cassettes."

"Well, go ahead, find out what they are."

"Got to rewind first." Alan set the two pairs of spindles whizzing backwards, and led Homer into Rosie's kitchen. "This is where the blood was. Right there on the floor."

"All cleaned up, I see." Homer knelt and looked at the quarry tiles. The uniform dull sheen was everywhere the same. "I suppose every surface has been tested for fingerprints."

"All I know is what it said in the paper. There weren't any prints they could match up with anybody in their files, except for the ones that were all over the place. They assumed they were Rosie's. They were surprised to find they matched a set in the police file."

Homer was astonished. "They did? Rosalind Hall was fingerprinted before?"

"Juvenile, that's all it said, with a date ten years back. I suppose there must be a way to find out what her prints were there for. Otherwise what's the point of having them in the file at all?"

Homer looked at the face of Rosie on the wall. "She must have done something naughty when she was a kid. I'll look into it. It's odd, but I don't see how it helps. Maybe it will come in handy later on. Then again maybe not."

Alan went back to the tape recorders and touched one of the play buttons. He grinned at Homer as the sober rhythms of a famous organ chorale prelude began pouring into the room.

"Nice," said Homer, wagging his head in time. Homer knew almost nothing about music.

"Listen, it's 'Wachet Auf,' a chorale prelude by Bach. Every organist plays it. It's an old warhorse."

They wandered around the apartment. "What a great place," said Homer. "She must be rich, Rosalind Hall."

"I don't know. According to the paper she inherited the house from her parents, and rented out most of it. I gather she wasn't working full time as an organist, she was mostly just taking care of Charley. That's what Mrs. Garboyle told the reporter. Maybe Rosie inherited a lot of money from her family."

"Mrs. Garboyle? Who's Mrs. Garboyle?"

"She lives here. The rest of the house is sort of a dormitory for girls at Boston University. Mrs. Garboyle's in charge, that's what it said in the paper."

Homer screwed up his big face, searching his memory. "Mrs. Garboyle—it sounds familiar somehow."

They inspected the kitchen, Rosie's bedroom, the bathroom. In the baby's room Alan was overcome by the memory of Charley's fat cheek against his own.

They returned to the living room as the steady merriment of the sixteenth notes of the chorale prelude rollicked to a close and the tape recorder fell silent. Alan extracted the tape and read aloud the handwritten inscription, *Wachet Auf, Harv. Mem. Church, RH.* He looked up at Homer. Once again he felt bereft. "It's her own performance on the Fisk organ at Harvard."

Homer watched with inquisitive interest as Alan stroked the cassette and put it back in the tape recorder. "You said you didn't know her?"

"No. I'd heard of her, of course, but we've never met. Let's hear what's on the other one." Alan touched the PLAY button on the second recorder. Homer was amused to see him lean his hands on either side of the picture of Rosalind Hall and stare at her as he listened. There was something a little goofy about his obvious obsession with the woman. Homer controlled an impulse to kid him about it.

Instead he waved his hand at the second cassette recorder. "Isn't that the same thing?" he said, feeling clever.

"Right, it's 'Wachet Auf.' She must have been copying it." Alan switched it off.

They left by the rear entry. On the way out Homer obeyed a nosy instinct and lifted the lid of the trash barrel. "Trash is always so revealing," he said softly. "Hmmmm, how strange." He pawed in the barrel with a big hand.

"Candles. A lot of perfectly good wax candles. And ashtrays. Look, a lot of ashtrays. And a couple of unopened packs of cigarettes."

"Maybe it's not trash. Maybe she was going to give that stuff away. To the Morgan Memorial or something. Maybe she stopped smoking and decided to give away all her ashtrays."

"But there's trash in here too. See?" Homer picked up a wad of greasy paper towels and dropped them again. "It was all supposed to be thrown out. Wasteful, wouldn't you say?"

"Well, you know how people are when they make a vow to quit smoking. Everything connected with it seems dangerous." Alan opened the outer door and they went out into the cold air. "I ought to know. I quit smoking myself a couple of years ago."

This time Homer managed to get over the brick wall without incident, and they parted on Clarendon Street. "I'll see what I can find out about those old fingerprint records of Rosie's," said Homer. "I doubt it will help, but I'll look into it. And maybe I can throw my weight around in the Department of Social Services and find out what's happened to the baby."

Alan thanked him, surprised at the strength of his gratitude, and hurried off in the direction of the Public Garden.

Homer made for the subway in Copley Square, striding along Commonwealth Avenue past a young couple walking their Dalmatian, a pair of Boston ladies bundled up in fur coats, and an old woman stepping timidly along the sidewalk with a cane, avoiding the slippery places.

He couldn't help smiling at the way young Alan had revealed his interest in the missing mother and child so nakedly. The kid was fond of the baby, that was obvious, but his attachment to the missing Rosalind was also absurdly apparent. And he didn't even know the woman! She might not be lovable at all. Who could tell? Rosalind Hall might be a genuinely ghastly girl.

CHAPTER 12

. . . thus the strong member may serve the weak, and we may be sons of God. Martin Luther

A s it turned out, Homer didn't need to throw his weight around at the Department of Social Services. Alan discovered the whereabouts of young Charley Hall on his own.

After his meeting with Homer at Rosie's apartment, Alan crossed Clarendon Street and glanced down at the excavation, where the pile driver still sat idle on its treads, its crane reaching high in the air, its hammer poised to fall. It pained him to think of the day when it would begin its work, dropping the hammer again and again to pound a thousand pilings into the ground, *kerwham, kerwham, kerwham.* How would he hear the subtle variations in the sound of his pipes with that racket going on across the street?

The cold had increased with the afternoon. Alan walked fast. At the Public Garden he started to run—past the frozen duck pond and the equestrian statue of George Washington, kitty-cornered to the intersection of Charles Street and Beacon, straight along Charles to Mount Vernon and up the steep hill to Louisburg Square.

And there he found Charley Hall.

Alan didn't recognize him at first. Charley was just a blob in a rickety stroller. But when a ray of low winter sunshine streaked through the narrow opening of Walnut Street and landed on his face, Alan was reminded of the baby in the Three Kings window in the Church of the Commonwealth. This infant too was a bright object against a shadowy background. A thin girl pushed the stroller up the hill, struggling to maneuver the small wheels on the uneven bricks of the sidewalk. Another child dragged after her, clinging to her parka.

Something about the baby brought Alan to a halt. He stared at it curiously, then crossed the street and passed in front of the stroller as if he were heading for one of the handsome doorways on the other side. To his delight he saw that the child was indeed none other than the baby he had rescued from the traffic on Clarendon Street two weeks before Christmas.

The baby recognized Alan. His solemn expression brightened. He gurgled and threw out a mittened hand. Alan smiled at him, then climbed the steps of the house as though about to enter. The girl pushing the stroller frowned and increased her speed, bumping the little buggy over a cavity in the sidewalk. The child at her side whimpered and fell back. The girl spoke to her sharply, "For shit's sake, Wanda, come on."

Alan waited until the three of them were several yards ahead of him, then followed. He feared that if he spoke to the girl she might be just as suspicious as Mrs. Barker in the Department of Social Services, but if he followed them home, he would know how to find them again.

They kept going, on and on, up and up. The little stroller bumped and rattled on the uneven bricks, making its way out of the fashionable part of Beacon Hill, jolting past Alan's own street and jouncing all the way through the tunnel beside the State House, where parking places were reserved for THE GOVERNOR, THE CHAIRMAN OF THE HOUSE WAYS AND MEANS COMMITTEE, THE STATE AUDITOR and other luminaries of the political establishment in Massachusetts. At last the girl tipped up the buggy on two wheels and careened left on Bowdoin Street and started down the steep hill with the tearful child toddling in her wake.

Alan too had an appointment on Bowdoin Street, in the

church of St. John the Evangelist, where the organist was troubled by a ciphering pipe. Was the girl heading for the same church? What a coincidence!

She was not. She pushed the stroller past *Joe and Nemo, Hot Dog Kings,* and made a sharp left into a yellow brick building called Bowdoin Manor.

Following her half a block behind, Alan grinned to himself, and noted the name of the place in his head. Now he would know where to find Charley. Satisfied, he went on down the hill, leaning backwards on the steep slope.

St. John the Evangelist was not like the other Episcopal churches in the neighborhood—nothing like Trinity, Emmanuel, Advent or Annunciation. It was a distinguished but shabby edifice catering to the poor, lavishing its funds on the hungry and homeless rather than on its soot-darkened interior. Under the church steps four elderly men were ac-

cepting sandwiches and soup from a woman who carried on a joshing exchange with her old regulars. Alan grinned at them and went inside.

The organist was glad to see him. Alan apologized for being late, and got to work at once on the ciphering reed. It turned out to be a simple matter. A cockroach had wedged itself under the pallet of the pipe, fixing it in the open position, so that it sounded all the time whenever the oboe stop was pulled. Alan repaired it, and urged the organist to do something about the infestation. "There ought to be something you could try. Oh, I know they're incorrigible on Beacon Hill, migrating from one house to another. How does the church usually handle cockroaches?"

The organist rolled his eyes upward. "We pray for them."

"Oh, I see." Alan laughed and packed up his tools. It was time to find Charley.

CHAPTER 13

I should have no compassion on these witches; I would burn all of them.   Martin Luther

The door of Bowdoin Manor was open. The hall smelled of lavatory disinfectant. Alan wandered past a Pepsi machine and a row of doors, listening for children. All was silent. He climbed the worn rubber treads of the steep stairs. At once he was rewarded with the sound of a television and a crying child behind the first door. A slip of paper was taped to the door, with the name *Deborah Buffington* scribbled on it in pencil.

He knocked. The cries increased. In a moment the door opened a crack. It was still held by a chain. A thin child with a sharp face looked out at him. "What do you want?"

It wasn't a child, it was the girl who had been pushing the stroller. Alan was ready with his story. "I've come to see Charles Hall. I'm a friend of the family."

"Oh, sure, a friend of the family! An inspector, you mean, from Social Services. Well, I'm busy right now."

"No, no. My name's Alan Starr. I just want to see the baby."

The pale eyes narrowed. "Are you the father?"

"No, no, the father's dead. I told you, I just want to see the baby." He had to speak up because the television was making a racket and Charley was bellowing.

The girl did not unchain the door. She stared at him sourly. "Why would you want to see the baby? What the hell for?"

Exasperated, Alan tried to explain. "I'm just interested in him, that's all. I was the one who found him on the sidewalk after his mother disappeared. I'm fond of him. I just want to be sure he's all right."

The girl was insulted. "Why shouldn't he be all right?" She turned her narrow face aside and shouted, "Shut up. Just shut up." She had been driven past some point of endurance. Relenting, she wrenched at a bolt, pushed back a bar, undid the chain and opened the door.

At once Alan went to Charley, lifted him out of his playpen and held him at arm's length. Charley stopped crying with a final hiccuping sob, and smiled.

A scrawny little girl in pink tights stared at Alan, then turned back to the tumbling cartoon animals on the television screen. Excited music scrambled around the room.

"He knows you," said the foster mother in surprise, folding her skinny arms across her chest.

"Of course he knows me. We're old buddies." Alan held Charley against his shoulder and looked anxiously at the girl. "How's he doing?"

"Who, him? Oh, Jesus, like he eats everything in sight."

"No, I mean, how are his spirits? Having his mother disappear like that, it must be hard on a little guy."

"Oh, Christ, he never stops crying. God."

"Well, you can't blame him." Alan kissed Charley's damp cheek.

"And he's stupid," said the girl vindictively. "He doesn't even talk or walk."

"Well, isn't he pretty young for talking and walking?"

"My daughter Wanda"—the girl jerked her head at the pale child in front of the TV—"she's been walking since she was a year old, and talking too."

Alan wanted to stick up for Charley's intelligence, but he didn't know anything about babies. "Well, he looks pretty smart to me," he said lamely.

"Well, he's not. He's probably retarded. I'll bet his mother left because she couldn't take it any more. God!"

"Look," said Alan, anxious to give Charley a vacation from this poisonous atmosphere, "may I take him for a walk?"

It was obvious that the girl was torn. How could she let a stranger go off with the child entrusted to her care? On the other hand, with Charley out of the house she'd have a few moments of peace. Alan watched her wrestle with her conscience. Lighting a cigarette, she hurled the match into the sink, took a deep drag and opted for peace.

On the street, with Charley snugly tucked into the stroller, Alan made for 115 Commonwealth Avenue. They were going home. It was a long walk, but it never occurred to him to take the baby anywhere else. He wanted to surround him with his old familiar life and show him his mother's face on the wall.

Up the hill they rushed toward the State House with its gold dome, and turned left on Myrtle Street. Alan bounced the stroller past a mattress leaning against a street lamp and a burlap bag that looked as if it might contain body parts, then turned onto Joy Street. Here seediness gave way to intense refinement and Bostonian charm, at—God!—how much per month?

The ascent was steep. Alan had to drag the stroller behind him all the way up to Mount Vernon Street at the crest of Beacon Hill, but from there it was downhill all the way. The stroller jounced on the cold bricks of Louisburg Square and raced past the shops on Charles Street. As they crossed the Public Garden, Alan ran the little stroller around the Ether Memorial on two wheels, and the baby squealed with joy.

In the alley behind 115 Commonwealth he had to face the problem of getting the baby over the wall. The problem was solved at once. There was a woman in Rosie's garden, a thin old lady with dyed black hair. She was manipulating a trash barrel, dragging it through the open gate into the alley.

She recognized the baby at once. "Oh, it's little Charley!"

she cried with delight. Bending down, she cuddled his face with her hands. "Such a lamb. Where is your sweet mama, Charley dear?" She stood up and looked sadly at Alan. "Such a tragedy, that sweet girl! You're taking care of him now? How nice that he has a foster father!"

Alan cobbled up a lie. It was remarkable how easily it came to him. "No, no, I'm not the foster father. I'm just a friend of Rosie's. I thought I'd keep an eye on the baby, and bring him back home now and then. My name's Starr, Alan Starr."

The old woman put out her hand. "Doris Garboyle." Mrs. Garboyle's eyes were enmeshed in wrinkles, but they were clear and frank.

"Oh, yes, Mrs. Garboyle. You're a housemother here, isn't that right?"

"Upstairs, yes. The ground floor is all Rosalind's. She grew up here when it was a real house. An elegant home." Mrs. Garboyle sighed, and a tear ran down one cheek. "Have you heard anything from the police?"

"Not a thing."

"Well, I hope they find her soon." Mrs. Garboyle leaned down and kissed Charley. "This little chickabiddy needs his mother."

"Is it all right if we go in? The police gave me a key to the back door." Once again Alan was surprised at his easy disregard for the truth. "Oh, Mrs. Garboyle, I don't suppose you have an extra key for the gate?"

"Of course, dear! I'll get one at once. I've got four or five extras." She hurried ahead of him, hugging her skinny arms to her sweater in the cold. The back entry was open. Mrs. Garboyle bustled through the second of the inner doors, and Alan caught a glimpse of the hall he had entered with the wandering baby on that eventful night before Christmas. "Back in a minute," promised Mrs. Garboyle, closing the door behind her.

Alan unlocked Rosie's back door and dragged the stroller into her apartment. At once he picked up Charley and carried him to the picture on the wall. Charley's education began at once. "Look, Charley, there's your mama. See Mama? That's Mama, Mama, Mama!"

The truth was, Alan felt a parental sense of competition with little Wanda, who had walked and talked when she was only twelve months old. By God, he'd teach Rosie's infant son to talk.

CHAPTER 14

Thus am I long since condemned to die, and yet I live.
Martin Luther

"*Call them again, Mother. You've got to try them again.*"
"*For Christ's sake, Helen, hold still! How can I comb your hair if you don't control yourself?*"
"*Oh, dear God, take me out of here. Oh God, please God, let me go.*"
"*Oh, wonderful, Helen, that's just wonderful. That's the thanks I get for sacrificing myself, when I might have been anything, anything! Helen, stop it! Hold still!*"
"*Please, God, let me go.*"

Alan called Homer Kelly to tell him about finding Charley. A woman answered the phone. "I'm sorry, Mr. Starr, Homer's not here. This is Mary Kelly. You're the organist? Homer's told me all about you. Oh, forgive me, perhaps he shouldn't have."

Homer's wife had a rich warm voice. Alan found himself eager to confide in her, to tell her everything. "Tell Homer I found the baby."

"The baby! Rosalind Hall's baby? How wonderful."

"I just happened to run into him. There he was, big as life on Mount Vernon Street. His foster mother was pushing him along the sidewalk in a little stroller, you know, one of those collapsible things on wheels. They live on Bowdoin Street. I don't know if it's a good arrangement or not. Her name's Debbie Buffington. She let me take him out for a while, and I brought him home. You know, to his own place on Commonwealth Avenue. Did Homer tell you? I've got a key."

"Yes, he told me. He's been looking into the matter of Rosalind's fingerprints."

"He has? Did he find out why she was fingerprinted before?"

"No. They lost the files. It was a computer error. Somebody punched a wrong button and wiped out five years of statistical records."

"My God."

"It was probably some dumb thing she did," said Mary soothingly. "She doesn't seem like the kind of girl who would have had a wild youth."

"No way."

Mary thanked him and promised to tell Homer the good news.

"Don't tell anybody else though," said Alan. "Debbie Buffington's afraid she'll get in trouble with the Department of Social Services. I gather they've got a really fierce woman in charge of foster care."

"Well, naturally they've got to be careful with other people's babies. You must be attached to the little boy, to want to see him again."

"Oh, yes," said Alan eagerly. "And it isn't only that." He was on the verge of telling Mary Kelly about his obsession with the picture of Charley's mother, but he checked himself in time. It was true that the picture haunted him, the tape recording of her playing enchanted him, and her handsome apartment seduced him, but what kind of a jerk would say anything like that out loud?

Extracting Charley from Debbie for another expedition to 115 Commonwealth Avenue was easier than the first time. Lazily Debbie said, "So long," and slammed the door.

It was the middle of January, but the sidewalks were still clear. The sun shone, the sky was blue. In the alley behind the church Alan surprised a woman who was unloading her car behind the church, dumping things on the pavement, a stack of small plastic chairs, a tricycle.

"Want to sign up?" she called to Alan gaily as he squeezed the stroller past her car. "We've got an opening in our new daycare center. Somebody cancelled out at the last minute."

"Oh, no thanks," mumbled Alan.

"Cute little kid," said the woman.

"Oh, right," said Alan, pleased with the compliment in spite of himself.

With this second visit to the apartment Alan and Charley established a pattern. The talking lesson came first, *Mama, Mama, Mama,* in front of Rosie's picture. Charley still didn't say anything, but he looked at the picture solemnly. To Alan he was less like an uncomprehending child than a wise old person who listened and kept his own counsel. In spite of the rancid opinion of Debbie Buffington—"Jesus, I think he's Mongoloid"—Alan knew the baby wasn't stupid. His rubbery little face was expressive, his eyes gleamed with good humor. There was a real person somewhere inside that plump infant body, communing with himself. One day he'd throw his bottle on the floor and say, "Here I am."

After the lesson it was time for a solid meal. Alan had seen the sort of food Debbie Buffington dished up for Wanda and Charley—macaroni, ice cream and potato chips. Surely the kid needed something healthier than that. Alan found little jars of spinach and apricots in a kitchen cupboard, and fed them to Charley with a tiny spoon. Charley smacked it all down.

After lunch it was naptime. Alan laid the baby down in the playpen, covered him with a blanket, then roamed around the apartment, looking in drawers and closets, wanting to know everything about Rosalind Hall. In her bedroom closet he looked at the clothes on the hangers, but they told him nothing. A thin nightgown hung on a hook, and it told him too much, not about Rosie but about himself. He lifted the transparent tissue and held it between his fingers and let it go again.

From the bedroom he went back to her collection of tape-recorded music. He took the two cassettes of "Wachet Auf" from the tape recorders, tucked them away in plastic boxes, and looked at the rest of her collection. It was a pity she didn't have better equipment. If she ever came home again, he'd show off his high-tech apparatus. She'd find out what she was missing.

Then for the first time since he had stolen it from Rosie's drawer, Alan remembered her notebook. He had stuffed it in the inside breast pocket of his jacket. Was it still there? It was. He pulled it out eagerly. Plumping himself down on the sofa he began leafing through it. The first pages were lists of organ registrations for pieces he recognized, chorale preludes from Bach's *Little Organ Book*. Some were in Castle's handwriting. Castle had made out similar lists for Alan.

What did Castle really think about Rosie? It was common knowledge she had been his favorite pupil. But everybody assumed he wasn't really interested in women. Most of the male organists in Boston weren't interested in the opposite sex. It was a fact of life.

But then it occurred to Alan with a rush of blood to his head that Rosie and Castle had disappeared at almost the same time. And Castle's parting from the church had been mysterious. He had not said where he was going or when he'd be back. His mother was supposed to be ill, but he had not deigned to tell anyone the exact nature of her illness or where she was lying at death's door. It was very strange. Alan had a vision of Rosie locked up in Castle's basement, wherever that might be, pounding on the door, crying, *Let me out!*

It was an unpleasant picture. Ridiculous, anyway. Respectable men of fifty with impeccable reputations, freckled bald heads and exalted careers did not carry women away by force, especially if they weren't attracted to women in the first place.

Once again Alan flipped the pages of the notebook. This

time he found a list of addresses. They were all organists. To his surprise his own name was among them.

Turning the page, he found the strangest of Rosie's lists. What the hell was it all about?

Self-sounding bells
Echoes in different languages
Boxes in which sounds can be locked up
Mirror fugues
Puzzle canons
A prison shaped like an ear, to carry the prisoner's secrets to the keeper
A domed chamber in which a whisper can be heard from one side to the other
The Little Harmonic Labyrinth, BWV 591
The music of the spheres
The Well-Tempered Clavier

The last item on the list made him laugh—

Noah's ark

What sort of fantasy was this? Most of it had to do with sounds—bells, whispers, echoes, music by Bach—BWV 591 was #591 in the *Bach Werke-Verzeichnis*. Puzzle canons and mirror fugues—the composer had been famous for playful inversions of melodies, musical themes turned backwards and upside-down. They were a sign of his teeming inventiveness, his frolicsome delight in tossing balls in the air, bouncing them on his head, catching them in his mouth, his hat, turning a somersault while the ball was in the air. But what was Noah's ark doing on the list?

Charley whimpered. He was waking up. Alan looked at his watch. They had been away from Debbie Buffington for two hours. It was the darkest time of the year, and dusk was falling. When would she begin to worry?

He bent over the playpen and looked at Charley. If only

the kid could talk. He must know what had happened to his mother. "Where's Mama, Charley?" said Alan, reaching down to pick him up. "Where's Mama?"

At once the baby did something clever. He turned his head and looked at the picture on the wall.

Alan swept him up and hugged him. What a smart little kid! Charley might not yet be talking, but his mind was there, all right, in spite of what his surly foster mother said. Hastily Alan carried him into his bedroom, changed his diaper, shoved him into his puffy outdoor clothes and plopped him into the stroller.

At the last minute, on impulse, Alan took Rosie's notebook to the window, turned to an empty page and made an entry:

January 5: Charley understands the word "Mama."

EPIPHANY

◆ ◆ ◆ ◆ ◆

"In Dich hab ich gehoffet, Herr"
Chorale harmonized by J. S. Bach

Thy splendor fills the blackest hour of night,
The solemn dark is all alight.
O set our feet upon Thy way!
That we may see
Eternally
Thy star forever bright as day.

◆ ◆ ◆ ◆

CHAPTER 15

It is said: "Preach thou, I will give strength."
Martin Luther

It was the day called Epiphany, the sixth of January, the
feast honoring the journey of the Wise Men to Bethlehem. This year it happened to fall on a Sunday. Thus
the annual special service celebrating the window of the
Three Kings in the south wall of the Church of the Commonwealth was better attended than usual.

The congregation was a mixed lot, as always. They sat elbow to elbow in their heavy winter coats, glancing up at
the window now and then. It was a cloudy day. The colored glass was muddy, the chalices dim, the naked infant in-
distinct.

Looking down at the crowded pews from the balcony,
Alan studied the occupants—male and female, old and
young—and wondered why they were all there. Some had
come for friendship, some sought metaphysical enlighten-
ment from Martin Kraeger, some were sturdy regulars from
way back, some were James Castle groupies—disappointed
this morning to find a string quartet fiddling in the balcony.
A few were elderly Brahmins like Edith Frederick who had
lived in the Back Bay all their lives. The surrounding uni-
versities were responsible for the students and professors, the
hospital complex for doctors, nurses and health administra-
tors. There were couples from the suburbs who had paid fifteen dollars to park their cars, and homeless people grateful
for the steaming radiators under the sanctuary floor and the
five-thousand-gallon oil tank in the basement.

Martin Kraeger preached to them all. He did not need a
microphone. His voice was strong, almost a bellow. In the

pulpit he often quoted a remark of Martin Luther's, *I cannot pray without at the same time cursing,* because all his sermons contained this paradox. On the one hand the nation was in decline and the planet was going to hell, but on the other, his own wit and his huge laugh and the strength of the good will that flowed from his combative spirit urged his congregation to plunge into the fight.

They emerged from one of his services mauled but refreshed. A sermon by Martin Kraeger wasn't a twisting of the arm, it was a wrenching, a powerful shove. They went out from the glowing darkness of the sanctuary into the daylight, feeling dazed, discovering that the trees along the divided street had taken other shapes, the cars were not the sort they remembered, the traffic lights were different shades of red and green.

This morning Kraeger's sermon was not a moral harangue, it was a psychological study of three sorts of journeys—those that tracked unmistakable stars, others following erratic and wandering lights, and a third sort probing for secret smoldering fires underground. It was a good sermon as sermons went, poetic and full of meaning of some sort or other, although perhaps there had been too many metaphors.

After the service Alan took four envelopes out of his pocket and paid the string quartet, handing over the checks he had requisitioned from Jenny Franklin.

On Sunday afternoon he took Charley for another ride in the stroller. It was a warm and blustery day. The winter streets were dry, the sidewalks still negotiable for the little wheels of the stroller. Alan gave Charley a giddy flight of wild bumps and bounds down Mount Vernon Street, and the baby screeched with delight. In the Public Garden they flew over the bridge across the Duck Pond and rushed in the direction of Arlington Street. There they had to stop because three men were blocking the sidewalk.

They loomed over the baby, three derelicts with ruined

faces. The tallest had a red nose and dirty denim trousers. "Gawd," he said, bending down, breathing gin into Charley's face, "he sure is cute."

"What's his name?" said the man in the green Day-Glo jacket.

"Charley."

"Mine's Tom," said the tall man, beaming proudly at Alan. "This here's Dick." He clapped the shoulder of the man in the green jacket.

They were harmless, Alan could see that. They only wanted to put their old faces close to Charley's, as one might smell a flower. "I suppose you must be Harry," said Alan, smiling at the third man, who was kneeling in front of the buggy.

The man looked up at him with small red eyes and grinned evilly, exposing three missing teeth. "Harry it is. I was christened sixty-four years ago by a Christadelphian Baptist."

The words came hissing out through the vacant teeth, but his accent was not like Tom's or Dick's. It was a soft whiskey baritone with cultured vowels.

"Hey," said Tom, "tell you what. I got something for the baby. Gawd, he's cute." He pulled down the zipper of his jacket and extracted a limp stuffed animal of no particular species.

Charley took it, turned it upside-down and hugged it to his breast.

"Well, thank you," said Alan, wondering how to get away.

"Jeez," said Dick, "I got something too." He rummaged in a sagging pocket and pulled out a lollipop to which a good deal of lint was stuck.

Alan felt a parental twinge of doubt, but he made no protest as Charley took the lollipop, perceived at once what it was for, and stuck it in his mouth.

Harry had a gift too. Getting to his feet with difficulty,

he groped in his coat and produced a shiny silver object. He put it to his lips, and a clear sweet note threaded its way down the street. Charley let go of the lollipop stick and held up his hand. "Wait a minute, kid." Removing the lollipop from Charley's mouth, Harry inserted the whistle. "Now blow."

My God, the germs, thought Alan. He watched anxiously as Charley sucked on the pipe, then blew a tentative breathy note.

"Smart kid," said Harry. "Maybe he'll be a flutist."

It was the first time Charley's intelligence had been praised by the outside world, and Alan felt a surge of pride. *You hear that, Wanda?*

Tom poked Charley's stomach with a dirty finger, Dick patted his woolly cap, Harry winked at Alan, and they shambled away into the Public Garden.

"The three kings in person," murmured Alan to the winter air.

Charley sucked in his breath and blew a tremendous blast.

A t the main office of the Massachusetts Department of Social Services on Causeway Street, Mrs. Marilynne Barker was harassed by another phone call about the infant Charley Hall.

"Mrs. Barker? This is Diana Weatherby calling. I am an attorney. How are you today?"

There was a pause while Mrs. Barker controlled her temper. An inquiry about her health by a total stranger meant a dumb phone call. "I'm just fine. Why do you want to speak to me?"

"Well, we have a court order, you see, requesting information about a foster child named Charles Hall. We need to know where he is residing."

The smell of rat was very strong. "Tell me, Ms. Weatherby, when did you pass the bar?"

"When did I—? Oh, last year, I mean the year before that."

"Okay, what's the second amendment to the Constitution?"

There was a gasp at the other end.

Mrs. Barker snickered and hung up, congratulating herself on preventing another criminal interference with her system of foster care. Why on earth were these phony people so inquisitive about young Charles Hall? Was there a disgruntled father hiding in the wings somewhere? No, there wasn't any father. The father was dead. Could it be some infertile couple desperate to steal a child? But why this particular child?

Mrs. Barker got back to work, but she couldn't get young Charley off her mind. The truth was, his foster home was extremely marginal. Probably she never should have accepted that dreary young woman Deborah Buffington as a foster mother. It might be a good idea to drop in on her one day with a surprise inspection.

Not today, of course, or tomorrow. For the moment Mrs. Barker was overwhelmed. As an administrator she shouldn't have had a case load of her own at all, but Social Services had been drastically cut back. They were trying to do twice as much work with half the former staff. It was impossible.

But this morning she had foiled an intruder. She had done one good deed this day. For once her occupation seemed more like the humane and compassionate calling she had expected it to be in the beginning.

CHAPTER 16

The world remains the world it was thousands of years ago; that is, the spouse of the devil.   Martin Luther

H omer studied the blue pages in the Boston telephone book, then dialed a number.

"'Vestigative Services," said a bored voice on the line.

"Department of Missing Persons?"

"Jussamin'."

It took Homer three tries, two transfers to other departments, one disconnected line, one wrong number, and four long pauses while he was batted around from one reluctant departmental employee to another, until at last a certain Lieutenant Middleton accepted the responsibility for knowing something about the disappearance of Rosalind Hall.

"You a relative?" said Lieutenant Middleton.

"No, but I'm looking into the case. My name's Homer Kelly."

"Homer Kelly?" Lieutenant Middleton sounded interested at once. "Oh, sure, I heard of you. What can I do for you, Mr. Kelly?"

"Well, I just wondered if you've made any progress in finding Rosalind's whereabouts?"

"I'll be honest with you. We've been so busy with the Cheese case, we haven't had much time for anything else."

"The cheese case? You've got a runaway cheese?"

"You know, Roberta Cheese, her case."

"Roberta Cheese?"

"The movie star. You mean you never heard of Roberta Cheese? Christ, where you been? Didn't you see the story on TV last week? She disappeared from Boston Common. They were shooting on Boston Common, this big Hollywood director, and all of a sudden their big star turns up missing."

"So you've been working on that, instead of on the disappearance of Rosalind Hall?"

"Well, Christ, the mayor's on our back. If we don't find her, the whole city looks bad on the national news. Everybody in the country, they're all following the case. God, Roberta Cheese disappears and it lands in our laps!"

"Mmmm, yes, I see. But Rosalind—"

"She wasn't kidnapped anyway. She probably left voluntarily. Ninety-eight percent of missing persons turn up someplace, they left on their own hook, they aren't missing at all."

"But what about the blood? It was her blood, right? That's what they found out. And some of her hair was in it, so she must have suffered a head wound."

"Oh, sure, but she probably slipped and fell, then got up and walked out. She packed a suitcase, right? Because there isn't any luggage in her closet, although that old lady in the house claims she had some, and she told us some of the clothes are gone. I don't know why we should spend our time looking for a woman who walked out on her own baby."

"What about her friends? Did you talk to any of her friends?"

"Oh, sure. Well, I mean, we talked to the old lady in the building. I told you, with this big Hollywood· case—"

"The Big Cheese case. I see. Well, thank you, Lieutenant Middleton."

Homer put down the phone and looked out the window at the frozen surface of Fair Haven Bay. There had been perfect skating on black ice ever since Christmas, as the cold continued and the snow held off. Yesterday he had skated upriver with Mary all the way to Framingham. Now he went looking for his wife, depressed by the exigencies of political life in the city of Boston.

"Well, of course I've heard of Roberta Cheese," said Mary. "Homer, where have you been? She ran off with her publicist last week, everybody knows that."

"She ran off with her—? You mean she didn't just disappear?"

"Well, her publicist disappeared at the same time, and his wife is hopping mad. It's common knowledge."

"Then why is Missing Persons so wrought up? Oh, well, never mind. Listen, those people didn't even bother to talk to anybody who knew Rosie Hall. So I've got to do it. Alan gave me a list. I've got an appointment with Barbara Inch. Want to come along?"

Barbara Inch waited for Homer in her apartment on Marlborough Street. It was a small apartment, dark and bleak, giving on the alley at the rear of the house. Even so, Barbara could not have afforded it without a roommate to share the expenses. Roommates were transitory and various, and sometimes infuriating, but there was no help for it. Barbara put up with them, doing her share of the housekeeping without complaint.

She had been on her own for years. Her parents had paid for her education at the Conservatory and then they had quietly died, leaving her to fend for herself. For a while Barbara had worked as a nurse's aide, and then she had found a part-time job teaching music in a private school. Last year her troubles had seemed to be over when she was hired as organist and choir director at the Church of the Annunciation.

But she had just been fired. When the phone rang, Barbara tried to get her voice under control before murmuring a choked hello.

It was Alan Starr. "Am I calling at a bad time? You sound as if you've been crying."

"Me, crying? The Inch family never cries."

"Oh, excuse me."

"It's okay. The truth is, I've lost my job at Annunciation."

"Oh, God, I'm sorry. What happened?"

"Incorrigible behavior."

"Oh, Jesus, Barbara, what did you do this time?"

"Failed to show respect for the assistant rector, not to mention to Jesus Christ, Our Lord. Mr. Binnacle turned around and caught me genuflecting when he was genuflecting."

"Good grief, during a service?"

"No, no, it was just a rehearsal for the first Sunday after Epiphany, but it was in front of the whole choir, accompanied by various titterings, gigglings, chucklings and other misdemeanors. I admit it was disrespectful, but he's such a pompous ass."

"Well, look, don't worry. They're having auditions for Castle's job. They need a substitute while he's away."

"No kidding? Well, I'll try, but Pip Tower will get it. He's better than I am."

"Well, try anyway. Oh, Barbara—"

"Yes?"

"I'm sort of interested in trying to find out what happened to Rosalind Hall. You knew her, right? Could you tell me about her? I mean—like, I never met her. People kept telling me I ought to, but I never did."

"She knew about you."

"Well, that's because we were supposed to have had a date once. My sister arranged it—you know my sister Betsy—but Rosie go. sick, or at least that's what she said, so I told Betsy to forget it."

Barbara's voice grew animated. "You know, that's just like Henry James. He wrote a story, 'The Friends of the Friends.' This man and woman are always being told they should meet each other, and their friends make arrangements but they never work out, and then she dies, only she comes back after death to get a good look at him. It's one of his ghost stories."

Alan shivered. "That's a very sad story."

"Oh, there's the doorbell. I have to go."

Alan had wanted to ask more questions about Rosie, but now he was glad to hang up. The ghost story had chilled him to the bone. "Well, thanks. So long."

Barbara slammed a door on her roommate's unmade bed, hurried out into the hall and looked over the railing, half expecting to find a private eye from the movies climbing the stairs, a short thickset character in a fedora with a cigarette dangling from his lips. She was surprised to see instead a very tall man and woman ascending the last flight of steps. They had middle-aged faces and scholarly-looking spectacles.

The man was out of breath. "Ms. Inch?—Homer Kelly here—I've brought along—my wife Mary."

Barbara sat them down on her two butterfly chairs and pulled up a folding chair for herself. She hoped her eyes didn't show she had been crying. "What can I tell you about Rosie? I really want to help."

Homer folded one long leg over the other. "Your friend Alan Starr gave us your name. He said you knew more about Rosalind than anyone else."

"Oh, yes. I've just been talking to Alan. You people are working together?"

Homer tried to organize his arms and legs in the butterfly chair. "That's right," he said, rocking back dangerously. The chair tipped sideways. Mary lunged, the chair tipped back again, and Homer continued with dignified aplomb, "All we know is that she was an organist, a widow with a young child. She rented rooms to students in a house she inherited from her parents, next to the Church of the Commonwealth. Anything else you can tell us about Rosie would be helpful."

Barbara looked down at her clasped hands. "I feel awfully guilty about her. She was one of my closest friends, but I confess I hadn't seen her for several months before she disappeared. Not since the fire, in fact. I can't remember anything after that. Oh, I should have gone to see her. She was housebound with the baby. I was busy with my job, but I should have made time somehow."

"The fire? You saw her at the fire in the church last spring?"

"Oh, yes, I did. Well, everybody in the neighborhood was there. We heard the sirens, my roommate and I, and we saw the red sky to the south, so we got dressed and ran over there." Barbara shook her head in sickened recollection of the noise, the confusion, the blocked street, the police barriers, the crowds, the fire trucks, the hoses lying everywhere, the firefighters silhouetted against the flames. "Have you ever seen a big fire? Well, it seemed thrilling at first, all those really brave firemen going into the burning building to make sure nobody was inside. But poor Martin Kraeger, they had to hold him back. He kept trying to go in too. His face, you could see it so clearly in the light of the fire." Barbara closed her eyes, remembering the anguish on Kraeger's face. "And then, oh God, they brought out the sexton."

"He was dead?" said Mary Kelly.

"Oh, he was dead, all right, a blackened body on a stretcher. They covered him with a rubber tarp right away, but we'd all seen it. It's something I wish I could forget. That's when I noticed Rosie. She was standing in front of her house with the baby in her arms, wearing a coat over her nightgown. Her face was—well, it was terrible, just like Kraeger's. I saw her try to get closer, holding the baby, but they wouldn't let her through. There were all these people crowding in, wanting to see, and the fire chief yelled at them and the ambulance pulled up, and I tried to get to Rosie, but the police barriers were in the way and I couldn't reach her." Barbara's voice shook. "I should have called her next day, but I didn't. I was busy, preparing for a concert. I'll never forgive myself."

"Who else was there?" murmured Homer. "What about James Castle? He should have been as upset as Reverend Kraeger. It was Kraeger's church that was going up in flames, but it was Castle's organ."

Barbara smiled bitterly. "Jim Castle? You don't understand. He got a brand new one out of the fire, that wonderful new tracker organ from Marblehead. He should have been dancing with glee. But he wasn't there. At least I didn't see him. I didn't recognize anybody but Rosie and Mr. Kraeger."

Mary Kelly sat back quietly while Homer asked question after question. She was interested in the look of Barbara Inch, the long brown hair hooked behind the ears, the owlish glasses, the long lank shape under the loose dress, the refusal to prettify. There were things one could do with the woman—one could cut her hair, try different sorts of clothes and throw away those big flat sandals.

But why interfere? She was all right as she was, with a keen edge like a well-sharpened tool. Let her alone.

CHAPTER 17

The word of God ... meets the children of Ephraim lik
a bear in the way and a lioness in the woods.

Martin Luther

It was Alan Starr's turn to play the midday Friday con
cert at Trinity Church in Copley Square.

The electropneumatic organ was not to his taste, although it was an enormous one with seven thousand pipes.
The console had a place of honor at one side of the broad
chancel, below Henry Hobson Richardson's golden walls
and arching golden heavens. Beyond the chancel rose the
massive piers supporting the giant tower. The decoration of
the church was a combination of Byzantine mosaic and
painted stencilling and sumptuous frescoes and brilliant
stained glass, with a superimposed touch of Art Deco. Alan
could never make up his mind whether it was a magnificent
masterpiece or just plain awful. Its reputation was too august
to question, its effect on the beholder too intimidating.
*BLESSING AND HONOUR AND GLORY AND
POWER,* thundered a legend high on the wall.

Now, sitting on the organ bench, Alan felt giddy, poised
all alone in shimmering air. Beyond the railing he could see
the entire audience, a slim scattering in a forest of oaken
pews. In the last decade of the twentieth century few people attended organ concerts but other organists. All Alan's
friends were there—Pip Tower, Barbara Inch, Peggy Throstle, Martha Moore and Jack Newcomb—and some of the
older professionals—Arthur Washington, Melanie Chick,
Gilda Honeycutt.

And as always in the wintertime, a few street people had
come in out of the cold. Alan was amused to see the three
dingy derelicts he had met the other day in the company of

little Charley—Tom, Dick and Harry. Tom was asleep, Dick was crouched over a comic book, Harry sat with bowed head.

Alan played Buxtehude and Franck. The thick, muffled quality of the organ was fine for the Franck, less fine for the Buxtehude, but the audience applauded politely as he finished the concert and came forward to the chancel rail to bow.

Then his friends walked up the chancel steps and clustered around the organ to praise his performance. "How's the job search coming?" said Alan, making polite conversation with Pip Tower. "Are you still working at that hospital?"

Pip looked grave. "Oh, sure. I'm a lowly hospital orderly. I deliver X rays, I wash mattresses upon which people have gone to a better world, I bathe dead bodies. Super. And I just started working in a copy center at night." He brightened. "I heard about the interim job at Commonwealth. I understand there'll be auditions."

"That's right," said Barbara Inch. "I'm going to try out too, but you're a shoo-in. The rest of us haven't got a chance."

Pip looked at Alan anxiously. "What do you know about the committee?"

"Well, I suppose Mrs. Frederick's in charge."

"Oh, Jesus, she doesn't know a fucking thing about music. What about you? Are you going to audition?"

"Me?" Alan laughed. "And compete with you? Heck, no. I'd have to be out of my mind."

Barbara and Pip drifted away. Everyone else had vanished too. The vast acreage of pews was empty. Alan gathered up his music, but as he slid off the bench and stood up, he was surprised to find the man who called himself Harry slouching against the wall behind him.

He looked worse than ever. He had pulled off his knitted cap, and his thin hair stood straight up on end. His eyes

were bleary and cunning. "You can do better than that," he said. "The registration on the Buxtehude, it was pure shit."

He lunged forward and switched on the organ. Alan looked on, flabbergasted, as Harry sat down and fumbled with the stops. He played a chord, and a threadlike Dulciana spiraled out of the organ and floated in a delicate veil over the dark spaces of the church.

Stunned, Alan listened as the gray man with the ruined face ran through the Buxtehude, then launched into a Bach fugue. His feet raced over the pedals in a monumental walking bass, and then with a surging combination of reed stops, his hands gave chase.

His touch was faultless. Without the evidence of his eyes Alan would have thought he was listening to James Castle's perfection of pace and sparkling clarity. But here there was something more, something unleashed, something transfigured, something free and wild.

The last measures crashed out of the pipes and ricocheted from the golden walls and the mosaics of prophets and the glassy surfaces of the windows and the lofty curvatures of the barrel vaults, and died away at last after seven long seconds.

Awestruck, Alan leaned toward Harry and whispered, "What did you say your name was?"

Harry turned off the organ. The pneumatic wind died down. His small red eyes glanced at Alan, then darted away. "Oates," muttered Harry. "Harold Oates. You might have heard of me."

Alan gasped. "Oates, Harold Oates? But I thought you were—?"

"Dead?" Oates laughed. "Well, you're right. I died a long time ago. What you see before you is a stinking corpse." Sliding off the bench, he stood up.

Tom and Dick appeared from nowhere. "Don't he play good?" said Dick.

"Gawd!" said Tom.

"AA, that's what done it," said Dick. "You should've seen him, last year when he first come. Welfare sent him. Tanked." Dick waved his hand. "Tanked up to here. Really stewed. Tom, he brought him in." Dick clapped Tom on the back. "Of course Tom's mostly half-pissed himself."

"Right," said Tom. "Gawd!"

"But where have you been?" said Alan. "It must be twenty years since—you know, since you were giving regular concerts."

"Dead," said Oates again. "I told you." He turned away and moved down the chancel steps with Dick and Tom.

Alan leaned over the railing. "How can I get in touch with you? Where do you live?"

"Among the lilies," snarled Oates.

◆ ◆ ◆ ◆

CHAPTER 18

*I hold the gnashing of teeth of the damned to be . . . despair,
when men see themselves abandoned by God.*

Martin Luther

His mother confronted him at the door. You'd think she couldn't always manage to be right there at the door when he came in, but she always was. Behind her at the end of the hall his sister huddled in her wheelchair, her eyes closed.

His mother began complaining at once. "Sonny, you've got to take over. I've got to get out of here, just for an hour."

He brushed past her, heading for the stairs. "I can't," he said coldly, "I'm going out again."

"Can't it wait? I've got to get out, Sonny, just for a little while. Helen, she's driving me nuts."

"No, I tell you. I've got to meet someone."

"Well, my God, when can I get out of here? You never think of me, trapped in here all day and all night with these two!"

He ran up the stairs impatiently, then leaned over the railing and spoke to Helen, who was looking up at him with glowing eyes. "How is she?"

"Better," murmured Helen.

"Better!" broke in his mother angrily. "I don't know if you can call it better, when all she does is whine about her kid."

"Well, for Christ's sake, why don't you call that woman? Try again."

"You try," shouted his mother. "Why is everything always left to me?"

He slammed his bedroom door.

No sooner did Mrs. Barker walk into her office than the phone rang.

She said, "*Damn,*" and dropped into the chair at her desk.

"Department of Social Services, Mrs. Barker speaking," she said wearily, unbuttoning her coat.

"Oh, Mrs. Barker, my name is Pettigrew, Mrs. Sharon Pettigrew."

"Yes, Mrs. Pettigrew?"

"I'm a volunteer at the—you know—the Home for Little Wanderers. We need to find one of the kiddos transferred to your department."

"Which kiddo?" said Mrs. Barker warily.

"Its name is—" There was a pause, as if Mrs. Pettigrew were consulting a list. "Hall, Charles Hall."

"Oh, no, not Charley Hall, not again! Well, what is it? What do you want him for?"

"His cousin wants to see him, with an eye to possible adoption. His first cousin, just returned from—ah—abroad."

"Oh, is that so? Just a minute." Mrs. Barker put down the phone, pulled Charley's file out of a drawer, and riffled through it. "I'm sorry," she said triumphantly, picking up the phone again. "That child has no living relatives but a couple of great-aunts, and they are both childless. Get lost, sister."

* * * *

CHAPTER 19

The Holy Spirit is a fierce thunder-clap against the proud.
Martin Luther

Alan felt like a fool for letting the great Harold Oates slip through his fingers. Why had he let him go? He should have run after him when he walked out of Trinity Church. Alan suspected it had been some kind of unconscious snobbery on his part, Oates had looked so sleazy and weird.

He had to be found. Alan tried the phone book, but of course it contained no entry for Harold Oates. He sat on his bed and stared at the telephone. There were now two voids in his life. Rosie Hall and Harold Oates.

But next day Oates turned up in the Church of the Commonwealth while Alan was experimenting with one of the newly voiced ranks of pipes in the Great division, the four-foot Clarion. He had set up a voicing machine in the balcony, a shelf of slots with a keyboard, so that he could sometimes work without a partner.

He set the smallest pipe in one of the holes and listened to it. Was it out of tune? The whole rank was apt to go sour in wet weather.

Fortunately the winter had continued to be cold and dry. People were complaining about the lack of snow. Ski resorts were desperate, farmers were afraid of an entire winter without moisture, nurserymen dreaded the drying out of their stock.

Alan romped through the merry allegro from an organ concerto by Handel. The Clarion sounded fine, a little strident and nasal the way it should. When he rollicked through the last measures, he heard a dry clapping from the

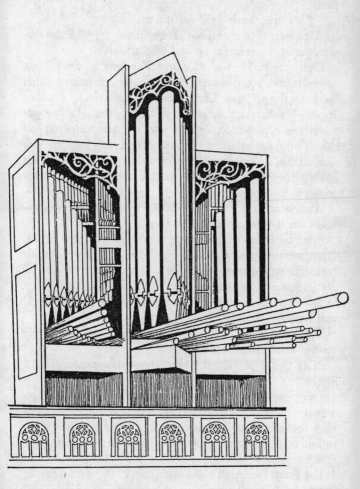

floor below. He turned to see Harold Oates looking up at him.

"What else can it do?" said Oates.

Alan wanted to cheer, but he was afraid to spook the elusive master. "Come on up and take a look."

Oates came. He looked worse than ever in a too-large overcoat and a too-short pair of trousers. But his clothes were not the problem. Oates could be fitted out by Louis or Brooks Brothers, and he would still look gross. His face was a study in decrepitude. Twenty years of heavy drinking had dulled his small eyes and sunk them into their sockets. The skin of his face drooped in swags and pouches. Even his balding forehead looked odd, flushed with patches of color as red as his nose.

Alan wanted to kneel at his feet. He merely slid over casually on the bench as an invitation.

For two hours they experimented with the new organ. Oates muttered and said little, but his eyes glittered, and his combinations of stops were clever, startling, a revelation.

"Fucking thing's got no bottom," complained Oates.

"Most of the sixteen-footers are still in the shop. Wait till you hear the thirty-two-foot Contra Bombarde."

"What's this here?" growled Oates, putting a dirty finger on the knob labelled DIV INSP.

"Oh, that. It was Castle's idea. Divine Inspiration. It's just a joke."

Oates uttered a sharp bark of laughter, which brought on a fit of coughing. He coughed and coughed. His coughs were terrible hacking explosions. In dismay Alan leaped up to find a glass of water. The man seemed to be expiring before his eyes.

But Edith Frederick stood at the top of the stairs, looking shocked. "Is he all right?" she whispered.

Oates stopped coughing. His face was purple, his eyes streaming. He glowered at Mrs. Frederick and wiped his nose on his sleeve.

"Oh, Mrs. Frederick," said Alan nervously, "I'd like you to meet my friend Harold Oates, the—ah—distinguished organist."

"How do you do, Mr. Oates," said Edith. Her tone was frosty. It was clear that she had never heard of him.

Oates leered at her, then pulled out a couple of stops and played a deep blatting chord like a Bronx cheer.

Alan closed his eyes and Edith scuttled down the balcony stairs.

◆ ◆ ◆ ◆

CHAPTER 20

We are gone from the clear fountain to the foul puddle, and
drunk its filthy water . . .   Martin Luther

"Mama," said Alan, holding Charley up in front of the picture of his mother on the wall. "Mama, Mama, Mama."

Charley studied the picture with his usual gravity. The teaching session had become a ritual. Twice a week Debbie Buffington was sullenly willing to take a respite from minding somebody else's baby. Twice a week, on Wednesdays and Saturdays, Alan took Charley for a ride in the stroller, whisking him across the Public Garden, ducking into the alley behind 115 Commonwealth and entering by the back door.

After the lesson it was lunchtime. Alan was experimenting with hard-boiled eggs and bits of apple. Charley opened his mouth willingly. His cheeks seemed pinker, his eyes brighter.

On the way back to Bowdoin Street Alan bought a bag of expensive peaches. When he gave them to Debbie, she dumped them on the table. She was excited about something else. Her eyes were alight. "Hey," she said, "I got news for you."

Alan plopped Charley down on the rug. "News? What kind of news?"

Debbie thrust a newspaper at him. It was the lurid front page of the *Boston Herald*. "Hey, did you see this? The kid's mother, she's burned up."

"What?"

"Burned up in her car. It says here they found her burned to a crisp in her car."

Alan couldn't believe it. "Rosalind Hall? Does it say Rosalind Hall?"

"Right. Rosalind Hall, the organ player." Debbie was taking a grisly pleasure in delivering shocking news. She read the article aloud.

Organist Rosalind Hall, missing since December 11, was found dead yesterday, a victim of the fire that destroyed her car. The '92 Ford Escort was discovered this morning in a gully beside a sharp curve on Route 62 in the town of Hudson. The car was registered in Hall's name, and her driver's license was found in her handbag. Officials could give no reason for her December disappearance.

Alan's eyes filled. He took the newspaper from Debbie and looked at the thousand gray dots of Rosie's picture. It was the same one he was using to teach Charley his first word.

"Hey, what do you care if she's burned up or not?" said Debbie suspiciously. "I thought you like never even saw her. That's what you said."

Alan couldn't speak. He picked up Charley, held him tightly, and sobbed twice.

"Christ," said Debbie. "You never met her? Give me a break." Little Wanda whimpered, and clung to her mother's leg.

Alan went back to Rosie's apartment, telling himself wretchedly that it didn't matter now if he trespassed on private property, because it wasn't private property any more, it didn't belong to anybody. He went at once to the picture of Rosie and Charley and leaned on the desk and gazed at Rosie's face, trying to get it through his head that she had died in a blazing car. What a horrible way to die! Yesterday, while he and Oates had been experimenting with the organ, or perhaps while he was lying in bed watching some dumb thing on television, Rosie's car had gone out of control and spun into the ditch and gone up in flames, and she had burned to death, *burned to death.*

Then Alan remembered Barbara Inch's story about the two people who met only after the woman was dead, the ghost story by Henry James. He had to sit down and hold his head in his hands. Rosie Hall and Alan Starr should have met in life, everyone had said so. Now the only way they would ever meet was if she turned up as a ghost. It was a bitter joke. Pulling himself together, Alan called Homer Kelly and told him the news.

Homer's voice on the line was sepulchral. "I've just been reading about it in the *Globe.*" There was a grieving pause. "I'm sorry."

"So that's it then," said Alan, his voice flat.

"I wonder how it happened. It doesn't say whether or not the car turned over. You don't get a fire unless the gas tank ruptures and the fuel leaks out and meets a hot surface, like the exhaust manifold."

"I don't know what happened," said Alan bleakly. "Cars burn up all the time. How did they know it was Rosalind Hall? Did somebody identify the body?"

"Credit cards, the paper said, in her pocketbook." Homer was about to add that burned cadavers were often so unrecognizable that only a forensic pathologist could identify them, by examining the teeth, determining the age of the skull, and so on, but he thought better of it. "Well, there'll be an autopsy. I'll look into it."

There was a final hollow pause, and then Alan said, "Well, thank you for all you've done. Don't forget to send me a bill."

"Relax. I'm not through yet. I'll let you know about the autopsy."

But the next time Alan picked up Charley at Debbie Buffington's apartment, she gave him another shock. "She's cremated already," she said. "All the kid's got for a mother is a pile of ashes."

"Sshh," said Alan angrily. "He can hear you."

"Bullshit. He's retarded, I tell you. He doesn't understand a thing. Look at this." Debbie held up another copy of the *Herald*. She seemed to enjoy gloating over depressing news.

Alan looked at the headline, *MIXUP IN MORGUE, AUTOPSY FOILED*. "I don't understand."

She explained as if to an idiot. "They cremated her by *mistake*. They got the *papers* mixed up. So there won't be any way of identifying it. You know, like they look at the *teeth*, so they can identify the *corpse*, even when it's all burned up. *You* know."

"Look," said Alan, controlling himself, "it's cold outside. Charley's going to need more clothes."

Debbie gave him Wanda's woolly hat and a thick blanket. Wanda whimpered, and tried to snatch the blanket back. Her mother slapped her hand.

"Sorry, Wanda," said Alan. He knelt in front of her. "I'll bring back some ice cream, okay?" Wanda stopped sniffling.

Outdoors the day was bright and clear. Rays of low winter sunshine slammed down on the steep sidewalk. A chill wind whistled down the hill. Alan pulled the knitted cap low over Charley's face, and tugged the blanket up around his ears until only his nose was visible.

In Louisburg Square the windows of the Greek Revival houses glowed with soft lamps and firelight. Alan could imagine the prosperous and comfortable scenes within, so different from the sad frowziness of Debbie's gloomy apartment. He trundled the stroller past the little park and plunged down Mount Vernon Street to Charles. In the Public Garden the cold breeze tossed the bare branches of the trees, blowing a couple of seagulls high above the roof of the Ritz Carlton Hotel. Charley giggled with joy, unaware that his life had been half-destroyed by the death of his mother. Alan wondered if a single man could adopt a child. Probably not. They'd give Charley to some rich married couple. Well, anything would be better than the tender mercies of Debbie Buffington.

The stretch of sidewalk between Arlington Street and Clarendon was empty of pedestrians. Alan galloped faster and faster. Charley shrieked with laughter. At the corner of Clarendon, Alan paused before heading for the alley behind the church. The sidewalk was thick with little kids, round blobs in puffy winter clothes. There were babies in pushcarts, mothers organizing a winter walk. It was the student body of the daycare center, all assembled. More kids were emerging from the church and toddling down the stairs. Music streamed from the open door.

Alan turned his head and listened. Somebody was practicing on the new organ. Probably one of Castle's pupils. Everybody wanted to try it. Could it be James Castle himself? Had he come back without warning? Who else could play like that? Bach's Dorian Toccata was flooding out onto the street, plunging like chariots, galloping like horses, racing like bloodthirsty cheetahs.

No, of course, it wasn't Castle. It was Harold Oates, playing without permission. Alan turned to one of the mothers. "Would you keep an eye on him for a sec? I'll be right back."

"Sure," said the mother, bending down to look at Charley. "What rosy cheeks!"

Alan ran into the church to take a look.

Charley sat in the stroller patiently, muffled to the ears. Under the blanket he held the grubby stuffed animal given to him by the man called Tom. Looking down at himself he could see the furry strands of his blanket standing up in the sunlight. Looking up he saw the tall shapes of women talking. A bird flew onto a tree and peered down at him, then flew away. Loud music curled around his head, then more and more of it in a big wave.

Looking along the sidewalk in front of him, he saw a

man and a woman come out of a house and hurry toward a car. The woman was wearing a white hat.

Charley was electrified. He leaned forward in the stroller and called out his first word.

"Mama!" shouted Charley. "Mama, Mama!"

Alan came running back to him down the steps of the church.

"Mama, Mama," wept Charley.

Alan looked up and saw a woman in a white hat in the back seat of a car. "Wait," he cried, but the driver pulled away from the curb and drove swiftly down Commonwealth toward Dartmouth Street.

"Mama," sobbed Charley. "Mama, Mama, Mama."

◆ ◆ ◆ ◆

CHAPTER 21

A man's word is a little sound, that flies into the air, and soon vanishes; but the Word of God is greater than heaven and earth.   Martin Luther

Homer and Mary Kelly responded to Alan's plea at once. They drove into Boston and parked in the alley behind Number 115. Homer shouted for Alan, who came out and unlocked the gate.

"What a nice place," said Mary, admiring the harpsichord and the view of the garden.

Homer peeled off his coat. "It's beginning to feel like home."

Mary pulled off her gloves and ran her hand along the railing of the playpen. "Poor little kid, he's an orphan now."

"But maybe he isn't an orphan," said Alan eagerly. "I told you on the phone, he saw his mother."

"Now calm down," said Homer. He lowered himself into a chair. "Start from the beginning."

Alan repeated it all patiently, his lessons with Charley in front of the picture of Rosie, the baby's obvious understanding that the word *Mama* meant his mother. He went on to describe the episode on the street, the woman getting into the car, her white hat, Charley's insistence that this was indeed his mother.

"But why did she drive away from him?" said Mary softly. "And if she was really his mother, how could she have left her baby in the first place?"

"She didn't leave of her own free will. There was blood on the floor, remember?"

"But what about this time?" said Homer. "Why did she drive away this time?"

"I don't think she even saw him. He was sixty feet away at the corner, all muffled up in a blanket, just one of a crowd of little kids. And she couldn't hear him because there was music pouring out of the church and the bells were ringing, that amplified carillon from the Lutheran church—and the traffic! You know what the traffic sounds like."

Homer stared at the floor, Mary gazed at the ceiling. The dusk of early winter twilight filled the room. Alan couldn't bear it. Impulsively he jumped up and went to the bookshelf and fiddled with one of Rosie's tape recorders. "Listen," he said. "Here she is."

The cheerful counterpoint of Bach's chorale prelude streamed over them, the jolly reed stops predominating, the ponderous pedal notes resounding underneath. Rosie's presence came warmly into the room. They could all imagine her fingers frisking over the keys, her feet dancing on the pedals. *Burned fingers turned to charcoal, blackened feet charred like logs.*

"Suppose Charley was right," said Alan loudly, waving his arms. "Just suppose he was right. Look at it his way. What if he really saw his mother? What if somebody else was burned up in that car? What would it mean?"

Homer and Mary stared at him. Then Homer looked solemnly out the window at the little yard, where a rag flapped in a tree. "If that's true, if Charley really saw his mother, then she isn't dead. And that would mean another person was burned in the fire, with Rosie's credit cards in Rosie's pocketbook on the seat of Rosie's car. It would mean somebody's trying very hard to make us believe Rosalind Hall is dead. Is that what you're saying? That's what you really think?"

"I don't know what I'm saying. But I think Charley saw her. I mean, I think he *thought* he saw her. I know he's only a baby, but I believe him."

There was a knock at the door. They all jumped. Reluctantly Alan went to the door. "Oh, Mrs. Garboyle, hello. Come in."

"Why, of course, it's you, Mr. Starr." Mrs. Garboyle's old face wreathed itself in a wide smile. "You're here with little Charley."

"Well, no, not today, as a matter of fact." Alan led Mrs. Garboyle into the presence of his two towering guests. "I hope you won't mind our being here, Mrs. Garboyle. We're"—hastily Alan decided to tell the truth—"we're looking into the death of Charley's mother. Mrs. Garboyle, Mr. and Mrs. Kelly." Mary and Homer stood up courteously, and loomed over Mrs. Garboyle. "Mr. Kelly is sort of a—" Alan looked at Homer for help, and Homer obliged.

"Lieutenant detective," he lied promptly, resurrecting his ancient connection with the district attorney of Middlesex County. Then he beamed and grasped Mrs. Garboyle's hand. "Oh, Mrs. Garboyle, we've met before. Do you remember me?"

Mrs. Garboyle looked up at him with dawning recognition. "Why, of course I do. You were a boy in that house on the Fenway, where I was the super, right? You wanted to see your boyhood home."

Mary Kelly gave a polite snort, and Homer hastened to explain. "I must apologize, Mrs. Garboyle. It wasn't my boyhood home. I was investigating a crime. I just used that as an excuse."

Mrs. Garboyle forgave him at once, effacing his crimes from memory, acquitting him of all wrongdoing. Hers was a sturdy soul, softened rather than hardened by a life that had been no picnic. "Oh, Mr. Kelly, that's all right. I don't mind. I don't mind at all." Then she turned to Alan, her expressive face drooping, her eyes filling with tears. "Oh, that poor baby! Poor darling Rosie! What a dreadful way to die! What will happen to little Charley now?"

"Don't worry about Charley," said Alan grimly. "I'll see that he's all right."

Mrs. Garboyle blew her nose and turned to go. "Thank you, dear. Forgive me for knocking on the door. I just wondered who was here, for dear Rosie's sake."

"Of course." Alan accompanied her out into the hall, patted her arm awkwardly, then returned to Homer and Mary, who were gloomily putting on their coats.

"What a nice woman," said Mary solemnly, pulling her car keys out of her pocket.

Homer said nothing. He made no suggestions, no promises. Once again, as the sky turned dark outside, Alan went back to Rosie's picture. But this time he found himself looking instead at a blank space beside it on the wall. Hadn't there been another one there? Yes, it had been a snapshot of Charley, a small fat object sitting on a blanket against a background of green bushes. Alan remembered it perfectly. It was gone. The thumbtacks that had held it in place on the bulletin board were still there, neatly replaced.

Alan pulled the desk away from the wall and looked behind it. He found nothing. Someone had removed the little snapshot. Who would want a picture of Charley but his own mother? Grinning to himself, Alan shoved the desk back against the wall.

Rosie *had* come back to the apartment. She had taken down the picture of Charley and gone away, but not before Charley had seen her and cried out his first word.

It was a small thing, a very small thing, but Alan was convinced. Rosalind Hall was still alive.

On the way home Mary Kelly said nothing until the car was safely heading west on Storrow Drive. Then she glanced at Homer. "Do you believe the baby?"

"Do I believe the baby?" Homer grinned. "I don't believe or disbelieve the baby. Let's just take it as a temporary hypothesis that he said *Mama* because he really saw his mother. The chances are a thousand percent against it, but I like the idea of one little kid against the world."

Mary smiled, and steered smoothly in the wake of the long line of red taillights. "I liked the music she was playing. It's a hymn, we use it in church." The car skimmed along Storrow Drive, and Mary began to sing:

> *Wake, awake, for night is flying,*
> *The watchmen on the heights are crying,*
> *Awake, awake, Jerusalem!*

◆ ◆ ◆ ◆

CHAPTER 22

They once showed here, at Wittenberg, the drawers of St. Joseph and the breeches of St. Francis. The bishop of Mayence boasted he had a gleam of the flame of Moses' bush.   Martin Luther

Waking up the next morning in his messy apartment on Russell Street, Alan felt his confidence sag. A sleety rain was falling. It was a day for pessimists. Was Rosie Hall alive or dead? On a morning like this, Charley's cry of *Mama* seemed only a squeak beside the roar of the evidence on the other side.

He got dressed and ate some healthy cereal his mother had given him. The chunky grains were hard to swallow without milk. Looking out the window he could see the rain turning to ice. Alan didn't own a winter parka, in spite of his mother's constant concern about his wardrobe. *Strong men don't wear overcoats.* What a dumb idea. What a jerk. He didn't have an umbrella either, having left it somewhere. He pulled on three sweaters and a windbreaker and ran up Russell Street and down Myrtle, taking a couple of hard falls on the icy sidewalk.

At the Church of the Commonwealth rain rushed along the gutters, poured down the copper drainpipes and gushed into the gravel-filled ditches below. All over the Back Bay, janitors and building superintendents were congratulating themselves on the natural recharging of the water table. At Trinity the building manager turned off the expensive supply of city water pouring into the manhole. Perhaps it was the start of a normal winter.

Alan was glad to throw open the door and shake himself like a wet dog inside the warm church. The stairs to the balcony were dim, and he had to feel his way upward in his squelching sneakers. The sanctuary too was dark. In the stained-glass window to the south the Three Kings knelt in a murky purple fen.

Pip Tower was waiting for Alan. He seemed energetic and excited, unaffected by the dismal weather. He sat cheerfully at the console and began the tedious job of depressing keys, while Alan huddled among the pipes, working on them one by one. "C-sharp?" called Alan. "D-sharp?"

Kneeling beside the rank of four-foot Chimney Flutes, Alan glowered at the open mouth of the pipe and found himself wondering why churches existed at all. They didn't do anything in particular. All they provided were Sunday morning lectures, a mysterious set of hieratic gestures, some meaningless gettings-up and sittings-down, a succession of foolish hymns, and occasionally (it was true) a little good music. The Protestant church as it existed in Boston at the turn of the second millennium was a withered survival from centuries past, a vermiform appendix on the social body of the state.

Yet there was Martin Kraeger, somewhere downstairs, shouting cheerfully in his powerful bellow. From the deep crevasse of Alan's morning cynicism he wondered if Kraeger's forceful manner was false heartiness—a clap on the back, a bone-crushing handshake—nothing more. And then his inner vision shifted, and he saw again the blazing car and heard Rosie scream. If things like that could happen, how could any clergyman make sense of it? Alan blew into a two-inch pipe and it peeped like a chicken.

There was a call from Pip Tower. "Hey, Alan, I've got to go."

"Wait a sec," said Alan, "I'm coming out." He worked his way along the catwalk beside the Chimney Flutes, taking care not to brush against them, knowing they would bend like flowers.

Pip pulled off his sweatshirt, revealing a shirt and tie. "My God," said Alan, "what's that for?"

"The audition," said Pip. "Didn't you know? It starts in

ten minutes." Nervously he pulled on a blazer with gold buttons. His hands were trembling.

"No kidding." Alan grinned at him. "Well, don't worry. You're the best there is." *Unless by some fluke Harold Oates turns up.* Alan shuddered at the thought, and Pip ran softly down the stairs.

So the rest of the morning would be wasted. Loretta Fawcett's schedule for the use of the organ was worse than useless. There was nothing on the schedule about the audition. Alan should have remembered it himself, but since he was an organ builder rather than a professional organist, he had no intention of trying out. This morning he had hoped to finish the voicing of two more ranks, but there was no chance of it now. He sat down on the bench and played the whole Chimney Flute scale on manual two. Yes, it was all right, bright and crisp, with a barely audible chiff.

Then for the hell of it he pulled out a showy collection of stops, including Castle's joke stop, DIV INSP, and launched into Handel's "Entry of the Queen of Sheba." He played it with cynical fervor as the composer had never intended it to be performed, with continuously changing registration, piling this mutation on top of that. Hilariously he threw in the Zimbelstern and the Glockenspiel and then he invented a ridiculous coda of hippity-hops like leapfrogging rabbits and a mighty set of pedal octaves. The Queen of Sheba entered Solomon's throne room, a towering woman thirty feet tall, accompanied by a thousand slaves with ostrich feather fans and two thousand warriors in brazen helmets. As a final flourish Alan snatched out the stop for Trumpets en Chamade. The din was terrific, yet every rank sounded clear, the resolution of one stop from another was precise. The pandemonium was not a swarm of giant wasps, it was this note and that note, every one distinguishable from every other. *Hail, O queen, all hail!*

As the last mad blast pierced the air, Alan lifted his arms high and listened for the echo, but instead there was a flutter of applause. Was Harold Oates down there again? Turning, Alan saw a row of people standing in the aisle below, looking up at him. They were beaming. One was Edith Frederick. Old man Partridge was there, and couple of portly men in dark suits.

Alan waved at them, then shoved all the stop knobs back in place, turned off the organ, switched off the light over the music rack, slid sideways off the bench, snatched up his windbreaker, and ran down to the vestibule, where he found a cluster of old friends—Pip in his gold-buttoned blazer, Barbara Inch, Peggy Throstle, Jack Newcomb and Arthur Washington.

They were the auditioners, waiting to be summoned. "Listen," said Alan, "you've only got a dozen stops. I'll make a list. Has anybody got a piece of paper?"

They stared at him blankly. "My God, was that you?" said Jack.

"Me? Oh, you mean the Queen of Sheba? Hey, how did you like the Principal eight? I threw in everything but the kitchen sink."

"We noticed," said Pip dryly. Barbara smiled at him faintly. Peggy Throstle said, "Honestly, Alan," as if in anger, and Arthur turned his back and stared at a plaque on the wall dedicated to the memory of the saintly Walter Wigglesworth.

"Who's going to be next?" said Mrs. Frederick, pushing open the door to the sanctuary, smiling at them brightly. "Which of you is Miss Inch?"

"I am," said Barbara, and she started up the balcony stairs, clutching her music.

Mrs. Frederick disappeared, and they all waited silently for Barbara to begin. When she did, she fumbled the opening measure and had to start over. Alan winced, but he could imagine that the others were thinking, *All the better for me.*

The rest of Barbara's performance was creditable. Alan

stood with the others listening, head down. When Barbara came downstairs, shaking her head, they all clapped politely and reassured her. "It was great," said Peggy Throstle. "No, it wasn't," said Barbara.

Jack Newcomb was next. He played a showy toccata by Widor, with all Alan's available stops pulled out and the shutters of the Swell box wide open. "Wow," said Alan kindly, when Jack came down, looking pale, his arms shaking. Then it was Peggy Throstle's turn. "God," she said, climbing the stairs, "my fingers are so cold." Peggy had chosen a concerto by Vivaldi, but it was too difficult. She muffed it badly, and came downstairs trying not to cry. Barbara put an arm around her and made soothing noises. Unfortunately Peggy's failure unnerved Arthur Washington, and he made a hash of his fantasy by Franck.

Pip Tower was last. Pip was magnificent. His Bach Toccata and Fugue was precise, the variations eloquent, the final movement overwhelming, his performance flawless from beginning to end.

When he came down, beaming, the applause from his rivals was genuine. "No contest," said Arthur Washington generously. Barbara said, "Proud to know you," Peggy hugged him tearfully, Alan clapped him on the back, and Jack did his best not to show his disappointed envy.

Alan wished them all good luck and started home, trudging in his damp sneakers back to Russell Street. It had stopped raining, but the wind was raw and penetrating. At home he hauled off his wet clothes, draped them here and there, and pulled on a dry shirt and a wrinkled pair of pants. Then he began going through his closet, looking for something decent to lend to Harold Oates, wondering how to get him out of the shelter where he holed up every night.

When the phone rang, he answered it absentmindedly, while examining a doubtful pair of khaki trousers. It was Mrs. Frederick. She was eager and vivacious. "Alan, dear, I want to be the first to tell you, we have unanimously chosen you as our interim organist. We want you to take over right away."

Alan spluttered into the phone, "But I wasn't auditioning this morning. You misunderstood. I was just testing the voicing."

"I don't care what you were doing, it was marvelous. That's the sort of music we want at the Church of the Commonwealth."

Oh, God, they didn't understand a damn thing about it. Alan didn't know whether to laugh or cry. "Mrs. Frederick, I'm not looking for a job. Philip Tower is a far better musician than I am. Or Barbara Inch, she's really good too."

"Alan Starr, we want *you* to play our splendid new organ. After all, you're already more familiar with it than anyone else."

"But Philip—"

Mrs. Frederick's voice turned frosty. "I'm afraid he is out of the question. My dear Alan, don't you understand? *You're* the one we want. May we consider it settled?"

Alan was torn. He felt uneasy about being chosen through the committee's total lack of musical judgment. And, good God, poor Pip! But then it occurred to him that the generous salary would pay for housing for the greatest organist of them all, Harold Oates. "Well, thank you, Mrs. Frederick. I'm grateful."

"Oh, I'm so glad. I know Jim will be pleased."

"Jim Castle? Have you heard from him? Do you know where he is?"

"Oh, no. I mean, he'll be so pleased when he comes back to know we chose you to fill in."

"Oh, I see." Alan was disappointed. *Where in the hell was Castle?*

He hung up politely, and at once guilt overwhelmed him. He remembered the scandalized faces of the auditioners after his crazy escapade with the Queen of Sheba, all that silly tinkling of the Zimbelstern and the cuckoo clucking of the

Glockenspiel. They must have thought he was throwing in that cornball registration for the benefit of the Frederick Endowment trustees. Alone in his apartment, Alan felt his face flush with embarrassment.

He called Barbara. It was plain that she had already heard from Mrs. Frederick. "Oh, hello, Alan," she said, her voice sounding strained.

"Look, I wasn't trying out. I didn't know those people were downstairs listening. I was just testing the voicing. I threw in every nutty combination I could think of. I went a little silly."

Barbara laughed. "Well, I'm glad to hear it. I didn't think it sounded like you. And don't worry about me. It's still not hopeless. They're going to hire a choir director. There'll be a tryout with the choir and an interview. It's the interview that worries me. They'll ask if I'm married, and I'm going to invent a boyfriend, so they won't think I'm a lesbian."

"Are you a lesbian?"

"I don't know. I'm not sure. Listen, Alan, it's not me that feels gypped. It's Pip. He's going to be so disgusted."

Alan hung up, feeling worse than ever. He screwed up his courage and dialed Pip's number. Would he be home yet? Probably. All the auditioners would have hurried home to await the verdict. Alan hoped to God he had already heard the bad news.

But Pip's "Hello" was too eager. Quickly Alan asked if he had heard from Mrs. Frederick. He had not. "Who's this?" he said, sounding irritated. "Alan Starr?"

"Yes, and I'm sorry to tell you, they chose me. Now listen—"

"*You!* They chose you? My God!"

"Listen, Pip, I didn't know they were there when I played that damn thing. I was just trying out crazy combinations of stops to see what they sounded like."

"Oh, sure." Pip's voice was thick. "They chose you. My God."

"They were wrong, of course," said Alan, trying to explain himself. "I told Mrs. Frederick they should have picked you."

"But you're taking the job, right?" said Pip angrily. "You couldn't turn it down."

"Well, yes, but don't forget it's only temporary, just until Castle gets back. And there's a permanent opening at Annunciation, Barbara Inch's old job."

"They've already got someone," said Pip bitterly. "They promoted the principal tenor. It seems his hobby is playing tiddly bits on the organ. Another great Music Committee."

Dismayed, Alan fell silent, and Pip crashed down the phone. There was a savage click in Alan's ear.

◆ ◆ ◆ ◆

CHAPTER 23

If you are a servant, a maid, a workman, a master, a housewife,
a mayor, a prince, do whatever your position demands. . . .
That is a right holy life.   Martin Luther

D onald Woody spent the morning overseeing the re-
      moval of the east window in the sanctuary and its
      replacement with four huge pieces of plastic. Then
he ran downstairs to the new daycare center to consult with
the director, Ruth Raymond.

He was pleased to find the big rooms full of children,
women, play equipment and small plastic chairs. Red paper
hearts dangled from the overhead pipes.

Ruth took him aside. "The thermostat isn't working."
She flapped her hands in front of her face. "It's too hot.
Phew! We can't even open the windows. They're swollen
shut."

"No problem," said Woody. "I'll get right to it."

As usual, Donald Woody was attending to the monstrous
complex of buildings in his care with instantaneous attention to problems small and large. Unfortunately he still had
no understanding of what lay below the daycare center, below the pattering feet of the children, deep down below the
boiler room with its oil-fired furnaces and the chamber
housing the elevator engine with its cables and solenoids,
below the hall where the AIDS support group met, below
the chancel end of the sanctuary with its panelled pulpit and
the portrait of Walter Wigglesworth holding the book *Di-*
vine Inspiration, below Jeanie Perkupp's arrangement of pulpit flowers—this morning they were roses and carnations.

In the dry weather the water table under the Clarendon
Street corner of Commonwealth Avenue had sunk another
inch. Yesterday's rain had done little to improve the situa-

tion. It merely bounced on the hard ground and ran off in trickles and rivulets. Behind the church offices the raindrops struck the pavement and poured into a catch basin and flowed into the combined sewer running along the alley.

Below the manhole across the street the switch to the buried sump pump was still stuck in the *on* position—there it hung, the on-off button, beside the cable that sent electric power down to the pump and a pipe lifting twenty-five gallons a minute to the level of the storm drain. A flick of the finger would have turned off the switch, but no finger came along to do the job. The lawsuit that had stalled the construction of the new hotel had blossomed. Now it was in full and furious flower. The case was moving through the courts at a snail's pace.

There was another hidden reason for the drastic lowering of the water table, a cracked connecting pipe from the church to the main sewer line. It was part of the history of the Boston sewage system.

Once upon a time Bostonians had meditated in lonely dignity in outhouses, little isolated buildings out-of-doors, and their waste products had mingled with the soil in single personal batches, flowing at last into the Charles River. But all the noble houses erected in the Back Bay in the nineteenth century had been supplied with indoor plumbing. Henceforth the output of Bostonian bladders and bowels swirled at the pull of a chain down and away into clay pipes connected to sewer lines, and surged in a foul democracy of excremental fellowship to a pumping station far away, from which it was discharged into a treatment plant.

But now the clay pipes were old. For a decade before Donald Woody's time the parking area behind the church had been a muddy yard. Trash and delivery trucks had backed up to the rear doors, their heavy wheels compacting the soil, pressing down on the buried connecting pipe until the joints between the sections no longer met. Groundwater had been flowing into the cracks for years, deepening the drawdown. In the drying wood of the pilings under the east wall of the church clusters of borer's eggs were hatching, releasing microscopic insects that spread themselves far and wide.

Woody was oblivious to the rot below. Above ground he was creating an earthly paradise. After fixing Ruth Raymond's thermostat, he ran lightly downstairs to his basement office to eat his bag lunch and feed his fish and inspect the tiny seedlings he was growing under lights. Today he was pleased to see little humps of blue salvia pushing their way out of the soil. The chrysanthemums were already sporting two pairs of miniature leaves. They were ready to be transplanted into pots.

One of the neon lights above the seedlings buzzed. Woody's canary chirped in its cage. Beneath his feet as he walked to and fro, tending his indoor garden, the round metal disks in the floor clinked softly.

◆ ◆ ◆ ◆

CHAPTER 24

Never have I seen a more ignorant ass than you.
                              Martin Luther

The baby lay asleep in the playpen. He was now a ward of the state, since his mother and father were both officially dead.

Alan sat in a chair beside the playpen in the shadow of Rosie's giant rubber plant and turned the pages of her notebook until he came to the list of musical oddities—

> Self-sounding bells
> Echoes in different languages
> Boxes in which sounds can be locked up
> Mirror fugues
> Puzzle canons . . .

Well, it was a crazy list. Flipping to a clean page, he took out his pen.

FEBRUARY 14, VALENTINE'S DAY

Today Charley stood up in the playpen, let go of the railing and took a couple of steps before he sat down. He's getting so big his clothes don't fit any more. I took him to an expensive place on Charles Street and bought him some overalls, but there must be a better way. I bought him a ball, and now he rolls it back to me.

For whom was he writing this record? For himself, for Charley, for Charley's mother? But Rosie was probably dead, burned to a crisp the way Debbie Buffington said. It was almost impossible to keep believing she was still alive.

Homer too was having a hard time believing in the continued existence of Rosalind Hall.

In the office of Lieutenant Detective Roger Campbell he kept up a good front, doing his best for Alan Starr. "Little Charley saw his mother, you see, and that's when he said his first word, Mama."

"The *baby* identified the woman?"

"Well, I admit it sounds a little crazy under the fluorescent lights in your office, surrounded by file drawers full of the testimony of adult witnesses, but listen here, Campbell, this infant is definitely precocious."

"Now let me get this straight. We're supposed to take the word of a baby—how old did you say this kid is? Not even eighteen months? We're supposed to take the word of an infant that the woman whose burned body was found in Rosalind Hall's car was not Rosalind Hall, even though she was carrying Rosalind Hall's pocketbook, credit cards and driver's license? Even though Rosalind Hall has disappeared from the face of the earth? It's true they botched the autopsy, but how could that piece of toasted flesh be anybody else?"

Homer waved his hand feebly. "Well, suppose foul play was involved? Suppose someone deliberately wants us to think she's dead?"

"Why would somebody want us to think she's dead, if she's alive and well and getting into cars? She was a woman of good character, right? Except for something unspecified on her record some years back—probably nothing, nothing at all. Why doesn't she come forward and say she's alive? Why doesn't she come back for her child? What kind of mother is she? What is this supposed to be, some kind of insurance scam? How much insurance did she have on her life anyhow? Wait a sec, I'll tell you. *Hey, Marjorie,* give me that file, will you? Here, Homer, listen to this, here it is. She had a very small policy. Young women like her, healthy, they don't usually go in for a lot of insurance."

Chastened, Homer said, "R-i-i-i-i-g-h-t."

Campbell leaned forward and patted Homer's knee. "Listen, friend, we've done a lot of good stuff together in the past, but sometimes, admit it, Homer, you go off the deep end. And this is the deepest you've ever gone. A kid still in diapers says 'Mama,' and you go berserk. Wait'll I tell Frankie what you said."

"Who's Frankie?" said Homer nervously.

Campbell snickered. "What do you mean, who's Frankie? Francis Xavier Powers, District Attorney of Suffolk County, that's who Frankie is." Campbell laughed again, and slapped his thigh. "He'll think it's a howl."

Mortified, Homer changed the subject. "Did you find out why the burned body was cremated before they could do an autopsy?"

"Honest mistake, the pathologist said. Somebody put the wrong identification on the refrigerator drawer, got a couple of stiffs mixed up. Fortunately it was what the girl wanted. She wanted to be cremated, that's what they told me at Boston City Hospital."

"What girl? You mean Rosalind herself? She'd expressed a desire to be cremated when she died? How did they know that?"

"Phone call from a relative."

"What relative?" said Homer sharply. "I thought she didn't have any relatives."

"Great-aunt, I guess. She had a couple of great-aunts. I met them at her memorial service. Here, do you want their names? I've got them right here someplace."

Homer kicked himself for forgetting about Rosie's memorial service. He knew perfectly well that it was always a good idea after any weird kind of unnatural death to go to the funeral and look over the dramatis personae. Humbly he copied down the names of the two great-aunts. "I think I'll just have a talk with the two of them."

"Ask them about the cremation notion," said Campbell,

"the girl being so explicit about wanting to be cremated. Remember, it wasn't until after the service that the mixup happened. The medical examiner was holding the body for autopsy when this woman called and said Rosalind had always wanted to be cremated, it was her dearest wish, and the M.E. said, that's fine, but not until we do an autopsy, but then there was that mixup, and the remains were sent to a crematorium, and that was that."

Homer shuddered, and said goodbye, and went out into the winter dark and looked for his car. He had parked it too close to a fire plug, and sure enough, Goddamn it, he had a ticket.

Furiously he snatched it out from under the windshield wiper and galloped back to Campbell's office, but Campbell held up both hands in a helpless gesture. "Sorry, pal."

When Homer got back to his car there was another ticket with a fine twice as large as the first.

On the other side of town Barbara Inch was lucky. She didn't own a car. For her interview with the Trustees of the Frederick Music Endowment she walked to the Church of the Commonwealth.

The interview went well. Martin Kraeger was present. Barbara had often heard him preach, but this was the first time she had actually been introduced to the officiating clergyman of the church in which she hoped to be chosen as interim choir director. The trustees gathered in the music room. Barbara was surprised to find how little they seemed to know about music.

"My husband was a lover of sacred music," said Mrs. Frederick, wondering why this young woman didn't do something about her hair.

"I've been singing in the choir for thirty years," said Eleanor Bertram, wishing Barbara had worn something a little smarter than that long shapeless dress.

"My father saw the first performance of *Salome* by Richard Strauss in Dresden," bragged Henry Mortimer, wondering why the girl didn't replace her thick glasses with contact lenses.

"I don't know anything about music," confessed Martin Kraeger, deciding to vote in Barbara's favor when the time arrived.

Afterward, walking blindly along the darkening street, her hair blowing in front of her, passing muffled figures huddled against the cold, Barbara came to the conclusion that she was not a lesbian after all. She admired those women, she respected them, but she wasn't one of them. No, she wasn't one of them at all.

‹ ‹ ‹ ‹

CHAPTER 25

*I have cracked many hollow nuts . . . they fouled my mouth,
and filled it with dust.*   Martin Luther

The first of Rosie's great-aunts was not what Homer
expected. Dr. Emmeline Ferris was not a dear old
lady with a lace collar and a cameo pin. She was a
tough cookie, a psychiatrist in charge of highly disturbed
patients at the state hospital in Danvers.

"No," she said firmly, "I never heard Rosie say she
wanted to be cremated. I doubt the thought ever entered
her head." Dr. Ferris snatched up a file folder and flipped it
open, as though willing Homer Kelly to go away.

Homer opened his mouth to ask another question, but
there was a disturbance in the hall. Someone shrieked. Dr.
Ferris leaped up, threw open the door and bellowed, *"Give
him what he wants."*

"But he's been through a whole pack since yesterday,"
gasped a young man in a white coat. He was wrestling with
a tall kid in a T-shirt. The kid shrieked again.

"Who the hell cares?" cried Rosie's great-aunt. She
slammed the door, returned to her desk and sat down with
a thump. "Anything else?" she said crisply, dumping the
contents of the file folder on her desk.

Homer was dismissed. But as he got up to go, he asked
an embarrassing question. "Oh, Dr. Ferris, do you have any
suggestions about what to do with Rosie's child? It will be
put up for adoption if none of her relatives take it."

"Don't look at me," said Dr. Ferris. "The girl was a fool
to marry that feckless young man. I told her so at the
time. What kind of care would a baby get from me? Re-

sponsible adoptive parents, that's the best thing for a baby girl."

"Baby boy," said Homer dryly.

"Well, whatever."

The second great-aunt was altogether different. Her name was Roberta Birdee.

Mrs. Birdee lived in a big chateau-like house on a broad tree-lined street in Newton. Homer was ushered in by a maid in uniform. She was the only uniformed maid he had ever seen outside a movie theater, except for his mother's sister, who had been in service in the household of Mayor Curley.

The maid led the way to a large living room in which Roberta Birdee lay on a puffy sofa, eating chocolates from a heart-shaped box. Homer was charmed.

Mrs. Birdee offered the box to Homer, and he took a round morsel containing a syrupy cherry. "Mmmm, deelishush," he said, sitting down.

"My hubby gave them to me for Valentine's Day." Mrs. Birdee, a chubby woman with dimpled cheeks, wore a frilly bedjacket and lay under a fluffy comforter. Everything about her was chubby and fluffy too. Even the word *hubby,* shaped by her tiny mouth, sounded cozy and plump.

Homer admired the way her mouth went around in circles as she worked her way through the box of chocolates. She offered it to him again. "Here, dear, try the square ones."

"Don't mind if I do," murmured Homer greedily, thinking of the snacks usually provided by his wife, healthy vegetables like carrot sticks and slices of green pepper. "Mmm, caramel, my favorite."

"You've come about poor dear Rosie," said Mrs. Birdee. "Oh, of course, *we* couldn't take the baby. The social worker, Mrs. Barker, asked us, but we couldn't possibly. I've been ill, you see." She put a pudgy hand to her breast, to indicate fragility somewhere inside. "Of course, if there's anything else we can do, we would be absolutely—" She paused while her little mouth went around and around, rotating clockwise, crushing and absorbing a piece of fudge. "Here, dear, have another."

Homer helped himself. "What I really want to know, Mrs. Birdee, is whether or not Rosie ever told you that after her death she wished to be cremated?"

"Cremated! Goodness! It's not the sort of thing you talk about, is it? So disagreeable. No, I'm sure we never discussed any such thing. Do try these, Mr. Kelly. Chocolate-covered almonds."

Homer's stomach was beginning to turn. Politely he waved away the heart-shaped box. "What about you?" he said evilly, probing in the soft flesh just for the hell of it. "Would you rather be buried in a coffin and just sort of slowly deteriorate over the years, or be burned up and have your ashes scattered somewhere? Although I gather you don't just burn down into ashes. I mean there are still big chunks of blackened bone, that's what they tell me."

Mrs. Birdee's little mouth stopped working. She stared at him. Then she took another chocolate-covered cherry and murmured around the edges, "Oh, deary me." This time her tiny mouth went counterclockwise, going around and around the other way.

"We've got to find him. We've just got to find him. I don't care what happens to me. They'll give him to me. I'm his mother."

"Look, what good would it do to find him if you're incarcerated for the rest of your life? They've got four charges against you—two or three cases of arson, one manslaughter, one first-degree murder. Now, listen, I've got something to tell you."

"Charley, he's all that matters. We've got to find Charley."

"Listen to me. You can't come forward and say who you are. That's what I'm trying to tell you. You don't exist any longer. So they're not looking for you any more. You're safe, but you've got to leave the country."

"Safe! Why am I safe?"

"Because, my dear, they think you're dead."

"Dead!"

"Dead."

"But why? Why do they think—?"

"Never mind. They do, and you can thank me for it."

"But, oh, God, dead!"

"All you've got to do is leave the country and be somebody else from now on. You can go to Germany, the way we planned it before."

"But I can't, I won't—not without Charley! We've got to find Charley! I won't go without Charley!"

"Oh, Christ!"

◆ ◆ ◆ ◆

CHAPTER 26

Ingratitude is a very irksome thing.
Martin Luther

A lan found a place for Harold Oates to live. It was a couple of furnished rooms on Worthington Street, a neighborhood not yet gentrified into high-rent condominiums. From his magnificent new salary as director of music at the Church of the Commonwealth, he paid the rent for both the first and the last month, a substantial sum.

Oates did not appear grateful. When Alan showed him his new quarters, he looked around suspiciously, pressed his long fingers into the mattress and pronounced it too soft, and complained about the sunshine. Then he went to the window and frowned down at the street, where some little kids were racing up and down on tricycles.

"Look, Mr. Oates," said Alan, "have you got anything in that suitcase you can wear to an audition?"

Oates turned around and looked at Alan savagely. "What do you mean, audition? Harold Oates does not audition."

"Look, I'm trying to arrange a series of concerts. It's been so long since anybody's heard you. Younger people, they don't know who you are."

Grudgingly Oates opened his suitcase. The contents were not encouraging.

"Well, maybe I've got something I can loan you," said Alan patiently, "although I'm pretty short on respectable clothes myself."

Leaving Oates to settle in, Alan took the T to Park Street and walked up the hill and down again to Debbie Buffington's apartment.

"Oh, hi there," said Debbie, letting him in, sounding almost genial.

"Hi," said Wanda, hugging him around the knees.

"Bye-bye," said Charley, chuckling and beaming as Debbie swathed him in layers of outdoor clothes.

Alan look on, feeling sorry for her. Debbie was living close to the edge of disaster. It was true she was doing a lousy job of taking care of Charley, but at least by becoming a foster mother she was trying to make her own way. She wasn't depending on the welfare system of the city of Boston, she wasn't a hooker, she wasn't selling drugs. You had to give her credit for standing on her own feet.

"Look," said Debbie, "I still don't get it. What you're doing this for, I mean. You didn't even know the kid's mother. It's weird." Her tone implied some perversion on Alan's part.

He laughed, pulled the hat down over Charley's head and tweaked his nose. "Oh, I don't know. I just like him, that's all."

Charley chuckled, happy in anticipation of another romp. There was a knock at the door.

"Oh, God," whispered Debbie. "Son of a bitch." Galvanized, she raced around the room, snatched up a couple of brimming ashtrays, dumped them in the wastebasket and switched off the TV. There was a howl of protest from Wanda.

"Just a minute, I'll be right there," called out Debbie, in a sweet unnatural voice. "Come on," she muttered to Alan, "get in the goddamn closet." Dragging him by the arm, she tugged him into the bedroom.

Alan guessed it was a surprise visit by Debbie's social worker. Dumbfounded, he allowed himself to be chivvied into the bedroom closet, which was only a curtain hanging across a corner of the room. Inside, squeezed among Debbie's clothes, he felt laughter building in his chest. But it was no joke. Suppose he were found hiding in this little bitch's closet?

The legs of a pair of tights wrapped themselves around his neck. Alan slumped against the wall and listened to the social worker's brisk, "Good morning, Debbie. I'm Mrs. Barker. How's everything going?"

There was a murmur from Debbie. Alan could hear Charley beginning to whimper, deprived of his outing. Wanda whined, and the TV came on loud and strong. Debbie spoke to Wanda sharply. The noise from the TV stopped. Charley sobbed.

The voices came closer. The social worker was only a few feet away, inspecting Debbie's bedroom with its unmade bed, its scattered clothing. Did she guess at the hidden Lothario in the closet?

She did. The footsteps came closer. Mrs. Barker flung aside the curtain. Light flooded the closet.

Debbie flared at Alan. "Asshole," she hissed. "Your foot was sticking out."

Alan unwound Debbie's tights from his neck and grinned foolishly. "I can explain," he said, feeling like someone in a comic opera.

"He's just a guy who takes the baby out," said Debbie sulkily.

"He's what?" Mrs. Barker stared at Alan. She was a neatly dressed thickset woman in designer glasses.

"It's true," said Alan sheepishly. "I take Charley out for walks."

"Debbie," said Mrs. Barker, "this is a very serious violation of our agreement."

"It's not my fault," wailed Debbie.

"It's true," said Alan, "it's nothing to do with her. I come here twice a week to take the baby for a run in the stroller. I'm not a friend of Debbie's, I'm a friend of Charley's, that's all."

Mrs. Barker's eyes narrowed. "Just what is your relation-ship to the child? You're not the father. The father's dead. Are you the mother's boyfriend?"

Alan ran his hand through his hair. Poor Charley was still crying. "No, no, I didn't even know Rosie Hall. I know it's hard to believe, but I don't know anybody in her family but Charley. I was the one who found him after his mother was kidnapped. I called you about it, way back before Christ-mas. Look, may I pick him up?"

Mrs. Barker stared at him with eyes that had seen every kind of human folly. "Why," she said softly, "were you hid-ing in that closet?"

Alan shrugged, feeling more idiotic than he had ever felt before in his life.

"It was me," said Debbie sourly. "I knew what you'd think, some guy in my apartment. I knew you wouldn't be-lieve that stuff about Charley."

Alan picked up the baby and soothed his crying. "Is it okay if I take him out for a while?"

Mrs. Barker looked at Debbie. "How long has this been going on?"

"A couple of months."

Mrs. Barker patted Charley's tearstained cheek. His face was red, his nose was running. He was anything but cute. Her shoulders drooped. Appalling human problems were her daily lot. Even her own home life was a problem. Marilynne Barker's family consisted of a senile mother wait-ing to be tended by her exhausted daughter every evening as soon as the expensive caregiver left.

Sometimes everything was too much, just too much. Mrs. Barker waved a helpless hand. "Well, go ahead. I guess it's all right." She gave Alan a tired, half-amused look. "But for heaven's sake, from now on don't go hiding in closets."

A light snow was falling on Mount Vernon Street as Alan pushed Charley down the steep brick sidewalk. They stopped to admire a poodle on a leash. Charley was delighted. "Doggie," said Alan, "that's a doggie."

Charley chuckled and said nothing, and they went on bumping down the street to the bottom, while Alan thought over the embarrassing scene with the social worker. It occurred to him that Alan Starr and Deborah Buffington were now on the same side. Had they persuaded Mrs. Barker they were telling the truth? He hoped so. If she were to remove Charley from Debbie's foster care, the baby would end up somewhere else, and Alan would never find him again.

♦ ♦ ♦ ♦

CHAPTER 27

When I preach, I sink myself deep down.
                                    Martin Luther

On the third Sunday in February Homer and Mary
Kelly attended the morning service in the Church
of the Commonwealth. Actually the important
destination on their minds that morning was a remote
wrecked-car lot halfway to Cape Cod, but the detour to the
Back Bay was part of the plan.

Homer was curious about the church. He hadn't entered
the building since the morning after the conflagration that
destroyed the organ and the balcony and killed old Mr.
Plummer. Reverend Martin Kraeger, of course, had confessed to starting the fire with his own carelessness, but Homer had his doubts about that. And it was certainly odd that
the missing Rosalind Hall had lived next door.

Anyway, this corner of Commonwealth Avenue was af-
flicted with fire, blood and death, and Homer wanted to get
closer to the scene.

They sat in the last pew, a little awed by the lofty space. It
made one feel small, and yet at the same time important, a
little puffed up. Normally, thought Homer, people lived and
worked in rooms only a little higher than their heads. This
place was big enough for elephants and giraffes, or for great
blue whales, if they should come swimming in to stand on
their giant flukes and sing their songs. Of course the sense of
sublimity was artificial, a phony spell guaranteed by so many
feet of colored glass and so many tons of stone vaulting. If
religion meant anything at all, and maybe it didn't, why did
it have to be propped up by so much grandeur?

Not that Homer had anything against churches on the

whole. In fact it had become a habit with the Kellys to go to church on Sunday morning. Homer sat grouchily beside his wife, Sunday after Sunday, disagreeing with everything, demurring in hoarse whispers, while she murmured, *Homer dear, shut up.*

The organ prelude was beginning. Mary looked at her order of service, showed it to Homer, and tapped the name of Alan Starr.

Homer raised his eyebrows and growled in her ear. "Hey, isn't that the same thing he—"

"Yes," whispered Mary. "Ssshh."

It was "Wachet Auf," *Awake, Awake,* the chorale prelude performed by Rosie Hall on the cassette in her apartment.

Mary and Homer sat quietly, staring at the packed pews in front of them as the music poured down. The piercing sound of the new organ in the stony chamber fell from the balcony upon the shoulders of the congregation, it rang in their ears, it ricocheted from the great round pillars, rolled along the arched aisles, cascaded in surges along the floor, then bounded in rushes and leaps to the vaulted ceiling. When it was over, the service began. Homer and Mary stood up and sat down with everybody else, bowed their heads, pulled money out of their pockets, sang hymns and listened to the anthem—it was the choir's first performance under the direction of Barbara Inch.

Then Martin Kraeger began his sermon. Homer remembered the big heavyset clergyman who had repeated so often, *It was my fault,* on that morning nearly a year ago, after the fire. Today he was a different man. His voice was strong and a little rough. He was speaking without notes.

His subject was repentance, because the season of Lent was about to begin. It was not the kind of repentance urged upon Homer in his Catholic youth. Kraeger began with a remark by Henry Thoreau, *If I repent me of anything, it is that I behaved so well.*

Homer whispered, "Hey," and Mary muttered, "Shut up," and Kraeger went on to demolish all traditional attitudes toward guilt and self-reproach, clawing down the entire history of sin and depravity until the moral law lay in ruins around the pulpit and his audience sat gasping, utterly deprived of ethical standards and the promptings of conscience. Then little by little he built it up again, adding stone after stone until a new morality rose before them like a tower. Kraeger finished with a calm remark about the coffee hour, and they all stood up to sing the last hymn.

Homer was speechless. He hauled on his coat and shuffled after Mary, following Martin Kraeger out into the broad vestibule facing Commonwealth Avenue.

Kraeger stood in the open door shaking hands. It was a thawing day. The light snow that had fallen the day before was exhaling from the ground in a milky mist, blowing off the trees. Sparkling flakes landed on Kraeger's black gown.

Edith Frederick was first in line. She stood beside Kraeger with the sunlight glittering down on her prim gray hair. Clearly under her delicate makeup Martin could see the fine blades of her skull. Almost as clearly he could imagine at her side the jolly Holbein skeleton, its bony arm hooked tenderly around her little jacket. Swiftly he banished the image and greeted her warmly, then turned to Homer and Mary Kelly.

"Ah," he said, grasping Mary's hand, "the Kellys of Concord. I met Homer last year. And I've read your book on the British suffragettes, Mrs. Kelly."

Mary was pleased. "Oh, have you?"

Homer grinned politely, expecting a similar compliment, because he too had taken pen to paper from time to time. Instead Kraeger introduced them to Edith Frederick. And then his attention was distracted by a woman who rushed up the steps from the sidewalk, dragging after her a small child.

"Why, Pansy," said Kraeger, bending down to the little girl, "I didn't expect to see you so soon."

Kay Kraeger was in a hurry. "I couldn't telephone because I've been so rushed."

"But I've got a budget meeting right now. Oh, well, it's all right. Welcome, Pansy, dear." Kraeger picked her up and hugged her. "Whoops, I think maybe Pansy had better—" Excusing himself, he pushed through the long line of smiling parishioners, carrying his small daughter.

"Had better what?" cried Kay Kraeger, craning her neck to stare after him. "Pansy had better what?"

But Martin and Pansy were out of sight, hurrying to the bathroom. Pansy was four years old, but she was inclined to postpone important matters far too long.

Mary and Homer walked to their car, avoiding puddles on the sidewalk. "Homer," said Mary, "I've had a revelation."

"No kidding. It's amazing what a dose of religion will do to a person."

"No, no, it's Mrs. Frederick. Did you see the way she was dressed?"

"Well, no, I guess not."

"Right. Do you know why you didn't notice? Because she dresses just like me. Look at me, Homer! My jacket, it's just like hers, it's got silver buttons just like hers, my pleated skirt, look, Homer! So ladylike! And the shoes, she had proper little low-heeled shoes with pompoms. Look at mine, they've got pompoms, they're just the same."

"No, they're not. Yours are three times as big."

"Oh, Homer, I'm so ashamed. We're both so ladylike, so horribly, dreadfully ladylike. Both of us, we're part of a vast horde of respectable women, all marching timidly through life in identical uniforms. I'm just not going to do it any more. Do you hear me, Homer?"

"Good Lord, my love, of course I can hear you. They can hear you in Copley Square."

Someone was shouting at them. "Homer? Homer, wait."

It was Alan Starr, racing after them. "The burned car, Rosie's car, did you find out where it is?"

"I did indeed. Matter of fact, we're on our way there right now. Want to come along?"

"Yes, yes." Impulsively Alan climbed into the back of the Kellys' car and leaned forward between the front seats as Mary pulled away from the curb. "How did you find out where it is?"

Homer groaned with self-pity. "It's supposed to take only five phone calls to learn anything, isn't that right? Well, this took fifteen. Campbell passed me along to Bleach, and Bleach passed me along to McArthur, and McArthur said talk to Smithies, and I forget all the rest. And all the time I could distinctly hear the shuffling of paper going on in the background. You know, *slip, slap, slop,* and red tape has a special sort of slippery sound when they tie it in bowknots on stacks of flabby interoffice correspondence."

"Pay no attention to Homer," said Mary. "The point is, he finally found out. The only question is, does Rosie's car still exist? Maybe they've sent it to Korea by now, mashed into a little cube."

◆ ◆ ◆ ◆

CHAPTER 28

Experience has proved the toad to be endowed with valuable qualities.
                                        Martin Luther

The sign beside the turnoff said, WRECKED CARS.

The surrounding landscape was a sad rural slum, old farmland turned into mattress salesrooms, car dealerships, Hawaiian restaurants and sinister-looking road-houses. Over New England the wintry cloud cover had come back. It was hard to imagine the sun ever shining on this landscape. As they turned in to the dirt road there was a distant rumble like war in another country, thunder in winter, ominous and unnatural.

The swamp beside the rutted driveway was wild and mysterious, but miscellaneous car parts rose out of it here and there like metallic eruptions of skunk cabbage. Mary slowed down on the bumpy track and grieved for the violated countryside. "What a shame."

"Well," said Homer, "you gotta have balance. You want a lotta pretty little New England farms and fields? Gotta balance 'em with wrecked-car lots. It says so in the Bible."

Rounding a curve they came upon the whole panorama of the wrecked-car emporium. It was a landscape of disaster. The relics of a thousand tragedies lay bent, burned and twisted in drifts and heaps—natty bashed-in sports cars in which harebrained young guys had perished, crumpled station wagons in which whole families had been wiped out, the smashed remains of ghastly collisions at railroad crossings. The place was a melancholy testament to human reck-lessness.

They sat for a moment, mesmerized, then got out slowly, just as another vehicle bumped up beside them and came to a stop. It was a shining black limousine, a hearse with a buckled side. The driver climbed out and grinned at them. "Hiya, you want shumping? My name'zh Brown, Boozher Brown."

For a moment Homer was speechless. So was Mary. They recognized Boozer Brown. "Mr. Brown, Boozer Brown," said Homer, reaching out a hand, "is it really you?"

Boozer smiled hugely. "Hey, ri' you are. Whazh your name? Nantucket, ri'? Zheezh! Hey, you shtill got the shame mizhush, ri'? Zheezh."

"But Boozer," said Homer, "what happened? What are you doing here on the mainland? I thought you were Nantucket born and bred?"

"Oh, Jheezhush, I losht the battle. You know. Nantucket real eshtate intereshtsh, they took away the lizhench for my garage, bought me out for a shong. Sho here I am." He gestured proudly around his new empire. "All mine. Thizh whole thing you shee here, it'sh all mine." Boozer took a bottle of Old Fence Rail out of his pocket and offered it around.

Alan declined politely. So did Mary and Homer. "Now tell me," said Boozer, "what can I do for you? Mush be shumping."

"We're looking for a particular car, Boozer," said Homer, "sent over by the Boston Police Department. It's a Ford Escort, destroyed by fire, registration number two-two-one-H-O-K."

"Oh, that one, oh, zhure, I know that one. Don't tell nobody, but it'sh full of all kinzha good shtuff. Alternator's shtill okay, and sho'zh the air conditioner, radio, water pump. And, Jheezhush, the engine'zh shtill pretty mush okay." Boozer gestured vaguely at a distant part of his domain. "You wanta shee it?" He waved hospitably across the sea of wrecked cars. "Ri' thish way."

They followed him along a narrow path between heaps of wrecked automobiles. The ground was littered with bits of upholstery, rags of stuffing, stained bucket seats, contorted bumpers, flattened gas tanks, rusted exhaust pipes and gasoline engines crushed as if by falling from the moon.

"Here she izh." Boozer stopped and waved dramatically. "Help yourshelf. It'sh all yourzh." He wandered away and lifted the hood of a smashed pickup truck.

Rosie's Ford Escort was a uniform velvety black. The windows were cracked and splintered.

"Awful, awful," murmured Mary, sickened. Alan turned away, seeing all too clearly the inferno that had consumed the soft flesh of someone who might once have been Rosalind Hall.

Homer, careless of his churchgoing clothes, turned the door handle on the driver's side and looked in. The interior too was black, and the vinyl seat was cracked and curled. But the knobs and switches on the dashboard had not melted. It was as though the sudden flare-up of fire around the car had quickly subsided.

He climbed in, squeezing himself into the front seat. His wife began to protest, then shrugged and smiled wanly at Alan, who stood watching grimly with his arms folded.

Homer tried winding down the window. The handle worked. He looked up at Alan. "Was Rosie a tall woman?"

Alan shook his head. He didn't have any idea.

"Because the seat's pushed pretty far back. The driver must have been fairly tall."

Homer tried the windshield wipers. They didn't budge. He swabbed at the face of the clock. It showed the wrong time, but maybe it had never worked. The horn beeped. There was a tape deck, its black plastic surface bubbled by the heat. Homer touched a button, and a cassette slid out silently. The label was barely legible—it was a Haydn horn concerto—but the tape itself was congealed into black strings. He put the cassette back and tried the radio. At once a huge racket boomed out of the loudspeaker, an immense roar, *SHE TOLE ME! SHE TOLE ME! SHE TOLE*

ME I-I-I WAS HER LOVER MAN! SHE TOLE ME! SHE TOLE ME!

"Turn it off," shrieked Mary. Homer turned it off, then sat staring at the radio dial in the pulsing silence. "You'd think she'd listen to one of the classical stations," said Mary. "I mean, a girl with her musical background."

Alan put his pale face into the car and looked at the radio. "She would never have been tuned to that station. It's hard rock all day long."

"But you didn't know her," Homer reminded him, looking him in the eye. "Maybe she liked all kinds of music."

"I just can't believe it."

"Well, the fact is," said Homer, struggling to get his big frame out of the car, "neither can I."

"Oh, Homer, look at you." Mary made a feeble attempt to brush some of the black from his trousers, then laughed and gave up.

Boozer Brown came back and grinned at them proudly, the lordly proprietor. "Hey, how you like it?"

"Oh, fine, Boozer," said Homer, "just fine. No, really, you've been a big help. Thanks so much."

On the way back to Boston, Homer waxed eloquent on the subject of the music in the air. "Here it is, all around us. I mean, look at it, the air looks empty, right? But it's full of electromagnetic radiation billowing in all directions, and all you have to do is stick up a little wire and you can hear it. I mean, it's not just radio stations, it's short-wave messages from around the world, it's cosmic rays, it's random noises from outer space, and it's all right here in this car."

"She wouldn't have been listening to that station," insisted Alan, who had a one-track mind. "There's just no way she would have turned it on. Somebody else was driving."

When they dropped him at the corner of Russell Street, he galloped upstairs and called Barbara Inch.

She was surprised by his question, but she knew the answer. "How tall was Rosie? Oh, not very tall, not very short. She was a couple of inches shorter than me. Five feet four, maybe? Why do you want to know?"

"Oh, nothing special. Thanks, Barbara."

Five feet four, thought Alan with satisfaction. *Too short for the seat of the burned Escort*—and then he couldn't help adding, *but not too short for me.*

◆ ◆ ◆ ◆

CHAPTER 29

*Ah, loving God, defer not thy coming. I await impatiently
the day when the spring shall return.*   Martin Luther

The fading winter continued to be dry. Homer and
Mary began to hope they might creep through the
rest of the season without a snowstorm if they kept
their heads down. One Wednesday afternoon Homer arranged to meet Alan Starr and little Charley Hall in the
Public Garden.

"He certainly is a cute little guy," said Homer, bending
down to smile at Charley. Charley smiled back.

Homer melted, feeling a pang at being childless himself,
a twinge that came over him now and then. Fortunately the
feeling vanished whenever other people's children fought
with their siblings or screamed in supermarkets. Mary and
Homer had settled the matter long ago, telling themselves to
look upon their shelf of books as offspring. The books
weren't cuddly and cute, but on the other hand they didn't
keep them awake at night and they weren't about to be arrested on a drug charge. It was only when some particularly
plump cherub came into view, gurgling cheerfully, chuckling when prodded, that Homer's equilibrium was upset.

Charley Hall was just such a child. Homer and Alan
stood beaming down at him beside the duck pond, while
pigeons waddled around them on pink feet, looking for
handouts. Other pigeons flew over the pond and landed on
the roof of the little Chinese temple. "Next month," said
Homer, "the swan boats will be out of drydock. I'll take
him for a ride."

They started around the pond. "Tell me about autopsies,"
said Alan, pushing the buggy along the asphalt path. "Sup-

pose the burned body hadn't been cremated? Could they have identified it, even when it was all charred like that?"

"Oh, yes. They can determine how the skull corresponds with photographs, and how the teeth compare with dental records. And what's more—"

"Wait a minute." Alan swerved the stroller out of the way while a flock of small children toddled past, roly-poly in their snowsuits, sporting orange tags. They were led by a stout young woman in a purple jacket. Another woman held hands with two of the children in the middle, and a third brought up the rear.

Alan waved at the woman in the purple jacket, and explained to Homer as the small crowd trudged by, "It's Ruth Raymond, from the new daycare center in the church. All those little kids spend the day in the basement."

Ruth Raymond was blowing a whistle, shouting at her charges. "Okay, you guys, time to feed the ducks." The little kids shrieked with joy and followed her to the shore of the pond. At once a fleet of mallards paddled up to them, expecting to be fed.

One of the children clung to Ruth Raymond's legs. Homer had seen the little girl before. It was Martin Kraeger's daughter Pansy.

"Where was I?" he said. "Oh, I was going to say there are ways you can tell whether or not a person was killed by smoke inhalation and fire, or if she was already dead when the fire occurred."

"You can?" Alan turned the stroller so that Charley could see the ducks. The three women were passing around a bag of bread crumbs, and the children were throwing handfuls into the water with delighted cries.

"They test the blood and see if it contains carbon monoxide from inhaling the fumes, and look for soot in the air passages and for vital reactions in cutaneous burns. It's tricky, but a good pathologist knows how to do it."

"I see," said Alan. "You mean the body in the car might

have been dead *before* the car burned up? Somebody might have put the corpse in the car and set fire to the whole thing?"

"That's right, only now we'll never know, because it was cremated before the pathologist could get his hands on it. I must say, it seems a little strange. You know, I've got a morbid fascination with morgues, cadavers in drawers, labels on frozen toes, dissecting tables, livers plopped onto steel trays. The pathologist said it was a regrettable mistake, but you can't help but wonder."

Alan trundled the stroller to the edge of the pond. "See the ducks, Charley? *Ducks*, Charley, *ducks.*"

Charley obligingly said his second word, "Doggy!"— embracing all zoological species under one stupendous heading, and they laughed.

"Just a minute, guys," cried Ruth Raymond, "Pansy needs the ladies' room," and she went rushing off, dragging Pansy by the hand.

"It's time to take Charley back," said Alan. Turning the stroller, he led Homer across the bridge and along the path in the direction of Charles Street. Above them the tall trees were still leafless. They bore signs, *Ulmus Hollandica Belgica, Fagus sylvatica.* Alan stared at the path, then glanced sideways at Homer. "Do you believe Rosie really said she wanted to be cremated?"

"I don't know. Who called the morgue and told them that? It wasn't either of her great-aunts."

"I'll tell you why I don't believe she said it. She was young. I mean, she was about my age, and I never give the matter a thought. Oh, I can see you might start thinking about it at your age, Homer, but I'm only twenty-nine."

Homer took the insult graciously. "Well, maybe she was more philosophical than you are, Alan, and she had a skull on her desk like St. Jerome, and contemplated her own end, the *terminus ad quem,* the last days, the final judgment, the eschatological conclusion to—"

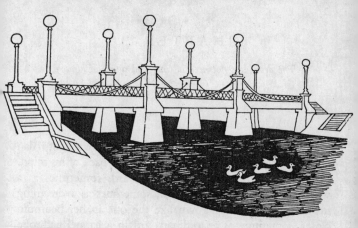

"Oh, Homer, I don't think she'd think of stuff like that. I doubt she said anything to anybody about it at all. Somebody wanted the body cremated before it was examined, so they wouldn't discover that it wasn't Rosalind Hall, it was somebody else."

"So this mysterious person called the morgue and told them it was what she wanted, is that it? And then it was just good luck that they made a mistake and got the stiffs mixed up and cremated her anyway?" Homer shook his head doubtfully, and reached for the stroller. "My turn now."

CHAPTER 30

The devil does not need all the good tunes for himself.
Martin Luther

Next morning, lying in bed in the dawn light, Alan tried to put the lost Rosie in the back of his mind. But she kept surging forward, sometimes as a woman on fire in a blazing car, sometimes as a dreaming image in a filmy nightgown like the one in her bedroom closet, sometimes as an ordinary girl in a flannel bathrobe brushing her teeth somewhere right now. At last, throwing his legs over the side of the bed, he told himself he had no choice but to depend on Homer Kelly's inquisitive nose.

At the moment he had enough to do on his own—practicing for Sunday services in the Church of the Commonwealth, voicing the organ, repairing a gasping wind chest in King's Chapel, adding a rank of Krummhorns to the organ at Annunciation, and now there was this daunting new undertaking, the rehabilitation of Harold Oates.

Alan was trying to arrange a series of concerts for the great man, beginning at Commonwealth. And maybe the *Boston Globe* would do a story on his musical resurrection. Come to think of it, why shouldn't there be appearances on television? Then, pulling on his clothes, Alan changed his mind about television. Better not. Much better not.

This morning Oates was to face his first challenge. He was to play for Edith Frederick. The all-powerful Mrs. Frederick would decide whether or not to grant Oates a festive, well-advertised concert, a celebration welcoming back into the world the most distinguished organist in the United States since E. Power Biggs. Her decision would have to be rubberstamped by the other members of the

Music Committee, but the deciding voice was always that of the Great Provider of All Funding.

The man would have to look respectable. Once again Alan ransacked his closet, looking for something tweedy. He pulled out a gray suit he had bought in college for a court appearance on a pot charge, six years back. He had never worn it since.

It didn't look too bad, although there was a moth hole on the collar of the jacket. Alan groped in his bureau drawer and found a tin button with the legend, SAVE OUR RIVERS. He pinned it over the hole. He found an Oxford-cloth shirt and a regimental necktie, more gifts from his ever-hopeful mother. At the last minute he threw a shoe-polishing kit into the paper bag and set off for the Church of the Commonwealth.

He had arranged to meet Oates fifteen minutes before the appointment with Mrs. Frederick, but Oates was late. "Overslept," he said jauntily, showing yellow teeth. Two were conspicuously missing. He looked awful. Alan rushed him into the men's room and made him take off his loud shirt and sleazy polyester pants. Oates fumbled with the shirt buttons and protested.

"Look, do you want a concert here or don't you?" Alan grinned, remembering scenes like this with his mother. "Let's see your shoes. Christ, Mr. Oates, where are your socks? Oh, God, I didn't bring any socks. Here, you can have mine."

Alan whipped off his shoes and tore off his socks. Oates put the socks on reluctantly, while Alan gave his shoes a quick swipe with the polishing kit. "Now, let's take a look at you. God, you look like a stockbroker." Alan laughed, wishing there were some way to spruce up the sagging face, the wicked little eyes, the hideous grin with its missing teeth. "The next thing we've got to do is get a dentist to fill in those gaps."

"Damn you," said Oates.

Mrs. Frederick was waiting for them on the balcony, graciously pretending they weren't late.

"Sorry," said Alan. He introduced Oates to her again, then hustled him onto the organ bench, hoping to keep silent the vile tongue of his great protégé. "Let's get started, shall we?"

Mrs. Frederick sat down nervously and gripped the clasp of her handbag, as Oates pulled out stops and began to play. There had been an argument over the music. Alan had nagged him into performing "Jesu, Joy of Man's Desiring," because he guessed it would be familiar to Mrs. Frederick. Oates had objected. "Oh, for shit's sake, why not the C Major Prelude and Fugue? Something every kindergarten kid can't play while wiping the snot off his nose?"

"Look, all we're doing right now is persuading one old woman. I tell you, Mr. Oates, this is what will do it."

Oates played it briskly, without sentimental languishing. The triplets danced up and down, his shiny shoes moved with certainty up and down the pedals, and at the beginning of the cantus firmus the Spire Flute and Violin Diapason serenely played their part. With a wink at Alan, Oates added a light Mixture and pulled out the stop that promised Divine Inspiration.

As he finished, Alan glanced at Mrs. Frederick. It was clear that she was overcome. "Oh, Mr. Oates," she said, rising from her chair, "that was simply magnificent."

Oates slid off the bench and lunged toward her. "Kind of makes you shit your pants, right?"

Alan closed his eyes, but Mrs. Frederick seemed not to have heard. She beamed. "Of course I have to bring it before the Music Committee, but I know they'll agree. We must pick a date. We must advertise and let everyone know."

Alan saw her out to the street, singing the praises of Oates on the way. To his surprise he saw that she was looking down and frowning. Perhaps Oates had insulted her after all. But as she said goodbye the truth came out. She wasn't dissatisfied with Harold Oates, she was disappointed in Alan Starr. "Really, Alan, I'm shocked. Coming out without your socks! It won't do, dear, it just won't do."

◆ ◆ ◆ ◆

CHAPTER 31

By these monstrosities I am driven beyond modesty and decorum.
Martin Luther

L ike Alan Starr, Mary Kelly was rummaging through
her closet. In her case it was a matter of finding a
new persona. She had sent away to the Morgan Memorial her jacket with the silver buttons, the one that was
so much like Mrs. Frederick's, along with her pleated skirt
and her shoes with the pompoms. Everything else in the
closet now seemed suspect. Her entire wardrobe was exces-
sively respectable.

Abandoning the closet she looked through her dresser drawers and pulled out a snaky black garment and a pair of black
tights. On the floor of Homer's closet she found a pair of black
sneakers that had once belonged to her nephew John. As a last
touch she twisted a red bandanna around her forehead.

In the meantime Homer was on the phone, trying to
find the cranny of the Boston Police Department in which
Rosalind Hall's burned pocketbook was lurking, along with
its identifying credit cards and driver's license. After eight
calls, he succeeded.

"The faceless bureaucracy has yielded up its secrets," he
told his wife as she came out of the bedroom. Then his jaw
dropped. "My God, woman, what's that?"

Mary hunched down and hurried past him, heading for
the kitchen. "Oh, it's just my new outfit."

"My dear, you look like a pirate."

"Good. Just so I don't look like that woman at church
the other day. You know, Mrs. Frederick."

"My dear, if there's anyone on earth you do not resem-
ble, it's Mrs. Frederick."

"Will you be ashamed to be seen with me?"

"Good Lord, no. My insane wife, I'll say, and everyone will nod their heads and smile and be kind to me, saddled as I am with an unsuitable mate."

"Oh, Homer, you do see, don't you? You see what I mean?"

"Of course I do, my darling." Homer embraced her. "And I don't care what you wear. You always outqueen everybody else, just by being yourself. Damn them all." He backed off and looked at her again. "It's true, you look really swashbuckling. All you need is a cutlass. Do you want to come with me?"

"Oh, no, thank you, Homer." Mary made nervous dashes around the room, collecting coat, bag, car keys. "I'm going to lunch with Ham Dow. He's invited some of the women faculty to lunch."

"You're having lunch with the president of Harvard?"

Mary looked down at herself again. "Oh, don't worry. Professor Dalhousie will be wearing her shroud, like Emerson's aunt, and Jane Plankton will be there in a velvet gown, the one that trails along the floor, and Julia Chamberlain will be wearing something smashing. I couldn't wear my prim little Johnny Appleseed outfit in that company. Thank God, I've burst out of my chrysalis at last."

"Well, congratulations, Mary dear. The butterfly flaps her wings."

The Evidence Locker for the Boston Police Department was housed in a building on Berkeley Street. Homer found the right door and walked in and put his hands on the counter and smiled ingratiatingly at the police officer in charge, a shapeless woman with dull eyes and a gray face.

Her voice was flat. "You got a form?"

"Yes, I do." Homer produced his request for AUTO FIRE 986702, Exhibit H, Rosalind Hall, deceased victim; handbag.

The form was signed by Francis Xavier Powers, District Attorney of Suffolk County.

"Just a minute." The woman strolled out of the room with the form. From the next office he could hear her in lively conversation. She had been on a winter cruise. There had been dancing and shuffleboard, a shipboard romance. Homer heard envious squeals. At last the gray woman came back and dumped a large plastic bag on the counter. A tag was attached, CHAIN OF POSSESSION OF EVIDENCE, with the signatures of the several officials through whose hands it had passed.

"Don't touch," she warned him, withdrawing a flattened black object. "I got to do all the handling. Like, nobody else is allowed."

The pocketbook belonging to Rosie Hall had once been brown, but now it was black. Most of the leather surface had been scorched. The gray woman reached in and drew out the contents, one article at a time. They were blackened but recognizable.

"May I see what's in the wallet?"

The woman shrugged and raised her eyebrows. She pulled open the billfold carefully, displaying scorched twenty-dollar bills, a couple of fused plastic credit cards and a warped driver's license. The sober face of Rosalind Hall was dimly visible on the license.

"What's in the zippered bag?"

"It's just cosmetics. I already looked."

"Please may I see?"

The woman was displeased. She tugged back the zipper with a petulant motion and shook out the contents with a violent gesture.

A fragrance of cheap perfume rose from the heap of cosmetics, mingled with the acrid smell of scorching. Homer was baffled. He could recognize the lipsticks, the melted comb and the cracked mirror, but what were all the other things? There were flat round containers, small square

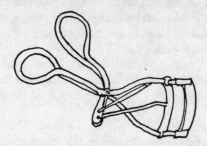

boxes, cylinders and pencils, and a device like an instrument of torture.

"What's that?"

"That? It's an eyelash curler."

"An eyelash curler?" Homer was stunned. "How does it work?"

The woman came to life. "Wait a sec. There's one in my bag." She turned away swiftly, took a shiny pocketbook from the drawer of her desk, reached in, pulled out a nearly identical cosmetic case, and emptied it on the counter next to Exhibit H. Picking up her eyelash curler in one hand and a pocket mirror in the other, she crimped the pale lashes on her upper lids until they stood straight up, kinked at right angles.

"Good Lord." Homer waved a hand at all the rest. "Could you demonstrate these too?"

"Well, okay." She got to work with a will. The subject of cosmetics was the woman herself. It was something she was interested in. She jabbered, explaining. "First you got your foundation cream—then your powder—your blusher—your eyebrow pencil—your eyeliner—your eye shadow—your mascara. You got two kinds of lipstick, see? Like, you put this one on first, and then you frost it with the other one."

Homer watched like a neophyte in a temple to an unknown god. In five minutes the gray woman had transformed herself into a white and pink doll with phosphorescent lips like the mouth of a corpse and eyes like bugs with a thousand legs. She was a work of art.

Humbly Homer thanked her and went away. Heading for Storrow Drive he pulled over impulsively and parked on Clarendon Street beside the Church of the Commonwealth.

He found Alan Starr in the vestibule with his nose pressed against the glass doors of the sanctuary. "Baptism," he explained. "Always some goddamned interruption."

Homer looked too. "Ugly little kid," he said. "Not like our Charley."

Alan grinned at him. "Just what I was thinking myself."

"Look here," said Homer, "I've just come from the Temple of Cosmetic Craftsmanship, and I want to tell you all about it."

"The temple of what?"

"Evidence Locker, Boston Police Department. Rosalind Hall's burned pocketbook, I've just seen it." Homer told Alan about the credit cards, the driver's license, the money, the cosmetic case with its contents—the eyelash curler, the mascara, the eyebrow pencil.

"But that's ridiculous," said Alan. "Rosie would never have used all that stuff."

"Ah," said Homer, looking at him wisely, "I thought you might say that. But you never met the woman. How do you know what she would do?"

"Well, just look at her photograph," said Alan angrily. "She's not wearing a lot of trashy stuff. I can't believe she wore makeup. Give her credit for some consistency."

Yesterday Homer would have agreed with him. But this morning his wife had driven off to Cambridge completely transformed, a new woman. He shook his head doubtfully. "Well, I don't know. I just don't know."

"Oh, Homer, for Christ's sake, it's just like the car radio.

That didn't fit Rosie either. She would never have tuned to that station, and she would never have worn all that stuff on her face. And Charley saw her, don't forget that. She's still alive, I tell you. Somebody wants us to believe she's dead."

The baptism was over. Martin Kraeger came out into the hall, nodded at Homer, and held the door open for the mother, the father, the baby, the sister, the brother, the grandparents and godparents. Everybody was smiling. Even the ugly infant was smiling, surrounded by a whole population of parents and well-wishers—unlike poor handsome little Charley, bereft of loving relations.

Homer walked back to his car. Idly he glanced at the excavation across the street from the church. Nothing seemed to be happening down in the hole. The machinery sat motionless.

The truth was that the hotel project was in serious trouble. Things had gone from bad to worse. The majority stockholder in the realty trust had suffered an apoplectic stroke. All hell had broken loose. The other members of the board were bickering among themselves, unable to make a decision while his life hung in the balance. In the meantime the arrangement with the contractor had been slyly cancelled and a new document signed, awarding the job to the brother of an alderman. There were suits and countersuits, restraining orders, fistfights, court appearances for assault lodged by both sides.

The job engineer didn't give a damn. He was busy with another dirty job, way down Route 95, building a slurry wall, only there'd been hell to pay from the beginning. The clamshell bucket busted its teeth on a boulder, and then the concrete refused to sink to the bottom of the slurry and had to be pumped out again, and the pump got choked and jammed, and the whole thing was a bag of shit.

The buried sump pump under the excavation of Clarendon Street and the switch that had been left *on* instead of *off* were the farthest things from his mind.

CHAPTER 32

Behold, here is . . . faith really working by love.
Martin Luther

Alan made another entry in his record of Charley's progress:

> Charley walks like anything now, sort of pitched forward.
> He falls down, but then he gets up and staggers on. Last
> Friday he was sick. I don't think Debbie noticed a thing,
> but when I got him here he wouldn't eat and he felt hot,
> and then he threw up. I bundled him up and took him back
> to Debbie's and stayed with him the rest of the day. He
> seemed a lot better by evening, so I didn't call a doctor.
> Next morning I called Debbie, and she was still asleep, so
> she was really mad, but she took a look at him, and his fore-
> head was cool and he seemed fine, so I stopped worrying.
> When I saw him at noon he was back to his old self.

Alan read over what he had written, looked at his watch,
slapped the notebook shut, put it back in Rosie's drawer,
lifted Charley out of the playpen, wrestled him into his
snowsuit and popped him into the stroller. He had a
meeting in an hour with the Music Committee at Commonwealth, and an hour was barely time enough to get
Charley home to Bowdoin Street and run back by himself
to the church.

In the back entry he found Mrs. Garboyle lifting a trash
bag into one of the plastic barrels. Slapping down the lid,
she bent down to coo at Charley.

"Oh, Mrs. Garboyle," said Alan, plunging to the point
without the usual introductory conversational flourishes,
"this is sort of a strange question, I mean, it's really strange,

but did you ever hear Rosie say she wanted to be cremated when she died?"

"Cremated? Rosie? Good heavens, no." Mrs. Garboyle poked Charley gently in the stomach, and he laughed.

Barbara Inch too was on her way to the meeting with the Music Committee. It was her first encounter with the committee, and she was anxious and excited. It was to be in Martin Kraeger's office. Surely he would be there too.

She had taken particular trouble with her appearance, but there wasn't much she could do beyond washing and brushing her hair and polishing her glasses. She found herself wishing she had the whole spectrum of cosmetics at her command, the ones Alan had told her about, the ones in Rosie's pocketbook.

"No, no, of course those weren't hers," Barbara had told him. "Rosie never wore anything on her face at all."

"Well, that's what I thought." Alan had seemed pleased.

But now Barbara couldn't help wondering whether some of that stuff might not improve things in her own case—some of Peggy Throstle's blue eye shadow, for instance, and her black mascara and red lipstick. But probably not. Probably it would just make her look ridiculous.

Barbara Inch had the poised aplomb granted to some homely girls, a quality growing out of her homeliness. As a small child she had not been aware that she was plain. Her parents had been brisk and kind. Only at school did she discover that something was the matter. Luckily she had been a clever girl and a strong athlete. She sank baskets and played the piano with the same accuracy. In a small way she had become popular, because she didn't show off, she had learned to be funny, and she won a lot of games for the school. Her success at basketball and field hockey had thrown her with the jocks rather than the pretty feminine girls, and it had led to doubts about which sex she favored.

She was no longer in doubt. Rounding the corner of Exeter Street, Barbara slapped down her flat shoes and told herself that being in love was better than not being in love, even if the whole thing was impossible. It made the cold sky bluer, the blowing clouds puffier. Perhaps the piece of paper drifting across the street was a precious letter, not just a wrapper from one of those shrimp-salad sandwiches they sold in Copley Square.

In Martin Kraeger's office she greeted Mrs. Frederick and took off her coat and hung it over the finial of one of the colossal chairs around the table.

Mrs. Frederick looked at her critically. The recommendations on behalf of Barbara Inch had been impressive, and the choir was said to be enthusiastic, but the girl had no style at all. Her features were good, but those thick glasses made her eyes small and she had an awful lot of teeth. And her dress! It was impossible, another shapeless bag.

Barbara could feel Mrs. Frederick's eye upon her. Bravely she looked back at her and smiled.

Martin Kraeger too was looking at Barbara, but with friendly interest. He thought how different she was from his ex-wife, who was all tight curls and crisp cosmetics and sharp elbows and sleek fashions from the right boutiques. "Welcome," he said, smiling at her, reaching out his hand.

Barbara took it. It was large and warm.

They sat around the table between the computer in its shell-topped niche and the fireplace—Alan Starr, Barbara Inch, Dennis Partridge, Martin Kraeger, Dulcie Possett and Edith Frederick. Edith sat at the end of the table opposite the windows, facing the light. Her soft pink blouse ruffled under her chin, her rose-colored jacket was always becoming, the rippling purple pleats of her skirt trailed their knife-sharp creases to the floor. The low winter sunshine slanted in at her, and she could feel her lost beauty reassert itself.

The table was littered with papers and books and church bulletins and Martin's crystal ball. He swept everything down to one end except the crystal ball, which he thumped on the table to call the meeting to order. The first subject under discussion was music for Good Friday and Easter.

At once Barbara got off on the wrong foot. She couldn't control her swift decisiveness. "My choir is so terrific, I think we could handle one of the Bach Passions. We'd only need to hire a couple of extra soloists. We've already got a good bass, Harvey Pound." Barbara smiled around the table.

Martin Kraeger glanced at Mrs. Frederick. "What do you think, Edith? It sounds good to me."

"Well, that takes care of that," said Barbara, half rising. "Meeting's adjourned." She sat down again, grinning. "But which one? What do you think, Alan?"

Alan raised his eyebrows at her warningly and said nothing. There was a pause. Barbara had begun her career at Commonwealth with a mistake. She had ignored Edith Frederick.

Martin Kraeger leaped into the breach. "But perhaps Mrs. Frederick has another idea. Any suggestions, Edith?"

Edith was confused. She wanted to be consulted, but she didn't know enough to make another suggestion. "Oh, whatever you people want, it's all right with me." Her hurt feelings were manifest.

Barbara saw her mistake at once. "I was only joking." It was something she had said a thousand times before. "Do tell us, Mrs. Frederick, what you would like best."

"No, no. Carry on. Bach is always an *excellent* choice."

Always in good taste, Barbara wanted to say, but she held her tongue.

Martin Kraeger pitied Edith Frederick and wanted to comfort her. This afternoon she was looking particularly shriveled and old. Again he could almost see one of Holbein's skeletons sitting next to her, crowding up against her, its articulated hand patting hers, the shiny plates of its skull close to her head, its arm around her shoulder. "Edith has put her finger on it," he said. "An excellent choice. I agree."

There were murmurs of agreement around the table. Dulcie Possett spoke of a performance of the *St. Matthew Passion* she had heard in Kansas City. Old Dennis Partridge had sung in the chorus for the *St. John,* back in the nineteen-fifties.

They went on to choose between the *St. Matthew* and the *St. John.* Alan had long since learned which way the tactful wind blew. "What do you think, Edith? The *St. John* is shorter, but I guess the *St. Matthew*'s a little more sublime."

"Measuring sublimity on a scale of ten," joked Barbara. "But with only two months before Good Friday, it had better be the *St. John.*"

"Should it be in English or German?" said Kraeger. He looked at Barbara. Something in his manner was a warning, but she was too new and she didn't catch it.

"Oh, German of course," she said, "the way Bach performed it."

"Well," Alan said judiciously, "there are some good English versions."

"*I* think," said Edith, seeing a chance to oppose the arrogant new choir director, "it's so much better when people can understand the music, don't you think so, Martin?"

"Yes, of course." Martin looked at Barbara. "Would you mind if the choir sang in English?"

Barbara wasn't stupid. "Not at all. By all means, let's have it in English."

Alan cleared his throat. It was time to introduce the subject of Harold Oates. "Edith and I have made a discovery. One of the best organists in the world is right here in Boston. Harold Oates."

"Harold Oates?" said Dennis Partridge. "I thought he was dead."

Barbara too was astonished. "The great Harold Oates? James Castle's teacher? But he must be awfully old! At least seventy." Then Barbara glanced at Mrs. Frederick, who looked eighty, and bit her tongue. Once again she had blundered.

Deeply offended, Mrs. Frederick turned to Kraeger. "I assure you, Mr. Oates is magnificent. He played for me the other day. Until Alan discovered him, the poor man was living in a shelter for the homeless on Kansas Street. Imagine, a man of his reputation!" She beamed conspiratorially at Alan. "We think he should have a concert right here in this church."

"Well, good," said Martin, "why not?"

"Hear, hear," said Dennis Partridge.

"Great idea," said Barbara.

"And there's another thing," said Alan, following up on the success of Edith's suggestion, "why couldn't he play the organ for the *St. John?* I'm pretty overwhelmed right now. And Oates could do it with one hand tied behind his back. It's child's play."

"Well, I'd be honored to have him," said Barbara. "Do you think he can handle rehearsals?"

"Absolutely," declared Alan, sounding more positive than he felt.

"Talk about resurrection from the dead," said Kraeger, grinning around the table. He glanced at the crystal ball, which was reflecting the huge moony glasses of Barbara Inch, and suggested that other churches might sponsor concerts by the rediscovered Oates. "A series, a whole Back Bay series. What would you think, Edith, if I were to speak to my fellow clergy and try to fix it up?"

Edith clapped her hands. "How marvelous."

"Wonderful," said Barbara.

"Meeting's adjourned," said Kraeger, banging down the crystal ball.

◆ ◆ ◆ ◆

CHAPTER 33

*The heart of a human creature is like quicksilver, now here,
now there.*   Martin Luther

"Hey, Dick, hey, Harry," said Tom Duck, reaching into his coat pocket, "looky here, what I got."

It was a bottle of cherry brandy, half gone. Tom slapped it down on the table in the kitchen of the house on Kansas Street.

Dick snickered. "The boss wouldn't like that. Neither would his wife."

"They're out," said Tom. "So it's all right. Let's just finish it up, okay? In honor of Harry's being here today, right?"

"Hold it," said Dick. "Harry ain't supposed to have any. He's got a two-year AA badge, like he's working up to three."

Harold Oates closed his eyes to shut out the sight of the bottle. "What do you think I am, a fool?"

"Well, okay," said Tom. "You neither, Dick? Well, all right, but I got something else to show you. Come here." Tom led the way into the hall and opened the door of the coat closet. It was jammed with clothing donated by charitable organizations and churches.

"Back here," said Tom, "see what I got back here." He held aside the hanging coats and leaned over a box of blankets. "See this here case of beer? Whole case. Stranger brought it to the house. Never saw him before in my life. Gawd! So any time you want a beer, help yourself. Share and share alike, right?" Tom's happy generosity was his witness to the kindly nature of the whole world.

They all heard the sound of a key in the front door. "Oh,

Gawd," said Tom. Harry threw a blanket over the case of beer.

But it was only another resident, Dora O'Doyle. "Hello, Harry," she said. "Sorry I'm late."

Oates grinned at her. "Go right upstairs, dear. I'll be right up."

"Jesus," said Dick, "the boss ain't going to like that either."

The house on Kansas Street was a shelter for homeless people. Actually it was more than a shelter, it was a permanent home for seven chosen lodgers under the ultimate control of the Shelter Resource Unit of the Housing Division of the Massachusetts Public Welfare Department, a tax-supported institution on Tremont Street.

There were many ribs in the vast umbrella of the Commonwealth's concern with social welfare. Another was the Department of Social Services, in which Marilynne Barker held sway.

This afternoon she was once again holding the fort.

The phone call was from a certain Fortescue Biggs, who claimed to be an employee in another agency, the Office for Children, Region Six. "We've had a complaint about a foster family," he said, "from a neighbor who witnessed the beating of a child."

"Oh? What foster family was that?"

"That's just it. The person hung up without giving the relevant information. All we know is the name of the child—"

"Don't tell me, I know. It's Charley Hall."

"That's right, that's the name." Fortescue Biggs's voice faltered. "I—uh—how did you know?"

Mrs. Barker sighed and told him he was an imposter. "I'm going to call Region Six right now and tell them you're making false inquiries in their name."

"Oh, fuck you," said Fortescue Biggs, and hung up.

◆ ◆ ◆ ◆

CHAPTER 34

Everywhere I am hedged about with thorns.
Martin Luther

W hen the phone rang in Martin Kraeger's study,
Harold Oates lay sprawled on the Victorian
sofa. He was snoring. Martin looked at him en-
viously as he picked up the receiver. Oates lived by instinct,
like an animal.

"Is this the Reverend Kraeger?" The voice was strident
and harsh. "This is Mrs. Drathmore. I'm calling from the
office of Dr. Slot."

"Dr. Slot?"

"Dental surgery. Dr. Slot has a patient who has referred
his payments to you. Oates, his name is, Harold Oates."

"Harold Oates? Oh, yes, Mrs. Drathmore. I know Mr.
Oates. It's true, I understand he needs a number of dental
crowns."

Oates snuffled and turned over on the sofa. The voice on
the phone was hostile, as though Mrs. Drathmore suspected
Martin of planning to default on his bills. "And you will be
personally responsible for his dental work? It will be extremely costly, I'm afraid. We must have partial payment in
advance before Dr. Slot can begin the first post and crown."

Kraeger closed his eyes, remembering gloomily that Alan
Starr had asked if the church would pay to have Oates's
teeth fixed. It was part of Alan's campaign to rehabilitate the
man. And Martin had said, Why not?

Since that day last month, Harold Oates had become a
frequent visitor in Martin Kraeger's office. In fact he had attached himself to Martin with sullen affection. Martin's privacy was severely invaded, but he had begun to interest

himself in the restoration of the man to his former status as
a distinguished musician. Clearly it would require more
than dental surgery, but the gaps in Oates's yellow teeth
were a good place to start. "Oh, well, all right, Mrs.
Drathmore. I'll have to get it from the church treasurer.
You'll have it in a few weeks."

"I'm sorry, Mr. Kraeger." The voice was cold. "I'm afraid
we must have it at once before we can begin work on Mr.
Oates. He has no health insurance, I believe."

We have to hurry, Alan had said, *we have to fix him up before
the concert. Those dental crowns, they make a wax impression and
turn it into gold and finish it in porcelain, and it takes a while.*

And the concert was only two weeks away. "Oh, I see,"
Kraeger told Mrs. Drathmore. "The trouble is, you see, as
the minister of this church, I don't sign checks. None of my
staff signs checks. Only the accountant at the direction of
the treasurer. I'll get hold of the treasurer right away, Mrs.
Drathmore."

"Nine hundred and fifty dollars, Mr. Kraeger."

"Nine hundred and fifty dollars!"

"Made out to Roderick Slot, 726 Hereford Street." The
line went dead.

Kraeger put down the phone and stared at Oates, who
was sitting up on the sofa sleepily, rubbing his frowzy hair,
yawning, showing all the ghastly spaces between his teeth.
"Excuse me," said Oates, getting up. "Got to take a leak."

Kraeger put his head in his hands, imagining the dismay
of treasurer Kenneth Possett at a request for nearly a thousand dollars for some organist's dental work. And of course
Ken wouldn't okay a check of that size by himself. He'd
submit it to the church council, because it would be a policy decision. It could take a month or two. Which would
mean that Oates would appear before the congregation,
bowing and smiling after his concert, showing his ghastly
grin, hideous with holes.

Maybe Martin could speed things up with a personal appeal. He called the office in the State House where Ken was some kind of lofty servant of the Commonwealth.

"I'm terribly sorry, Mr. Kraeger," said a soft voice on the phone. "Mr. Possett is in Europe attending an international conference. He won't be back till next month."

"In Europe!" Martin said goodbye and put down the phone and reached for his own personal checkbook. But he had used the last check. He rummaged in his desk. In one of his drawers there was a Church of the Commonwealth checkbook. He found it at last on top of a file cabinet under a heap of orders of service left over from the Christmas season. Taking it to his desk, he uncapped his pen. The phone rang.

"Reverend Kraeger?" This time the voice was silky. "This is Dr. Slot's office again. We wish to make a correction in the billing procedure. Mrs. Drathmore is new. She was unaware of our new policy. It is being handled out-

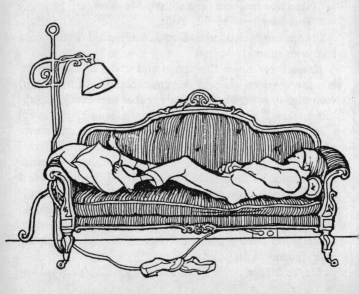

of-office. Would you please make out the check to Dora O'Doyle, and send it to 79 Kansas Street? Thank you, Reverend."

Oates had returned. He grinned at Kraeger and lay down once again on the sofa.

"Well, all right." Kraeger felt like a damn fool. Swiftly he wrote the check to Dora O'Doyle, addressed an envelope to Kansas Street, and took it out to Loretta, who was sitting at her desk, yawning and typing languidly with two fingers.

"Loretta, could you mail this for me? It's got to go out right away."

Loretta's eyebrows shot up. "You want I should go out in the snow?"

"Well, no, of course not. I'll just run over to the mailbox myself."

Actually it felt good to be outdoors. Martin ran all the way to the mailbox on the corner of Exeter Street. The snowstorm was only a flurry, but it outlined the architectural features of the rows of houses. Every molding, every knobbed gable and projecting cornice was defined in white. The slanting lengths of sandstone railings made a pattern of white diagonals. In the narrow park the trees held white tracings along their lifted twigs. Snow lay on the bronze mackinaw and visored cap of Samuel Eliot Morison as he sat on his rock, gazing in the direction of the Public Garden.

Back in the church the freshness vanished. Kraeger was enveloped at once in the warm rush of air from the two furnaces in the basement, surrounding him with a fragrance of floor wax and candles, of copy machine ink and potato salad, of Brasso and hymnbooks and the indefinable perfume of billions of particles suspended in the air from the congregations of the past, from broadcloth trousers, boned bodices, dragging hems, from feathered hats and fringed shawls—the dust of the ages perpetually sifting down.

There was intellectual dust as well, drifting into the nose of the mind, pressing upon Martin as he pushed open the door to the church offices. How was he to minister to his wildly mixed congregation? Some people wanted Bible study, some were eager for holistic self-awareness. It was a perpetual jumble. The mind's nose and the body's nose sniffed all of it in at once, so that the problem about self-awareness had the distinct aroma of furniture polish, of pews thrice coated with white shellac, of a pulpit well dressed in lemon oil.

From the sanctuary came the bleating of the organ, *bah* and again *bah*. It was still being voiced. Martin ran up the stairs. He was late with his weekly piece for the parish bulletin. He had to finish it in a hurry so that the printer could

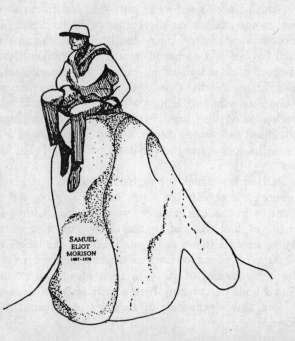

SAMUEL
ELIOT
MORISON
1887-1976

run it off for the retired men who did the collating on Thursday morning.

His study was empty. Harold Oates was gone. The crushed cushion of the sofa retained the imprint of his body, but the man had taken himself elsewhere.

Kraeger was relieved. He took Alan's word for it that Oates was a genius, a great master of the pipe organ, but there was no denying he was also something of a pain. His chummy familiarity meant a constant interference with Martin's daily schedule, it meant listening to obscene stories without end.

Oates had paid him the compliment of saying that he wasn't like other preachers. "You don't usually make me puke. I come to hear the organ, and then I'm stuck with your sermons, but Christ, sometimes I think you're a closet atheist. Congratulations."

"Not an atheist, no, that's wrong." And then Martin found himself explaining the precise nature of his imprecise faith. It was a battle of wits. Oates jeered and sank his javelins. Martin plucked them out and hurled them back. The man was a clever advocate of the devil, chief counsel in the bowels of hell.

But there was a fascination about him, a dazzle, a repellent sort of brilliance. And Oates needed a patron. Martin was determined to back him up with the all the good offices of the Church of the Commonwealth.

CHAPTER 35

A fiery shield is God's Word . . . this shield fears nothing,
neither hell nor the devil.   Martin Luther

I n the central office of the Department of Social Services on Causeway Street, Alan faced Mrs. Barker across
her desk. He was not getting much of her attention.

"Oh, God," she said into the phone, tipping back in
her chair, "we'll send somebody over right away." She put
the phone down and explained. "Mother on crack, she
OD'd, she's on her way to the emergency room, her kid's
been abandoned, the neighbors are outraged." Mrs. Barker
lifted up her voice in a shout to someone outside. A woman
assistant looked in, got the message, disappeared.

Mrs. Barker looked at Alan. Her eyes were tired. He
guessed it was a terminal tiredness, inflicted by the hopeless
misery of the world in which she moved, a place of drug-
addicted teenagers, babies with AIDS, women with black
eyes and bruised bodies, desperate mothers who beat their
children, suicidal mothers in apartments with backed-up
toilets and trash-filled yards, homeless mothers with toddlers
tagging after them in the cold. "What do *you* want?" said
Mrs. Barker.

"I just wanted to say it wasn't Debbie Buffington's fault
that you found me in her closet."

Mrs. Barker emitted a short laugh. "Debbie Buffington,
oh, right, the girl with that strangely popular child in foster
care."

"Popular? What do you mean, popular?"

Mrs. Barker's protective instincts rose up around her like
a cloud. She looked at Alan and narrowed her eyes. The

boy seemed sensible, and he certainly seemed dotty about the baby, but why? An unattached young man taking a shine to a stranger's child? Was there something a little sick about it? "Nothing," she said shrewdly. "I didn't mean anything by it." The phone rang, and she was once again waist-deep in someone else's sorrow. When she hung up and turned back to Alan, she had lost her train of thought.

"Debbie Buffington and Charley Hall," Alan reminded her.

"Oh, right. The trouble is, as a foster mother the girl was marginal in the first place. And we've just learned she abandoned a child of her own a few years back in Amherst. Fortunately the child was adopted by somebody else, but Debbie certainly isn't your ideal earth mother. I'm going to bring it up at our next staff meeting."

"But she's trying, she really is. And she needs the money. If she weren't a foster mother she'd be on welfare. And I'm helping with the baby a couple of times a week. You can depend on the two of us to provide good care for Charley."

Mrs. Barker slapped the desk, having made up her mind. "Tell you what, I'll look into it again myself. Now, if you don't mind?" She picked up the phone to make another call, having lost interest in Alan Starr.

He left, and went back to Debbie's apartment on Bowdoin Street. He found her reading a magazine and smoking a cigarette, while Charley dozed in the playpen and Wanda watched television, sucking her thumb.

"Hey, listen," said Alan, "we've got to clean this place up. Mrs. Barker, the social worker, I think she's going to come again. You know, without warning. Where's your vacuum cleaner?"

"Oh, Christ." Debbie flicked ashes into her coffee cup, "All I've got is an electric broom."

They got to work. Charley woke up and looked at Alan eagerly. "Doggie," he chirruped. "Doggie, doggie."

"He wants me to take him to see the ducks," said Alan. "Not now, Charley boy, later. Here, Wanda, you want to help? You can dust. See? Here's how you dust."

Debbie ran out of the house with a load of laundry, while Alan took charge of the electric broom. Then he rolled the TV set into a corner and sorted the toys, putting the educational ones front and center. By the time Debbie came back the apartment didn't look so bad. Alan bundled up Charley and folded the stroller under his arm. "Try to keep the place picked up," he said. "I'm positive she'll be here soon."

The next day, sure enough, Mrs. Barker fulfilled his prophecy. Alan found a message from Debbie on his telephone. Her voice sounded almost cheerful. "Like, hey! Call me!"

When he got back from an organ-tuning job in Allston, he called at once. "She came? Mrs. Barker came?"

"Right, and it was great. Like I was feeding Charley this hard-boiled egg, like you showed me, and Wanda was drawing with the crayons you bought, and it was only two o'clock, so the TV was off, and everything was, you know, nice and clean. And it's okay. She's not going to take him away."

"Hey, wow, good for you."

"Yeah, well, thanks." She sounded almost human.

CHAPTER 36

I offer no excuse. Let who will blame me. Perhaps I still owe
God and the world another folly.   Martin Luther

"A discrepancy in the books?" Martin Kraeger
looked at his church treasurer in surprise.

"Nine hundred and fifty dollars," said Ken
Possett.

"That's a lot. How could a thousand dollars go astray?"

"The fact is, it was your doing."

"*My* doing?"

"The check. It wasn't itemized anywhere, it wasn't au-
thorized, but there it was among the cancelled checks returned to us with our statement by the Boston Five Cent
Savings Bank, a nine-hundred-and-fifty-dollar check signed
by you."

"Me? But I never sign church checks. Oh, wait a minute,
yes, I did. I remember now."

"Who is Dora O'Doyle?"

Martin heaved a sigh, and explained about Dr. Slot and
Oates's teeth. The story sounded fishy, even to himself.

Ken's voice was quiet. "The check was not made out to
Dr. Slot. Martin, I thought we agreed you were not to sign
checks."

"Well, the trouble was, I couldn't reach you, I remember
that." Kraeger looked at Ken Possett with bravado, feeling
trapped. "I do have the authority to sign church checks."

Ken looked grave, and went away, and Martin tried to
gather his wits. But almost at once Loretta Fawcett came
into his office without knocking, leading his daughter Pansy
by the hand.

Pansy looked doubtful, as always. She had become a wary

little girl, living as she did in an uncertain world, subject as she was to the nervous unreliability of her sphincter muscles.

"Mrs. Kraeger had to go shopping," said Loretta, "so she dropped her off. She said Pansy has to be home at four o'clock sharp for her ballet lesson."

"Her ballet lesson?" Kraeger laughed, and gave Pansy a hug. He picked her up and whirled her around in a circle, then set her down. Pansy's solemn little face opened up in a wide grin. It was a gap-toothed grin. Two of her baby teeth were missing. She looked like a childish version of Harold Oates.

He plopped her on the sofa and sat down beside her and read her Babar the Elephant and a Tom and Jerry comic book. Then he tried to work on a sermon while Pansy played with the copy machine, copying her mittens, a pair of scissors, her father's necktie, and a sandwich from her lunchbox.

At three-thirty it was time to go. "Come on, Pansy, dear. Mama wants you home at four o'clock."

"Kay," said Pansy, correcting him. "Mama wants me to call her Kay."

"Oh, fiddle." Kraeger buttoned Pansy into her coat and carried her piggyback down the stairs, ducking hugely under doorways, to Pansy's delight.

His ex-wife was waiting for them on the sidewalk outside the big house in Brookline, the one he had once known so intimately. He knew how to tease hot water out of the shower, he knew the corner of the kitchen where he had replaced the rotten floorboards, he was familiar with the willow tree that dropped branches into the gutter.

"Hi, Mama," said Pansy, jumping out of the car.

"Kay," said her mother. "I told you to call me Kay."

"Okay, Kay." Pansy giggled.

Kraeger laughed. "That's a nice joke, Pansy."

"It is not a nice joke," snapped Kay. "You are never to say that again, Pansy."

"Well, okay, Mama." Pansy giggled again. Kraeger was pleased to observe a show of spunk in his little daughter. Driving away, he remembered what Martin Luther had said about marriage: *If I should ever marry again, I would hew myself an obedient wife out of stone; otherwise in desperation I obey all women.*

But Katharina von Bora had been a stalwart companion to Martin Luther, as well as a strong and independent woman. Kay Kraeger was merely—Martin said it to himself at last—a fool, and a dangerous one at that. She was bizarre and unpredictable, winding herself in crazy spirals like those bugs that whiz in wildly eccentric circles in the air.

CHAPTER 37

God has his measuring lines and his canons, called the Ten Commandments; they are written in our flesh and blood.
                                                    Martin Luther

"Okay, little guy, come to Daddy." Charley stumbled across the rug and fell against Alan's knees. His cheeks were sticky with strawberry jam. Some of it stuck to Alan's trousers. "Hey, watch it there, kid. These are my best pants. Come on, little guy, time for your nap."

While Charley was sleeping, Alan took Rosie's notebook out of the drawer and started another page.

I bought Charley a toy xylophone, and he really whacks it. I play it too, and give him concerts. His favorite is "Twinkle, Twinkle, Little Star." Rosie, where are you?

At once he erased the last sentence, but it had been ringing in his head. He put down the notebook and called Homer Kelly, struck with an idea.

"Homer's not here," said Mary. "He's teaching today. Can I help?"

"It's just that I've been wondering whether Rosie might have been calling the Department of Social Services to find out where Charley is. It's something Mrs. Barker said, the social worker. She said he was *strangely popular*—that's what she said. I wondered if they've been getting queries about him, and she's stalled them off the way she did me."

"I see. You're assuming Rosie is a good mother and wants him back. But don't forget, it's possible she just went off and left him in the lurch, and then somebody faked her death in that car, and now she's got a whole new life some-place else, and doesn't give a damn about Charley."

Alan was startled by the strength of his answer: "No, no!"

"Well, I don't think so either, but perhaps you and I are just being sentimental. Tell you what, I'll call that woman, what's her name? Mrs. Barker, and ask her if anybody's been inquiring after Charley's whereabouts."

"Good for you, that's great. Call me back. I'm at Rosie's apartment with Charley. Do you know the number?"

Mary wrote it down, then got to work at once.

Mrs. Barker's voice on the line was brisk. "Department of Social Services, Marilynne Barker speaking."

"Mrs. Barker, my name's Mary Kelly. My husband and I are working with the police department on the case of Rosalind Hall, whose infant son is in foster care under the auspices of your department. We—"

"Oh, no, not another call about Charley Hall!"

"Oh, you've had other calls?"

Mrs. Barker fumed. "Yes, we've had other calls, and I'm getting sick and tired of it. Oh, your stories are very clever, I must say, but you will not worm his whereabouts out of me."

Mary stared at the buzzing phone. She called Alan. "She hung up on me, but I gather she's had a number of inquiries about Charley, somebody wanting to know where he is, telling different stories. She thought I was another one."

"But that's good. Why would anybody but his mother want to know where to find him?"

"Well, all right, but why doesn't she just say she's his mother? Why the vanishing and pretending to die in a burning car?"

"I don't know. I don't know why in the hell."

It was time to take Charley home. Alan raced him across the Public Garden and up Beacon Hill, and handed him over to Debbie Buffington. Afterward, slipping and sliding back to the Church of the Commonwealth, he was pleased to see a truck double-parked in the street, unloading the sixteen-foot pipes, which had come at last from Marblehead.

Harold Oates was taking charge. "The thirty-two-footers are still missing, damn them. They won't get here until next month."

"Next month? God, I've promised to have the organ completed by Easter Sunday, all tuned and voiced and ready for the Bach Passacaglia."

"Hey, fella," said the driver of the truck, "how about taking the other end?" Alan grasped one end of a pipe tray and backed up as the driver slid it off the end of the truck.

Oates looked on, grinning. He was sporting a suede coat with a fur collar. The price tag hung from one sleeve. "That low C in the Passacaglia, it'll give those bloody Christians a thrill."

Alan glanced at him, then almost dropped his end of the pipe tray. There were still ugly black gaps in Oates's teeth.

"Hey, watch it," said the truck driver.

"Oh, sorry." Alan backed up the church steps. "Hey, Harold, what about your teeth? You were going to get your teeth fixed."

Oates made a grotesque face. "Fucking teeth." Then he cackled and made a joke about the old lady who had only two teeth in her head, but thank God they met.

"But what happened? We made an appointment with Dr. Slot. He was going to put in temporary substitutes while the new ones were being made."

"Bunch of bullshit, you ask me," muttered Oates, hunching his head down into his fur collar.

"Oh, God," said Alan, holding the door of the church open with his shoulder. "Sometimes, Mr. Oates—" He backed his end of the pipe tray through the door and left the sentence hanging.

Oates came in too, grinning sheepishly, his mouth full of godawful holes.

To Alan's surprise he found Pip Tower waiting for him in the balcony. "Oh, hi," said Alan, embarrassed. He hadn't talked to Pip since their painful telephone conversation after the auditions.

But Pip had come back to help with the voicing. Shame-facedly he admitted needing the money. "I'm sorry about what I said. I was pretty goddamn awful."

"No, no, it's okay. Oh, say, Pip, have you met Harold Oates? Harold, this is Philip Tower, another student of Jim Castle's."

"How do you do, Mr. Oates," said Pip smoothly, shaking Oates's hand.

Once again Oates displayed the holes in his yellow teeth in a hideous smile.

Next day Alan made a visit to the office of Dr. Roderick Slot. It was on the first floor of a handsome brick building on Dartmouth Street, adorned with patterned brick and jutting bays. In the waiting room Alan was confronted at once by the secretary-receptionist. She glowered at him. "Do you have an appointment?"

He recognized her at once as the dragon he had encountered so frequently in offices, libraries, schools and buses. Men or women, they were all the same dragon, with clawed bat wings and leathery scales. Her desk was a fortress between him and the dentist. Alan could see Dr. Slot in the next room, bent over a supine figure who had his hands clasped on his chest like a deceased person in a funeral parlor. "Can you tell me what happened to the appointment for Harold Oates? He was to have three crowns fitted last week."

The dragon glared at him. Little streams of smoke leaked from her reptilian jaw. "We received no prepayment. The appointment was cancelled."

"But the check was mailed to you. Mr. Kraeger told me he sent it. Reverend Kraeger from the Church of the Commonwealth, he sent you a check for nine hundred and fifty dollars."

Sparks flashed from the hooded eyes. "Young man, do you doubt my word?"

"Why, no, but there must be some mistake. Never mind, we'll just make another appointment."

"Until we receive an advance payment that will be impossible."

"But we could at least make the appointment. There's been some silly mistake."

The dragon reared up on her hind legs and flapped her wings. Flame shot from her forked tongue and seven rows of long sharp teeth. "Out," she said, pointing at the door with one claw. "Out, out."

The dentist looked up from his patient and met Alan's eyes. No message passed between them. The dentist looked down again, and Alan left the office of Roderick Slot, Doctor of Dental Surgery, driven from the field of battle by Mrs. Eloise Drathmore, Dragon First Class.

In the Church of the Commonwealth Donald Woody was shutting up shop, taking a last look around before turning the building over to the night sexton.

In the vestibule some of the new pipes still lay in their boxes, ready to be carried up to the organ in the morning. He glanced into the sanctuary, where the evening light slanted through the Burning Bush window above the balcony and fell on the picture of Reverend Wigglesworth on the east wall. The picture was crooked.

Woody wandered down the aisle and shifted it so that it hung straight. Then he saw with dismay why it had tipped to one side. There was a crack running up the wall. There had been other cracks, and he had repaired them carefully, using patching plaster and taking a lot of trouble to match the paint exactly. This time he vowed to replaster the whole wall, perhaps the entire sanctuary.

Alan Starr would be pleased. He'd been calling for it, because the present coating of plaster was filled with nineteenth-century horsehair. "It's terrible," he said. "It sops up the sound. It's like acoustic tile, the way it deadens the reverberation. They've got it in King's Chapel too. Big mistake."

The picture was again at a little angle from the vertical. Woody straightened it. Reverend Wigglesworth looked back at him vaguely, clutching his book. The gold letters of the title, *Divine Inspiration*, glimmered in the last rays of the afternoon sun.

CHAPTER 38

The church is more torn and tattered than a beggar's cloak.
Martin Luther

Alan burst into Kraeger's office. "It's Oates. He still hasn't had his teeth fixed."

"He hasn't?" Kraeger was sick of hearing about Harold Oates. "But I sent them a check."

"That gruesome woman in the dentist's office, she says they never got it. Maybe it was lost in the mail. Are you sure you sent it to Dr. Slot?"

Kraeger stared at Alan, then sagged in his chair. "No, I didn't send it to Dr. Slot. I sent it to somebody called Dora O'Doyle on Kansas Street." The miserable sequence replayed itself in his memory—the call from Slot's office while Oates lay listening on the sofa, the sly exit of Oates, the call from Dora O'Doyle. "Oh, my God, it was Oates, he did it. He diddled me. He called this woman O'Doyle and had her call me back and say she was doing the billing for Dr. Slot. She must be his girlfriend. Oh, lord, I should have seen through it. What an asshole I am." As a clergyman Kraeger had never used the word *asshole* before, but this was as dumb a thing as he had ever done, and it called for a new grasp on profanity.

Alan sank down on one of the huge chairs. "So Oates got the money, damn him. I notice he's been buying himself a whole ghastly new wardrobe. And Dr. Slot still wants his nine hundred and fifty dollars."

"I'll pay it myself," said Kraeger. "No point trying to explain it to Ken Possett. If he hears what happened, I'll be out on my ear. They'd hire some certified public accountant to occupy the pulpit."

"Look, I'll chip in. But Christ, it's only the first install-ment. There'll be more to come."

"Good Lord." Kraeger thought about his dwindling sav-ings account. The Church of the Commonwealth paid him a good salary, partly because it was a prosperous church with a large congregation, partly because propriety required his income to equal that of the director of music, so amply re-warded by the Frederick Music Endowment. But the shrewd divorce lawyer hired by his ex-wife had conned Martin Kraeger out of two-thirds of it, and his own rash charitable impulses often left him short. How would he pay for a new set of teeth for this musical shark, Harold Oates?

From the music room down the hall they could hear the choir beginning to work on the music for Good Friday. "That's good, sopranos," cried Barbara Inch, "but remem-ber, don't breathe except at the holds."

"What if I faint?" gasped Betty Finch.

"No problem. Just lie down quietly and crawl out of sight. Now turn to page one-forty, *We have no king but Caesar.*"

CHAPTER 39

. . . as if the eternal harmony were communing with itself, as might have happened in God's bosom . . . before the creation of the world.   Goethe, on the music of Bach

Harold Oates's temporary teeth were installed by a dental surgeon in Cambridge on a rush-rush basis just in time for his concert in the Church of the Commonwealth. They were only plastic, but they filled in the gaps while gold and porcelain were molded by a dental sculptor in Allston. Oates's smile was dazzling, a flash of yellow and white.

Alan came to the concert early, and looked over the organ. It was as ready as he could make it. He turned it on, then stood back to wait for Oates, looking with pride at the manuals with their white and black keys, the panels of stop knobs, the curving arc of pedals, the façade pipes with their bronze patina. In the last week he had tuned and voiced the sixteen-foot Double Trumpet rank in the Great division. Only the sixteen-foot pedal Trombone remained in the Pedal division, and of course the thirty-two-foot Contra Bombarde, if it should ever arrive.

When Oates turned up, he was wearing a sharp new suit. *That nine hundred and fifty dollars is going fast,* thought Alan, resenting the rent he was paying for Oates's room on Worthington Street. "Are you nervous?" he asked Oates.

Oates pretended to be insulted. "Me, nervous? Harold Oates nervous?" But he grinned at Alan and pulled out the DIV INSP stop knob. "No harm in calling on a higher power."

"Look, the place is filling up," murmured Alan, glancing over the balcony railing. "Look at your audience."

"Screw the audience," said Oates. He was polite to Barbara Inch and Martin Kraeger when they came up to wish him well, but he frowned at Edith Frederick. "I need," he told her, "a moment of prayerful repose."

"Oh, of course!" said Edith, and dithered down the stairs.

"Stupid old bitch," muttered Oates, unwrapping a stick of gum.

Alan shuddered. "For Christ's sake, Mr. Oates, don't insult Mrs. Frederick. She's the one who got all these people here. It's the biggest audience I've ever seen."

Oates sneered. "I have performed," he said, "in St. Peter's Basilica to crowds stretching as far as the eye could see." Then putting the stick of gum in his mouth, he began to play.

It was Bach's chorale prelude on Luther's hymn "A Mighty Fortress." At once Alan forgot his resentment and forgave Oates all his sins. Out of the man's profane heart poured strength and grandeur, power and might, filling the huge chamber with solemn beats of four, great columns towering to the vaults above, thundering in the floor below. All that was random and disordered in the life of Harold Oates was contradicted by these hammer blows of structure, tremendous undergirding pedal notes, THUS and THUS and THUS, while the scrambling rush of sixteenths thronged above them helter-skelter.

Alan flipped the pages for Oates and pulled out the stops, while through his head coursed the words of the hymn about the bulwark of God's power against the prince of darkness. In Oates's playing there was indeed something demonic, as though the devil himself were crouched on his back—a wildness, a recklessness, as if the music were about to destroy itself, only it didn't.

Most of the people crowding the pews below the balcony were ill-informed about the organ literature of Johann Sebastian Bach, but they knew something extraordinary was happening, and they responded with loud applause. Oates took a bow, popping up at the balcony railing to bend from the waist, withdrawing, popping up again.

Alan stood back out of sight, looking on. *Okay, Mr. Oates, don't overdo it.* But the applause continued. There were shouts of *Bravo.* Oates climbed up on the organ bench and capered.

He had cursed the audience, thought Alan cynically, but look at him now, he was pleased as punch.

◆ ◆ ◆ ◆

CHAPTER 40

Though earth all full of devils were,
Wide roaring to devour us;
Yet have we no such grievous fear,
They shall not overpower us.
    Hymn by Martin Luther

Homer Kelly ran into Alan Starr in the Boston Public Library. Alan was hunched over a table in the reading room. Books lay beside him, but he wasn't taking notes. He was writing to Rosie Hall in her notebook, writing about music.

Have you ever read what Schweitzer says about the way Bach uses certain patterns to express specific emotions? One of the motifs I like best is the use of dissonance at the end of a piece, resolved in harmony, as in O Sacred Head:

Those dissonant notes send shivers up my spine, and then it's so great when they smooth out in a major chord. It's sort of like banging your head against a stone wall because it feels so good to stop.

Alan leaped in his chair when Homer Kelly touched his arm. Guiltily he slapped Rosie's notebook shut and stood up, knocking over the chair. In the vast spaces of the reading room with its lofty barrel-vaulted ceiling, the crash echoed and re-echoed, and heads looked up from the other end of the room a quarter of a mile away.

Homer righted the chair and took Alan's arm and led him away into the Delivery Room, where books could be requested and where they sometimes, hours later, arrived.

Pale scholars leaned on the counter, worn down by years of waiting.

"Listen," said Homer, "I've been thinking about pairs of things."

The Delivery Room was resplendent with blood-red marble. Alan stared at the mural over the fireplace, a languid procession of Pre-Raphaelite noblewomen. Vaguely he remembered that they had something to do with the quest for the Holy Grail. "Pairs of things?"

"Two fires, the one at the church and the car fire, and two disappearances, Rosie's and Castle's."

"Castle's! But he didn't disappear. His mother—"

"Is ill, or so he gave everyone to believe." Homer looked at Alan gravely over his half-glasses, while ghostly scholars shuffled by, pursuing Holy Grails that were missing from the shelf or stolen by unscrupulous students or loaned to greedy professors with extended borrowing privileges.

"But it was overdue a month ago," whimpered an untidy man, who looked as if he had been sleeping in the library and hadn't eaten for a week. Homer gripped Alan's arm again and urged him out into the golden ambience of the great stair hall.

"What do you mean," said Alan, *"gave everyone to believe?* Why would Castle lie about his mother being ill?"

"Well, it's interesting that his departure nearly coincided with Rosie's. And we don't know where he is, any more than we know where she is."

Alan looked at the stone lions resting halfway down the stairs. They were gazing sleepily into nothingness, remote and disinterested in all human concerns, like those gods that created the world and abandoned it to its fate. "Well, you know, I've thought about that. I wish I knew more about Jim Castle. Martin Kraeger told me something sort of weird about him. He dropped in on him last Thanksgiving, and it was really embarrassing because he walked in on a screaming session. Castle's mother—you know, the mother who's supposed to be so sick—was there and she was really yelling, and there was this sick sister on the couch, and a bunch of other embarrassed relatives standing around. Martin left right away, and he never did find out what it was all about."

"Strange, the ways of families," said Homer. "You'd think a fine musician like Castle would come from a really supportive household."

"Like Bach's family," agreed Alan. "You know, the whole family all singing and playing instruments together."

"But it doesn't always work that way. Sometimes the family is a barrel of snakes, and the poor little genius has to escape and make his own way." Homer looked at Alan and added softly, "Could Castle have been in love with Rosie? You know, a teacher in love with his student? It's happened plenty of times before."

"God, I don't know. I guess I thought he was more interested in men than in women. Most male organists are gay. It's just a fact. I don't know why the hell it's true, but it is."

"Do you have any reason for thinking he wasn't heterosexual?"

"Oh, I guess I thought he liked me. He was very kind to me, and once—well, once he put his arm around me kind of, you know, lovingly, after I played something for him. I was too surprised to respond. Anyway, I didn't, and that was all there was to it."

Homer sat down on the marble balustrade and folded his arms. "Well, suppose he was heterosexual after all, and in love with Rosie? Do you think he might have carried her off by force, leaving her child behind and a pool of blood on the floor?"

Alan smiled and shook his head, telling himself once again that the idea was ridiculous. "I certainly don't think so." Then he remembered something he had forgotten. "Two fires, you said. Listen, he was in a fire before."

"Castle was in a fire?"

"He told me about it. His hand was bandaged afterward.

He couldn't play for a week or two. His whole house burned down. It's one of those town houses near Louisburg Square, and the fire shot up the staircase in the middle of the night, so he was lucky to get out alive."

"When was that?"

"Oh, a couple of years ago."

"He owned the house?"

"Right. He collected a lot of insurance, but not until he hired some expensive lawyer to sue the Paul Revere Insurance Company."

"Three fires then, but possibly unrelated. Of course I've

heard a rumor that Castle had a motive for setting fire to the balcony of the Church of the Commonwealth."

"You mean, to burn up the old organ on purpose? That's absurd. He'd never do a thing like that."

"Tell me, was Castle a smoker? Was he smoking along with Kraeger on the night of the fire?"

"He might have been, I don't know. He used to smoke, I remember that. But I'm pretty sure he gave it up."

Homer clapped Alan on the arm and said goodbye, then walked down the marble stairs and out into Copley Square. Before heading for the subway he paused to admire the bronze figures of Art and Science, graceful maidens in classical draperies seated on either side of the library steps.

It occurred to him as he boarded the Green Line that the city was full of allegorical women. It had been a fixation with painters and sculptors at the turn of the century. Jammed into the crowded subway car, grasping a pole, hurtling through the dark in the direction of Park Street, Homer wondered about Alan's idealized allegorical woman, Rosie Hall. It was true, her picture looked noble enough, but maybe she wasn't the goddess Alan thought her. Maybe she was nothing but a selfish young woman who had left her poor child in the lurch.

And maybe she wasn't anything at all, because perhaps—indeed probably—Rosalind Hall was dead.

Homer shuffled out of the car at Park Street in a thick mass of students and commuters. He was reminded of the snakes he had been talking about with Alan, the seething mass from which a talented person could sometimes escape. Where in the whole sprawling universe was James Castle? And where was the family of snakes, slimily crawling over each other?

"Oh-ho, Miss High and Mighty, now you're not going to speak to me either! I see, it's a conspiracy. You and Sonny, taking sides against me!"

"Oh, God, Mother, will you let her alone?"

"All I'm doing is following doctor's orders. Can't you see she needs a sedative?"

"Oh, no, oh, please, please, no!"

"Helen, you'll do as I say! You need a sedative and I need a rest. Come on, open your mouth!"

"Oh, for Christ's sake, can't you see she doesn't want it?"

"Helen, hold still!"

CHAPTER 41

Buckle to! Though you don't want to, you must!
Martin Luther

The Kellys' driveway was at its worst. In the month of March it was sometimes a skating rink and sometimes a rutted track. The car wallowed off the road and Homer had to gun the engine through a thicket of fern and blueberry to find his way back.

Was it worth it, living here at the end of a mile-long dirt road? No, by God, it wasn't. Paradise it might be, but one day he would plunge out of control down the embankment beside the house and crash through the ice on the Sudbury River and the car would fill up with freezing water and his drowned body would be hauled out with a boat hook. Serve him right.

He left the car at the top of the steep incline above the house and slid down the hill on the seat of his pants, his briefcase skidding ahead of him, landing in a snowbank.

Mary met him at the door. "Yes, it is too worth it," she said before he could complain, handing him a drink.

"No it isn't." Homer hauled off his heavy parka and collapsed into a chair with his whiskey. "Oh, God, I'm tired."

Mary sat down too, and leaned forward eagerly. "Homer, I've been thinking."

"Always a mistake." Homer sat up and looked at his wife appreciatively. Today she was wearing a monkish garment with a rope around the middle. "Your outfit," he said, "it's charming. You'd never see Mrs. Frederick walking around in a thing like that."

"Oh, thank you, Homer. Now listen, it's about the burned body in the car. If it wasn't Rosalind Hall, who was it? It had to be somebody. Somebody with a name, some-body who was missing afterward."

"Oh, God," said Homer, taking a swig of whiskey, "I don't want to think about women being burned alive in cars. Not now."

"But maybe the body was already dead. The question is, suppose you wanted to get hold of a dead body, so you could burn it up in somebody else's car, what would you do?"

"Well, you could practice self-reliance," said Homer sourly, "and kill somebody yourself."

"Or you could steal one that was lying around. The point is, there must be a record somewhere of all the people who died around the thirteenth of January."

"So we should be finding out about missing cadavers? Hmmm, a funeral parlor, perhaps, from which a stiff has been purloined." Homer groaned and tried to change the subject. "Look, this is deeply distressing to a man of my sensitivity and taste. Let's talk about noble ladies with pop-pies in their hair—Pulchritude! Youth! Sacrifice! Glory! Victory!—not gruesome repulsive swollen blackened bodies in somebody's burned-up car."

"Homer, what are you talking about? Look, we should be finding out whether a body turned up missing about that time. Because it certainly wouldn't go unnoticed, if it disap-peared. Deceased people have relatives with strong feelings about their nearest and dearest. They want coffins and cem-etery plots and tombstones."

Homer was feeling better. The whiskey had gone straight to his head. "That's true. The family mortician doesn't just flap his hands and say, 'Whoops, I'm terribly worry, but Aunt Dolly seems to have flown the coop. We were trun-dling stiffs here and there yesterday and somehow we lost track.' No, that wouldn't do at all."

"But suppose the person didn't have any relatives? So that nobody missed her? What about that?"

Homer set his glass down with a bang. "Okay, suppose it was a prostitute. Dangerous life, especially for the ones who are in business for themselves, so to speak."

"So what happens then? The anonymous body goes to a funeral home and somebody just helps himself to it?"

"It wouldn't be a funeral home, it would be a morgue. That's where they end up, the derelicts, in a morgue." Homer stood up to pour himself another drink. "The trouble is, they've got a system. You can't just walk off with a corpse. They keep track of every decomposing bit of protoplasm that comes their way. Tell you what, I'll talk to a pathologist in Boston. Dead derelicts would probably turn up in Boston. I'll try Mass General tomorrow."

Massachusetts General Hospital was one of the great medical institutions of the Western world, but it was a pain to get to. All the parking lots were full. The automobile civilization, decided Homer, had reached its peak and was now on the decline, and a moment was approaching when all the cars in the United States would collide in a giant smashup causing earthquakes throughout the world and a mountain of wrecked cars as high as the moon. Well, at least Boozer Brown would be happy.

He left his car in a doubtful spot and found his way to the office of the Chief of Pathology.

The pathologist didn't look the way Homer had expected. He didn't have long narrow fingers reeking of formaldehyde and a pale ivory complexion. He was tanned and healthy, as if he had just been on vacation in the Caribbean. Sweat pants showed beneath his green pajama top, and his feet were encased in huge athletic shoes.

"Absolutely not," he said, shaking his head. "We couldn't possibly lose track of a body. No way. You want a list? The names of all the cadavers that have come through here in the last six months? To whom they were assigned?"

"Oh, yes, thank you. But what about unidentified bodies? Derelicts, people like that? Anonymous people, nobody knows who they are? They haven't got any identification and nobody comes looking for them?"

"Boston City Hospital. We pass them along to Boston City. That's where the medical examiner's office is. He keeps them until they're identified."

"How long?"

The pathologist shrugged. "A year. Two years."

"In their—uh—deep freeze? Suppose nobody ever comes to identify them? Do they just stay there forever?"

The pathologist shook his head and moved to the door, eager to get back to extracting organs from some expired person—brain, liver, heart, stomach, spleen, pancreas, lungs, kidneys, adrenal glands, testicles and bladder, and then go out to a jolly lunch with fellow pathologists and gnaw on barbecued pork ribs, his fingers dripping with sticky sauce. Nodding at Homer, he dodged out of the room.

Homer jumped up and followed him as he swung down the foul-smelling corridor. "Well, suppose somebody came along and said, 'Hey, wait, that's my sister Madeline.' Could he take her away?"

"It would have to be an undertaker with a release form, everything signed out. If the cause of death was violent or uncertain, there'd be an autopsy and all the records would be available." The pathologist swung left into an open elevator. As the doors began to close he was still talking about microscope slides and fragments of tissue. The last words Homer heard through the crack were faint and far away, "Boston City Hospital, Mallory Institute of Pathology." Then the doors came together softly and the healthy young man was gone.

Homer went back to the parking lot, to find an outraged motorist backing and filling as he struggled to squeeze past his car. "You're damned lucky I didn't just sideswipe your goddamned automobile, you goddamned bastard," hollered the driver.

"You're absolutely right," said Homer humbly. "I agree with you completely. I'm all apology." Fuming, the man drove away, and Homer set off to find Boston City Hospital.

It was easier said than done. He spent the next half hour getting lost, cursing at the traffic, waiting at red lights, getting lost again, then coming upon the hospital at last by a miraculous accident.

The Mallory Institute of Pathology had a building to itself. It had once been grander than it was now. There were gold sphinxes in the lobby, but the place exuded an air of seediness and melancholy, as though every kind of human sorrow and degradation came here to a bitter end. Homer wandered without direction. One floor was sickening with the same smell that wafted gruesomely up and down the corridor of the Pathology Department at MGH. There were swinging doors with a sign, THESE DOORS MUST REMAIN CLOSED. Another floor was neat and well lit, lined with offices and a handsome library.

Homer poked his head into one of the offices, and a young black woman looked up inquiringly. "May I speak to a pathologist?" said Homer. "I'm from the office of the District Attorney of Middlesex County." As usual he neglected to say how long he had been trading on this defunct connection.

But the Boston City pathologist was just as discouraging as the man at MGH. "Impossible," he said. "Utterly impossible. The system is absolutely airtight."

Homer gave up and went home and complained to his wife. "They were so firm about it. It always puts my back up. Somebody says no way, and I always think there must be a chink somewhere. The human mind will think of something. The snake will crawl over the wall until it finds a hole, then slither through."

"It's that inquisitiveness of yours, Homer. You've got the longest nose in Massachusetts."

"I do?" Homer felt his nose. "It's not the longest, maybe, just the biggest."

Mary gave it a kiss. "Well, anyway, it's a splendid example of the human proboscis on a monumental scale."

✦ ✦ ✦ ✦

CHAPTER 42

*If you think rightly of the gospel, do not imagine its cause
can be accomplished without tumult, scandal, and sedition.*
Martin Luther

H arold Oates brought home to his room from the
Church of the Commonwealth one of the four-
foot Gemshorn pipes, because that dumb kid Alan
Starr hadn't got it right, and now you couldn't do a damn
thing about it without a blowtorch.

He put the pipe down on his bed and looked at the propane torch he had picked up in a hardware store. How did
the fucking thing turn on? Oates fiddled with the knob. At
once a blast of blue fire squirted out of the nozzle and ignited the window curtain.

Martin Kraeger was sacrificing his Tuesday afternoon to
promoting the welfare of Harold Oates. He usually devoted
the afternoon to putting together rough notes for a sermon.
During the rest of the week a rash would break out in his
mind and some of the notes would develop growths and
warts, which would effloresce and expand over half a dozen
sheets of paper.

But it was the only time available for obeying Edith Frederick's demand that he talk all his fellow clergymen into arranging concerts for Harold Oates.

"And be sure to inquire about practice time," Edith had
said. "Alan told me their pipe organs must be made available
ahead of time. And keys! He'll need keys to every single
church."

So Martin put aside his infant sermon and called the music directors at Emmanuel and Trinity, the rectors at Advent
and St. John the Evangelist, the ministers at Old South,

Arlington Street, King's Chapel, First Baptist and the Church of the Covenant, the presiding priest at the Cathedral of the Holy Cross, and the First Reader at the Mother Church of Christian Science.

He was almost totally successful. Nearly all of them were willing to fit a concert by Harold Oates into their schedules of spring activities. Even the cleaning woman at the Church of the Annunciation was enthusiastic. "I'll tell Mr. Baxter," she said. "I was there the other day, at that concert in your church. That Harold Oates, he's just fabulous."

But the consequences of Kraeger's success in arranging concerts were not entirely happy. Within a few weeks there were querulous complaints.

"He was practicing when the wedding party arrived," reported the music director at Trinity. "He refused to leave. We had to pick him up bodily and deposit him on the sidewalk."

"He's sleeping in the pews," said Ronald Baxter, the rector at Annunciation. "We can't have that."

"I caught him smoking in the Lady Chapel," said the assistant rector at Advent, "leaning against the bust of Bishop Grafton. His shirtsleeve was on fire."

"He invaded the chancel during Communion," reported the rector at Emmanuel. "We thought he was taking the wafer, like everybody else, but instead he snatched the cup from the celebrant and drank it down. I was horrified, I can tell you. The man must be mad."

"He drank the wine?" said Martin Kraeger. "That's bad news. He's supposed to be on the wagon."

Kraeger decided to speak to Oates when he next appeared at Commonwealth to rehearse the *St. John Passion* with Barbara Inch's choir. On the next Saturday morning he sat in a pew, waiting, while Oates played a continuo accompaniment and the choir took all the blame for the crucifixion upon themselves:

My own misdeeds were far more
Than grains upon the seashore,
Than multitudes of sand.
'Twas my misdeeds that maimed Thee
With agonies that shamed me,
As though they came by mine own hand.

"Don't screech, sopranos," said Barbara. "One doesn't screech a confession. Listen to the altos. Humility, that's what the altos have got. Good for you, altos."

It was a strange doctrine of faith, thought Martin Kraeger, that God's son should suffer a gruesome death in order to give human sinners a chance at paradise. He himself did not believe the doctrine, but Johann Sebastian Bach had been a devout follower of Martin Luther, and he had certainly believed it, and then he had poured all the intensity of his belief into his music. It didn't matter a damn whether he was right or wrong.

The rehearsal was over. Martin climbed up into the balcony and congratulated Barbara Inch. "The choir sounds wonderful. You certainly do a good job." She seemed absurdly pleased.

He took Harold Oates aside. "Look, Harold, we've done our damnedest to work up a concert schedule for you, but you're undercutting our best efforts. You can't interrupt services. You can't sleep all night in another church."

Oates glowered at Kraeger. "Well, where the hell am I supposed to sleep?"

"Well, why not go home and sleep in your own bed?"

"Oh, shit, they threw me out of there. Lousy place, anyway."

"They threw you out? Why did they throw you out?"

"Fire hazard. They told me I was a danger to public safety. Thought I'd burn down the house."

"Fire hazard? What were you doing?"

"Repairing a four-foot pipe. It was Starr's fault. He got

the voicing stretched too far. I had to use a blowtorch to get it right. Curtains caught fire. My landlady blew a gasket, called the fire department, threw me out."

"Well, damn it, Harold, now we have to find you another place. Listen, if you're going to sleep in a pew, sleep here."

Glumly he went back upstairs to his office to find Loretta Fawcett slapping down the mail on his desk. "I'm afraid some of this is old," said Loretta. "I was so busy finishing my needlepoint pillow. You know, the broccoli. Now I'm starting the cabbage." Loretta went back to her desk, and Martin sifted grimly through the mail.

It was the usual thing, appeals for the homeless, the starving, the addicted, the orphaned, the lost. This morning the wretchedness of the world's condition fell on his shoulders like cobblestones. At the bottom of the pile he found a week-old letter from his ex-wife, and he winced. Kay didn't write often, only when she wanted to announce some weird grotesquerie. This one was hard to figure out:

This time you've gone too far. I am going to sue.

What was that all about? Martin shrugged and threw the letter in the wastebasket. To his surprise, tears were brimming under his eyelids.

◆　◆　◆　◆

CHAPTER 43

The devil, too, has his amusement and pleasure.
                                    Martin Luther

Sleeping in pews was one thing. Vandalizing pipe organs was quite another.

At first the disasters were random and unrelated. Barbara Inch's trouble, for example, seemed to be her own fault. It was a Sunday in the middle of March. Alan Ştarr was sick with the flu, and therefore Barbara accompanied the choir and Pip Tower was hired as a substitute to play the prelude. In the middle of the anthem Barbara's feet blundered on the pedals and the tenors were thrown off-key.

She glanced down in horror, but her feet seemed to be in the right places. Then on the repeat the same thing happened. How could she be so clumsy? Normally her hands and feet were deft and nimble. Once she had mastered a passage it stayed mastered.

After the service Edith Frederick hurried up to Martin Kraeger and professed herself deeply disappointed. "She had such excellent credentials. I feel myself responsible. We should have chosen someone else as interim choir director, the Throstle girl, or Arthur Washington."

"Oh, no, surely not," said Martin, suddenly finding himself a partisan of Barbara Inch. "She's never made a mistake before." After shaking the hand of the last parishioner at the door, he went to look for her.

In the balcony he could hear her voice from inside the organ. "You mean they're all right, all of them? Well, then, it has to be my fault. Damn."

Kraeger put his head in the narrow opening and called

out, "Hello, in there." He had never looked inside before. He was astonished to see the organized complexity of the interior. It was like a city of pipes above a forest of wooden connecting rods, delicately hinged and jointed.

"Is that you, Martin?" Barbara came out, bending her tall frame, acutely conscious of his hand on her side, helping her through. She was followed by the substitute organist. Barbara introduced him. "Martin, have you met Philip Tower?"

"Good morning," said Kraeger. "Were you expecting to find something wrong in there?"

Pip shrugged his shoulders. "Barbara thought some of the pipes might have been switched by mistake, but they looked all right to me."

Barbara shook her head unhappily. "So it was my fault. I played a couple of wrong notes, that's all."

"Well, nobody's perfect." Martin smiled at her, and the idiot words made her laugh.

But in other churches the malevolence was more evident. At the Church of the Advent someone slit the leathers of the bellows with a knife. At Saint John the Evangelist hundreds of fragile tracker rods were crushed with a sledgehammer. At King's Chapel holes were drilled in a whole row of Brustwerk pipes. Even the enormous electropneumatic organ at the Mother Church was attacked—the solenoids on the solid-state switchboard were smashed.

A malicious vandal was at work. The alarm spread from church to church. And everybody said the same thing: *Oates, Harold Oates.*

The rector of the Church of the Advent called the rector of Emmanuel. "Did Harold Oates give a concert there? He did, didn't he? And he had a key?"

The rector of Emmanuel called the minister of King's Chapel. "Didn't Oates play for you?" And then the King's Chapel minister called the First Reader at the Mother Church.

"You had a concert for Harold Oates, didn't you? I thought so. Every place he plays, the pipe organ is seriously damaged. The man's got to be stopped."

In the meantime the vandalized organs had to be fixed. Alan Starr rose from his sickbed, coughing and sneezing, and scrambled from one church to another, making emergency repairs. He had to cancel some of his afternoon excursions with Charley Hall, and Deborah Buffington was miffed.

Three weeks before Easter he called Marblehead to order new pipes for King's Chapel. "And, hey, how about my Contra Bombardes? You keep saying they're nearly ready, and then they don't come."

"Oh, don't worry, we'll be loading the truck in a day or two."

Alan hung up, and at once the phone rang again. This time it was Martin Kraeger, sounding troubled. "Alan, could you get over here right away?"

He found Martin in another quandary about Harold Oates. "All those churches with damaged organs, they're the same ones where Oates has been giving concerts. They're blaming him. He's got keys to all those churches and all those organs. He could have done it, that's what they think. Well, you know what Oates is like. He doesn't exactly ingratiate himself. I'm afraid his nuttiness has become notorious."

"Well, my God, no wonder."

"I can't really say I put it past him." Kraeger stared disconsolately into his crystal ball, which was glassy and blank, empty of prophetic advice. "I mean, the man's so—" Kraeger held up his hands in a gesture signifying Oates's flagrant eccentricity.

"Oh, I know. But the fact that he has keys to those places doesn't mean anything. All the organists in Boston have keys." Alan looked out the window at the pale spring leaves on the trees along the avenue. "Castle had keys, I know that."

"Surely you don't think Jim Castle—?"

"Of course not. I don't suppose you have any news about when he'll be back? Pip Tower thinks Castle's back in Boston. He said he caught a glimpse of him on Boylston Street. So I tried calling Castle at home, but his phone's still disconnected."

"It sounds like those sightings of famous dead people. You know, the way Elvis Presley keeps coming back to father babies. Oh, excuse me." Kraeger's telephone was ringing.

"Reverend Kraeger?" The voice on the line was loud and overbearing. "My name is O'Rourke. I'm a prosecuting attorney for Suffolk County. My office has been asked to investigate the vandalism of a number of pipe organs in the vicinity of Copley Square. Several people have mentioned the name of an organist named Harold Oates. Are you acquainted with Mr. Oates?"

Martin raised his eyebrows at Alan. "Yes, I know Harold Oates."

"Can you tell us how to get in touch with Mr. Oates?"

"No, I'm afraid not." It occurred to Kraeger at once that his ignorance was lucky for Oates. The only way to keep the man out of jail was to prevent his being seen at all. An interview would land him in prison as a menace to civilized society. Martin summoned his stuffiest manner. "I can't tell you where he lives, but I can tell you that Harold Oates is the greatest organist in the world." He went on in this vein, implying that Oates was the living embodiment of Johann Sebastian Bach and Albert Schweitzer. "He has played for the crowned heads of Europe and for His Holiness in the Vatican."

"His Holiness?" O'Rourke was obviously impressed. "No kidding."

Martin suppressed his own doubts about Oates. "So you see, Mr. O'Rourke, he couldn't possibly have done any of those criminally foolish things."

"Oh, right, I can certainly see that." O'Rourke hung up, apparently satisfied.

Alan grinned at Kraeger. "You got him off the hook?"

"For now." Kraeger shook his head ruefully. "Maybe I shouldn't be protecting him. Maybe he should be locked up. Maybe the man's a menace. Did you know he's been thrown out of that place on Worthington Street?"

Alan was flabbergasted. "He has? What for?"

"He was using a blowtorch, repairing a pipe. He said you hadn't voiced it right. Somebody's got to keep an eye on him and find him another place to stay."

"Oh, God, I'll try." A solution to the Harold Oates housing problem arose in Alan's mind, a vision of Rosie Hall's beautiful apartment, but he squashed it at once.

"One more thing," said Kraeger. "All the clergy in the area are setting up vigils. You know, volunteers guarding the organs day and night, just until this thing blows over. Will you talk to Woody about it?"

"Well, of course. Good idea. I'll see him right away."

Alan found Woody in his basement office, adjusting the lights over his bushy little seedlings. He explained Kraeger's suggestion about keeping watch over the organ.

Woody was way ahead of him. "The night sexton's already spending all his time in the balcony. And I plan to do the night watch on weekends."

"But that's too much. Why don't I take Saturday night?"

"Well, okay, thanks a lot. That's great."

Alan walked around Woody's office, admiring everything, peering into the clear water of the fish tank. "Nice goldfish. What are those striped ones?"

"Angelfish. The fluorescent ones are neon tetras."

"Oh, I see. They're really pretty. Well, so long, Woody. I'll be here on Saturday night." Alan said goodbye and walked out of the basement office, his feet jingling the metal lids in the floor. Like Donald Woody he paid them no mind.

CHAPTER 44

When apples are ripe they must be plucked from the tree.
                                        Martin Luther

"Look at this," said Homer, handing his wife the Metro section of the *Boston Globe*. "Unidentified woman killed by a truck."

Mary took the paper and looked at the picture of a couple of medical corpsmen lifting a stretcher into an ambulance. There was a slight mound on the stretcher, under a blanket. "Poor old girl. Homeless woman sleeping on the street."

"The truck backed over her. The point is, she's just what you would need if you were looking for a dead body to burn up in a car."

"Ah, I see. Unidentified, so nobody would miss her. That is, except the people who keep records in the medical examiner's office. More coffee, Homer?"

He held out his cup. "I can't believe there isn't some way to get around all the rules and regulations. Suppose you needed a body. Here's one right here in the paper, nice and fresh, happened last night, just what the doctor ordered. What else would you need? A release from a fictional funeral home, requesting the body, signed by a fictional relative, who just happens to have turned up." Homer took a large bite of English muffin. "Mmmmph. Documents can be manufactured. Nothing to it. You'd get somebody like George Beanbag to do it."

"Bienbower." Mary blew on her coffee. "George Bienbower with his desktop publishing equipment. And you'd need something else. A hearse."

"Right, a nice cozy hearse. Now where would you

borrow a hearse if you wanted to do a bit of body snatching?"

"Back in the sixties," said Mary dreamily, "young hippies lived in hearses. Maybe some middle-aged hippie would lend you one."

"No, no, it's easier than that. Boozer Brown's got a hearse. And he's so easygoing, I'll bet he'd lend anybody anything, including the hearse. Tell you what, after I teach my class this morning, I'll go out Route One and speak to Boozer." Jumping up, Homer crammed the rest of the English muffin in his mouth, licked his sticky fingers and pulled on his coat.

Mary got up too. "Fine, and in the meantime I'll go to the library and look through their newspaper file. Oh, God, I'll bet it's on microfilm, and I'll get a headache from looking at all those pages whizzing across the screen. But we've got to find a nice serviceable unidentified dead woman. What was the date of the car fire? I'll try to find somebody who turned up dead immediately beforehand. If there isn't anyone, our whole theory's no good."

"Well, Boozer, good morning!"

"Oh, yeah! Hey, whasha know? Hiya!"

"Say, Boozer, that's a nice big limo you've got there. Used to be a hearse, right?"

"A hearshe? Oh, right, thash right. Usheta be a hearshe."

"It's in beautiful condition, I must say."

"Oh, sure. Only, shee, itsh got thish big dent on thish shide. Other shide'zh perfect."

"Nice inside, too. Mint condition. Beautiful."

"Oh, yeah, exshep for a few stainzh inna back. Embalming fluid. You know. Leaksh out shometimezh from the desheashed. You know."

"Of course. Common knowledge. Listen, Boozer, did you ever lend this thing to anybody? Say, back around the middle of January?"

"In January? Shay, you know, thasha funny thing, it dishappeared lash January. Gone overnight. Kidzh, thash what I thought."

"Really! It disappeared? Did you call the police?"

"Me? Call the polishe? No, no, uh-uh. Me and the polishe, we ain't got much in common. I clozhe my eyes, they clozhe theirzh. Better that way. Anyway, I don't need no limo. Plenty other good carzh around here. Shee that little Honda over there? All it needed wazh a new tranzhmission. And the Chevy, no kidding, itsh good azh new. And take a look at the Pontiac, honeshta God—"

"Boozer, you're amazing. It's a vehicular resurrection studio you've got here. I'm really impressed. Well, I'll be getting along. Tell me, did you get a look at the kids who borrowed the limo?"

"Not a glimpshe. One day she wazhn't there, nexsht day, zheezh! There she wazh, parked downa hill, can't shee the playzhe from here."

"Well, thank you, Boozer, you're a national treasure, that's what you are."

"Sho long. Hey, watchit, Mishter Kelly, watchit. Oh, whoopsh, shorry about that. Gotta move that ole axshel. I trip over the louzhy thing myshelf, alla time."

Homer picked himself up, hobbled to his car and drove home, congratulating himself. He found Mary trying to wrench a leaf rake out of the toolshed, where it was entangled in the coils of a garden hose. She was wearing a baseball cap and a long dragging skirt sprinkled with sequins.

Grasping the rake, she watched him limp up the porch steps. "Homer, what happened to you?"

"Tripped over bits and pieces of the starry heavens. You know that divine emporium of Boozer Brown's. Barked my fool shin."

"Good grief, are you all right?"

"I'm fine. And somebody stole Boozer's hearse in January, kept it overnight, brought it back."

238 + JANE LANGTON

"Really! Well, wait till you see my little collection of unidentified cadavers."

They sat at the kitchen table and looked at Mary's list.
"Three of them," she said, "only a couple of days before the
burning car was seen by that jogger, down in the ditch below the road."

"Three!"

"One was a homeless man, he froze to death. Remember him? There was a lot of flak at the time. People were
mad at the city for letting a citizen freeze to death on the
street."

"I remember. Pitiful case. But a man won't do. It's got to
be a woman."

"Okay, here's a woman, but she won't do either. She'd
been lying in the woods since last fall. Here, look at the
third one. A little note on the obituary page. It's just what
we're looking for. She's perfect."

Homer read it aloud: " 'An unidentified woman, about
thirty, was declared dead on arrival in the emergency room at Massachusetts General Hospital. The cause of death was listed as unknown. She was found on that part of Washington Street known
as the Combat Zone. No one has so far claimed the body, which
has been transferred to the Mallory Institute of Pathology at Boston
City Hospital.' "

Homer glanced at his wife. "The Combat Zone. Probably a hooker."

"That's what I thought too. Now suppose somebody read
the paper, learned about the body at Boston City, borrowed
Boozer's hearse and somehow managed to steal the body
from the morgue? Then it was shoved behind the steering
wheel in Rosie's car, the car was rolled into the ditch and
ignited, and afterward the police came along and took the
burned body back to the morgue, assuming it was Rosalind
Hall. That's all fine, but how did they avoid the autopsy?
The medical examiner would surely have discovered it
wasn't Rosie, it was somebody else."

"Well, there was that providential slipup, and they cremated her by mistake."

Mary looked at Homer wisely. "Accidental or intentional, that slipup?"

"Either way, it was a fortunate development for the sleazeball masterminding the whole thing."

Mary began plucking leaves from the hem of her long skirt. "Not the best gardening attire, I'm afraid. Of course we may be wrong. Maybe that poor hooker is still in the morgue, not burned up at all. You know, waiting for somebody to claim her. If she's still there, we're back to square one."

"I'll see what I can find out."

"By impersonating that young lieutenant detective from the office of the District Attorney of Middlesex County? Oh, Homer, isn't it a misdemeanor or a felony to impersonate a public official?"

Homer snickered. "You only get thirty years." He sat down at the telephone and worked his way through the bureaucratic hierarchy at the Mallory Institute of Pathology. There were delays, accidental disconnections, recorded messages, transfers to the wrong department. At last the Chief Medical Examiner for Suffolk County returned his call.

"Oh, Dr. Smythe," said Homer, "thank you for getting back to me. I'm looking into the death of Rosalind Hall, whose body was found in a burned car on the thirteenth of January in the town of Hudson. There's something we'd like to inquire about, if we might." Homer's editorial *we* implied an entire department of stalwart police officers standing beside him at the salute. "We wonder if you can tell us what happened to the body of a young woman turned over to you from MGH at that time. According to our records she was unidentified. Do you still have her in—ah—storage? Or has someone come forward in the meantime to identify her and remove the body?"

"Just a minute, I've got my book right here. Let me see.

November, December, January. Ah, here it is. No, Mr. Kelly, that particular body is no longer with us. It was removed on January sixteenth by—just a minute, the handwriting is hard to read—it looks like Kerliss, or perhaps it's Kooliss? Tooliss? Funeral home in Woburn. The signature of the driver is—well, it's totally illegible."

"Tell me, Dr. Smythe, do you know that particular funeral home? Is it one you're familiar with?"

"No, but that doesn't mean anything. We often transfer bodies to funeral homes we never hear from again. People seldom end up in the medical examiner's office from nice suburbs like Woburn."

"You don't ask for accreditation from the driver? Proof that he belongs to a legitimate outfit, the Academy of Accredited Embalmers, or something like that?"

"Perhaps we should, but we don't."

"Well, thank you, Dr. Smythe. Oh, one thing more, what was the name by which the body was identified when it was taken away?"

"Let me look. Yes, here it is. Opal Downing Dew. That's D-E-W, Opal Dew."

"Opal Dew! Well, thank you, Dr. Smythe."

Homer hung up, and went looking for his wife. He found her in the kitchen, turning pieces of chicken in a frying pan with a pair of tongs. "Opal Downing Dew, did you ever hear of a woman named Opal Dew?"

"Opal Downing Dew! It has a sort of familiar ring. One of those three-named women of days gone by, like Aimee Semple McPherson and Carrie Chapman Catt. Wait a minute, I'll try the encyclopedia." Mary wiped her hands on a towel and went to the kitchen bookcase, and groped on the bottom shelf for the D volume of the children's encyclopedia she had used in grade school. It was full of patriotism, optimism, incorrect information and pictures of beaming little girls with pumpkins and Boy Scouts saluting the flag. "Homer, look, here she is, Opal Dew. Look at her, the pince-nez, the marcelled hair, the immense bosom. Formidable! They don't make women like that any more. She died in 1955."

"Well, what was she famous for? Why is she in the encyclopedia?"

Mary looked up from the book and laughed. "She was an organist. I remember now. She used to play in music halls, big thunder-and-lightning concerts to immense crowds. Opal Dew!"

"No kidding. That's interesting. The body snatcher needed a name, and he came up with one that was lying around in his mind, a familiar one. An organist! The body snatcher was an organist! Who else would think of Opal Dew but another organist?"

♦ ♦ ♦ ♦

CHAPTER 45

*The last judgment draws nigh, and the angels prepare themselves
for combat.*   Martin Luther

As a reliable guard over the new organ in the balcony of the Church of the Commonwealth, Alan Starr was a failure. He couldn't keep awake. At three in the morning he fell asleep in one of the balcony pews, and he didn't wake up until Donald Woody shook him at dawn.

"My God," said Woody dolefully, waving at the façade pipes, "look what happened."

Alan jerked upright. "Oh, Christ," he whispered. The entire rank of Trumpets en Chamade had been pulled down by a merciless hand. They drooped at crazy angles.

"They're soft, right?" said Woody. "With a high lead content?"

Alan groaned and stood up, furious with himself. "No, they're mostly copper, but they can be manhandled. Shit! Goddamn the son of a bitch!"

"You must have been invisible," said Woody, "over here in this back pew in the dark. You didn't hear anything?"

"No, goddamn it, I can sleep through anything."

"Can't they be fixed?" said Woody hopefully. "You know, sort of bent back into shape? Like in a body shop?"

"Oh, hell no. They'll have to be taken apart and fixed with new metal and soldered back together." Alan looked at Woody angrily "Do you know how much a single rank costs? Thousands of dollars, that's what it costs."

Woody whistled through his teeth.

Alan called Martin Kraeger and woke him with the bad news. Twenty minutes later Kraeger came bounding up the

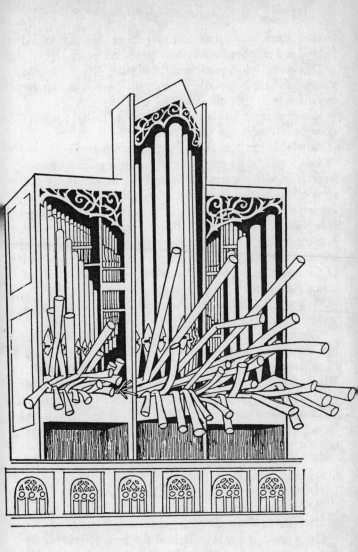

balcony stairs, his shirttail out, his necktie dangling around his collar. He looked at the bent pipes and swore.

"My stupid goddamned fault," said Alan. "I was asleep at the switch." He began taking down the bent pipes, removing them from their footholes.

Kraeger stuffed his shirt into his pants and asked a solemn question. "Where was Oates last night?"

Alan looked at him, and stopped removing the bent pipes. "I'll find out. I'll go next door and call that place on Kansas Street. Oh, don't worry, I'll be back for the eleven o'clock service." He rapped one of the folded pipes with his knuckles, and it gave back a dull clunk. "I guess my Couperin prelude will have to get along without Trumpets en Chamade." Hauling on his jacket, he ran down the balcony stairs, nearly colliding at the bottom with Dulcie Possett, the chairperson of the Flower Committee. Dulcie was carrying a big vase of spring flowers for the morning service.

"Whoops!" said Dulcie, swinging her vase out of harm's way.

"Sorry," said Alan. Dodging around Dulcie he went out into the spring morning. The air was earthy with the smell of softened ground, fragrant with the scent of the daphne Woody had planted beside the steps. Alan ran around the church and started up the alley, then stopped in surprise.

There was Oates, right there in the alley, sitting on Rosie's garden wall. "Harold," exclaimed Alan, "what the hell are you doing here?"

"What are *you* doing here is more like it, right?" said Oates insinuatingly, grinning down at him.

"Don't tell me you've been inside?"

"Might have been."

"But how? Where did you get the key?"

Oates gazed at the sky. "Behold the birds of heaven, we sow not, neither do we reap, but God provides all us birds with nice little brass keys."

"Keys! You've got a key to Rosie Hall's apartment?"

"No, *you've* got a key to her apartment. Or rather, you did have." Oates pulled it out of his pocket and held it aloft. "You should take better care of your coat pockets. I left the Lifesavers."

"Gee, thanks." Alan recognized the key by the yellow tag. He knew what it said, *115 Commonwealth, Rear.* "Goddamn it, Harold."

"Oh, it's all right." Oates tossed him the key. "You can have it back. I've got another one right here. Hardware store made a copy. Nice place you've got here. I thought I'd just bed down here once in a while. Perfect little home away from home. Belonged to your fried girlfriend, right? Place is in escrow, right? Month after fucking month those legal hacks think the thing over, and who's to know I'm here? Charming little place, really cute. Cunning little harpsichord. Your fried girlfriend on the wall, sweet girl, really sweet. Pretty little potted plants, they need watering, right? I'll be doing the executors a favor." Oates jumped down into Rosie's garden, trampling a bed of crocuses, and beamed at Alan over the wall, showing his brilliant teeth.

Alan reminded himself that Oates was the greatest organist in the world. "Why didn't you steal the gate key too?" he said, opening the padlock and walking into the garden.

Oates opened the back door with his hardware store key and led the way inside. Throwing himself on the sofa, he lay down full-length with his muddy shoes on the yellow cushions and pulled a pack of cigarettes out of his pocket.

At once Alan went to the back entry and groped in the trash can. He brought one of the ashtrays to Oates, dumped his feet on the floor, and pulled up a chair beside him. "Now look here, Harold, tell me the truth. Were you in the church last night messing around with the organ?"

Oates opened his eyes and blew smoke in Alan's face. "Jesus," he said, "what happened?"

"The horizontal trumpets, somebody bent them down, the whole rank."

Oates sat up, shook a clenched fist at the ceiling and uttered a stream of obscenities.

Alan was convinced. "All right, it wasn't you then. Tell me, I hear you've been sleeping in churches. Have you slept in Commonwealth? I assume you have a key?"

Oates sank back and closed his eyes again. "Well, naturally, I'm quite the chatelaine these days. The man of a thousand keys. I creep through walls into locked rooms, I open bank vaults with a whispered word. Which reminds me." Oates sat up again. "Did you know there's a safe in the bedroom?"

"A safe? No, where?"

"In the bedroom, behind an artsy-craftsy wall hanging. I looked for a key or a combination. No such luck."

So Oates had been groping in Rosie's drawers. Alan cringed, but it was no more than he had done himself. He went to the bedroom. Sure enough, under the handwoven Guatemalan fabric on the wall was a small metal door with a numbered dial. Alan dropped the hanging and returned to Harold Oates.

It was Oates's turn to ask embarrassing questions. "Cozy retreat, this place. Woman's dead, right?"

"Maybe," said Alan gruffly. "And then again, maybe not."

"Must cost you a couple thousand a month to live here?"

"Oh, God, Harold, I don't live here. I just come in now and then."

"You stole the key, is that it?" Oates gave him a hideous wink.

"Well, yes, I suppose I stole the key."

Oates grinned. He got up and shambled across the room to the picture of Rosie and Charley on the wall. "Your fried girlfriend is adorable," he said, leaning on the desk, "but altogether too sunnyside-up. I like 'em over easy myself." He glanced around slyly. "Just your type, right?"

Alan couldn't be responsible for the look on his face. He turned away, feeling too well understood. The man was too many kinds of a genius.

Oates wandered away from the picture and ran his finger along one of the bookshelves. "Christ, here's an old friend, Chiapusso on the life of Bach. Good book. Your girlfriend seems to have read it carefully. Notes in the margin. Girl after my own heart, fried or not fried."

"For God's sake, Harold."

Oates chuckled, then flipped the page and gave a loud guffaw. "Look at that, she underlined the cat cantata."

"Bach wrote a cat cantata? I never heard of it."

"No, no, it was somebody else's nutty idea. You lined up a row of cats, pinched their tails, you got a cantata. Joke." Oates yowled like a cat and flipped another page. "All the other crazy stuff too, she's underlined the rest of it, the self-sounding bells, the echoes in different languages." Oates threw his head back and put his hands beside his mouth, calling from one mountain to another, *"Good m-o-o-o-o-o-o-o-r-n-i-i-i-i-ng!"* Then he put one hand to an ear and sounded the echo in German: *"Guten mo-o-o-o-o-o-o-r-g-e-n!"*

"Echoes in different languages? Self-sounding bells? Does it say that?"

"Of course. Good old Chiapusso. Great book. All the stuff Bach grew up with, the things he read, his philosophical friends and beer-drinking buddies."

Entranced, Alan reached into an inside pocket of his windbreaker and extracted Rosie's notebook. His fingers were shaking. He felt on the verge of understanding something important. "But they're here. She wrote them down, the very same things, the self-sounding bells and the echoes. She made a whole list of strange things. Listen to this, *Boxes in which sounds can be locked up, a prison shaped like an ear, a domed chamber in which a whisper could be heard from one side to the other.*" Alan read the entire list to Oates, finishing with Noah's ark. "Well, of course some of it's Bach himself, the mirror fugues, the puzzle canons. I understand some of it, but the rest's so crazy. What's Noah's ark doing here?"

Oates took the notebook and looked at it, chuckling. "Clever girl, whether pan-broiled or lightly toasted."

"Oh, shut up, Oates."

"It all goes together, you see. Even Noah's ark. It was remnants of old medieval superstitions, with a dab of Kepler and a smidgeon of Pythagoras. You know about the music of the spheres? The whole universe distributed according to notes sounded by the different lengths of a vibrating string? Mercury at middle C, Venus at G, Mars at the octave? That kind of thing is still around. Folk superstition, you can't get rid of it. Bach was as much a prey to it as anybody else. And Noah's ark fits right in. It's in the Old Testament, the length, height and width of the ark, it's a major chord. You know about Bach's mirror fugues, don't you?"

"Oh, sure. He'd turn a tune every which way to make a variation. Upside-down and backward."

Oates hurled his lighted cigarette on the rug. Alan snatched it up. "And *The Art of the Fugue*, it's so Germanic, the discipline, the thoroughness, writing canons and fugues in every damned key." His wasted face alight, Oates groped in his pocket and lit another cigarette.

Alan was spellbound. Rosie's cryptic list was no longer mysterious. He reached for the ashtray and parked it on Oates's knee.

"You know what drove me to drink, don't you?" said Oates. "It was the crap I had to listen to every Sunday morning. The only goddamn place you can play a pipe organ is in a fucking church. But I had to, I mean I had to play the organ. Ever since I was a kid, it was what I wanted to do. But Christ! The feeble old farts I've had to listen to, the hogwash, the horseshit." Oates leaned forward and took Alan by the arms and shook him. "All those gaseous discharges from the pulpit, the whining hymns, the gutless hoity-toity feeble cries for morality and moderation. Listen, kid, moderation never got anybody anywhere. It's overdoing it that counts, it's going beyond. You've got to eat too god-

damn much, drink too goddamn much, fornicate too goddamn much, I don't give a shit what you do too much as
long as you do something too goddamn much. You've got
to go beyond, I tell you. Look at Bach, you think he was
content with moderation? The man was a hearty trencher-
man. His belly was full of beer. Do you think some lily-
livered sissypants wrote the B-Minor Mass? Was it a
goddamned mild-mannered asshole who invented the *St.
Matthew Passion* and those demented crowds howling for
blood? Passion, my God, what's passion but going beyond?"

Dazed, Alan made up his mind. Fate had him in its grip.
Oates was a tidal force, you couldn't hold him back. And
anyway the man had his own key. There was no way to
keep him out. "Listen, Harold, why don't we both live here
from now on? You can have the bedroom, I'll camp out on
the couch and do the cooking. Wait a minute, I hear Mrs.
Garboyle. Come on, I'll introduce you."

Opening the back door of Rosie's apartment, Alan found
Mrs. Garboyle in the entry, depositing trash in one of the
barrels. As usual she seemed delighted to see him.

"Oh, Mrs. Garboyle, I hope it's all right with you if we
move in for a while. We're keeping an eye on things until
the court decides what to do with the place. There's been
a lot of vandalism lately. Last night the church next door
was broken into and somebody damaged the organ."

"Oh, no!" said Mrs. Garboyle.

Alan introduced Oates, and as usual Mrs. Garboyle was a
pushover. "Oh, I'm so grateful that you're concerned. I
know dear Rosalind would be pleased, if she were alive."

"We'll pay the full rent of course," said Alan, throwing
himself headlong into the practice of overdoing things. Mrs.
Garboyle ran off to get a couple of front-door keys.

Thus did the great Harold Oates become a resident of
115 Commonwealth Avenue. And so did Alan Starr, to
keep an eye on him.

CHAPTER 46

Whoso climbs high, is in danger to fall.
                        Martin Luther

T he forked career of Harold Oates continued its dou-
      ble path. On the one hand his new concerts at Old
      South and Trinity won him rapturous acclaim. On
the other, the destruction that followed the concerts
brought more enraged suspicion down on his head.

At Old South all the stop knobs were disconnected and
removed. At Trinity a bucket of paint was emptied over the
keyboards. The sacrilege seemed worse at Trinity, under the
gold walls and lofty prophets. The paint looked blasphe-
mous, a grubby reminder of the pitiful corruption of the
human race.

There were frantic calls for Alan's repair services. He did
what he could, but there was too much going on. There
was hardly time around the edges to work up new preludes
and postludes for Sunday services, and it was all he could do
to snatch an hour or two once a week to see Charley. The
heaviest pressure was the completion of the voicing of the
Commonwealth organ for its dedication on Easter Sunday.
The new Prestant rank hadn't come yet, nor the giant Contra Bombardes for the Pedal division.

It was no surprise when the music director at Annunciation cancelled the concert by Harold Oates, the one that
was to have taken place on Palm Sunday. But it was a dismal
shock when the vandal retaliated. Philip Tower fell from a
high ladder inside the organ. The ladder had been sabo-
taged.

Pip had been hired to sub for the regular organist, who
was on vacation. Fortunately, although there was no service

in progress, he wasn't alone in the church. When he shouted for help he was taken to the emergency room at Mass General.

Alan went to see him. He found Pip hobbling on crutches along the hospital corridor, accompanied by a nurse. "My God, Pip, what happened?"

"Goddamn Oates anyway." Pip looked at Alan, his eyes round in his pale face. "For God's sake, get him locked up. He cut the ladder supports. I was climbing up to turn off the motor for the tremulant, you know, the vibrato paddle above the pipes. When I got to the top the ladder tipped backwards and I fell into the tracker rods. They busted under me, but, thank God, they broke my fall."

"Just a lot of cuts and scratches," said the nurse cheerfully, turning Pip around and heading him back the other way. "He'll be right as rain in a day or two."

Alan walked beside them. "You don't know for certain it was Oates?"

"Well, who the hell else would it be? They cancelled his concert, so he struck back. The man's a menace."

Alan agreed glumly. "But I can't believe he'd destroy an instrument he cares so much about."

"Well, what about Michelangelo?" Pip waved one of his crutches and almost fell down. "Michelangelo destroyed some of his own sculpture. What about that?"

Alan went back to Rosie's apartment to call Homer Kelly. It was true that the destruction of pipe organs in the Back Bay didn't seem to have anything to do with the disappearance of Rosalind Hall, at least on the face of things, but to Alan everything had begun to seem entangled.

This time Alan went boldly in the front door of 115 Commonwealth. When he unlocked the apartment door, he thought for a moment that the plumbing had gone berserk. There was a great splashing noise within. He ran to the bathroom and looked in the open door and laughed. Harold Oates was lounging in the tub in a luxurious foam of bubbles and scented bath salts. "Enjoying yourself, Harold?" said Alan, with a hint of sarcasm, thinking of poor Pip limping painfully down the hospital corridor.

"Tub's too goddamned short," growled Oates.

Alan went to the kitchen and held the phone close to his mouth and murmured his news to Homer Kelly.

"I'll come and take a look," said Homer, interested at once. Alan hung up, smiling to himself. He had begun to think of Homer as a big dog sniffing the air, nosing at trees and bushes and telephone poles. For him the world must be a symphony of bizarre and curious smells.

Homer had never seen the interior of the Church of the Annunciation. The place was even more medieval than the other Episcopal churches in the Back Bay. Every excuse for sacerdotal finery had been grasped. The suppliers of religious merchandise had done a land-office business. There were banners with lambs and crosses, rood screens and baptismal fonts, and a high pulpit shaped like a tulip. There were altars with candlesticks, needlepoint kneeling stools, and wooden figures in generic saintly robes, their classic features pursed in holy wonder. Homer supposed that if he were to sit down with the rector and grope his way past the liturgical trappings, they might find themselves more or less in agreement on fundamental things. It was just that there were so many layers to get out of the way first. You'd have to come in with a wheelbarrow and roll it all away, trailing gold fringe and purple velvet and the rattling chains of thuribles.

"Hey, Homer, up here." Alan was leaning out like an angel from a forest of organ pipes. Homer found his way up a side stairway and found Alan peering out of the great square case enclosing the pipes. "Follow me," he whispered.

Below them someone was rearranging the altar. There were thumps and clinkings. Homer wedged himself through the opening and edged after Alan along a narrow plank, fearful of bumping into something fragile. They found the ladder lying on its side behind the façade pipes at the front of the organ.

"Look up there at the top," said Alan. "See those clean cuts in the framework? Somebody sawed right through that two-by-four."

Homer stared upward. "I see what you mean. Why did they bother with a saw? They could have unscrewed it with a screwdriver." Cautiously he turned around on the plank and looked at the wreckage of the tracker rods into which Pip Tower had fallen.

"They broke his fall," said Alan, "but it must have been painful. That's a fifteen-foot drop."

Moving carefully, they worked their way out. At the opening Alan gave Homer a brisk shove, and he popped out on the other side. Downstairs they found a priestly person in an embroidered cope arranging articles on the altar. Women bustled about with flowers, genuflecting as they crossed the center aisle.

"It's vespers," whispered Alan, "in honor of Saint Etheldweeda or somebody."

"Martyred in the year 500," murmured Homer, "for protecting her virtue from the godless barbarian."

They escaped, and went outside. Homer looked up at the amethyst sky of late afternoon rising over the brownstones across the way, with the crystal shaft of the Hancock tower soaring behind them. "So what about Oates? Did you talk to him? What did he say?"

"He said he didn't do any of this stuff." Alan looked at Homer defiantly. "And I believe him. Oh, by the way, Homer, Oates and I have moved into Rosie's apartment. Oh, sure, I know we shouldn't be there, but Oates has got a key, so I thought maybe I'd—I mean, I'm going to pay the rent."

"Well, it's all right with me."

"What do you really think, Homer? You don't really think it's Oates—all this, I mean?"

Homer tried to come up with a sensible reply, but instead of weighing the evidence against Oates, he thought of his concert in the Church of the Commonwealth. It had felt like a natural force. He had been reminded of the law of gravity, the rules governing the behavior of gases, the spidery intersecting lines of geometry, the physical constants of Planck and Avogadro and Newton. "No, I don't," he said, hoping he was right.

◆ ◆ ◆ ◆

CHAPTER 47

A liar is far worse, and does greater mischief, than a murderer on the highway.   Martin Luther

"Send her away, Sonny, she's all right now."

"Not until we find the goddamned baby."

"Tell her we need more money. She owes me, Sonny. I saved her life. She would have died."

"Oh, it was you, was it? You saved her life! You did it all by yourself!"

"Of course it was me! Where were you when she was having convulsions?"

"Mother, for Christ's sake, don't you give any credit to Helen? Who do you think restored her sanity?"

"God! Is that what you think? You think Helen did it? Look at her, she's insane herself. She's a hysterical cripple."

"Christ, Mother, shut your fucking mouth!"

Another voice, pleading: "Oh, stop it! My God, please stop it!"

Marilynne Barker lolled back in her office chair, half asleep. It was two o'clock, a time when she often felt drowsy. When her phone rang, she sat bolt upright and stared at it. It rang a second time before she answered it, wary of the human misery about to pour out of the receiver.

"Marilynne Barker speaking."

"Mrs. Barker, my name is Truesdale. I'm a physician at Boston City Hospital. I have here the results of a test conducted on an infant, Charles Hall, which indicate he should be receiving medication. We would like to deliver it to the foster home where he is in care, if you would kindly oblige us with the address."

Mrs. Barker twirled in her chair and looked out the window at the boys playing baseball in the schoolyard next door. Their thin cries came through the window. *Smack,* went the bat. "How is it that you don't have the address, if you were doing tests?"

"I have no idea. I can only tell you that if this child does not receive a dose of Haemoplateletsaroxin immediately, he will be in danger of asphyxiation from the collapse of his right lung."

The ball was a grounder. It went between the legs of the pitcher, while the hitter, a fat boy with red hair, lumbered to first base. "It's strange," said Mrs. Barker, "how many missing pieces of paper there have been lately. Well, all right, just a minute." Reluctantly she went to her files and returned to read Deborah Buffington's address to Dr. Truesdale.

"Thank you," he said, with formal gratitude, and hung up.

Almost at once, Mrs. Barker had second thoughts. She called Boston City Hospital and asked for Dr. Truesdale.

"Jussaminute," said the woman at the switchboard. Well, at least Dr. Truesdale actually existed.

"Ophthalmology," said another voice.

"Ophthalmology? Is this Dr. Truesdale's office?"

"This is the office of Dr. Truesdale and Dr. Clementine."

"But ophthalmology, that's eyes, isn't it? Not lungs?"

"I'm sorry?"

"May I speak to Dr. Truesdale?"

"Dr. Truesdale is attending a conference in Barcelona."

"In Barcelona! Oh, damn it all!"

"I beg your pardon?"

"Oh, God, never mind."

Marilynne Barker hung up, furious with herself. She had

been hornswoggled. It was just another example of male supremacy. A male doctor, even a phony one, could get his way. All he had to do was throw out a few bogus medical terms and she grovelled at his feet.

Mrs. Barker looked out the window at the boys playing baseball. They looked healthy and happy, they weren't abandoned, they weren't pregnant, they were not about to require the services of the Department of Social Services, and she was grateful for it.

CHAPTER 48

Love is the cause of his sickness.
Martin Luther

Dear Rosie,
Charley's vocabulary is larger every day. He says *guck* for
truck and *Aree* for Charley. That's ten words altogether.

Actually it was eleven, but Alan didn't add the eleventh, which was *Daddy.* Without thinking about it, he had begun saying, "Give it to Daddy," and "Daddy wants you to go to sleep now," so it wasn't surprising that Charley picked it up. But it would be presumptuous and embarrassing to write about it in a letter to Charley's mother.

Alan sat at the counter in Rosie's kitchen and looked up through the south window at the Baptist church across the street. The trumpeting angels on the corners of the tower were blowing up a wind that tossed the leafy branches of the trees in the park. Cars drifted silently past, heading west. Oates would be getting home any minute. Alan's peaceful communion with Rosie would be over. Hastily he went on writing:

I can't bring him here any more, not with Harold Oates living here now. I've been taking him to my place on Russell Street. Charley doesn't seem to mind. The poor kid doesn't know the difference between splendor and squalor.

Oates's key was rattling in the lock. Swiftly Alan scrawled three foolish words at the bottom of the page. Then he slapped the notebook shut and jumped up and shut it in the desk drawer.

Oates came in, his thin hair windblown, his eyes watering from the blustering wind. He looked keenly at Alan, and then at the desk drawer, as if he knew every word Alan had been writing to his fried girlfriend.

Alan retreated innocently from the desk. "How was the concert at the Church of the Covenant?"

Oates snorted. "They fell on their knees, naturally. They slaughtered lambs and laid them before me as bloody sacrifices. It was fine."

Charley Hall woke up in his crib in Deborah Buffington's apartment on Bowdoin Street. Afternoon sunlight slanted through the window and lay in splashes on the floor.

There were noises in the next room. Charley rolled over on his back and looked across at Wanda, napping beside him in the next crib. Her eyes were closed, her mouth open, her pale hair frowzy around her face.

He craned his neck as someone pushed open the door and hurried to him across the room. "Mama," whispered Charley.

Rosie swept him up and held him close. "Oh, Charley, you're so big. Oh, Charley, Charley."

CHAPTER 49

I never thought the world had been so wicked.
Martin Luther

"Gone?" Alan stared at Debbie Buffington. "What do you mean, gone?"

Debbie's eyes were rimmed with red. "Just what I said. The kid's gone. He's disappeared." She was braiding Wanda's hair, jerking it this way and that.

Alan strode past her into the room Charley shared with Wanda. His crib was empty. There was no small boy clambering over the railing. He went back to Debbie and shouted at her, "For Christ's sake, tell me what happened."

Debbie wrenched at Wanda's hair, making the little girl cry. "Well, Jesus, I just got back. I had this, you know, doctor's appointment. I was only gone half an hour. He's right down the street."

"You mean you left them alone?"

"Of course I left them alone. They were both sound asleep. Oh, shut up, Wanda."

Alan couldn't believe it. "You left two babies alone, all alone?"

Debbie let go of Wanda's pigtail and began to sob. "You don't know what it's like. I had to get out. I just had to get away for a few minutes. This shitty apartment, nothing but kids all day, kids all night."

"It wasn't a doctor's appointment, was it?" said Alan cruelly.

She sobbed and sobbed. His rage subsided. "Well, who could have taken him? Did you see anybody? How did they get in?"

"Oh, I always leave the door unlocked," sniffled Debbie.

"This neighbor downstairs, I knew she'd look in if they really screamed."

"So you've done this before?" There were more sobs. "Well, listen, did the neighbor see anybody? Did she know anything had happened?"

"Oh, shit, she wasn't home either."

Alan gasped, and forbore to say, *You mean you went out without checking whether or not she was home?* "Well, look, have you told Mrs. Barker? Have you called the police?"

Debbie merely shook her head miserably, her eyes brimming with tears.

Alan stopped his furious inquisition. Putting an arm around her, he patted her shoulder. "Well, it's okay, it's okay. Don't cry."

Debbie responded violently. She threw her skinny arms around his neck and clung to him and kissed him wildly.

Alan took her wrists and thrust her from him. "No, Debbie. No, no."

She stared at him with streaming eyes, her face patchy from crying. "Asshole," she hissed. "You goddamned asshole."

CHAPTER 50

I may compare the state of a Christian to a goose, tied up over a . . . pit to catch wolves.   Martin Luther

"What do you think," Homer asked Mary, "should I slick down my hair and part it in the middle and wear thick glasses, like an undertaker in the movies?"

"No, no, they'd catch on right away. Undertakers don't really look like that. They're ordinary people. It's a service industry, like running a garage or fixing teeth."

Homer was ready for a day of body snatching. With the help of George Bienbower's electronic home-publishing equipment he had acquired a piece of paper with the logo of a phony funeral home printed at the top. And then genial Boozer Brown had loaned him his hearse.

It was luxurious. The shock absorbers made a smooth ride, the engine was almost inaudible. Homer sang all the way to Boston about his merry Oldsmobile, although actually it was a Buick.

At the Mallory Institute of Pathology he drove into the parking lot and paused to scan the situation. Another hearse was standing beside a big open door. Homer thought it best to wait until it was gone, fearing the driver might engage him in shop talk. "Hey, fella, have you tried the Wozzick system yet? You know, the new way of congealing the vitals? Recommended in *Mortician's Monthly*?" "Sorry," Homer would have to say, flapping his hands, "I'm just transport. I deliver stiffs, that's all. Don't ask me." But it would look bad. Homer turned off the engine and hid his face in the *Boston Globe*.

Not until the other hearse left the parking lot did Homer drop the newspaper and back Boozer's limo around so that the rear end faced the door, which was now closed. He got out and rang the bell.

Someone flung up a window and said, "Just a sec, okay?" The window crashed down. An attendant in a green cotton jacket stood looking at him. "Who you here for?"

Homer looked at his phony release order. The name Horace Roland Danby had appeared in yesterday's obituaries. Wordlessly he held out the piece of paper, which was

---

SHADYGROVE MEMORIAL CHAPEL

EVERETT MASSACHUSETTS

HOSPITAL AUTHORIZATION FORM

To ...... *Mallory Institute of Pathology* ....

This will authorize ...... *Michael Morrissey* ...... Funeral Director

to take charge of ...... *Horace Roland Danby* ...... Deceased

Lois D. Danby
Name

...... *Wife* ......
Relationship

...... *23 Prescott St., Everett* ......
Address

Date ...*4/12/93*......

artfully decorated with some of George Bienbower's cleverest oversize fonts.

The attendant snatched the piece of paper and raced away down a sloping corridor, a long sad tunnel leading to the room where the bodies were stacked in refrigerated drawers. Homer had seen it. The room was windowless and lined with tile. He opened the back doors of the hearse and flicked a speck from the floor of the interior. Before long the attendant was back, rolling before him a gurney on which lay an object loosely wrapped in cloth. He brought it to a stop at the door and whisked another piece of paper out of his pocket.

Homer took it carelessly as though after tedious years of cadaver transport, glanced at it, scribbled his name at the bottom, and handed it back.

"Give me a hand, okay?" said the attendant.

"Oh, sure." Homer got a grip on the wrapped feet. He was shocked by the chill, which sucked the warmth from his fingers. Shivering, he dropped the feet and backed away. "Look, never mind. I just wanted to find out if I could extract a corpse with phony papers. My name's Kelly, Homer Kelly. I'm investigating a criminal matter."

"Jesus *Christ!*" The attendant in the green jacket dropped the other end of the body, and it flopped back on the gurney. He snatched the release from his pocket and threw it at Homer. "Oh, God, don't tell anybody. Jesus, don't let my supervisor know."

"Oh, don't worry. It's okay. This is a private investigation. I'm not part of any police department or anything like that."

Without another word the attendant whirled the body around and raced back down the corridor, propelling the gurney before him in the dark satanic tunnel, pursued by all the devils of hell.

Homer drove away through the unlovely streets of Roxbury, remembering once again that the university where he taught and the suburb where he lived and the handsome

streets of the Back Bay were merely a thin skim over the
deep waters of the inner city. His unease was a typical sickness of the suburban soul in its genteel isolation from the
dangers of urban life—*We're sorry, of course, really sorry, but it's
not our fault, is it? Well, maybe it is our fault, but we don't know
what to do about it, and anyway we're busy.* He drove for miles,
gradually cheering up as countryside succeeded city, aware
that his guilt would soon vanish.

At home he found his wife bowed over her books. "It
worked," he said, tearing off his jacket. "He swallowed it,
the guy at the morgue. He handed over the body, never
questioned a thing. I almost came home with it. We could
have propped it in the yard like a piece of garden sculpture.
The point is, somebody else could have swiped a body and
nobody would have made a fuss. How do you like that?"

"Well, good for you," said Mary, but she didn't look
pleased. "Homer, something else has happened. Charley's
disappeared. Alan called and told me. The baby's gone."

Homer gasped. For a moment they looked at each other,
and then both of them said, "Rosie."

Homer dumped his jacket on a chair and wrenched at his
tie. "Well, there you have it, the doting mother after all.
We've been wondering how she could endure being sepa-
rated from her child, if she was alive. Well, now that's no
longer an issue."

Mary slammed the book shut and stood up. She was wearing an old-fashioned pair of golfing knickers. "Exactly. Who else would kidnap a baby?"

"Oh, any number of people. Some young couple desperate to adopt a child. Or somebody in the business of supplying babies to couples like that. Or some affection-starved old lady on the street. They're always extracting infants from baby carriages."

"But Homer, Charley wasn't snatched from a baby buggy. Somebody entered the foster mother's apartment on Bowdoin Street and took him away, leaving Debbie's little three-year-old behind—Debbie was AWOL."

"Good Lord. So the next question is, how did Rosie know where to find him? That woman at Social Services, Mrs. Barker, she said people were phoning about him, only she wouldn't ever tell them anything."

"Maybe she finally did. I'll call and find out. Maybe she'll talk to me this time."

"After lunch?" pleaded Homer. "I've been all over the East Coast this morning without a bite to eat. Take pity on a starving man."

"Look in the fridge," said Mary heartlessly. "There's all kinds of stuff in there. Liverwurst, cheese. Take a look."

When the phone rang in Mrs. Barker's office, she was interviewing a pregnant teenager and the teenager's mother. The mother looked more like the teenager's sister.

"I want to keep the baby," wept the teenager.

"An abortion, Sandra," said her mother firmly. "You're only fourteen." She turned to Mrs. Barker. "Tell her. She's only fourteen."

The phone rang again. Mrs. Barker sighed and reached for it, staring at the mother and daughter. She felt like Solomon giving judgment. If she agreed with the daughter, another wretched child would be born into an unstable family to be reared in bad circumstances and end up a costly bur-

den to the state. If she sided with the mother, a human being would be denied existence, and who could tell what
sort of flower might have blossomed from this unlikely
ground?

Mrs. Barker held the phone against her breast for a moment and closed her eyes, remembering a Right to Life
poster she had seen somewhere, THE LIFE YOU SAVE MAY SAVE
THE WORLD. It was sheer sentimental nonsense, but still—
"Hello? Marilynne Barker speaking."

"Mrs. Barker? My name's Mary Kelly. My husband and I
are investigating a recent case of kidnapping."

"A kidnapping? What kidnapping?"

"Yesterday. A ward of the state was stolen from a foster
mother named Deborah Buffington."

"Oh, yes, of course. You mean Charley Hall." Mrs.
Barker shook her head despondently and looked at the
fourteen-year-old in front of her, whose pink cheeks were
trickling with tears. "That child has been a problem from
the beginning."

"Can you tell me, Mrs. Barker, whether or not you've
given out his address to anyone recently?"

"Oh, yes, I'm afraid I have. Normally we never give out
addresses unless we're positive the person has some legitimate connection. I refused the information several times,
but then when someone called claiming to be a doctor, I
told him. Well, what could I do? He said the child was in
danger of suffocating from a collapsed lung. Naturally I gave
him the address. And next day the child was gone. I blame
myself. Although I must say Deborah Buffington is a careless creature. We've crossed her off our list."

"Do you know the name of the doctor?"

"Oh, it wasn't a real doctor. The real doctor's in Spain.
The whole thing was just a ruse to get the baby's location
out of me. Unfortunately it worked."

"Thank you, that's a big help."

Mrs. Barker returned to her clients. "Look, honey," she

said to Sandra, "I'm afraid your mother's right. Wait till you're a little older and can give a baby a proper family life. You should be enjoying yourself now, going to school and having fun with your friends."

"You see, Sandra?" said her mother. "I told you, you're too young."

Sandra began to sob in earnest. "I want to keep the baby! I want to keep the baby!"

Mrs. Barker put her head in her hands and closed her eyes.

CHAPTER 51

. . . truth goes a begging.
Martin Luther

Coming from his apartment on Dartmouth Street, Martin always entered the church by the basement door on the alley. It had been painted royal blue as a welcome to the mothers and children of the daycare center, which now occupied the three bright rooms so recently brought to life by Donald Woody.

Through the open door of the biggest room came a babble of cheerful voices, the sound of small children singing. Kraeger nodded through the door at Ruth Raymond. To his surprise she glowered at him and turned her back.

Upstairs he found Barbara Inch rushing along the corridor. Seeing him, she stopped so quickly her hair swung forward and her skirt swirled around her knees. "Oh, good morning," said Barbara.

Kraeger stopped too. "How are the Good Friday rehearsals coming along? What about Oates? Is he cooperating?"

Barbara grinned. "If I don't watch out, he'll steal the show."

Kraeger took a shortcut through the kitchen, and there he had to stop and pass the time of day with Marian Beggs and Jeanie Perkupp, because they were old stalwarts who had been part of the congregation since long before his time. This morning they were preparing coffee and bouillon for newcomers.

"Oh, Martin," said Jeanie, "I wish you'd try one of these macaroons." She held out a plateful. "They came out a wee bit limp."

Kraeger took one. "They taste fine to me. Delicious."

Then he had a thought. "How many macaroons have you people made for this church? I mean in all the years you've been coming here? And cookies and so on? Make a wild guess."

There were protests and bursts of laughter as they tried to calculate. It turned out that Jeanie's entire record was some thirty thousand, Marian's forty-five.

"And if you took everybody else's and added them in," said Martin, "it would mount up to half a million. That's what's held this place together all these years, not bricks and mortar. Not those rock-solid pilings under the church. Macaroons, cakes and pies. It gives me an idea for a sermon."

"Oh, Martin," said Marian impulsively, "I want you to know I'm on your side."

"So am I," cried Jeanie.

Martin was surprised and pleased by these testimonials. But then his lifted spirits were dispelled by church treasurer Ken Possett, who was waiting for him in Loretta Fawcett's empty cubbyhole outside his office. Loretta was taking her sick cat to the vet. "Oh, Martin," said Ken gravely, "I'd like to speak to you."

If Martin had a taskmaster in the congregation, an authority figure towering over him, it was Kenneth Possett. Ken was a sturdy old parishioner like Marian and Jeanie. He was one of the staunchest contributors to the budget, he had chaired many an annual canvass and moderated innumerable annual meetings. He had been head of the search committee that had chosen Martin Kraeger from a long list of applicants. As the congregation had changed in the last thirty years from a parish of wealthy local residents to a mixed and transient population of students, professionals, suburbanites and street people, Ken had kept up. He had even adapted to the idea of a Tuesday evening service for gays and lesbians, and a pastoring group for sufferers from

AIDS. His wife Dulcie was another pillar of the church, and their children were active in the youth group. Ken had earned his authority, and Kraeger had often bowed to it in the past. This morning it nearly knocked him down.

"Of course," he said, "come on in." He pretended to unlock his door, because Ken would be shocked to think he ever left it open.

Ken sat down in one of the six massive chairs. He had bad news. An anti-Kraeger group, he said, was forming in the congregation.

"Oh," said Kraeger, the light dawning, "is that what those two women were saying in the kitchen? They said they were on my side. You mean there's another side?"

"I'm afraid so." Ken looked at him solemnly and began listing their grievances. "First, the fire in the balcony that killed Mr. Plummer. You said it was your fault. Some people still hold a grudge."

Kraeger's bravado vanished. "Of course they do," he said, wincing. "I don't blame them."

"Second, your support for Harold Oates, who is manifestly a dangerous vandal. A lot of people think he should be locked up, or at least no longer permitted to perform on our valuable new organ at sacred services."

Kraeger opened his mouth in protest, but Ken held up another finger. "Third, political preaching. Some people complain there's too much of it. They come to church for spiritual comfort, they say, not to be harangued."

Kraeger smiled. This one was easy. *"I cannot deny that I have been more vehement than is seemly. They ought not to have stirred up the dog."*

"What?"

"Martin Luther. That's what he said when people told him he should stop shaking his fist at Leo the Tenth."

Ken shook his head in warning. "It's no joke, Martin."

"Of course not. But all members of the clergy worth their salt run into the same thing." For a moment a note of bitterness edged Kraeger's voice. "There are people like that in every congregation. They want everything sunshiny. They don't want to hear about other people's problems. They don't understand that the future is made out of wretched material"—Kraeger waved his arms and thought up crazy examples—"like lost hubcaps and sticky sandwich wrappers and mildewed Bibles and the disreputable causes of long-dead men and women."

Ken stared at him blankly, and Kraeger went on wildly, reciting a hymn by James Russell Lowell about truth being forever on the scaffold and wrong forever on the throne, but fortunately it was the scaffold that swayed the future, because God was standing in the shadow keeping watch above his own. Then he shook his head sorrowfully. "The trouble is, maybe God isn't keeping watch at all. Half the time the scaffold tumbles down and the hanged men fall into the pit and so do the women." Kraeger stopped ranting, and made a gesture like brushing away a fly. "Listen, let those people who want spiritual solace go to Annunciation. Things are pretty soulful over there." It was the wrong thing to say, and Kraeger knew it.

"Love it or leave it?" said Ken. "You don't mean that, Martin?"

"No, of course not. But I'm not going to stop preaching the way I do. The soul isn't some little closed-up walnut inside you. It's part of a whole world of trouble."

"Fourth"—Ken held up another relentless finger—"Dora O'Doyle. She has been identified. It seems she's a notorious prostitute. You wrote out a check for nine hundred and fifty dollars to a prostitute."

Kraeger stared at him, speechless. It came to his lips that it was not he who had engaged the woman's services but Harold Oates, but he quelled the impulse just in time. It wouldn't help matters to have another cause of complaint against Oates. "Look, Ken, you don't think I'd pay a prostitute on a check labeled Church of the Commonwealth and have it turn up among your cancelled checks? It was supposed to be for Oates's dental work, I tell you."

"It did not reach the dentist."

"No, that's true. I paid the dentist's bill a second time myself, later on. But at the time this woman told me she was the dentist's accountant. Do you mean the whole congregation thinks I consort with prostitutes?"

"Fifth—"

"Oh, good God, what else?"

Ken spoke with extreme distinctness, separating the syllables. "Child mo-les-ta-tion."

Kraeger laughed in disbelief. "What are you talking about?"

"Your former wife accuses you of molesting your daughter."

"Pansy? She says I molested Pansy?" Kraeger laughed again. "You don't really take that seriously?"

Ken spoke with distaste. "I don't know anything about these things. But one reads about it in the papers. It seems to be fairly common." Ken looked accusingly at Kraeger.

"But she's only four years old. She's my daughter. How could I do such a thing? What exactly does she say I'm supposed to have done to Pansy?"

Ken's mouth worked. The details were apparently too repulsive to say aloud. "I think you'd better ask your ex-wife."

Kraeger sat stricken in his chair, and Ken Possett said a grim goodbye. He did not say, "Carry on, old man," or "We'll work it out together," and therefore Martin knew what a dangerous gulf had opened in his congregation. Was Ken Possett on the other side? If Ken were to come out against him, Martin Kraeger's time at the Church of the Commonwealth would soon be finished.

Alone in his office, he fumbled blindly for the morning mail. Among the appeals for charity he found an envelope with a menacing return address, *Pouch, Heaviside and Sprocket*. With a sinking heart Kraeger recognized those pitiless extortionists, his wife's divorce lawyers.

He tore open the envelope and found a summons to an arraignment for child molestation.

He called his ex-wife. "Kay, for heaven's sake, what the hell are you doing? You know I never did a single damned thing to Pansy."

"Oh, no? Well, Pansy and I know better. You're an animal, a beast."

"Oh, come on, Kay, be reasonable. I can't believe this. What am I supposed to have done?"

"My attorney has instructed me not to speak to you on this or any other matter," said his ex-wife, slamming down the phone.

♦ ♦ ♦ ♦

CHAPTER 52

Music is the best solace for a sad and sorrowful mind.
                                                    Martin Luther

The Boston Chapter of the American Guild of Organists was conducting an organ crawl. They were touring the churches in the Back Bay, getting acquainted with each other's instruments.

"Jeez, listen to the Krummhorn."

"How do you bring in the Contrabassoon? Oh, here it is. God, it's like Judgment Day."

"Peggy? Your turn. Try the Cornet on the Swell."

At the Church of the Commonwealth Alan explained the virtues of the new tracker from Marblehead and talked about the voicing.

"You've replaced the Trumpets en Chamade, I see," said Gilda Honeycutt.

"Contra Bombardes still missing?" said Pip Tower.

Alan was glad to see Pip back on his feet, fully recovered after his fall from the ladder. "Right. I'm getting kind of frantic. What have we got, two weeks? The whole thing's supposed to be ready by Easter."

During the afternoon there was a good deal of grumbling about Harold Oates. "I don't know what they're waiting for," said Jack Newcomb. "He ought to be put where he can't do any more damage."

"But my God, can you imagine him in prison?" said Arthur Washington. "What a waste!"

"And he's so old," said Peggy Throstle. "He ought to be allowed to play while he can, right?"

Pip Tower turned to her angrily. "Suppose every time he

plays, some good instrument is ruined or somebody's back is broken, is that what you want?"

Alan changed the subject. "Listen to this. I've been working on the sixteen-foot Trombone." He ran his feet down the pedal scale. Deep braying notes shuddered in everyone's bones and shook the walls. "Wait a second, I'll play fifths. Listen to the resultant."

They stood around the console, watching Alan's feet on the pedals, while across the sanctuary the spidery cracks in the east wall branched delicately upward, and the picture of Walter Wigglesworth slowly tipped askew.

Afterward Alan persuaded Pip to join him for a drink at the pizza place on Boylston Street. He was anxious to mend their shaky friendship. It was probably vanity, he told himself, a case of not wanting to be disliked. But it was more than that. Pip had always been fun to talk to. He had a gift for intimacy and he told wonderful stories, funny anecdotes about mutual friends. One of his friends had been Rosie Hall. Alan felt an urge to confess his obsession with Rosie, his conviction that she was still alive. He wanted to ask what she was really like.

They walked up Clarendon Street past the Baptist Church, past old men walking timidly among crowds of students, old women daring the sidewalk for the first time since the ice storm in March. "Did you know I'm renting Rosie Hall's apartment?" said Alan. "Harold Oates and I, we're staying there while it's in escrow, or whatever you call it. You know, while they settle her estate."

Pip looked at him in surprise, and said nothing. His customary flow of talk was not forthcoming. Maybe, thought Alan, he was still too angry about the audition.

In the pizza place Alan ordered beers, and tried again. "How's the job situation? Any new ones opening up?"

Pip was vague. "Oh, I get along. When I'm not at the hospital I work in a copy shop."

The waiter delivered the beers. Alan couldn't think of

anything else to say. Fortunately Pip knocked his glass over, and in the confusion of mopping up the spilled beer, things relaxed a little. Alan ordered another, and asked him about Rosie. "You knew her pretty well, isn't that right?"

"Oh, sort of."

Alan had hoped for more. "She meant a lot to you, I'll bet?"

"Well, naturally. Just as a friend. I mean we didn't—"

"No, I didn't mean that. None of my business anyway." This topic wasn't working either. "More beer?"

"No, thanks."

Alan offered him the basket of corn chips. "I'll be joining you in the ranks of the unemployed before long, when Castle gets back."

Pip blinked. "Castle's coming back?"

"No, no, but he will sooner or later. I don't know why the hell he doesn't let us know when."

At last Alan had touched a chord. Pip leaned forward across the small table. "Suppose he doesn't come back, will they keep you on?"

"I don't want the job. By rights they should give it to Harold Oates, but I doubt they will. You know what he's like."

"You don't want the job?"

"I want to build organs, not play them. I'd say you were the prime candidate." Then Alan remembered Mrs. Frederick's antipathy. Maybe he shouldn't raise Pip's hopes. The poor guy would have to find a permanent place in some other church. Of course another church wouldn't pay anything like as much, but it would be better than making hospital beds and flipping pieces of paper in and out of copy machines. Alan stood up and said an awkward goodbye.

Pip did not get up.

On the sidewalk Alan looked back through the glass door and was surprised to see him getting out of his chair with difficulty, as though still suffering from the effects of his fall.

✦ ✦ ✦ ✦

CHAPTER 53

*Bear not false witness, nor belie
Thy neighbor by foul calumny . . .*
From a hymn by Martin Luther

In his office Martin Kraeger could hear the organ guild experimenting. The building quivered. Behind him a book fell from a shelf with a thump.

He paid no attention. All he could think of was the grotesque suit brought against him by his ex-wife. He sat at his desk staring into his crystal ball, visualizing one face after another, the scandalized members of his congregation. By now the entire parish must have heard that he was doing repulsive things to his little daughter. His name in the city of Boston must be mud. Worse than mud—filth, foulness and obscenity.

But surely the people who had known his ex-wife were aware she was a nutcase. And surely little Pansy would stick up for him. *Pansy and I know better,* Kay had said, as if Pansy were on her side.

Then it occurred to Kraeger that Pansy was enrolled in the daycare center in the church basement. At this moment she was probably frolicking with the other children, playing ring-around-the-rosy, or whatever it was they did down there.

He leaped up from his desk and ran past Loretta, who had just arrived. She was taking off her coat. "Good morning," he called over his shoulder, but from the way she looked back at him with huge accusing eyes, he knew she had heard the story too.

It was the same with Ruth Raymond. When Martin opened the door to the daycare center, she looked at him blankly and clutched the child in her lap, as if he might snatch it from her and do something unseemly. It was naptime. Most of the children were stretched out on blankets on the floor. Pansy was not among them.

"Pansy isn't here today?" he whispered to Ruth.

She looked at him suspiciously. Her manner was defiant. "I'm sorry, but I'm not supposed to tell you where she is."

"But she's my own daughter."

"I'm sorry." Ruth looked away and hissed at one of the children, "Cecily, lie still."

But Cecily was kneeling upright on her blanket. "Pansy's at Mother Goose Land," she said brightly. "They have a pony at Mother Goose Land."

"Cecily, lie down!"

Martin went back to his office and looked it up in the phone book. Mother Goose Land was on Hereford Street, not far away. He ran as far as Exeter, then slowed down and walked the rest of the way.

Mother Goose Land occupied a basement below the level of the pavement, like the daycare center in the church. Martin opened the door and entered a sunny room with windows overlooking the alley. Through one window he could see a small paved area at the back, where an aged donkey hung its head, its winter coat coming off in patches.

There was a cheerful babble of childish voices, a tumble of small children doing exercises on rubber mats. Two hardworking women were stuffing some of their charges into jackets and tying their shoes. One of the children was Pansy. At once she ran over to hug Martin's knees and give him a huge gap-toothed smile.

He picked her up and hoisted her over his head. Then he sat down on a small chair and held her on his lap and inserted her feet into her Donald Duck cowboy boots.

"You're Mr. Kraeger?" said one of the women, smiling at him, apparently unaware he was a lecherous monster. "I can see you're an old hand."

Martin set Pansy on her feet and drew her toward him until her small face was close to his. "Listen, Pansy, dear," he whispered, "your mother says I was mean to you. What did I do, Pansy? Can you tell me? I don't think I was ever mean."

Pansy lowered her eyes. "My panties," she whispered. "You took off my panties."

"Well, of course I took off your panties. Because—you remember, Pansy—they were wet. They needed to be changed."

Pansy was silent. She stopped up her mouth with her thumb. At once she was swept up by a whirlwind.

"Pansy, don't you speak to him," cried her mother. "I told you, Pansy, not one word." Kraeger's ex-wife looked at him, clutching Pansy to the front of her coat. "How dare you? How dare you talk to Pansy behind my back?"

The children of Mother Goose Land stopped milling around. They stared. The two teachers exchanged glances, then went on shepherding their flock out to the playground. Through the window Martin could see the donkey shamble away into the farthest corner.

"For heaven's sake, Kay, I'm just trying to find out what this is all about. Pansy says I took off her panties. Well, of course I did, but Pansy knows why. She wet her panties, that's why."

"Pansy does not wet her panties. That is a complete fabrication. Pansy is completely toilet-trained. She has been toilet-trained since she was one year old."

"Oh, now, Kay, you know she has accidents all the time."

"I know no such thing. You took her panties off, you pervert, and did something to her!"

"Did something to her? I put on clean panties, that's what I did to her."

"Pansy," said Kay Kraeger, plopping Pansy down on the

floor again and looking at her fiercely, "did you wet your panties?"

Pansy shook her head violently, and looked at the floor.

"Pansy, did your father *do* something to you?"

"Oh, for Pete's sake, Pansy," said Kraeger, "tell your mother what happened."

"Pansy," whispered her mother, "you told me he did something to you, something unspeakable, didn't he, Pansy? Didn't he?"

Pansy was trapped. It *had* been unspeakable, what had happened, and she couldn't possibly mention it. Her mother had threatened that if she ever wet her panties again she would be spanked. So Pansy had suppressed the evidence.

Her mother's threats about lapses in perfect behavior had made her an adept at concealment. There were petrified meat patties tucked behind the furniture, and fossilized baked potatoes in the back of the bookcase, and dusty brussels sprouts under the grandfather clock. One day last month when her father had been taking care of Pansy in her mother's house, repairing a plugged-up sink at the same time, there had been an unfortunate calamity. Her father had tut-tutted gently and cleaned her up and found her a pair of clean panties, and then he had washed out the old ones and put them in the laundry basket. Afterward Pansy had removed them carefully and tiptoed downstairs and carried them under her sweater to the trash barrel. With her fragile fingers she undid the plastic tie of one of the trash bags, dropped the panties inside and twisted it shut again.

The case against her had vanished. Not until her mother undressed her that evening did she discover that Pansy was wearing panties with bunnies on them instead of teddies. Pansy had answered her mother's outraged questions as cautiously as she could, and by saying as little as possible had shifted the blame to her father.

Now Pansy looked sideways, left, then right, and then, slyly, she nodded.

"Oh, Pansy," moaned Kraeger.

"You beast, you beast," cried Kay, making shuddering sounds of revulsion. "I'll see you in court." Snatching her daughter's hand, she rushed away, with Pansy half-flying behind her.

CHAPTER 54

Why strengthen your walls—they are trash; the walls with which a Christian should fortify himself are made, not of stone and mortar, but of prayer and faith.

Martin Luther

W oody looked with dismay at the new cracks in the east wall. They had crept up and fanned out like forked tendrils of lightning. He couldn't understand it. He left the sanctuary and descended two flights of stairs to look at the foundation. In the furnace room he worked his way through the warped scenery left over from a Christmas pageant until he uncovered the supporting walls of the east end of the church.

The stones were not rectangular blocks but ragged boulders fitted neatly together. In his basement office they were painted white. They looked immensely heavy and strong, mighty enough to hold up a building ten times the size of the Church of the Commonwealth.

Ah, here was the problem. A fissure had opened in the wall where the mortar had given way. Nothing to it. Woody went to the closet where he kept bags of sand for the winter sidewalk and sacks of lime and fertilizer for the garden, and hauled out a bag of cement. Dumping some of it into a bucket, he added water from the set tub in his office and stirred up a batch. Then he applied it to the fissure, using a putty knife to shove it deep between the stones. There, that was taken care of. Now he could concentrate on resurfacing the walls of the sanctuary.

Woody didn't trust anybody else to do it. Who else could restore the William Morris trim of vine leaves around the windows? It would be a full-time job, and it would have to be done by Easter Sunday. He'd have to call in a retired friend of his to take over the usual cleaning and daily upkeep. Woody cleaned out his bucket and called up the friend, who said he'd be right over, toot sweet.

When Martin Kraeger came striding in next morning, the place was noisy. A stranger was running a waxer in the vestibule, making shiny circles on the floor. Above the whine of the waxer there was a high buzzing from the sanctuary, and the loud *bah-bah* of the organ.

Feeling uneasily at loose ends, Kraeger climbed the steps to the balcony. From there he could see Woody on a high ladder at the far end of the sanctuary, using a power sander on the wall. Alan Starr sat at the organ console, his eyes closed, trying to hear above the racket while he played a pedal scale. Kraeger sat down and listened. *Whah,*

  whah,

    whah,

      whah,

        whah, droned the sixteen-foot Prestant.

Kraeger found it comforting. The nice thing about music was its abstractness. It was totally unconcerned with human problems and nasty little random perversions.

Alan hit the lowest note and held it. The balcony shook. On his ladder Woody was surprised to see the crack he had filled with Spackle open up again. Below the dried surface it must have been still a little wet.

Alan turned to Kraeger and said, "Good morning." His greeting was friendly and natural, not tainted with loathing.

Kraeger was grateful. "Nobody's been bending any more pipes?" he said, just to say something.

"No, everything seems all right. Woody's hired a doctoral candidate from Boston University for weekend nights. He writes his thesis in here, doesn't fall asleep like some of us jerks."

"Well, good."

Alan looked at him keenly. "Are you all right?"

Kraeger was surprised at the way it flooded out of him,

the whole crazy story about his ex-wife's unsavory accusation.

"But nobody will believe it, will they?" said Alan. "I've heard that your former wife is—forgive me—some kind of a fruitcake."

Kraeger grinned painfully. His wife was a fruitcake, all right, but the wrong kind of fruitcake. If she were huddling in a corner with her head drooping on her breast, she would have been hauled off to a psychiatric ward long ago. Instead she was a totally self-confident megalomaniac, and it would take a war to stop her from ruling the world. "Maybe so," he said, "but her lawyer isn't a fruitcake."

The sander buzzed again. Alan looked down thoughtfully at his feet and ran up the scale again. Then he stopped and turned to Kraeger. "You need a lawyer too."

"I suppose so. I haven't got one."

"I know a good one. So do you. Homer Kelly used to be an attorney, back when he was a lieutenant detective in Middlesex County."

"Oh, yes, I remember. Does he take an interest in this kind of—repulsive sort of matter?"

"I don't know. Why don't you ask him?"

"Well, all right, I will."

"I see him pretty often. He's working on the disappearance of Rosie Hall."

"Disappearance? But she's dead."

"Well, maybe, maybe not. Did I tell you, I'm staying in her place now? You know, right next door. So is Harold. We're staying there together."

"Is her child still missing?"

"I'm afraid so." Alan looked gloomily at the DIV INSP stop knob, reached over and pulled it out. A little DIV INSP was what he needed right now. "Here," he said, fishing in his pocket, "I've got Homer's phone number right here."

Kraeger went to his office and called the number. Mary Kelly answered the phone. When she spoke, Martin remembered meeting her at the church door after a service last month. He remembered her great height and sympathetic face. Once again his story poured out of him.

"Tell you what," said Mary Kelly. "Homer isn't here, but he'll be back later on. Why don't you come out for supper?"

Kraeger paused, remembering the church council meeting he was supposed to attend. Well, those people would have a better time of it if he weren't there. They could tear him to shreds in absentia. "Sure, I'd love to."

"Good. Now, listen closely, here's how to find us."

It was no joke. Finding Fair Haven Road in Concord was tricky in itself, and then you had to choose fork after fork in the woods and look for a faded sign on a tree. It was like going deep into the forest to find the cottage of the wise witch.

He found it at last, a small house at the end of a long dirt road. "What a beautiful lake," said Martin, looking out at Fair Haven Bay.

"It's not a lake," explained Homer. "It's a big bend in the Sudbury River."

"Oh, I see. What's that bird in the water? See the one with its head sticking up?"

"No. Oh, yes, I do. Oh, my God, it's a loon. Look, Mary, a loon."

"So it is. Well, good for you, Mr. Kraeger. We're off to a lucky start."

They sat down in the narrow living room under the map of the river, and once again Martin went over his sordid little story, his tongue loosened by whiskey. At the end he said, "Do you people have kids?"

"Well, no." Homer glanced at Mary. "But we've got a little nephew named Benny."

Mary grinned. She was wearing flowered shorts over stockings with red horizontal stripes. "So we know all about it. My sister and brother-in-law had already reared six kids when Benny came along. He was the last straw. They sort of gave up, with Benny. He's ten now, and he goes to baseball camp every summer, but there was a time"—Mary gazed dreamily into the past—"he was three before he was out of diapers, although he could spell *metamorphosis*. In first grade he was doing algebra, but he always got to the boys' room too late. Darling child." Mary looked at Martin. "Pansy has the same problem?"

"Exactly, but her mother refuses to recognize it. That day I met you two people in church, Kay brought Pansy to spend the afternoon with me, and Pansy was wearing wet panties. I washed them out and dried them on the radiator in my office, and then put them back on Pansy, so Kay may not have noticed what happened. But the occasion she's so furious about was the weekend she wanted me to stay with Pansy because she was going away, and I was supposed to fix the drain in the kitchen sink. Pansy wet her pants, so I washed them out and put them in the laundry basket. My wife must have found them there, and of course she would have known right away what happened."

"So you think she made up this story about your molesting Pansy?" said Homer.

"Well, of course, she must have. But she's so angry, she really seems to have convinced herself I'm a monster."

"I don't suppose the panties would still be there in the laundry?" suggested Mary.

"Oh, no, I'm sure they've been thoroughly scrubbed in scented soap by now."

"Look," said Mary, "don't bother with Homer. This is right up my alley. Benny spent a lot of time with us, and I was the one who handled the problem of his excitable urinary tract. Let me handle it."

"Wonderful," said Martin. "I feel better already. Mrs. Kelly, I put my entire future in your hands, like a holy chalice. Speaking of chalices—" He held out his glass.

◆ ◆ ◆ ◆

CHAPTER 55

This affair will not have an end, if it be of God, until all my friends desert me . . . and truth be left alone.

Martin Luther

Edith Frederick heard the whispered stories with disbelief and shock. It was true that everything in her background should have condemned the man who could generate such rumors. But Edith was not altogether a conventional woman. In dress she was conservative, in musical judgment ignorant, in social intercourse old-fashioned, in action timid. But the changes of the last thirty years in the city of Boston had administered innumerable small jolts, painful but instructive. And the changing nature of the congregation of the Church of the Commonwealth was an education in itself.

No longer was it made up of her own dear friends. It was a cross-section of a larger world. And the sermons of Martin Kraeger had chivvied her, nudged her farther and farther from the preconceptions with which she had been nourished. His beneficent ranting from the pulpit and his courtesy to her as a colleague had made of Edith Frederick a devoted advocate, anxious for his welfare.

She came to him at once. "Is Mr. Kraeger in?" she asked Loretta Fawcett, who was typing at her desk.

"Oh, he's in," said Loretta. Her eyes opened wide. Leaning over her desk, she whispered, "Did you hear—?"

Edith cut her off. "I don't believe it for an instant." She knocked on Martin's door, he called, "Come in," and Loretta was deprived of her sensational revelation.

For the next twenty minutes the conversation in Martin's study was conducted in tones too low for Loretta to overhear, although she stopped typing and tried to listen. When

Edith came out, Martin came with her. Edith's soft old face was damp, and his was turned down to her with solicitude.

Loretta watched them walk together to the stairs. When Martin came back he smiled at Loretta, but she only stared blankly back at the monster who had molested his own little daughter.

He went into his office and shut the door. It was clear to him that Loretta's response was a sample of what the entire congregation must be feeling. This morning Ken Possett had told him frankly that he had joined the opposition. Martin was grateful to Edith for remaining loyal, but she was only one old woman, even more fragile than she had seemed last week. Holbein's bony skeleton was clinging to her more closely than ever, its grisly skull nudging her hollow cheek, its loving arm gripping her shoulder.

Martin could not help comparing her brittle old age with the plump good health of Kenneth Possett. Her elderly goodwill could never outbalance the strength of Ken's hostility.

◆ ◆ ◆ ◆

CHAPTER 56

Ah! how bitter an enemy is the devil.
Martin Luther

Next day Mary Kelly took up the crusade, the question of Pansy Kraeger's problematical panties. She began with the daycare centers. The women in charge would be surely be experts in the toilet training of small children.

Pansy had been enrolled in a couple of different places, the center at the church and another one called Mother Goose Land on Hereford Street. And Martin thought there had been another before that.

Mary began with the church. But Ruth Raymond was too busy to talk. She was trying to handle a group of fifteen small tots with the help of only one other woman. "Cecily, stop talking. Scott, put that down. Karen, leave Becky alone." In answer to Mary's question about Pansy Kraeger, she said, "Oh, isn't it dreadful? How could he? We're all so upset."

Mary suppressed a sharp retort and said blandly, "Well, some of us think the charge isn't true." Folding herself double, she sat down on a tiny chair.

Ruth wasn't listening. Darting forward, she helped a small girl clamber to the top of a pint-sized jungle gym and climb down again. "Oh, we made such an awful mistake last month," she said, plopping down beside Mary in another small chair. "I don't know how long I can stand it. Cecily, stop that noise!"

"An awful mistake?"

"We took in eight more children, all at once, just like that."

"Eight more, in the middle of the year?"

"Well, we had extra help then. But Marcia resigned because she was getting married, and then Joanie got mono, and Ann and I—well, we had a fight, we were both so tired, and I said something I shouldn't have said, and she left, so here I am. Sometimes I can get a mother to help, like today—thank God for Mrs. Benjamin—but most of the mothers are working. I mean, that's why the kids are here, so their mothers can work. I'm only barely legal. Some days I'm not even that, like today."

"But why were there suddenly eight more children?"

"Oh, the other daycare center in this neighborhood, Kiddy Kamp, closed down. The kids had to go somewhere, and we thought we could handle them—we were glad of the extra money, so we took them." Ruth lowered her voice and whispered in Mary's ear, "Mrs. Benjamin had her little boy there. See, there he is, climbing into her lap. I asked her what the trouble was. I mean, I heard there was some sort of scandal, but she buttoned her lip and wouldn't tell me. Cecily, I don't want to speak to you again!"

Mary had another question, but it was interrupted by a noisy argument over a tricycle. It took both Mrs. Benjamin and Ruth Raymond to handle it. Then a small moppet bashed another one with a tin pan from the toy stove. Ruth darted away to comfort the victim.

Mary went to Mrs. Benjamin and sat down beside her, folding her long legs once again. "Oh, Mrs. Benjamin, I understand there was some sort of trouble at Kiddy Kamp. Can you tell me what happened?"

Mrs. Benjamin was a black woman with a smooth kindly face. She looked at Mary and shook her head, but Cecily piped up brightly. "It was Pansy. Pansy went to the bathroom in her—"

"Ssshhh, Cecily." Mrs. Benjamin touched Mary's arm. "Talk to Millie Weideman. It was her daycare center. She'll tell you all about it." Mrs. Benjamin opened a book and held it up for the children to see. "Now look, everybody, who's that?"

"HORTON THE ELEPHANT," shouted all the children, crowding close to her knees, eager to climb the first rung of the ladder of education.

"Thank you, Mrs. Benjamin. Thank you, Mrs. Raymond." Mary left the daycare center and found her way to the public phone in the vestibule of the church. She was pleased to find Kiddy Kamp in the phone book, even though it was defunct. "Is this Millie Weideman?"

"Speaking."

"My name's Mary Kelly. My husband and I are friends of Martin Kraeger, the minister of the Church of the Commonwealth. I understand his daughter Pansy was enrolled in your daycare center. Might I come to see you and talk about Pansy?"

"Talk about Pansy?" Millie Weideman made a sound that was half laugh, half snort. "Why not? Come right over. I'd be delighted to talk about Pansy Kraeger."

It was only five blocks up Clarendon Street to Millie Weideman's apartment. The day was mild. Mary swung along, enjoying the way the mirrored surface of the Hancock Tower reflected the blue sky and Trinity Church and the pedestrians on the sidewalk. She crossed St. James Avenue toward her own wobbly reflection, then broke into a run.

Millie Weideman's building was one of a row of town houses that were downmarket versions of the grand dwellings on Commonwealth Avenue. Her apartment was small, crowded with paraphernalia from the discontinued daycare center.

"Don't trip over the cats," said Millie, leading the way to a couple of chairs laden with toys and blocks. "Here, I'll just shove all this stuff aside." She picked up a plastic egg box filled with tiny plants growing in eggshells. "Look at that. What am I supposed to do with all these little clovers? The kids planted them. I suppose I should take them over to Commonwealth, but I don't want to set eyes on Pansy Kraeger ever again."

Mary made her way past a guinea pig in a cage full of shavings and a gerbil whirling on his exercise wheel. Picking up a Raggedy Ann she smoothed its apron and sat down. Four half-grown kittens tumbled over each other on the floor. "Tell me, what is it about Pansy that's so disturbing?"

"Oh, Lord, it wasn't Pansy, it was her mother." Millie put her head in her hands. "Where to begin?"

"Can you tell me why you had to close down?"

"Mrs. Kraeger accused one of our mother-helpers of molesting one of the children. White child, black mother-helper. Pain."

"Well, was the accusation true?"

"Of course it wasn't true. The little kid couldn't control her bladder. We had to keep changing her pants. We told her mother we couldn't keep her because our kids had to be toilet-trained. I mean, we had a long list of children waiting for an opening. Their mothers needed to be working. They really needed a good daycare center. And we were good. Damn!"

"But why would Mrs. Kraeger make such an accusation?"

"Oh, she was insulted. She refused to believe her perfect little four-year-old needed her pants changed all the time. She accused us of—you know—wanting to handle her genitals or something."

"But couldn't you fight back?"

"Oh, God, we tried. We called in her complaint to Social Services immediately—you have to do that—and sent in a report, and then an inspector came and talked to everyone on the staff, and they exonerated us. But it didn't make a hell of a bit of difference. That slimy woman called all the other mothers and got them excited too, and they all snatched their children out of Kiddy Kamp, so we had to close down. And now I've got this crazy thing on my record as a daycare administrator. I'm so mad I could spit."

"So it was all Kay Kraeger's doing," murmured Mary, getting up to go.

"Kay Kraeger," agreed Millie Weideman. "I hope she fries in hell."

PALM SUNDAY

❖ ❖ ❖ ❖ ❖

"Alle Menschen müssen sterben"
Chorale harmonized by J. S. Bach

Everyone on earth must perish
All our flesh must fade as grass.
Only through Death's solemn portal
To a better life we pass.

CHAPTER 57

The Lord drags me, and not unwillingly do I follow.
Martin Luther

Alan's bank account was shrivelling. He was paying two separate monthly rents, one for his room on Russell Street, the other for Rosie Hall's apartment. The fact that Harold Oates was sharing the apartment didn't seem to give him any qualms of conscience about helping with the expense, even though his concerts were bringing in substantial sums of money. Well, the hell with it. Grudgingly Alan told himself that the greatest organist in the world had a right to float on his greatness.

Mrs. Garboyle took Alan's rent checks graciously and set them aside. She promised to turn the money over to the executors whenever the house made its way through probate—to the executors or to anybody else who was concerned with the matter out there in the dry stretches of barren desert where courts convened and judges ruled and estate attorneys earned large fees.

Oates was completely at home in Rosie's apartment. He deposited cigarette ashes everywhere, complained about Alan's cooking, splashed in the bathtub and played the harpsichord. Alan was bewitched by his harpsichord technique. His fingers were as precise and delicate on the plucked notes of the keyboard as they were powerful on the keys of the tracker organ, where two coupled manuals called for strength of hand and arm.

Alan listened with pleasure, but at night he insisted on sleeping on the sofa, while Oates took the bedroom. It wasn't generosity, it was harpsichord protection.

But there was no way to protect Rosie's drawers and closets from the inquisitiveness of Harold Oates. He pried and poked, examining prescription medicines, fingering her underwear, reading letters, uncovering a bedside book on female hygiene. Alan couldn't blame him, because he himself had examined everything in the house, but he was infuriated just the same. And what about Rosie's notebook? How could he protect it from the meddling fingers of Harold Oates?

Alan wandered around the house looking for a hiding place, then slipped it among the cookbooks in the kitchen. Oates was no cook. He wouldn't be consulting Julia Child or studying *One Hundred Ways to Cook Zucchini*.

On Palm Sunday Alan came home from an exhausting service at the Church of the Commonwealth to find Oates rewinding a tape on one of Rosie's old-fashioned tape recorders. He was fuming. "Horrible low-tech. A recording of a recording. Wrong registration. And the repeat is a mess. Background noise. Disgusting."

Alan felt resentful for Rosie's sake. "What's that, 'Wachet Auf'? I thought she played it very well."

"Who, your fried girlfriend? Oh, her technique's okay, but, shit, the registration. She should have come on strong with a gutsy reed in the cantus firmus." He looked at Alan and jerked his head toward the bedroom door. "Hey, somebody opened the safe while you were gone."

"What?" Alan ran into the bedroom and stared at the wall where the little woven fabric from Guatemala had covered the small safe. Now it was hanging cockeyed. The door of the safe was open.

"Empty," said Oates, trailing after him. "I thought they might have left a stray thousand-dollar bill. No such luck."

Alan turned on him. "Where were you while this was happening?"

Oates plopped down on the unmade bed and closed his

eyes. "Visiting old pals on Kansas Street. Where do you think?"

And Dora O'Doyle, no doubt. Alan didn't care. He went to the kitchen and phoned Homer. "It had to be Rosie," he said eagerly. "Who else would know the combination?"

"Good," said Homer. "Is anything else missing?"

"I don't know. I'll look around and call you back."

At once Alan turned to the shelf of cookbooks. He ran his fingers over the books, and pulled out the zucchini book and *The Joy of Cooking*. Surely he had put Rosie's notebook between them? It wasn't there.

The notebook was gone, and so were a number of other things. Alan made a list and reported it to Homer. "Charley's blanket, his spoon, his ball, his vitamins, his xylophone. Whoever took him from Debbie Buffington's place must have come here, opened the safe, and taken stuff for the baby. It had to be Rosie."

"Well, I'll be damned," said Homer.

Alan went back to the church and spent the afternoon voicing the eight-foot Octave. Only the thirty-two-foot Contra Bombarde remained in the Marblehead shop.

Returning to the apartment late in the afternoon he found himself alone. Oates was somewhere else. Once again Alan ransacked the cookbook shelf. The notebook was nowhere to be found. Perhaps Rosie was flipping through its pages right now, reading his notes on Charley's progress and the letters he had written to her in his sentimental folly. Alan winced as he thought of the dumb things he had said. He tried to picture her walking away down Commonwealth Avenue carrying a bag of Charley's things and turning over the pages of the notebook.

The picture refused to materialize. Rosie was absent. Until now she had been a presence lurking just around the corner somewhere, if he could only find the right corner. Now she seemed remote, removed to the farthest star, as though she did not exist in Boston at all, or in New York City, or Pittsburgh, or Santa Fe, or Milwaukee, or San Francisco, or Detroit.

She was more gone than she had ever been before.

"They're gone? Oh, thank the Lord!"

"I dropped them at Lufthansa in plenty of time. Helen, for Christ's sake, don't cry. You know they had to go."

"Here, Sonny, your coffee's hot. Pay no attention to Helen. Her mind's going. I've noticed it a lot lately. Yesterday she forgot to take her medicine, didn't you, Helen? Oh, God, stop that whining!"

"Christ, Mother, will you kindly shut up?"

"Oh, that's right, Sonny, blame me, when I'm only telling the truth. Oh, Sonny, look out, you broke the cup! Oh, God, Sonny, what happened?"

"Nothing. For Christ's sake, let me alone. Nothing happened."

"But you dropped the cup! Your hands are shaking! Sonny, Sonny, tell Mother, are you all right? Oh, Helen, shut up! Do you hear me? Just shut up!"

◆ ◆ ◆ ◆

CHAPTER 58

*The ungodly have great power, riches, and respect . . . we
. . . have but only one poor, silly, and contemned Christ.*
                                        Martin Luther

T he Monday before Easter was freakishly hot. Homer
        took off his jacket as he walked past the Church of
        the Commonwealth. He nodded at Donald Woody,
who was removing a dead pigeon from his lush garden of
daffodils, and Woody said, "Hi, there, nice day." Across the
street a beach umbrella had blossomed on a sunny rooftop.
Joggers were out in force.

Homer had an appointment at 115 Commonwealth Avenue. It wasn't with Alan Starr, it was with Mrs. Garboyle.
Homer had turned over the matter of Pansy Kraeger's panties to his wife. His own concern this morning was with the
whereabouts of Rosie Hall, who was now fully alive in his
mind. Somewhere the woman was living and breathing,
with warm blood pulsing in her veins. She might be as lovable as Starr thought her, or she might be an awful person,
but she had certainly not been burned up in that flaming
automobile. Where was she?

Mrs. Garboyle's apartment was on the third floor. On the
way up the stairs Homer passed a couple of girls on the way
down, plump young students in curly permanents. They
were laughing at some joke, their arms full of books. Exams
must be in the offing.

Mrs. Garboyle opened her door at once, and beamed at
him. "Oh, come in, Mr. Kelly. Isn't it a lovely day!"

Homer made admiring remarks about her apartment,
which was the same shape and size as Rosie's, but altogether
different. Gathered under her bay window was a cactus garden. Prickly objects sat on tables. Every sort of geometric

shape thrust out dangerous-looking spines. A ceramic dachshund sported a thorny tail. Pots of African violets had a place of honor on the television set, beside a photograph of a young marine.

"Your son?" said Homer, bending to look at it.

"Yes, that's Scottie. He was killed in Viet Nam."

"Oh, I'm sorry."

"Never mind, dear." Mrs. Garboyle pointed at another picture, a large framed color print. Homer recognized the portrait of Isabella Stewart Gardner. "I found it," said Mrs. Garboyle, "and brought it back to the Gardner Museum, remember?"

"Of course I do. That was a great day for the museum, after all they'd been through." Homer turned to look solemnly at his hostess. "Mrs. Garboyle, Alan tells me you used to babysit for Rosalind Hall."

She nodded enthusiastically. "Oh, yes, many times. Such a good baby." Her face fell. "I pray to the Lord someone's taking good care of him, that dear little boy."

"Well, I hope so too. Tell me, Mrs. Garboyle, did Rosie go out often?"

"Almost every night."

"Every night? She went out every night?"

"Oh, yes. She went next door to the church to do her organ practicing. She played the organ, you know, the king of instruments. She practiced late at night when there weren't any weddings or funerals or novenas. Oh, no, I suppose this church doesn't have novenas." Mrs. Garboyle's voice trailed off sadly.

Homer thought it over. "You mean she practiced on the old organ, before the fire?"

"Yes, that's right." Mrs. Garboyle's face screwed up in pain. "The fire, oh, that was a dreadful night."

"You saw it, Mrs. Garboyle?"

"Yes, I did. Oh, dreadful, it was dreadful."

"Was Rosie practicing that night?"

"I'm not sure. I'm afraid I've forgotten. She was certainly at home when the fire started. We all woke up when the fire engines came, what with all the noise and the sirens. Then when we saw that it was right next door, we were afraid we might be next. All the girls took their best clothes out-of-doors. I took my hedgehog outside."

"Your hedgehog?"

Mrs. Garboyle picked up a large potted cactus with rosettes of dagger-sharp spines and held it in her lap. "I've grown it from a baby."

"But this house was safe, wasn't it? The fire confined itself to the balcony of the church, as I recall. I saw all the damage next morning, when they called me in, and it was clear that it was mostly the balcony and the pipe organ."

"That's right. We were in no danger after all." Mrs. Garboyle thanked the good Lord. "But it killed that poor man. I'll never forget it. The tears! We all cried and cried."

"I understand Rosie saw the fire? She was pretty upset too, I gather?"

"Oh, yes. She wrapped little Charley in a blanket and stood there watching beside me. But it was too much for her. Well, it was a terrible sight, that poor man. They brought him out, all burned." Mrs. Garboyle's eyes filled with tears.

"Mrs. Garboyle, try to remember whether or not Rosie practiced in the church that evening. Because if she did, if she was there *after* Mr. Kraeger and James Castle, then they couldn't have been responsible for the fire, do you see?"

"I'm sorry, but I just can't recall. All I remember clearly about that night is the fire and smoke, and poor Mr. Plummer." Mrs. Garboyle covered her face with her gnarled old hands. "Oh, it was terrible, terrible."

Homer reached out in sympathy and drove his thumb into one of the hedgehog's spines. He cried out in pain.

Mrs. Garboyle put the cactus on the floor and leaped up for a bandage, her tears forgotten.

❖ ❖ ❖ ❖

CHAPTER 59

I will do whatever the Lord gives me to do, and, God willing, never will I be afraid.   Martin Luther

It was a Saturday morning rehearsal for the soloists.

"That's right," said Barbara Inch, pushing back her hair, "just free and easy. Take your time."

The tenor Evangelist put his foot on the balcony railing and sang one of the narrative passages from Bach's *St. John Passion*, *"The soldiers platted then for Him a crown out of thorns."* He broke off to complain that he couldn't see the damn music. He'd lost one of his contact lenses.

"And put it upon his head," prompted Barbara.

"Oh, right." The soloist closed his eyes and went on singing, *"And put it upon His head and put on Him a purple robe."*

Homer Kelly sat below the balcony in a pew halfway to the pulpit, looking at the bowed back of Martin Kraeger a dozen rows in front of him. Was Kraeger listening or praying? Whichever it was, his own crown of thorns must be sticking into him like one of Mrs. Garboyle's cactuses, with the blood trickling down over his ears. Mary had reported to Homer what she had learned about the Pansy affair. It wasn't helping. Kraeger's malicious wife was obviously a screwball, but she still had the upper hand. You couldn't laugh off a putrid lawsuit like this one.

The alto soloist came puffing onto the balcony, a large woman in mammoth blue jeans. Barbara sent the tenor home for a pair of glasses, and the contralto took a deep breath and let loose with a rippling succession of deep trills, *"From the shackles of my vices to liberate me, to liberate me, they have bound my Saviour."*

Kraeger stood up, nodded gravely at Homer, and walked out through the door behind the pulpit, passing the portrait of Reverend Wigglesworth without a glance, although it offered him DIVINE INSPIRATION. In the gloom the gold letters on Wigglesworth's book sparkled with uncouth exaggeration. Above the painting half the wall was freshly painted, the other half a labyrinth of patching plaster.

Homer turned in his pew and looked up at the balcony, where Barbara and the soloist were crouched over the music, talking in low voices. Above them the pipes of the new organ rose in profusion on either side of the window of Moses and the Burning Bush. The fire in the bush was a tour de force of colored and painted glass. The late afternoon sunlight slanting through the dancing boughs along the avenue made the flames flicker as though the window were really on fire.

On fire. Homer focused his mind on all the fires he had heard about lately. There had been the one in the church balcony, the fire that had destroyed the old organ and killed Mr. Plummer. Kraeger had taken the blame for that, but perhaps he had been wrong. Castle had been there with him, and they had left together, leaving behind them, perhaps, a smoldering cigarette. But suppose there had been no cigarette, and Castle came back later and started the fire by himself, in order to destroy the organ and get himself a new one? Of course if Rosie Hall had been practicing in the church later on, both Kraeger and Castle were in the clear.

Fire number two was the car fire, the one that had destroyed the body of an anonymous woman, a substitute for Rosie.

Fire number three was in Castle's own house, which had been partly destroyed by fire a couple of years back.

Fire number four wasn't a major conflagration, it was the general carelessness of Harold Oates. For one thing he had used a blowtorch in his rented room, and for another his sloppy smoking habits made him a walking incendiary bomb.

For the first time Homer decided to take seriously the strangeness and unpredictability of the great Harold Oates. Suppose he really was the culprit? Suppose it was really Oates who had vandalized all those organs, the way most people thought? Perhaps the destruction of the old organ at the Church of the Commonwealth last spring had been the first in the series. It was true that Alan Starr hadn't discovered Oates until last January, but that didn't mean he wasn't hanging around town before that.

But why in hell would he be burning up bodies in cars? Or destroying Castle's house? Could it be that he raged against the competition? He was of course the greatest organist within a thousand miles, but James Castle and Rosie Hall were next best. Had he tried to finish them off, in order to reign supreme? No, no, it was impossible. Homer scoffed at his own conjecture. Surely Oates was too erratic to carry out anything as complex as the burning of the body in Rosie's car.

Homer stood up and stretched, and walked out of the church. On the way to his car he was surprised to see Martin Kraeger sitting on a park bench across the street. He wondered if Martin was neglecting his duties. Maybe he should be writing a sermon or visiting shut-ins.

Probably the poor man was always doing something he shouldn't be doing, or not doing something he should be. It must be god-awful to be a clergyman.

CHAPTER 60

Antichrist attacks with fire, and shall be punished with fire.
                                                Martin Luther

Homer had a dream that night about fire. It was an astonishing dream. There was God, awful, immense, towering up and up, filling the cosmos, his face dark and hidden under a flaming diadem. His crown was a vast ring of church spires, smoldering, blazing, sending up columns of black smoke against the stars. Rousing himself sleepily in the morning, Homer made up his mind to spend the day in the Boston Public Library trying to learn something about arson.

He didn't find much that was of interest, beyond the fact that arsonists began young. As infant pyromaniacs they played with matches. They set fire to mattresses and wastebaskets and later on they lit bonfires in the drawers of their teachers' desks. In ripened maturity they ignited automobiles and houses and people.

That was your garden-variety arsonist, the kind with a passion for flaming infernos. There was another kind, the respectable owner of a failed enterprise, who set his property ablaze as a matter of business. People like that experienced no thrill from sticking around to watch the flames mount to the heavens, they hastened from the scene to establish alibis a hundred miles away.

Which kind of arsonist had set the Church of the Commonwealth on fire, and perhaps also Rosie Hall's car with the cadaver in the front seat?

Doggedly Homer abandoned the library and set out to find the headquarters of the Boston Fire Department on Southampton Street. His destination lay somewhere between Boston City Hospital and the Southeast Expressway. By the time Homer found it he had acquired a bashed fender and endured humiliation and contumely from the drivers of other cars, whose lanes he had wandered into in desperation, trying to turn left when he was on the right side of the highway, and right when he was on the left.

"Sure," said the officer behind the information desk, "we've got a whole department of archives. Third floor, down the hall on the right. Sergeant Drum, he's in charge."

The room was full of file cabinets. A pink-cheeked kid in a blue shirt looked up from a computer as Homer walked in. "Sergeant Drum?" said Homer.

"That's me."

Homer introduced himself, and flashed his long-defunct card from the office of the District Attorney of Middlesex County. "What I want to know is, do you have any sort of system, so you can trace fires that have similar characteristics?"

Sergeant Drum stood up. "Sure, we've got a system. Categories, you know? Warehouse fires, car fires, space heaters, insurance scams, everything cross-referenced. Like what have you got in mind?"

Impulsively Homer said, "Churches, have you got a history of fires in churches?"

"Oh, you bet. Churches burn down all the time. Painters using acetylene torches to remove old paint, flame gets under the clapboards, place burns down. Careless use of candles, you name it. Here, just a sec."

He pulled out a file drawer and unfolded a printout. "See here, Baptist church, Shelburne, ten years ago, March seventeenth. Entire edifice one hundred percent destroyed, suspected arson, thirteen-year-old juvenile arrested, indicted, convicted, conviction suspended on appeal. Same kid, a year later, First Baptist, Thornton, ninety percent destroyed, fourteen-year-old served six months in a house of correction."

"My God, what was the kid's name?"

"Not listed here because it was a juvenile. Unfortunately the juvenile arsonist file"—Sergeant Drum made a face—"well, it no longer exists. My predecessor punched the wrong button and the whole thing went poof." He clapped his hands to show the finality of the disaster. "I mean, that's why I'm here. The poor klutz got fired."

"Do you remember it, I mean in your head?"

"Sorry, I was in grade school at the time."

"Well, maybe there's somebody older who was here then, who might remember?"

"Wait a sec. I'll get Heinrich, Fred Heinrich, he's really old, been here since day one." The pink-cheeked sergeant bounded out of the room and came back a moment later with Heinrich.

Homer had expected a bent and crippled old fossil. He was shocked to see that Sergeant Drum's idea of an old man was this strapping fortyish youth in a pair of pink athletic pants tied around the middle with a drawstring.

"Well, I sort of remember," said Heinrich. "It was architectural, that's all I recollect. The name of the kid was kind of architectural."

Homer pounced. "Castle? Was his name Castle?"

"Castle? Well, I'm not sure. Was he a juvenile ten years ago?"

Homer tried to remember the vague face of the organist he had met only once, a year ago, among a crowd of other people on the scorched balcony of the Church of the Commonwealth. Surely the man had been bald. Did some men go bald in their twenties? "I don't think so, but I'm not positive."

"Wait a minute," said Sergeant Drum, "I'll see if he's in the regular file." He bent over his file drawers again and snatched out another printout. "Hey, here he is, James Castle."

"That's it! James Castle!"

"House fire, One-two-one Mount Vernon Street, nineteen April, 1992. Inspector from the insurance company declared it was of accidental origin, problem with wiring, they paid up."

"Anything else under Castle?"

"One other thing, Church of the Commonwealth, last year, fatal fire, one victim, careless smoking by pastor, Castle present at the time. That's all on Castle."

Homer racked his brain for more people with architectural identities. Then, with a pouncing sensation in his head, he remembered one. Softly and tenderly he said the name of the girl with the mysterious juvenile police record, the woman who might have been present in the Church of the Commonwealth after Kraeger and Castle had left it on the night of the fire. "Rosalind Hall?"

Sergeant Drum ransacked the file drawers again, and extracted another printout with a flourish. "Say, now you're talking. Look at this, two entries, a couple more churches."

Homer tried to restrain his excitement. "I thought you said the juvenile entries were lost."

"These aren't juveniles," said Drum. He held up the printout for Heinrich to see.

"They're not exactly arson," said Heinrich, staring at it. "This one, Preston Falls Methodist, Christmas Eve service, five years ago, candles on the organ, music caught fire. Didn't amount to much. Smoke damage to the ceiling, that was all."

"My God, what's the other one?"

"Wedding," said Heinrich. "Candles again. Damnfool brides, they've always got to have candles."

"Where was it?"

"Malvern," said Sergeant Drum, running his finger along a line. "Church of the Holy Redeemer, destroyed a bunch of music. Organist couldn't see without a whole row of candles, knocked over a couple. Same female, Rosalind Hall."

"Interesting," said Heinrich, "both fires started with candles. Arsonists, they usually establish a pattern. Like you've
got your kerosene arsonists, they always use kerosene. Other
people, they stick to a cigarette lighter, or maybe an acetylene or propane torch. Or like they ignite a bunch of oily
rags, try to make it look like spontaneous combustion, only
they use an accelerator, throw it out to spread the fire, you
can tell what they've done. Those church fires a while back,
in Shelburne and Thornton, that was really clever. The kid
dissolved some kind of incendiary chemical in water, sprinkled it around, so when the water evaporated long afterward, the stuff caught fire when nobody was there. It was
polka dots, like. Polka dots of combustible material. It
flamed up in spots where the stuff was sprinkled."

"Polka dots," exclaimed Homer. "You mean those two
church fires that were set by some kid with an architectural
name? The one whose records were wiped out by mistake?"

"That's right," said Heinrich. "I was present at the
Shelburne fire. I remember seeing the flames coming up in
a lot of different places, just like, you know, polka dots."

"What about the fire at the Church of the Commonwealth?" said Homer. "Was that polka dots too?"

"Don't know. That end of the building was really ablaze
by the time Engine 33 got there from Boylston Street. They
managed to save the rest of the church, by some miracle.
Great bunch of guys, Engine 33. They had a tower unit
there too from Purchase Street and everything from Colum-
bus Ave. One fatality though, right?" Heinrich shook his
head. "Too bad."

Homer left the headquarters of the Boston Fire Department half frustrated, half excited. Something was heaving
and tumbling in his mind like a cat in a bag. Before long he
knew what it was, the trash can in Rosie Hall's back entry.
It was full of ashtrays and candles.

Had she been throwing away the evidence of her interest
in incendiary materials? Had she entered the church late at

night, after Kraeger and Castle were gone, bringing along her innocent little candles, and set fire to the balcony?

Afterward, poor dear, she had been deeply distressed by the charred body of the sexton. The dear girl had only meant to cause a pretty blaze, she hadn't really meant to kill anybody, and it weighed upon her mind and tormented her soul, and finally she couldn't stand it any more, so she ran away.

Homer couldn't help a bitter laugh as he drove cautiously back to Storrow Drive. Poor old Alan Starr with his fixation on the sweet girl in the photograph! Perhaps she was a pyromaniac, a killer, a careless abandoner and kidnapper of babies, a really ghastly woman after all.

CHAPTER 61

The mouth of fools doth God confess,
But while their lips draw nigh him
Their heart is full of wickedness
And all their deeds deny him.
Hymn by Martin Luther

Homer had his hands full. Ninety-eight of his students had written final papers, and they had to be graded by Friday. He could dump half of them on Mary, but forty-nine undergraduate papers were still a hell of a lot of papers. The whole terrifying heap was stacked on the back seat of his car, along with a potted Easter lily, a present from a graduate student who was sweet on Mary.

He parked his car on Clarendon Street—the sign said NO PARKING, but surely it didn't mean it. Homer locked the car and peered over the fence at the excavation, where everything still seemed to be on hold. Then he walked across Clarendon to the Church of the Commonwealth. He had an appointment with Alan Starr.

Alan wasn't going to like what he had to say, the news about the two churches in which Rosalind Hall had started a couple of merry little fires. He wasn't going to like it at all.

As Homer walked into the church he felt the floor shiver under his feet. A huge dull booming resounded from the sanctuary. "My God, what's that?" he asked Donald Woody, who was shouldering a tall ladder.

Woody grinned at him. "The thirty-two-foot pipes have come. Listen to that, did you ever hear anything like that? Shakes the whole building. My plaster wall, the cracks keep opening up. I have to keep fixing 'em all over again."

Homer ran up to the balcony and found it cluttered with long wooden pipes. "Wow," he said, "so this is what you've been waiting for."

"I've got to work fast," said Alan. "They've got to be mounted and voiced and tuned before next Sunday. We don't need the new ones for the concert on Friday and Saturday, but I've promised the complete organ for the Easter service. Hey, listen to this." With his feet on the pedals he played MANY BRAVE HEARTS ARE ASLEEP IN THE DEEP, SO BE-WARE, BEE-EE-EE-EE-WARE.

The floor trembled. "Look here," said Homer, gripping the back of a pew, "I'm afraid I've got bad news."

Alan listened soberly to his account of Rosie's previous involvements with burning churches. As Homer had expected, he brushed them aside. "That's ridiculous. It's just a coincidence. Those fires were accidents. They didn't amount to anything anyway."

"And there's another thing. Mrs. Garboyle tells me Rosie used to practice in the middle of the night. Maybe she was here on the night of the fire. If she came in to use the organ after Martin and Castle left, it would mean they weren't responsible for what happened. If they had accidentally started a fire, she would have seen it. She wouldn't have sat here innocently playing scales with flames shooting up around the organ. Does anybody keep a practice schedule? Might her practice times be listed somewhere?"

"Yes, Loretta keeps an organ schedule. Loretta Fawcett, Martin's secretary."

"Superb! Where is the magnificent Loretta?"

Alan made a face and got up from the bench. "She's not very magnificent, I'm afraid. Don't get your hopes up."

They found Loretta at her desk. She was working on her needlepoint cabbage. It was leafy and green and enormous.

"Good morning, Loretta," said Alan. "Might we have a look at the organ schedule?"

"Certainly." Loretta stuck her needle into the cabbage and groped in the drawers of her desk. After a few wrong drawers she found the right one, and pulled out a piece of paper. "This is for March. April must be in here some-where."

"That's all right," said Alan. "I just want to show Homer Kelly how it works. See here, Homer, the days of the month are along the top, and the times of day down the side." Alan looked up at Loretta. "But it's hardly filled in at all."

"Oh, well, I didn't put you in because everybody knows you're there from eight in the morning till noon."

"But what about the choir? They're not marked down for Thursday night?"

Loretta turned huffy. "Well, everybody knows that too. Look, see this line here? It's all filled in, midnight to one in the morning, because that's Peggy Throstle, and not every-body knows about Peggy Throstle."

Homer put his big hands on Loretta's desk and looked at her keenly. "What about last year, Miz Fawcett? Do you have the schedules for last year? For the night of the fire in the church, for instance?"

Loretta looked blank. Swivelling on her chair she made a pawing motion at the empty shelves behind her desk, then turned and whisked away the crumbs of yesterday with a sweep of her arm. "Oh, I don't keep the old schedules. Out they go! Out with past history! No room for useless old stuff. Get rid of it before it multiplies, that's what I always say."

Homer was disappointed. He had been hoping to provide proof that Martin Kraeger was innocent. Then maybe all those old fusspots in his congregation would calm down.

Alan too was chagrined, having hoped to prove to Homer that the fire could not have been started by Rosie.

Silently they parted company. Homer found his way outdoors and headed for his car, depressed by Loretta Fawcett's cavalier attitude toward history. *No room for useless old stuff!* Nothing mattered to Loretta but the passing moment, this instant right now, this fleeting second. *Now,* as I put down my right foot. No, *now,* as I put down my left foot. No, forget about my left foot, the only important moment is *now* as my right foot comes down on this manhole cover in the street.

Homer paused in his metaphysical speculations on the nature of history and the passage of time, and stopped to listen. He could hear a throbbing noise coming from somewhere, deep down under the iron disk of the manhole cover. What was going on down there? Was it part of the past or part of the future? Well, what did it matter? Only this instant mattered, right *now,* as he put his left foot up on the curb.

He found a meter maid standing beside his car. She had

a pad of ticket forms in her hand. "Oh, please," said Homer, "I'm really sorry. I'll never do it again."

Heartlessly the meter maid wrote out a ticket for fifty dollars and handed it to him, grinning.

CHAPTER 62

. . . a fine understanding . . . that seeks after truth, and loves that which is plain and upright, is worthy of all honour and praise.   Martin Luther

Mary Kelly was restless. She had finished grading her half of the final papers. She was free to return to the problem of Kay Kraeger's vicious attack on her ex-husband. Mary had followed the Pansy track as far as Kiddy Kamp, but now—it was the Tuesday before Easter—she was stuck. She dropped into the Church of the Commonwealth to report her stalled progress to Martin Kraeger.

It was spring on Commonwealth Avenue. The trees along the narrow park were like tall flowers, their branches airy and transparent, their gold-green tassels hanging like strands of gossamer. The tassels were pollen cases, and the pollen lay beneath the trees like a bright shadow. Beyond the trees on either side of the avenue the houses were distinguished presences, their windows dark, their occupants invisible. Mary imagined majestic personages sitting in great chairs, gazing at the light.

Kraeger wasn't in church. Loretta Fawcett didn't know where on this earth he was. "If you ask me, he's neglecting his duty. He's never in his office. He doesn't answer the phone. And there's, like, people in trouble probably, trying to reach him, people on their deathbed."

Loretta was partly right. Martin was in a crisis of passive despair. The things that usually occupied his time seemed empty and futile. His unpopularity was clear. There were conspicuous absences in the pews on Sunday mornings. After the service, people shook his hand feebly, failing to meet his eyes.

His only escape from the sense of approaching doom was to sit in the sanctuary when Barbara Inch was putting the Good Friday soloists through their paces. Only then was there worth in the world, only then did chaos part to reveal a marvel flowering in the wilderness.

For her part Barbara was acutely aware that Martin Kraeger was sitting below her, listening to everything that went on in the balcony—the plea of one of the tenor soloists to cut out all the *da capo* parts from the arias, and her reply, "Why not? The purists will hate us, but everybody else will be grateful." He heard the kidding between the two bass soloists, he heard the soprano muff an entrance over and over.

Hour after hour Kraeger sat with folded arms, while through all the reworking of tricky places and the breakings off and startings again, the burden of the music of the Pas-

sion according to St. John threaded its way. *What is truth?* sang Pilate. What indeed, wondered Martin Kraeger.

But this morning there was no rehearsal. In Loretta Fawcett's little office Mary could hear only an occasional hooting note from the organ. Martin was elsewhere.

She wandered into the corridor, and at once found another restless soul, Barbara Inch. "Oh, good morning," said Mary. "We've met before. I'm Mary Kelly. Homer and I came to see you, to ask about Rosalind Hall. Remember?"

"Of course I remember."

"We're coming to hear the *St. John* on Saturday night. You don't happen to know where I can find Mr. Kraeger, do you?"

"No, I'm afraid not. Sometimes when we're rehearsing he comes to listen. But there are no rehearsals today. There's just one more on Thursday night, and we're not ready. There's so much to get done." Panic-stricken, Barbara hugged her arms to her breast. She glanced anxiously at Martin's office door. "I hope he's all right."

Her voice was strained. Mary sensed an ally. "How about a cup of coffee? Have you got time to walk over to Boylston Street?"

Barbara seemed pleased. "There's a coffeemaker in the music room."

They sat down amid the cellos and basses, the tangle of music stands, the leaning rows of folding chairs. Barbara poured two cups of coffee and brought them to the table, shoving aside a choir robe.

Mary got down to business at once, probing carefully. "What do you think about the rumor that's going around, about Mr. Kraeger and his little daughter?"

Barbara showed her colors at once. "It's ridiculous. Anyone who knows him can see how silly it is. His wife sounds like a dangerous woman."

Mary smiled. "Good. I was hoping you'd say that. I agree completely. Homer and I are trying to help." Grasping her coffee cup, she leaned forward and told Barbara what she had learned about Kiddy Kamp from Millie Weideman, whose daycare center had been closed after Kay Kraeger's malicious insinuations.

Barbara gazed intently into her coffee cup. "You know there's always gossip around a church. Jeanie Perkupp told me Mrs. Kraeger's made trouble before. Her son worked in the same office with her once. He told Jeanie that Kay was always accusing people of one thing or another, trying to get them fired. She finally got herself fired."

Mary sipped her coffee. "That's very interesting. Perhaps there's a pattern, some kind of repeated—what do you call it?—neurotic conduct."

Barbara jumped at the idea. "Let me help. I'll see what I can find out about her. I'll have plenty of time after Easter Sunday."

"Good. We'll track down her entire history. I suspect she's a professional predator who gets her kicks by smashing crystal vases."

"That's right," said Barbara, thinking of the crystal vase that was Martin Kraeger.

CHAPTER 63

*God shows His power in our weakness; He will not . . . break
in pieces the bruised reed.*   Martin Luther

"H i."

Alan winced. The whining voice on the
phone was Debbie Buffington's. "Oh, hello,
Debbie."

"I got to see you right away."

"I'm sorry, not now. What about next Monday?"

Debbie whimpered. "Just for a while. Can I come over?
Like right now? I know where you live."

Alan tried to control his irritation. "How do you know
where I live?"

"I followed you. When you used to take Charley, I followed you half a block behind. That house on the alley beside the church, One-fifteen Commonwealth, where that
girl used to live. I looked her up in the phone book."

"Look, I've got a deadline. Honestly, I won't be free until
Monday."

"Oh, shit, nobody works like that."

"Well, I do. Right now anyway. I'm sorry."

Debbie turned plaintive. "Like I don't know what to do.
Wanda and me, all we've got is this bag of Fritos. I haven't
got a cent."

"Didn't you call the welfare office? Child support? Aid to
mothers with dependent children? Emergency services? I
gave you the phone numbers. Didn't you call them?"

"Oh, shit, bunch of bureaucrats."

"Bureaucrats with money for people in trouble. Look,
have you got a pencil? I'll give you the numbers again."

The day had begun badly. It went on badly. Harold Oates was missing. He hadn't slept in Rosie's bed for days. Would he show up for tonight's rehearsal? Damn Oates anyway.

And then Alan was stunned to find the church milling with people. The vestibule was full of middle-aged men and women talking at the tops of their lungs. Through the glass doors he could see another mob thronging the aisles in the sanctuary. They were all carrying folders, opening them to show what was inside. Someone was hooking up a microphone on Martin Kraeger's pulpit. It was some kind of a meeting.

Alan couldn't work on the Contra Bombarde while somebody was giving a speech. "What's all this?" he asked an excited-looking man.

"American Philatelic Society, annual meeting."

"Philatelic? You mean stamps? It's a meeting about stamps?"

The stamp collector's shiny lenses snapped with reflected light. "We always rent this place in April. You interested in stamps?"

"I'm afraid not."

The stamp collector was undeterred. Under Alan's nose appeared a sheet of green sixty-five-cent Graf Zeppelins. "Perfect condition. I've been offered three thousand. I'm holding out for five. Interested?"

"But it's Thursday. I'm supposed to have the organ to myself all day."

Alan went to Loretta Fawcett and complained. "Look, Loretta, it wasn't on the schedule. I always have Thursday mornings, and I signed up for the afternoon too, remember?"

"Oh, sorry, I forgot. I mean it just slipped my mind. I mean, everybody knows about the stamp collectors. They come every year."

"But, oh God, Loretta, I need the time. Well, never

mind." It did no good to bawl her out. He was just going to have to work through the next three nights.

The stamp collectors were gone by five o'clock, and at once Alan bounded up into the balcony and got to work. He had only a scant two hours. At seven, people began to gather for the final rehearsal of the music for Good Friday.

Reluctantly Alan slid off the organ bench and stood aside, watching the instrumentalists fumble among the chairs, set up music stands, breathe into flutes and oboes, tune violins and cellos. The chorus arranged itself noisily in the rear. The soloists arrived. They were wearing jeans and sloppy sweaters like everyone else, as though they were no better than ordinary mortals, in spite of their glorious voices.

Barbara Inch called to Alan over the heads of the tenor section, "Have you seen Harold Oates? He's late again."

"Oh, Jesus," said Alan. "I'll see if I can find him."

He plunged down the balcony stairs, narrowly avoiding a woman carrying a priceless antique gamba, raced next door, let himself into 115 Commonwealth Avenue, and found Oates collapsed on the sofa, snoring loudly. The room was yeasty with the smell of beer.

"Hey, Harold, wake up. You're supposed to be next door. Come on, wake up."

Oates didn't want to wake up. He rolled over and hid his face in the cushions. Only when Alan hauled him to a sitting position did he wake up and belch. Alan worked him over, mopping his face with a wet washcloth and helping him into a clean shirt, but Oates kept closing his eyes and slumping.

"Oh, God, Harold, can't you stand up? Wait a sec, I'll make some coffee."

By the time Oates shuffled up the balcony stairs with Alan urging him from behind, he was more or less sober.

Alan watched him blunder through the chairs of the violinists and take his place at the organ, while Christ in the garden of Gethsemane asked of the chief priests and Pharisees, *Whom seek ye here?*

Alan held his breath. There, it was all right. Oates was coming in at the right place without hesitation. He sighed with relief.

GOOD FRIDAY

+ + + + +

"O Haupt voll Blut und Wunden"
Chorale harmonized by J. S. Bach

O sacred Head now wounded,
With grief and shame weighed down,
Now scornfully surrounded
With thorns, Thy only crown!
How pale art Thou with anguish,
With sore abuse and scorn!
How does that visage languish
Which once was bright as morn!

◆ ◆ ◆ ◆

CHAPTER 64

I always loved music; whoso has skill in this art, is of a good temperament, fitted for all things.   Martin Luther

The next night Oates was not merely late, he was nowhere to be found. The church was packed. Every pew was filled, and Donald Woody had found a miraculous new source of folding chairs for the overflow crowd at the back.

In the balcony the chorus members were lined up in their black robes. The instrumentalists held fiddles on their knees, and flutes, English horns and oboes across their laps. The soloists were somber and distinguished in black gowns like those of the choir. They waited.

Barbara's patience was giving out. She grasped Alan's arm. "Where is he?"

Alan had been dodging next-door, looking for Oates, running up to the balcony to report. "I don't know where the hell he is. He's not at home. I'm afraid he's back on the bottle."

Below them people turned to stare up at the balcony. In the front row Mrs. Frederick frowned, and whispered to Martin Kraeger. Barbara looked at Alan severely. "You'll just have to take over."

"Oh, God," said Alan, who had never even glanced at the organ accompaniment to the *St. John Passion*.

"You've got to. It's not difficult. Really, there's nothing to it."

Alan groaned. But then the problem vanished. A familiar figure walked out onto the balcony, plump and beaming, his bald head glowing with sunburn.

It was James Castle.

It didn't matter that he had left the Church of the Commonwealth in a state of precarious doubt. Nor did it matter that Homer Kelly suspected him of having something to do with the fire in the church, and with the disappearance of Rosalind Hall. All that mattered now was their immediate need.

"Oh, Jim," said Barbara, throwing her arms around him, "will you help us out?"

"Of course," said Castle.

He sat down on the organ bench and pulled out a few stops—Stopped Diapason eight, Prestant four, and Div Insp—and nodded at Barbara.

At once she raised her arms, the instrumentalists began to play, and the choristers drew breath to sing "Lord, Lord, Lord, Thou our Master." From that moment they were possessed. Everything flowed out of them into the music, torrents of controlled feeling. For a little while on an April evening at the end of the twentieth century they existed together in the mind of the eighteenth-century composer. The bows of the string players went energetically up and down, the flutes and oboes tweedled contrapuntally, the organ gave harmonious support, and the voices rose and fell and cried out, resolving splendid dissonances in harmony and beginning the story again. Barbara stood at the front of the balcony, transported, while sixty-seven men and women obeyed every motion of her lifted hands, lamenting the anguish of the cross, bewailing their grievous sin, uttering their majestic wonder.

And then it was all over. There was applause for the chorus and the musicians and the soloists, and Barbara was presented with a bouquet of flowers. Then the instrumentalists put away their fiddles and flutes and oboes, and everyone left the balcony but Barbara. She sat down on the organ bench, and depression washed over her.

She didn't need the applause, she didn't want a bouquet of flowers. She wanted only one thing. But Martin Kraeger had not even shaken her hand in congratulation. He had come up to the balcony to welcome back James Castle, he had nodded at her and smiled, and he had gone out with Castle.

She felt washed-out and hollow. What did life hold for her after this, after tomorrow, after Easter Sunday morning? Castle would take over his old position, and once more she would be out of a job.

She heard a step on the stairs. Quickly Barbara stood up, and looked for her coat.

"Barbara Inch?"

She didn't know the woman who stood staring at her and frowning as though it were a crime to be Barbara Inch. "Yes, I'm Barbara Inch."

"I just want you to know a few things about my ex-husband."

Barbara shook her head, bewildered. "Your ex-husband?"

"A word to the wise. I'm here to warn you. Steer clear."

"I'm sorry, but I don't know what you're talking about." Barbara looked at the stairway, wondering if she could dodge past this insane person and get away.

"He wasn't married to me, he was married to the church. He did not attend my mother in her last illness. His parenting lacked discipline."

"You're Mrs. Kraeger," said Barbara, astonished.

"Lately he has revealed his bestial instincts, but I should warn you that in bed he seldom achieved my personal needs. I am a very passionate woman."

It was grotesque. "But why are you telling this to me?"

"I've heard rumors. I feel I owe it to you as a woman." Kay Kraeger's eyes narrowed. "I must say, you're not what I expected in a femme fatale. Why don't you do something about your hair?"

Barbara burst out laughing. Did it mean, could it possibly mean—? No, of course it didn't mean anything, but a crazy happiness welled up in her, and she couldn't control her laughter.

"Oh, you may well laugh." Kay Kraeger turned and pushed through the folding chairs. "I'm only trying to help, woman to woman."

Barbara found her coat and followed Mrs. Kraeger down the stairs. There was no one in the vestibule but Donald Woody.

"She came roaring in here and demanded to know where you were," explained Woody. "She's bonkers, if you ask me." He waggled his finger in a circle beside his ear. "What did she want?"

"You tell me," said Barbara. "I haven't the faintest idea."

Martin Kraeger took James Castle for a drink in the Copley Plaza.

"So it was you who was ill, not your mother? Why didn't you let us know?"

Castle looked down at his gin and tonic. "Pride, I guess." My doctor didn't hold out much hope, and I didn't want people feeling sorry for me."

"But where have you been? Were you at Mass General all this time?"

"No, no, Sloan-Kettering in New York. Then I went to Fort Lauderdale and strolled along the beach while my mother fed me up."

Martin remembered the woman who had turned her back on him, whose screams he had heard through the brick wall of Castle's house on Mount Vernon Street. Hastily he revised his opinion. The woman couldn't be so bad, after all.

"How about another one of these?" said Castle. He beckoned to the waiter. "Two more of the same."

Martin looked at him uncertainly. "Are you sure you're supposed to be drinking this stuff? After what your insides have been through?"

Castle looked surprised, and fumbled with his paper napkin. "Oh, no, it's fine. I mean this is a special occasion."

"Right you are. Here's to the special occasion. Welcome back."

◆ ◆ ◆ ◆

CHAPTER 65

He has all divinity at his fingers' ends.
Martin Luther

After the Good Friday concert, Alan went back to Rosie Hall's apartment and let himself in by the front door. He expected to find Harold Oates collapsed on the bed in an alcoholic stupor, and dreaded his waking up to curse the whole world. What could Alan say to him? Nothing. The failure of his effort at rehabilitation was miserably disappointing, but it wouldn't do any good to talk about it. The man was a hopeless case.

But Oates was not there.

Alan was in a queer mood. He was still under the spell of the music. After his rescue by James Castle, he had left the balcony and gone down to the front of the sanctuary to hear the concert from behind one of the piers separating aisle and nave. Listening to the scandalized narrative of the Evangelist, the solemn urgency of Pilate's interrogation, the wild clamor of the chorus demanding crucifixion, he kept remembering what Oates had said, *Passion, my God, what's passion but going beyond?*

Now he moved restlessly around the apartment, touching things—the harpsichord, the bookcase, the rubber plant, the wall. What did he care about in the same way, what was there that would pitch him into some other state of being, some mad condition of creative power and exalted understanding? He had to go beyond some barrier, he had to climb a ladder without rungs and hurl himself aloft without wings. What did he care about so much that it didn't matter whether it was true or false, right or wrong, worthy or unworthy?

Only one thing. He wanted to find Rosie Hall. Oates called her his fried girlfriend, Homer Kelly said she was probably a ghastly girl. Alan didn't care. She wasn't fried, and he didn't care what she was like. He had to find her. He sat down heavily on a chair and closed his eyes. Mentally he picked up Rosie's missing notebook and opened it and turned the pages as though it held an important secret.

There had been page after page about registration. And pages of addresses and phone numbers. He himself had filled in blank pages with news about Charley—and with his own stupid letters. And there had been the page of acoustic oddities.

Oates had explained the oddities, and at once they had lost their mystery—the music of the spheres, the echoes in different languages, Noah's ark, the self-sounding bells, the box in which sounds could be locked up.

The box in which sounds could be locked up. Alan rose and went to the mantelpiece and picked up the big conch shell. Here was a box with a sound locked inside it, the sound of the sea—or so people said. He put the shell to his ear, and sure enough, there was a whisper like the murmur of waves on a faraway shore. It was really only the exchange of vibrating air between the curled passages of the shell and those of his ear, but it was a pleasant notion. The tide breathed in Alan's ear and fell back and breathed again, as though the shell were a natural recorder, trapping the sound of the sea.

Well, for Christ's sake, a tape recorder too was a box that trapped the sounds you put into it, and released them whenever you wanted to hear them again.

Alan went to the shelf where dust was collecting on Rosie's old-fashioned audiocassette recorders. One of them held a cassette. It was the copy of her own performance of "Wachet Auf." Oates had played it. He had denounced her choice of stops.

Alan began a conversation with the composer. "Listen,

Johann Sebastian, it's true, I can open this box and your own music will come out. You wrote it two hundred and fifty years ago, and Rosie played it last year, but it's still in here. Listen to this, Herr Kappelmeister."

The music began, and Alan pictured Bach raising his eyebrows in astonishment. His great jowls would shake, his small eyes stare with envy. "*Gott sei dank!* Ah, if only *vee* had such a box!"

"The trouble is, Herr Kappelmeister, this apparatus isn't very good. You should hear it on something high-tech."

The music rollicked and bounded along, right hand and pedal notes teasing each other, and soon the left hand began the admonitory tune, *Wake, awake, for night is coming.* Then there were noises in the street and Alan had to turn up the volume.

But the noises grew louder.

That was strange. The noises must be on the tape. They weren't happening now, they had happened during the copying. Damn all low-tech sleazy paraphernalia. If the two gadgets had been wired together like the cassette recorders that were part of his own CD player, this wouldn't have happened.

Then he understood. The interference with the music had been recorded on the day he found the baby and brought him home for the first time. The two machines had been turned on when he walked into the apartment. Rosie must have set them going herself. She had been copying her

own music from one tape recorder to the other, and then—
Alan gasped—there were voices in the room, two people
shouting, the baby beginning to cry.

Swiftly he rewound the tape and listened again, holding
his breath.

The music was too loud, too insistent. He couldn't distinguish what the voices were saying. But one was a
woman's—surely Rosie's—and the other a man's. Whose
voice was it? Who was beginning to shout at her? What was
he saying?

Alan crouched closer, but Charley's cries grew louder,
blotting out everything. And then, oh God, the voices of
the man and woman suddenly stopped and the music came
to a close and the baby went on crying.

Alan listened, agonized, as Charley cried on and on.
Then with a click the crying broke off. The tape had run
out. There was only the low humming sound of the machine itself.

It was clear what had happened. Rosie had been making
a copy of her own performance of Bach's organ prelude,
"Wachet Auf," and the blank tape had mindlessly recorded
not only the music but whatever was going on in the apartment at the same time. There had been a wild argument,
and the baby had cried, and then Charley had been left all
alone. Rosie and the guy who had been shouting at her had
vanished, leaving the doors wide open. Poor Charley had
climbed out of his crib and crawled out of the house by
himself.

Alan rewound the tape, his hands trembling, and listened
a third time. The voices were no clearer. He gave up and
called Homer Kelly.

"Oh, hello, Alan," said Mary. "How was the concert?
We're going tomorrow night. Do you want to speak to Homer? He's gone to bed."

Hurriedly, breathlessly, Alan told her about the noises on
the tape.

She was interested at once. "Listen, there are people who know how to disentangle those things. Acoustics experts, they can sort out the frequencies. I'll bet they could erase most of the music and leave only the voices. Do you know anybody like that?"

"No, but I'll find someone. It will have to be on Monday. I've got to spend all day tomorrow finishing the voicing on those damned Contra Bombardes."

"You poor kid. Well, good luck. And don't lose the tape."

Alan went back to the tape recorder and extracted the cassette. Mary Kelly was right. Nothing must happen to it. It would have to be hidden where Harold Oates couldn't find it, no matter how much he poked and pried. Alan winced, remembering the way Oates had ripped all the tape from one of Rosie's cassettes. *Filthy shit, Castle playing Sowerby. Some philanthropist should buy up every Sowerby recording in the world, smash them all, destroy them, burn all the scores, obliterate the name of Sowerby from the face of the earth.*

Alan brought a chair into the kitchen, climbed on it, and laid the tape well back on the top of the cupboard.

CHAPTER 66

Mankind is nothing else but a sheep-shambles, where we are slain and slaughtered by the devil. Martin Luther

Pip Tower climbed the stairs to the balcony, where Alan Starr was sounding one pedal note over and over. Again and again a great roar boomed from the thirty-two-foot F-sharp Contra Bombarde.

Alan looked up and grinned and slid off the bench. "Thanks for coming. I've been dodging back and forth all morning, trying to get those tongues curved just right."

"No problem," said Pip. "Sorry to be late." He took his place at the bench, and Alan crawled back into the organ and picked up his burnishing knife. But then he had to come out again to say hello to James Castle.

"Oh, don't mind me," said Castle, looking up eagerly at the immense height of the new Contra Bombardes. "I'll just hang around. Don't let me interfere." He shook Pip's hand. "It's good to be back among old friends."

Pip mumbled something, and Alan remembered how anxiously Pip had wanted to take Castle's place. Now there was no place for him to take. Poor old Pip.

When Homer Kelly gasped his way up to the balcony, they were back at work. Again and again a single pipe in the rank of Contra Bombardes bellowed the same note. "My God," said Homer, "it sounds like a war."

"A foghorn," said James Castle from the back of the balcony. "That's what I always think." He stood up and introduced himself to Homer, and so did Pip Tower, and everybody shook hands.

Homer went to the narrow door in the organ case, put his head in and said loudly, "What's all this about noises on a tape?"

For a moment Alan was hidden in the forest of pipes, but then he put his head above a rank of Spire Flutes and spoke up excitedly, waving his burnishing knife. "Oh, Homer, I've been so dumb. It's been there all the time, the whole thing, and I never listened. It's on the copy, the music that was on one of the tape recorders when I came into the apartment that first time. I never played it all the way through before. There are voices on it, Rosie and somebody else—a man— and the baby crying."

"Whose was it? Did you recognize it?"

"No, it's too muffled. But Mary says you can get the frequencies unscrambled."

"So she tells me. That's good, it might be a break-through. For Christ's sake, don't lose the tape."

"Oh God, no. I hid it in the apartment where Oates won't come across it. I'll find a technician on Monday and then maybe we'll know who this bastard is."

Homer was crouched double, and his spine was killing him. He began backing out of the narrow opening. "How's the voicing coming? You're almost done?"

"Almost, but it's got to be finished for the Easter service tomorrow. I'll be at it all day. Well, I can't work on it during the concert this evening, but I'll keep at it all night. Hey, Pip, hit it again."

There was a pause. "Pip?" called Alan.

Once again the deep braying note of the F-sharp Contra Bombarde bellowed out of the pipe.

"My God," said Homer.

"You ain't heard nothing yet. Hey, Pip, play the fifth. There, how do you like that? That's a sixty-four-foot resultant."

BOOM, roared the organ. BOOM, BOOM, BOOM.

"Hey, Jim," yelled Alan, deep inside the case among the Spire Flutes, "how do you like that?"

There was no answer. Homer turned his head, but no one was sitting at the back of the balcony. James Castle was gone.

CHAPTER 67

*Cursed, damned, reviled, and destroyed be . . . everyone who
strives against Thy will.*   Martin Luther

I t was all very well to talk about working all day long,
but Alan couldn't do it. First he lost his helping hand at
the keyboard because Pip Tower had a doctor's appointment, and then by midafternoon he didn't trust his fingers.
He had been up all night, and he was exhausted. If his knife
slipped, it could ruin an entire thirty-two-foot pipe.

He walked wearily back to Rosie's apartment, picturing
the comfortable sofa and its soft cushions, hoping to avoid
a miserable scene with Harold Oates.

But when he opened the door he was shocked to discover that the apartment had been ransacked. Drawers had
been pulled out, their contents dumped. Half the books
were on the floor. Rosie's collection of cassettes had been
scattered right and left.

"Harold?" shouted Alan. There was no answer. Alan
looked for him in the bedroom. He found only a bare mattress. The sheets and blankets were tumbled on the rug.

The kitchen too was a mess. Everything in the cupboards
had been jumbled right and left. With a sinking heart Alan
climbed on the counter and looked at the top of the cupboard. But it was all right. The precious cassette was still
there. Had Oates been looking for it? Was the shouting on
the end of the tape the voice of Harold Oates?

Alan left the cassette where it was and spent the next
hour putting the apartment to rights. Adrenaline coursed
through his veins. He no longer needed a nap.

CHAPTER 68

These are knavish tricks and sophistical inventions.
                                        Martin Luther

For the Saturday night performance of Bach's *St. John Passion* in the Church of the Commonwealth, Mary Kelly wore a pair of pink harem pants over orange tights.

"It's strange," said Homer, admiring the general effect, "in that outfit you ought to look ridiculous, but you don't. I can't understand it. You look like Queen Victoria opening Parliament."

The evening was balmy. People drifted into the Church of the Commonwealth from the street, where magnolia petals lay on the ground like fragments of smashed porcelain.

The second performance was like the first. Once again Harold Oates failed to show up, but James Castle cheerfully took his place for a second time. He sat beaming at the or-

gan console while Barbara swung her arms and guided her singers through one tricky transition after another and the instrumentalists fiddled and puffed.

Alan watched grimly as Castle played the first measures in company with the wind instruments and the strings. Damn Oates anyway. He was out on a bender somewhere. All of Alan's tender devotion to the reclamation of the great man was going straight to hell.

When the concert was over, Homer and Mary Kelly strode down the aisle while everyone else was applauding, and plucked Alan out of the back row. "We want to hear that tape," said Mary.

"And I don't suppose you have any beer in the fridge?" said Homer. "All this frenzied Christianity, it makes a person thirsty."

But as soon as Alan unlocked the door of Rosie's apartment, it was apparent that something was wrong. Homer put his head in and sniffed. "That's a funny smell."

Alan thrust past him into the living room. "Look," he said, "the floor's wet."

Mary walked around, avoiding the damp places. "It's not wet all over, just here and there. It's the way my mother used to sprinkle laundry."

They stood bewildered, then all of them jumped back as a little flame shot up from the floor.

"Polka dots," cried Homer. "The wet spots are like polka dots. Those other fires, they started from polka dots, that's what the man said. It's some incendiary chemical mixed with water. When the water evaporates, the other stuff ignites."

Alan picked up Rosie's watering can and dumped it on the flame, which sizzled and went out. Mary ran to the kitchen and snatched up the kettle from the stove.

Homer grabbed it from her and dumped it on one of the damp spots on the rug. "They have to stay wet. They only start burning when they dry out."

"Watch out, there's another," cried Alan, as another blaze erupted under the harpsichord. Two more flickered up in opposite corners of the room.

Clumsily the three of them rushed back and forth, bumping into furniture and colliding with one another while new flames sprang up beside the sofa, the table, the bookcase. A blaze behind an armchair almost got away from them. For the next ten minutes they trampled small fires and soaked them with water.

"God," cried Alan, "the bedroom." It was a mass of small flames.

"Get those curtains," cried Mary, snatching at the smoldering bedspread.

There was no time to call for help. But when all the fires were out in kitchen and living room and bedroom and baby's room and bathroom, in closets and back entry and front hall, Homer picked up the phone. "As soon as they dry out they'll burn again. That chemical stuff, it's got to be neutralized somehow."

They waited, exhausted, looking at each other. Their faces were sooty, their shoes soaked. The apartment was drenched and scorched. Automatically Alan tramped on a final spurt of flame behind the rubber plant. With a start he remembered the tape. He ran into the kitchen, slipping and sliding on the wet tiles, clambered up on the counter and fumbled on the top of the cupboard.

The cassette was still there. Thankfully he put it in his pocket and climbed down again as the fire apparatus from Boylston Street came howling along Commonwealth Avenue.

Homer took charge, hailing them in, shouting his explanations, heaving another pitcher of water at a new blaze. At once the place was full of big men in rubber coats.

"The harpsichord," said Alan. "The water will ruin it."

Together they lugged it outside, struggling through firefighters and snarled hoses and Mrs. Garboyle and a stream of excited teenagers from the rooms upstairs. Then Alan helped Mary and Homer wedge it into their station wagon.

"Oates," said Homer, slamming down the rear door, "where the hell do we look for Oates?"

"Kansas Street," suggested Alan. "He's got a girlfriend there, and there's a couple of other guys. Twenty-four Kansas Street. It's a shelter for homeless people."

They squeezed into the car and Mary swerved recklessly away from the curb, while the harpsichord jiggled in the back, giving out plangent chords.

But Oates wasn't to be found at Kansas Street. "Gawd," said Tom, "we ain't seen him in a week."

"Where the fuck do you suppose he's at?" said Dick.

"That is a question the answer to which I would very much like to be informed of," said Dora O'Doyle.

Disappointed, they gave up on Oates. Mary and Homer drove Alan back to Rosie's apartment. The fire apparatus was just pulling away.

Homer and Mary followed Alan inside. Then, while Alan shuffled around dolefully among the wreckage of Rosie's possessions, Homer called Lieutenant Detective Campbell and urged him to set up a serious search for the missing Oates. "Try the bars around Copley Square. And all the local shelters, the Pine Street Inn."

The Kellys went home. Alan locked up the apartment and ran down the street to the church.

The Contra Bombardes were waiting. He had a long night's work ahead of him.

CHAPTER 69

One day will come a thick black cloud out of which will issue three flashes of lightning, and a clap of thunder will be heard, and in a moment, heaven and earth will be covered with confusion.   Martin Luther

The pandemonium was colossal. Alan ran his feet up and down the pedals, laughing, while the building rocked around him. The massive voices of the Contra Bombarde were majestic pronouncements from on high, booming decrees declaring authority over man and beast, they were proclamations of universal justice. *HEAR ME,* roared the thirty-two-foot pipes, rumbling four octaves below middle C, vibrating on the fifth, the octave, the fourth above the octave. Alan coupled in the sixteen-foot Prestant and a couple of trumpets and DIV INSP, just for the hell of it. Finally he pulled out the Bärpfeiffe, which was like a bear dancing.

The uproar was deafening. And it was all wrong. The unvoiced pipes were slow of speech and ragged. Alan shut off the extra stops and got to work, moving from organ bench to the forest of pipes and back, applying his tools to the tongues of the Contra Bombardes, hammering them delicately, stroking them with his burnishing knife.

It was wonderfully still in the church. There wasn't even a night watchman to look in and say hello, because the Ph.D. candidate was away on his Easter break. Alan was alone, working among the pipes in the light of a lamp hooked over a nail. The forty-watt bulb over the keyboards was a tiny glimmer in the cavernous darkness.

It was four hours before he laid down his tools and rubbed his eyes and crawled out of the organ case and stood up straight and stretched, arching his tired back. Sleepily he

thumped himself down on the bench, tried the last note
and found it perfect.

The Easter music lay on the rack, ready for the morning
service. Alan chose a set of stops, including the newly
voiced Contra Bombarde. Then he opened a folder and
leafed through it, looking for Number Seventeen.

Attracted by the clamor of the new pedal pipes, Harold
Oates fumbled with his collection of keys until he found the
one for the side door of the church. Stepping silently into
the hugeness of the dark chamber, he could see Starr on the
balcony silhouetted against the feeble lamp above the music
rack. The corners of the room were thickets of shadow.

As Alan began to play, Oates recognized the music at
once. It was a famous chorale prelude from Bach's Little
Organ Book, "In Thee Is Joy." Energetically the measures
bounded forward. Exuberant scales ran up and down in the
left hand, and the pedals repeated a single mighty passage:

Oates stood grinning in the dark, listening to the racing
tumult of right and left hands, while the pedal repeated the
same thunderous blessing again and again, *In thee is joy, joy,
joy.*

Joy was the right word. Joy was what it was. All the wild
rancor in the soul of Harold Oates gave way to the only joy
he had known in all his life, that of Diapason and Mixture,
of Gemshorn and Regal and Rohrpipe. He moved forward
and felt for the back of a pew and gripped it. The wood
shivered in his fingers. The floor moved under his feet.

Only then was he aware that someone else was listening.
A human shape moved in the dark. It was very near, gazing
upward at Starr as he piled on more ranks of pipes. The
crazy kid was summoning all the strength and variety and
power of the organ to magnify the tumbling merriment of

his rushing fingers, while his feet romped on the pedals and the great Principals and Contra Bombardes bellowed the same mighty phrase.

Joy, joy, and joy again. The speaking mouths of a thousand pipes whistled and wheezed and shouted and sang to Harold Oates, and he raised his hands in wonder. The building swayed. Instinctively he moved forward as the floor rolled beneath him. The other listener too raised his hand in a haunted gesture, a mystic tribute, reaching toward the source of the splendor.

The floor moved again, shaken by the long waves rumbling within it. Again Oates stumbled forward until he was close enough to see that the reaching hand of the other man was not held up in awe. It was holding something, and now the other hand came up to grasp the thing in both fists.

The music swarmed around them, the building shook, the spongy floor sagged and Oates shouted, "No," and threw himself at the gun as it went off. The reeling shape turned, and in another blast of noise and fire the rejoicing of Harold Oates died away forever.

At the organ Alan heard the shout and the shot and the *crack* as the projectile struck a pipe beside his head. The second shot was lost in the splitting noise of the timbers under the floor. The pilings under the east wall were crumbling into dust. The granite sills collapsed. Behind the pulpit the east wall crumpled and caved inward. A single block from the vault over the pulpit pitched down with a crash, and then the rest roared down together in an avalanche of stone.

In the balcony Alan tottered to his feet and stumbled to the west wall, taking refuge in a brick archway beneath the window. With a wildly beating heart he watched the second bay of vaulting droop and fall, the cut stones thundering down, plummeting like rocks in an avalanche. For a breathless moment the third vault held, and then it too went down in a cannonade of falling voussoirs, ribs and keystones. The vast wooden roof fell too, cracking and twisting sideways, tumbling in a burst of snapped bolts like rifle fire, slamming down in a jungle of felled timber and a shattering cascade of slate shingles from the roof. The shingles rattled and bounced and lay still.

The church was no longer in darkness. Looking up, Alan could see the limpid sky of morning. He shrank back against the wall and stared fearfully at the last remaining vault, which rose above his head in sexpartite perfection, poised on intersecting ribs. The architect of the Church of the Commonwealth had visited the continent in the year 1885, and he had come home enraptured by the stone vaulting of the Romanesque churches of southern France. Solidly, then, he had designed the four bays of his own vaulted ceiling, grandly he had buttressed and supported them like those of the ancient churches—but now only one of his massive vaults remained, clinging to the high walls south, west and north, trembling in empty air to the east, thrusting outward into nothingness its tons of arching stone.

Alan closed his eyes and waited, but the noise was dying away. Opening his eyes, he looked up fearfully. The vault was holding. Somewhere over his head the tower was still standing calmly erect. Below him dust rose in billowing clouds from the wreckage, thinning and dissolving, floating higher and higher into the pale morning sky.

The only sound was the heaving of the bellows. A single row of flue pipes whispered and sighed. Alan smiled. The lungs of the pipe organ were intact. In the midst of chaos and destruction it was still alive, and so was he.

The stairway from the balcony to the vestibule was in perfect order. Alan stumbled downstairs, his legs caving beneath him, and found his way outdoors. To the east the sun rose over Boston Common and the Public Garden, over the Ritz Carlton Hotel and Arlington Street and the trees along the avenue.

It was Easter morning.

EASTER

❖ ❖ ❖ ❖ ❖

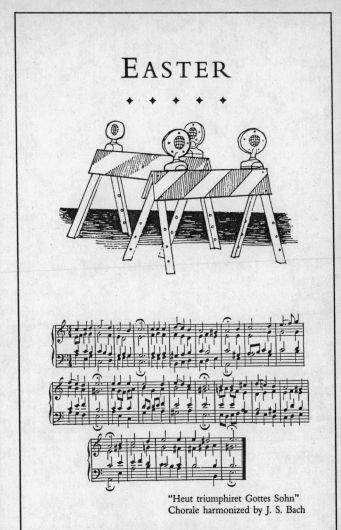

"Heut triumphiret Gottes Sohn"
Chorale harmonized by J. S. Bach

Crumbled to dust is Satan's power,
Vanished his passion to devour.
Alleluia! Alleluia!
By valor strong our champion brave
Flingeth our foe into his grave.
Alleluia! Alleluia!

◆ ◆ ◆ ◆

CHAPTER 70

*When we read that Judas hanged himself, that his belly burst
in pieces, and that his bowels fell out, we may take this as
a sample how it will go with all Christ's enemies.*

Martin Luther

The phone call that woke Martin Kraeger was from
Alan Starr. "What?" said Kraeger sleepily. "Oh, I
see. Thank you."
For some reason the news of the collapse of the Church
of the Commonwealth fitted right in with his apocalyptic
dream, and it didn't surprise him. Only when he got out of
bed and stood up did understanding smite him. Thunderstruck, he hauled on his clothes and plunged out the door
into the freshness of the morning on Dartmouth Street, and
began running in the direction of the church. As he turned
onto Clarendon he could hear distant cries and the spiral-
ling whine of overlapping sirens. Someone shouted at him
from a window, "What happened?"

It was like the night of the fire. Kraeger had run toward
the burning church with the same dread in his breast.

"The phone's ringing," said Mary, sitting up in bed. She
looked at her watch. It was only five o'clock.

"Mmph," said Homer.

Mary got out of bed and went out into the hall. A moment later she was back, walking slowly.

Something in her step alerted Homer. He lifted his head
and stared at her white face.

"That was Alan. He says the church has fallen down."

Donald Woody was already there. He nodded at Kraeger
and went on talking calmly to a uniformed policeman about
turning off the utilities. "It's all okay downcellar." Woody

gestured at the office building, which was still intact. "I turned everything off—electricity, gas, oil burner." He pointed at a fountain of water rising from the wreckage. "That geyser over there, they'll have to turn it off in the street."

There was a traffic jam at the intersection of Clarendon and Commonwealth. Barriers had been thrown up, yellow sawhorses with blinking lights.

Kraeger tried to get closer to the heap of shattered wood and stone that was his church, but he was only one of a crowd being shoved back onto Commonwealth Avenue. A couple of men in hard hats were throwing down more sawhorses, shutting off the westbound lane. An officer in an orange tunic stood in front of them, turning cars into the eastbound lane on the other side of the park, where two more cops blew shrill whistles and made huge pointing gestures, urging the traffic into two slow-moving streams.

Someone gripped Kraeger's arm. It was Alan Starr. His face was ashen. "Last night," he said, "all those people in the building last night."

"I know," said Kraeger. He was unable to say anything more. Together they looked at the heap of rock that could have fallen during the concert, crushing eight hundred lovers of sacred music, forty choir members, six soloists, a conductor, an organist, and twenty players of miscellaneous musical instruments. Kraeger found his voice. "You were here when it happened? Are you all right?"

"I was up there." Alan pointed to the balcony, which thrust out into the sunlight under the single remaining vault. "Listen, Martin, it was my fault. I turned on all the stops at once. All those thirty-two-foot pipes, they were all open at once, sending tremendous long sounds waves into the walls. I could feel everything shaking. All this"—he gestured at the wreckage—"it was all my fault."

Traffic was stalled, gridlocked. Frustrated drivers sounded furious horns. Martin had to shout. "No, no, it couldn't have been the organ. Not just the organ."

A police officer yelled at them angrily, "Get back." He bellowed at the crowd gathering in the blocked-off street, "Hey, you, all of you, move back. Come on, get back."

Alan and Martin had to retreat behind a barrier halfway down the block, along with a throng of inquisitive strangers who had come out of nowhere.

Someone plucked Alan's sleeve, an important-looking man in a business suit. "Mallory," he said, introducing himself, "building inspector. You're the one who was here, the witness? Was anybody else in the building? Like a janitor? Anybody?"

"I told them already, there wasn't anybody. I think I was all alone. I mean, I don't know about anybody else. There wasn't any night watchman, not last night."

"Good," said Mallory, turning to go. "I just wanted to be sure."

"Except, wait." Alan glanced at Kraeger. "Just before the roof fell in, I thought—"

"What?" said Mallory impatiently. "What did you think?"

"It was probably just the beginning of the collapse, a timber snapping, but I thought—" Alan braced himself and said firmly, "Someone shot at me. First there was a shout, and then I heard a shot. The bullet struck one of the organ pipes about a foot over my head. It made a hole in the pipe. Then everything fell down. But the expended slug must still be there somewhere. And if I'm right, somebody must be under all that rubble, whoever fired the gun."

Mallory stared at him, then turned away abruptly and gave an order.

They found Oates first. His body had been crushed by the collapse of the easternmost vault, but his face had lain in a hollow. It was white with dust, but unhurt.

Alan knelt in the cleared space around the shattered body. Oates's eyes were closed, his mouth curved in a smile. It was a strange smile, not a grimace, not one of the cruel grins with which Alan was so familiar.

"This is the man who fired at you?" said Lieutenant Detective Campbell. "Do you know him?"

Alan stroked Oates's thin hair in sorrow. "Of course I know him. It's Harold Oates. He was the greatest organist in the—oh, Harold, Harold."

"Uh-oh," said Campbell, "what have we got here?" He brushed the white dust from Oates's forehead, revealing a small hole. "I thought so. Look at that. Twenty-two-caliber, same as the slug in that organ pipe. Point-blank, probably. Where the hell's the firearm?" He turned to the men who stood at one side, looking on grimly. "There's got to be somebody else under here. Can't be far away. Keep looking. Hands only, no machinery."

The driver of the backhoe threw up his hands. "Christ! When can I get to work?"

By the time the second corpse was uncovered, Homer Kelly had arrived on the scene. He stood in the rubble with Alan and Martin, looking down silently at the crushed bloody body and the broken skull, as Campbell inspected the shattered target pistol beside the smashed right hand.

"Who is it?" whispered Homer, who didn't recognize the flattened face.

"Friend of mine," murmured Alan. "You met him, Philip Tower."

"But why would he fire at you?" said Kraeger.

"And Oates?" said Homer. "Why would he want to kill Harold Oates?"

"I'm not sure why he wanted to kill me. But as for killing Oates"—Alan looked at Homer gravely—"I think Pip shot him because Oates was trying to save my life."

◆ ◆ ◆ ◆

CHAPTER 71

A mighty fortress is our God,
A bulwark never failing . . .
Hymn by Martin Luther

Kraeger and Alan and Homer sat hunched on folding chairs in Donald Woody's basement office. Woody handed around cups of steaming coffee.

"He was listening," said Alan. "Remember? Pip was sitting at the organ when I told you about the noises on the cassette."

"Of course," said Homer. "I remember him now. And he heard you tell me you'd hidden it in Rosie's apartment. So he went there and ransacked the place."

"But he didn't find it, so he went back later and tried to set the apartment on fire, hoping to burn up the cassette along with everything else."

"And when that didn't work either, he came after you with a target pistol."

Martin Kraeger laughed grimly. "It reminds me of the martyrdoms of saints. What do you do with an aggravating and disagreeable saint who won't stop being a pain in the neck? You throw her in the fire, but unfortunately she refuses to burn, so you dump her in the water, only she won't drown, so you stick her full of arrows like a pincushion, but she goes right on praying, so in desperation you cut off her head, and that always works."

Alan's hand trembled on his coffee cup. "I owe my life to Harold Oates. He must have come to the church to help me with the voicing, and then he saw Pip getting ready to fire, and he shouted at him—I heard him shout—so the shot missed me. So Pip killed him, and then he would have fired at me again, but the vaults came down."

"But how could it have happened?" said Woody. "Everything collapsing like that? It couldn't have been the organ. I mean, you hear about high notes shattering glass, but I never heard of a pipe organ shaking down a building."

"I suppose it was the pilings," said Kraeger, gloomily shaking his head. "The pilings must have dried out." He looked at Donald Woody, trying to keep the note of accusation out of his voice. "Have you checked the water level lately? I suspect it must have gone way down."

Woody looked at him, bewildered. "Pilings? What pilings?"

There was a stunned silence. "The pilings under the church," said Kraeger. "The whole Back Bay is built on pilings, wooden pilings, because it's all filled land."

Woody's face turned gray in the light of the fluorescent ceiling fixtures. "I never heard of any pilings. I don't know what you're talking about."

"But I wrote it all down. Last summer, before my vacation. I wrote a whole big thick— You mean you never got my list of directions?"

"Directions? You didn't leave me any directions. I had to work everything out for myself. I remember, I was kind of surprised that nobody told me what to do."

Martin stared at him. "But I gave them to Loretta. She was supposed to give them to you. You know, type them up and give them to you when you came in, on your first day at work."

"Well, she didn't. I asked her if there was any sort of job description, to sort of tell me what to do, and she said maybe I'd find some down here in my office, but there weren't any."

"For Christ's sake," murmured Homer.

Kraeger jumped up and strode across the room to Woody's fish tank. The goldfish were circling idly behind the sparkling glass, unconcerned with the fall of the church.

It occurred to Martin insanely that they were nondenominational goldfish who didn't give a damn whether the
church remained standing or fell straight to hell. He shook
his head in wonder at the consequences of his failure to fire
the abominable Loretta.

Then he turned to Woody, who had risen and was standing with a stricken face. Martin pointed at one of the metal
lids in the floor.

"Look," he said gently, "that thing in the floor, there's a
pipe under it, going down into the fill. It's an observation
well. You lower a measuring tape into it, so you can find
out where the water table is, and if it's below the tops of the
pilings, you raise the level with a hose, so they don't dry
out. You mean, you didn't know what the metal disks were
here for? And the manhole in the furnace room?"

Donald Woody had been a solid rock of support all
morning. He had been a good right hand to the police department, the firefighters, the building inspector, the street
crew from the Water and Sewer Commission. Now he was
shattered. "Christ, no, I didn't know. Nobody told me. I'm
from Kansas. We build on stone foundations in Kansas." His
knees buckled, and he had to sit down. "Oh, God, it's my
fault. All those people last night, they could all have been
killed, and it's my fault."

"It sounds to me," said Homer wisely, "like somebody
else's fault, namely that woman Loretta Fawcett's."

"No, no," said Kraeger, "it's not anybody's fault but mine.
I should have fired her long ago. I gave her the handwritten
list of directions to type up, only she didn't type them up
because she was too busy embroidering pussycats or something, so she never did it, so you never got the list, and then
I never checked with you because you were doing such a
bangup job of keeping the place in perfect running order. I
should have realized Loretta never does anything right. It's
all my fault."

"It doesn't matter whose fault it is," said Homer. "What matters is what to do now." He looked at Alan. "You've still got the cassette?"

Alan patted his pocket. "I sure do."

"We've got to get it unscrambled. We've got to find out more about this kid Philip Tower. And we've got to find Rosie. Come on, Alan, it's ten-thirty. There's a lot of stuff we've got to do."

"Ten-thirty!" Kraeger leaped up. "My God, it's Easter Sunday."

Homer gaped at him. "Somebody tell this man his church fell down."

"No, no, it's all right. Come on, Woody, let's work something out."

Outside in the park across the street, they found the entire congregation of the Church of the Commonwealth. Some were dressed in their Easter finery, having come to church without knowing what had happened. Everybody was there—Edith Frederick, Barbara Inch and her singers, all the deacons, all the members of the committees for music, religious education, outreach, stewardship, all the church school teachers, and of course all the ordinary parishioners who came to church every Sunday, and also the ones who seldom really got there, having decided to stay home in bed. There were whole families swarming in the park with their fidgeting excited children. Even people who thought of the church only as a place to be married and buried had come running to see it in ruins.

They were all shocked, and some were weeping. They craned their necks to see across the street the rock-filled hole that had once been their church, while around them the impacted traffic clogged the avenue and police whistles shrieked above the mutter of engines idling in low gear and the disgruntled blowing of horns.

At once Martin was engulfed in tearful embraces. Momentarily, at least, his sins were forgotten. Disentangling himself, he turned to Barbara Inch. "I'm not going to preach," he told her. "Why don't we just sing?"

So Barbara ran into the office building to collect the discarded hymnbooks stored in the music room. Coming back down with a teetering pile she almost collided with Woody, who was dragging a trolley of folding chairs. In a moment the books were passed from hand to hand and the older parishoners settled in chairs. Barbara whispered to Martin, "What about hymn number three-six-three?"

Among the motorists stuck in traffic on Commonwealth Avenue were a husband and wife from Brookline, trying to make their way into the North End to visit their daughter. "Oh, Henry, look," said the wife, "it's the church that fell down. We just heard about it on the radio. Listen, they're all singing. See that? They're singing on the sidewalk. Isn't that *dear?*"

Her husband snorted. "What's that they're singing, 'A Mighty Fortress'? Some fortress! Look at it, it's a pile of rubble. I don't know what they've got to sing about. The place is totalled. You couldn't build a structure like that this day and age for twenty million dollars. No way."

Henry was a building engineer, and he spoke from experience. But he reckoned without the treasurer of the Church of the Commonwealth, Kenneth Possett.

Ken was a changed man. While the other men and women of the congregation sang with Barbara Inch and prayed with Martin Kraeger and embraced one another, sobbing, in a transport of emotion, Ken stood at one side doing figures in his head. When the impromptu service was over, he marched up to Kraeger and clapped him on the back. "Martin, old man, don't worry about a thing." Ken's cheeks were like cherries, he beamed as though a thousand tons of rock were not lying in a hole across the street, along with a million shards of stained glass and the splinters of a hundred pews and the smashed remnants of an antique pulpit and the wreck of a dozen marble memorials and the tatters of the precious painting of the divinely inspired Walter Wigglesworth.

Martin was stunned. He couldn't believe it. Was this the same Kenneth Possett who had opposed him at every meeting of the church council, who had cavilled at every expense and taken him to task over the repair of Oates's teeth, who had jibbed at bills for hundreds of dollars and gasped at expenses of thousands, and accused him of hiring a prostitute and molesting his little daughter? Somehow the disaster had turned the man around. Ken was in his element, he was galvanized, he was ready to go.

Mrs. Frederick was at Ken's side. "Dear Martin," said Edith, her old voice trembling, "we're forming a committee."

CHAPTER 72

They who take to force, give a great blow to the Gospel.
                                                    Martin Luther

I n one of Philip Tower's blood-soaked pockets Lieutenant Detective Campbell found a driver's license with his
address. "Anybody know he's got a wife? If there's relatives, I got to inform them what happened, and then somebody's got to talk to them. You know, find out what they
know."

"I don't think he's married," said Alan doubtfully.

"Well, whatever. I'll find out if there's anybody. Usually
everybody's got somebody."

In Philip's case the somebody turned out to be a mother,
Mrs. Howard Tower, living at the same Brookline address.

"Jesus," said Campbell, hanging up the phone, "I wish to
God somebody else would interview the woman. She went
ballistic. Screamed at me."

"Well, what do you expect?" said Homer reasonably.
"You told her her son is dead."

"Sure, I know, but this was— I mean it was really— Hey,
Homer, how about it? Why don't you handle it? Right
away, okay? We need a report right away."

"Me?" Homer was taken by surprise. His curiosity rose
to the surface. "Well, all right. I'll bring Starr along. Friend
of the deceased. Where does Philip's mother live?"

Campbell wanted a quick report, but even Homer Kelly
didn't have the gall to interrogate Mrs. Howard Tower on
the very day of her son's death. "We'll go tomorrow," he
told Alan. "Tell you what, we'll bring Mary along. She's
good at soothing tortured souls and comforting the be-
reaved."

Mary didn't want to go. "Oh, Homer, the idea of talking to the mother of a recently deceased murderer doesn't appeal to me at all. She'll be in a pitiful emotional state."

"My dear, that's why we need you."

"Womanly sympathy, is that it? Well, why can't men by sympathetic?" But she gave in.

They picked up Alan at the church. It was only the day after Easter, but already a scaffolding had been erected. Huge diagonal timbers buttressed the tower and the one remaining vault.

"There he is," said Mary, pointing up at the balcony where Alan and Donald Woody were struggling with huge sheets of plastic, draping them over the organ console and the pipes, protecting them from the weather. The plastic sheets kept flapping up in the wind, refusing to be fastened down.

Alan glanced down at them and yelled, "Just a sec."

"I've got it," said Woody. He grasped a loose corner and stapled it to the floor with a bang.

Alan crowded in next to Homer on the front seat of Mary's car. "Thank God, now I can stop worrying about the organ." He pointed down the avenue. "Straight on. Take Beacon Street at Kenmore Square."

Mary glanced at him as she pulled away from the curb. He was obviously wrought up. His fingers gripped his knees. Reaching across Homer, she squeezed his arm. "Do you think they'll know what happened to Rosie?"

Homer made a discouraging noise. "Pip Tower's mother may not know anything at all. How many first-degree murderers talk things over with their female relatives? I doubt they sit down and chat about things over the teacups."

Homer was half right and half wrong. Philip Tower's family had not discussed things quietly at teatime—they had screamed them at each other, day in and day out. Mrs. Tower was expecting them. Her small face was elaborately made up, her great hips shrouded in yards of fleecy fabric.

She led them into the kitchen and introduced another member of the family, her daughter Helen, who sat in a wheelchair and looked up at them with eyes puffy from crying.

"Lieutenant Detective Campbell has spoken to you, I believe," said Homer to Mrs. Tower with formal politeness.

At once she began to talk. "He didn't understood a thing. He didn't understand my boy at all. I told him Sonny was a genius, but do you think he was listening? All he wanted to know was where Sonny worked, the copy center and Boston City Hospital, and then he kept asking about fires, things like that, and I just kept saying, God, I didn't know, what did I know? I didn't know anything! But he kept asking and asking. Police! I should have known. What can you expect from law enforcement in the city of Boston? God!"

Homer stopped listening. He was mesmerized by Mrs. Tower's large staring eyes. They reminded him of someone. They were rimmed with black, and her eyelashes stuck stiffly up like wires. Of course, she was like the woman who guarded evidence for the Boston Police Department, the one who had demonstrated the uses of the cosmetics in the scorched and blackened pocketbook.

The cosmetics must have belonged to Mrs. Tower. It was she who had supplied the contents of the pocketbook. Homer turned his attention back to what she was saying. Words gushed out of her, whining words of self-pity. The girl in the wheelchair crouched with bowed head while her mother poured out the misery of her life, the injustice of her lot, the sacrifices she had made for others.

"Of course my children get all their talent from me. I was a coloratura soprano, I sang for the Boston Pops when I was seventeen, but then I made the mistake of getting married, and after the kids were born I lost my beautiful voice. The anesthetic, you know, it ruined my voice. I could have sued for malpractice. I could have gotten millions."

Homer felt bewitched. He unstuck his eyes from Mrs. Tower's and looked at the ceiling. At once she transferred her gaze to Mary. "My husband was not a good provider. I had to work as a practical nurse. I lived for my children. They were both so gifted. Helen played the violin. She was a genius, my poor little girl."

There was a murmur from the young woman in the wheelchair. Mrs. Tower glowered at her. "What did you say?"

"I said, stop, please stop."

Mrs. Tower did not stop. She turned her headlamps on Alan. "Oh, we had problems. Did any woman ever bear such a cross? My husband, did you hear about my husband? Huntington's disease! He had Huntington's disease for fifteen years before he died. Look at Helen, she's got it now, she got it from him. She'll be a basket case too, just like him. Bedpans, how would you like to spend your life changing bedpans?"

Homer tried to turn the agonizing monologue in a useful direction. "Mrs. Tower, can you tell us anything about Rosalind Hall?"

The flood of words stopped. Mrs. Tower looked craftily away. "Never heard of her."

It was Alan's turn. "We happen to know, Mrs. Tower, that Pip went to Rosalind's house on the night she disappeared. We have a tape recording of her screams as he dragged her away against her will. There was blood on the floor."

Mrs. Tower blinked, and looked sidelong at her daughter, who had closed her eyes and clenched her fists. "I don't know anything about that. He never told me." Then she burst out, "My poor Sonny, he was so gifted." She looked at Alan spitefully, and raised her voice. "And they gave his job to you, the job he should have had!"

Doggedly Homer returned to the subject of Rosie. "Do you mean to say you never saw the young woman called Rosalind Hall?"

Mrs. Tower looked at him sullenly. "I don't know anything about any Rosalind Hall. My boy didn't need women. He had his mother, he had his sister."

And then Pip's sister screamed at her mother. She writhed in her wheelchair, and shrieked, "Oh, God in heaven, shut up." She threw her head back and closed her eyes as if praying, and shook her crumpled fists at the ceiling. "Oh God, oh God, oh God."

Mrs. Tower leaped to her feet and snatched up a bottle from the kitchen counter. "She needs her medication. Helen, it's time for your medication."

"No, no," wept Helen, "no, no." But her mother came forward with a spoonful of brown liquid and gripped Helen's head and brought the spoon to her mouth. Helen wrenched her head away and threw up her arm, knocking the spoon out of her mother's hand.

"Sometimes," said Mrs. Tower through her teeth, "we have to use force. Now, Helen, hold still." Pinning her daughter's fragile arms together with one hand, she held the bottle to her lips.

It was terrible to see. Helen fought and tossed her head from side to side, her mouth clenched shut. The liquid ran down her chin.

Mary touched Mrs. Tower's shoulder. "Wait," she said. "Let her alone. She'll be all right."

Panting, Mrs. Tower stepped back. Helen reached forward and gripped Mary's hand.

"Why don't I take her around the block?" Mary's voice was calm, ordinary. Homer looked at his wife in wonder. Alan stood up to help, as Mary released the brake and began pushing the wheelchair out of the room. It was the most natural thing in the world, as if she had taken Helen for a spin a thousand times before.

"Now, listen here," said Mrs. Tower, her voice rising in anger, "Helen, remember what Mother said. You hear me, Helen? Answer me, Helen!"

Helen said nothing as Mary skimmed her out into the hall. Alan dodged ahead of them and opened the door and helped lower the wheelchair to the sidewalk. Then to his surprise Helen thanked him. Her ravaged face cleared in a heavenly smile, and she said, "The xylophone."

"The xylophone?"

"It's in the kitchen drawer."

"We'll be back sooner or later," said Mary breezily. Alan watched them speed merrily away along the sidewalk, bouncing over uneven places, leaving the house of torment behind, the tyranny of the mother, the controlling medication. He had the impression of escape, of freedom, of a couple of tramps taking to the open road.

He grinned, and went back indoors, to find Mrs. Tower delivering a lecture on the subject of her daughter's unreliability. "Poor child, her mind is gone. She doesn't know the difference between truth and falsehood. I hate to say this about my own daughter, but she's a liar. It's her illness. Huntington patients, they all lie."

Homer persevered. "Rosalind Hall was not burned up in that car, was she, Mrs. Tower? That burned body was somebody else, wasn't it? Tell me, how did your son get hold of it?"

Mrs. Tower shook her head and closed her huge eyes. Her thousand-legged lashes with their caked mascara lay on her cheeks. "You're not going to get me to say anything when I don't know anything."

But when Alan opened the kitchen drawer beside the sink and found the toy xylophone and thrust it under her nose, she lost her nerve. "Oh, Lord," she said.

"It was Charley's, wasn't it?" said Alan. "He was here. Rosie was here. Where are they now?"

Mrs. Tower stared at the xylophone dolefully. "Oh, my God."

Triumphant, Homer took the xylophone and ran a finger up the scale. The metal notes tinkled cheerfully. "She was here, the baby was here. Where are they now? Tell us, Mrs. Tower, and then we'll go away and leave you alone. Where is Rosalind Hall?"

Mrs. Tower shriveled and crouched. She lowered her eyes and stared at the floor. "In Germany. She went to Germany."

"She's in Germany?" Alan whispered it, hardly daring to say it aloud. "Then she's all right?"

"Her? Oh, *she's* all right. Thanks to me. How do you think I felt when Sonny brought home a stranger with a fractured skull? *Me,* he expected *me* to bring her back to life. It was up to me! After what I'd already been through with my husband and Helen! But I did it. She can thank me she's still alive. Only she never did. She never thanked me. *Oh, Mrs. Tower, you saved my life, I'm so grateful.* Never, not once." Mrs. Tower broke off, and her eyes shifted away. Her self-pity poisoned the air.

Alan could hardly contain his excitement. "Where is she in Germany, Mrs. Tower?"

She looked at him slyly. "Sonny didn't want me to know. He knew I'd write, asking for money. But I knew where she was, and I knew what she called herself, her new name, so I wrote every now and then, and usually she sent something, not much. Well, she owed me, right? I saved her life, didn't I? If I tell you where she lives, will you let me alone?" Eagerly Mrs. Tower lifted the strap of a large hand-bag from a hook on the wall, and groped inside. "Here it is. Heidelberg. She's living in Heidelberg."

She handed the slip of paper to Alan. He looked at Rosie's new name and address, and learned them at once by heart.

◆ ◆ ◆ ◆

CHAPTER 73

*From deep distress I call to Thee,
O God, I pray Thou hear me!*
Hymn by Martin Luther

"What did she say?" Homer wanted to know. "Did Helen tell you anything? She must have said *something*."

Mary shook her head. "Wait," she said. "Not now."

Alan and Homer sat in silence while Mary drove fiercely along Beacon Street, plunging around double-parked delivery vans, jolting to a stop at intersections. Waiting for a green light in Kenmore Square, she turned angrily to Homer. "She won the Prix de Rome, she was so good. There she was in Paris, off to a brilliant start, and then she began noticing the symptoms of her father's disease. It's inherited, Huntington's, and each child has a fifty percent chance of getting it. But it's not just the disease." The light changed. Mary jerked the car forward and glowered at the oncoming cars.

"You mean her mother," said Homer softly. "Life with a disappointed coloratura."

Mary thumped the steering wheel. "The torments of hell, that's what it's been like."

"Well, that was pretty obvious," said Alan. "Look, why don't you come up to my place? How are your brakes? It's really steep on my hill."

Alan's room was a mess. "Sorry," he said, shoving things off the bed, which was the only place to sit down. "Oh, God, I've only got one bottle of beer. Here, we'll divvy it up. I've got some corn chips somewhere."

Mary waved away the beer and the corn chips. She was ready to talk, to pour out everything Helen had told her. "First about the fires."

Homer gasped. "The fires! Was that Philip? The fire in the church, that was his work, wasn't it? It wasn't Rosie, it wasn't Kraeger, it wasn't Castle?"

"Of course it wasn't," said Mary. "Helen said Pip had been setting fires since he was eight years old. First it was just wastebaskets. She'd find a flaming wastebasket full of her dolls. He was paying her back for being her father's favorite. You know, the cute little curly-headed tyke with a tiny violin. Next he burned up the violin."

Homer shook his head sadly. "Pyromania, it's an addiction like gambling. Once you get started, you can't stop."

"Then he got more sophisticated. In high school he studied chemistry and figured out that trick about mixing incendiary material with water, and then he burned down a couple of Baptist churches. This time he was getting back at his parents. They were both strong churchgoing Baptists."

"My God," said Alan.

"Ah, yes," said Homer, remembering the printout from Sergeant Drum's cross-referenced file drawer. "He went to prison for one of those."

"But what about his music?" said Alan. "When did he start playing the organ?"

"I'm coming to that." Mary heaved herself off Alan's bed and began walking around the room, stepping over scattered books and shoes and a nest of coffee cups. "Helen said Pip was musically gifted too, he could play the piano like anything, so after getting out of Concord Reformatory— no, they don't call it a reformatory, what do they call it, Homer?"

"A correctional facility." Homer emptied his bag of corn chips. "Only I doubt they do much correcting, or reforming either. They used to be penitentiaries, only nobody ever repented."

"Anyway," said Mary, "Pip had this musical gift, and he got serious about it and started taking organ lessons. And from then on, he did better and better. There were no more fires. He won a scholarship to the New England Conservatory. They were all so proud of him. By this time his father had lost so much strength he couldn't work any more, so his mother got a job as a practical nurse and supported the family. She really did sacrifice herself, working twelve hours a day while Helen went to Paris and Pip studied with James Castle and won a big national award—"

"Annual competition, American Guild of Organists, big honor." Alan found another bag of chips and handed it to Homer.

Mary sank down on the bed again. "Then everything went to hell. It was Helen's turn to get sick."

Homer offered her the bag of chips. "She was studying in Paris then?"

Mary waved the bag away. "Oh, God, Homer, imagine what it must have been like. She couldn't hold a fiddle bow. She'd watched her father waste away, and now it was her turn. She had to go home and take his place as an invalid in her mother's care—and you've seen what that's like." Restlessly Mary unfolded herself from the bed and went to the window to look down at the cars slowly negotiating the hill, creeping down to Cambridge Street. "It was so extraordinary, listening to her, there in that little park at the end of the block. She sat in that wheelchair gesturing with her cramped little hands and poured it all out. I just stood there leaning against a tree, listening. I hardly had to say a word. She wanted to tell me. She was dying to tell me."

For a minute they were silent. Then Alan asked a sarcastic question. "Was it true her mother could have been an operatic soprano?"

"Oh, I doubt it, don't you?" Mary couldn't keep the scorn out of her voice. "It was just something to add to her list of grievances. Oh, she'd sacrificed for her kids, all right, but I doubt she gave up a great career."

"So from now on everything depended on Pip?" Nervously Alan began picking up dirty dishes from the floor and dumping them in the sink.

Mary handed him Homer's empty glass. "From now on it's pretty sickening. Pip had a few organ students, but it wasn't enough income, so he worked in a copy shop and at Boston City Hospital. Well, you know what hospital orderlies do. They run errands and clean up operating rooms after surgery, grubby jobs like that. But then one day he happened to see James Castle come out of the office of one of the cancer specialists in the hospital, and then the doctor asked Pip to go for Castle's X ray. So on the way back Pip took a look at it, and there was a big shadow on it."

"Stomach cancer," murmured Homer. "Oh, Alan, that reminds me. I found out about that barrel of snakes."

"Snakes? What barrel of snakes?"

"Castle's family. Remember, you told me his mother was yelling at him, and his sister was sick and his whole family were standing around looking green, last Thanksgiving when Martin walked in on them? Well, Castle told Martin what it was all about, and Martin told me. The doctors had told Castle his chances of survival were poor, so he told his family he wasn't going to have the surgery, he was just going to let things take their course. So his mother got all excited and started screaming at him. She wasn't some kind of a hysterical person, she was a normal mother wanting to save her son's life. So he gave in and had the surgery and everything went well."

"What about his sister?" said Alan. "Did she have some kind of dangerous disease too?"

Homer laughed. "The only disease his sister had is called pregnancy. A few days later she gave birth to a nine-pound baby girl. Martin's going to baptize her next week."

Alan tried to gather his wits. "But back before he went to New York to have the surgery, Pip Tower saw his X ray in Boston City Hospital, and so he knew what none of the rest of us knew. He knew Castle was very ill."

"Right, and he assumed he would die."

"Castle would die and his organ bench would be empty. Permanently." Alan picked up a shirt from the floor, then dropped it again. "That's why it was so important to be his substitute. Oh, Jesus, and they appointed me. I played that damnfool music and the stupid committee appointed me."

"Hold it," said Homer. "Let's get back to Boston City Hospital. That's where Pip was working, and that's where the morgue is—the morgue where that useful body came from, the morgue where it turned up again after it had been burned, the very same morgue where somebody made a mistake and sent the body to be cremated. Am I right?"

"Of course you're right." Mary winced and shrugged her shoulders. "Pip knew his way around, he knew how to fill out the proper forms, he knew how to switch them around. It was all his doing."

"Then it was Pip who stole Boozer's hearse and came to the morgue to pick up the body of that poor hooker. He must have had phony papers, just like me. But how did he—ah!" Homer slapped his knee. "He worked in a copy shop. He created the phony papers in the copy shop. Nothing to it."

"Helen said he didn't drive the hearse himself, because the man who hands out bodies might have recognized him. So his mother drove it. Talk about maternal self-sacrifice— you have to hand it to the woman."

"Well, all right," said Homer. "So now he had the miscellaneous cadaver, and he put it in Rosie's car, and drove it into a ditch and set fire to it."

"No, Pip didn't drive it. He hired one of his fellow orderlies, a guy who owed him money."

Alan laughed bitterly. "So I was right. It wasn't Rosie who turned the car radio to that hard rock station. It was somebody else, some sleazeball."

Homer looked down regretfully at his empty beer glass. "Sleazeball is right."

Alan tipped up the can of beer and emptied the last drops into Homer's glass. "Well, okay, so Pip went to all that trouble to get rid of Rosie, because she couldn't very well get Castle's job if she was supposed to be dead, right? But what about the rest of the good organists in Boston? They were competitors too. What about Oates? Oh, I get it—those messed-up organs, that wasn't Oates, I knew it wasn't Oates!"

"No, it wasn't Oates, it was Pip." Mary shook her head angrily. "What really makes me mad is the way he got Oates drinking again. He kept sending him booze. That was terrible. And he double-crossed Barbara Inch. He switched a couple of pipes on the Commonwealth organ during a service, so it sounded like her own awful blunders. That was a mean trick."

Homer held up a cautionary finger. "But what about the ladder in the organ at Annunciation? Pip fell victim to that dirty trick himself."

"That was to throw us off. He didn't really fall from the ladder. He stood on the tracker rods and fell into them *very carefully.*"

"Damn him anyway," said Alan. "But look, why didn't he sabotage me? There I was, smack in his way, holding down the job he wanted. Why didn't he try to get rid of me?"

Mary laughed. "Luckily you saved yourself. You told him you didn't want the job anyway. As soon as Castle came back, you were going into organ building full time."

"But what about Charley?" said Homer. "On the night Alan found him, why was Charley still there? Why didn't Pip take Charley too?"

"Panic. There he was, with Rosie on his hands, bleeding and unconscious, so he carried her out of the house, leaving all the doors open, and while he was dumping her in the car a neighbor leaned out a window and said, 'Hey, what's going on down there?' So Pip jumped into the car and drove away and turned Rosie over to his mother, the practical nurse."

"A neighbor saw him?" said Alan. "Why didn't the neighbor call the police?"

"Oh, neighbors," grumbled Homer, "they witness muggings and rapes and murders, and say tut-tut and go back to baking cookies, or whatever. I'll look into it. How badly was she hurt?"

"I gather it was pretty bad. Helen thought Rosie was dying. Fortunately her mother knew the most essential things to do right away, and kept her alive."

"Thank God," whispered Alan.

Mary was suddenly ravenously hungry. "Alan, you must have something in this place besides corn chips." She poked in his cupboard. "Look, I thought so. There's a lot of baby food in here, yummy little jars of apricots and peaches, and here's a can of soup. I'll heat it up. Have you got a pan around here somewhere?"

Alan found one on the floor under a phone book. He had to ransack the room for the can opener, which turned up at last wedged under a closet door. Mary opened the can and stirred the pot. Warm smells of vegetable soup rose from the stove.

"What about Helen and Rosie?" said Alan. "They were living there together, with Helen's mother taking care of them both. What was that like?"

Mary made a face. "Well, you can imagine what it was like. A domineering embittered woman, feeling trapped once again, taking it out on the two of them. But for Helen it was a relief. They were friends. In that grim household, the two of them clung to each other."

"So what about Charley?" said Homer, gratefully accepting a bowl of soup. "Remember that day when Alan said he saw his mother? Did Rosie really go back to her house that day?"

"I asked Helen. She said Rosie did go back. She persuaded Pip she needed more of her own things. Actually she just wanted to be sure Charley wasn't still there, abandoned and starving."

"Her hat!" Alan waved his soup spoon triumphantly. "Remember, I said she was wearing a white hat? It was a bandage around her poor head. It was Rosie, all right. Charley was one hundred percent correct."

Homer finished his bowl of soup and licked the spoon. "Are you sure this young woman was really telling you the truth? How did she know what Pip was doing?"

Mary shook her head, as if she didn't believe it herself. "He told her things she didn't want to know. He whispered things to her, he bragged about everything. If she gave him away, he said, he'd set fire to her bed while she was asleep." Mary looked angrily at Homer. "We've got to do something about her, Homer. We've got to get her out of there."

"I can see that, but how?"

It was late. They were all exhausted. Mary smoothed Alan's bed, Homer pulled himself upright with a groan, and they said goodbye.

Alan listened to their footsteps receding down the stairs. Then, reaching eagerly into his pocket, he found the slip of paper with Rosie's address, and took it to the table where his typewriter was gathering dust. He had a letter to write.

But at once he jumped up and went to the window and threw up the sash and shouted down at Mary and Homer as they climbed into their car. "He had it too, didn't he? I saw it, but I didn't recognize it. I saw him knock over a glass, and then he had a hard time standing up. Huntington's disease, he was getting it too?"

Mary looked up at him. "Yes, that's right. Helen told me she knew what was happening to him. She recognized the symptoms so well. It was the only time she cried."

Alan wanted to say that it was horrible, but he couldn't utter another word. He could only shake his head and slam down the window, while the car pulled out from the curb and crept down the steep hill, heading for home.

CHAPTER 74

These hard heads need sound knocks.
Martin Luther

Barbara Inch was as good as her word. Even with her professional career crumbling around her, Barbara kept her promise to Mary Kelly. She spent the week after Easter pursuing the past history of the ex-wife of Martin Kraeger.

The trail of wreckage was easy to follow. In every workplace, classroom or institution in which Kay Kraeger had set foot, the broken glassware was still bitterly remembered. Resentment rankled. Every victim displayed the scars Kay had inflicted, and pointed in the direction of another sufferer.

Barbara invited Mary to lunch, and showed her the list.

They sat sipping sherry in the living room of Barbara's dark apartment on Marlborough Street, while her roommate whispered on the telephone in the next room. Leaning back in her chair, Mary read the first page of the list aloud. "Oh, this is choice." By the time she had read all six pages they were doubled up with laughter.

"I could do more," said Barbara. "Her high school adviser said there was some sort of weird incident in the eighth grade."

"No, no." Mary stroked the sheaf of pages and stuffed it into her briefcase. "This is enough. I'll give it to Homer. He'll take care of it."

"Pouch, Heaviside and Sprocket, legal firm," said Martin Kraeger, holding the phone in the crook of his shoulder, trying to open an envelope at the same time. "This is the letter accusing me of child molestation. It's signed by Archibald Pouch."

"Archie Pouch!" Homer was overjoyed. "At last I'll get my own back. I've tangled with that rat before. I can hardly wait."

From the wreck of his ruined church next door, Martin could hear the grinding of trucks backing and filling, the jarring thump of rock rattling from the shovel of a bucket loader, the shouts of working men. He murmured something into the telephone.

"What?" said Homer.

Martin spoke up. "You say Barbara Inch discovered all these things?"

"That's right. Mary started it, but Barbara carried on."

"Well, thank you, Homer. Thank all of you." Kraeger hung up. His church lay in ruins, his career was surely at an end, but at this moment he felt strangely pleased.

The glossy offices of Pouch, Heaviside and Sprocket were on Federal Street. Homer remembered them well. On an earlier occasion he had been humiliated by Archie Pouch. Today he was eager for revenge.

"Hey, like I remember you," said Pouch, reaching out a finger and prodding Homer in the chest. He was a vilely handsome goon in cowboy boots and a sharp three-piece suit.

"Your client is a nutcase," said Homer. "Allow me to recite her colorful history. Item one, at the University of Vermont she accused a fellow graduate student of climbing in her dormitory window for purposes of assault, burglary and sodomy. Charges dismissed. Item two, your client charged a number of her fellow students with indecent exposure in the same women's dormitory. Case laughed out of the dean's office. Item three, she accused her professor of sociology of trying to kidnap her when he stopped his car to ask if she needed a lift. Resulting scandal rocked the university, your client was expelled. Item four, she was thrown out of another institution of higher learning for reasons described as good and sufficient. Item five, she accused a fellow employee in the Ten Cent Savings Bank on Milk Street of making sexual advances. He proved his innocence with a witness, and your client was fired. Item six—"

"Oh, shit," said Archie Pouch, "tell you what. We'll settle for seventy-five thousand."

"Item six, your client accused a delivery man of drugging a bottle of milk in order to commit rape—you know it's very odd," said Homer, interrupting himself, "when you consider that your client is a very homely woman. Well, never mind, that's beside the point. Item seven, she accused her mother's physician of—what? You tell me. You lost the case in court."

Pouch looked chagrined. "Oh, yeah, it was kind of dumb. Necrophilia, having sex with a dying woman."

"Item eight, your client sued the night nurse in the obstetrics ward of Brigham and Women's Hospital for failing to attend to her crying baby. Items nine, ten, eleven and twelve, your client attempted to close four separate and distinct daycare centers by spreading rumors about child molestation. Items thirteen, fourteen and fifteen, she brought tumult and interdepartmental strife to three different places of employment with absurd accusations against colleagues, namely—"

"Oh, the hell with it," said Pouch. "Tell Kraeger we're dropping the case." He turned on his heel and shouted at an underling and went out and slammed the door.

CHAPTER 75

Jerome, in his excitement, used to beat his heart with stones but could not beat the maiden from his heart. Francis made snowballs. Benedict lay among thorns, Bernard had so mortified his body that he stank abominably. . . . These great men were as much slaves to it as we are.   Martin Luther

Alan wrote his letter to Rosie seven times. The first letter ran to fourteen wild gushing pages. The second was a single page of cold hard fact. In the end he filled three typewritten sheets with a straightforward account of all that had really happened, from the true story of the fire at the Church of the Commonwealth to the day he found Charley on the steps of the church, to the collapse of the vaulting, the death of Philip Tower and the confessions of Pip's sister, Helen.

Reading the letter over, Alan wondered if Rosie would believe it. She herself had witnessed some of it, but Pip Tower had warped the truth, and frightened her, and sent her fleeing across the Atlantic.

When she called him from Germany, her voice was tentative, almost inaudible. "Alan Starr? This is Rosie Hall."

Alan had been getting dressed. He held the phone in one hand and his left shoe in the other. "Oh, hello," he said, and then his throat closed and he could hardly say anything more. It was an unsatisfactory conversation. Rosie said she was coming home with Charley as soon as she finished at the university. She would write. He said a squeaky goodbye.

The day of Rosie's transatlantic phone call was the very day when the litigation over the construction of the new hotel on the other side of Clarendon Street from the Church of the Commonwealth was settled out of court.

Neither side in the negotiations was happy. Each accused

the other of misrepresenting the facts. But now, at last, work could begin again on the digging of the excavation and the shoring up of the steel sheeting lining the hole with rakers and tie-back anchors.

On the first day back at work the construction engineer walked around the site, getting a feel of the place again. It had been months since he had seen it last. As soon as the lawyer called to say that construction could go forward, his mind had leaped ahead, he had thought of everything. He rehired the bulldozer and the fleet of dump trucks and the pile driver, and he even remembered to notify Boston Edison that he needed access to the switch for the pump under manhole 277.

But it was strange. This morning when he got down inside the manhole he found the pump switch in the *on* position, rather than *off.*

"Shit," he said conversationally to the guy from Boston Edison, "the fucking thing's been on the whole time. Well, what the hell." Shrugging his shoulders he climbed out of the manhole and the Boston Edison guy whanged the cover back down and went away.

Only later in the day did the construction engineer look across the street to the wreckage of the Church of the Commonwealth and think about the continuous uninterrupted drawdown of groundwater by the sump pump. Twenty-five gallons a minute had been sucked up by the pump, night and day, week after week, ever since that morning last March when they had been ordered off the job.

For a moment his face went blank. Then he reached into the bulging pocket of his down vest, jerked out his lunch bag, pulled out a sandwich and hollered at the driver of the ten-ton truck that was backing into the hole, "Jesus Christ, you sonofabitch, why don't you look where you're going?"

Hell, if the assholes across the street didn't know enough to check the water level on those old wooden pilings, it was their own goddamned fault.

CHAPTER 76

Seven times tried by fire will prove
Thy silver undefiled:
Await with patience too God's word
And find it pure and mild.
Hymn by Martin Luther

After such a catastrophe as the violent destruction of the Church of the Commonwealth, the collapse of a thousand tons of stone, how could a congregation ever settle down and become itself again?

Kenneth Possett did it. His aggressiveness and financial know-how, combined with the energy and will of Martin Kraeger, were an upward force more than equal to the downward pull of gravity that had dropped three neo-Romanesque vaults into the wreckage of the granite footings beneath the sanctuary.

Ken was a dynamo from the beginning. On the very day of the disaster he whipped together a fundraising committee with Edith Frederick as chair. For the next two months the two of them bustled around the city of Boston, talking to people of enormous distinction, appointing them to the committee—the mayor, the governor, six college presidents, four museum directors, three Pulitzer prize–winning economists, a dozen directors of international investment houses, and seventeen regional heads of multinational corporations. In addition they sought out particular people famous for their wisdom and insight—Putnam Farhang of the Paul Revere Insurance Company, Harvard Fellow Shackleton Bowditch, and even that legendary financier Jane Plankton of the Cambridge firm of Janeway and Everett.

Miss Plankton came to the site of the devastation with Ken Possett and clasped her old hands in horror, remembering from her girlhood the window of the Wise and Foolish Virgins that had sparkled so gaily, high in the east wall. A wise virgin herself, she cried out with sympathy and swore to lend a hand.

At once they took her into the undamaged part of the building and up the stairs to Martin Kraeger's study. There, seated at Kraeger's desk while he looked on in wonder, Miss Plankton wrote out a list of her best bets, obscure little firms that were about to surge skyward. Her two brothers in the firm of Janeway and Everett were well known for their experience and acumen, but Jane was famous for the inspired and mystical nature of her predictions. She was seldom wrong.

Ken tested one of her suggestions with his own funds, and tripled his investment in three days. Then, greatly daring, he transferred some of the blue-chip investments in the church portfolio to the next item on Miss Plankton's little list. This venture also blossomed, doubling the income of the church in a single week.

"You did *what?*" cried Bill Foose, another member of the church's Investment Committee. "You made an executive decision to transfer funds without consulting the rest of us?"

Ken blushed. "Well, of course if it hadn't worked so well, I would have replaced the sum myself."

They stared. Ken Possett, of all people, saying a thing like that. But they couldn't deny their pleasure in the result. "What else is on her list?" inquired Marybelle Trotter.

Ken opened his pocket notebook. "She seems to have a lot of faith right now in automobile services—Howie's Rebuilt Engines, Acme Auto Body, Moody's Mufflers and Brake Shoes, Victory Electronic Tune-ups."

In a moment they were crowded around him, staring earnestly at Miss Plankton's precious list, taking down her infallible strokes of genius on the backs of envelopes.

In the meantime, with something as gigantic as the rebuilding of the church to think about, the complaints against Martin Kraeger melted away. It was strange, but in the presence of such an overwhelming physical disaster the congregation settled down, its peeves forgotten. The usual crowd came to Sunday services in the rented school auditorium and listened calmly, while James Castle played simple preludes on a portable organ and the choir sang anthems under the leadership of Barbara Inch. Barbara had been asked by Castle to stay on as choir director because his doctors had urged him to slow down a little.

Thanks to Homer and Mary Kelly, most of the old complaints against Martin Kraeger had vanished. It was true that he still preached powerful sermons against the administration in Washington. And he went right on denouncing the same international corporations from which his money raisers were wheedling capital funds. But this sort of truculence was a long-standing failing on his part, and everybody was used to it.

It was too bad that Edith Frederick did not live long enough to see the new edifice for which she was raising so much money, and to which she was contributing so much of her own wealth. In the year following the collapse of the church, Martin kept a close eye on his old friend. He couldn't help noticing her growing fragility, the hesitation in her step. Strangely enough, he found a new attractiveness in her wasted face as the pure structural outlines showed beneath the skin, and the lineaments of vainglory fell away. He was intensely moved by her tireless efforts to help with the capital drive, to make a hundred personal visits to wealthy men and women of her own generation. Who but Edith Frederick could charm such massive contributions out of their pockets? In the last days of her life she accomplished one more good thing, although the consequences were not at all what she intended. She went to Martin's office to warn him about that dangerous woman Barbara Inch.

"I see Loretta's gone," she said, noticing the empty desk outside Martin's door.

Martin beamed. "Thank God. I fired her, bang, just like that. It was a pleasure. I didn't know firing people could be so satisfying. She didn't seem to mind. She gathered up all her spinach and Brussels sprouts and whatnot and walked out. I'm looking for a replacement."

"Actually," said Edith, "I came to warn you about someone else. I think you ought to know, Martin, that you should watch out for Barbara Inch. She's after you."

Martin was thunderstruck. "My dear Edith, you're out of your mind. Nobody in this world is after me. I'm too fat and old and ugly."

"Nonsense, you are very attractive to women." Edith smiled at him. "If only I were thirty years younger! But honestly, Martin, I think you should be aware that Barbara Inch has her eye on you. A word to the wise. I mean, a woman can always tell."

Martin scoffed at her gently, and kissed her, and changed the subject. But he was profoundly affected. Feelings he had suppressed for months came rushing to the surface, and this time he let them flood his consciousness, and send warm blood all over his body. At once he went looking for Barbara.

He found her in the music room, riffling through stacks of music, choosing anthems for the choir to sing in November. She looked up as Martin came in, and the music slipped from her fingers.

He crossed the room and stood close to her and came to the point at once. "Edith Frederick thinks you have your eye on me. Is it true?" He took her hands. "My dear, is it true?"

Barbara could say nothing. She merely looked at him, and in a moment he reached out his great bearlike arms and drew her in.

The first word to the wise had been delivered to Barbara by Kay Kraeger, the second to Martin by Edith Frederick. The two words had been enough.

Edith died without knowing of the failure of her advice. One Sunday during the morning service in the borrowed school auditorium her bony companion pressed closer and closer, ever more tender and attentive, and then as the sermon began he lifted his arm and struck her kindly on the breastbone. Martin hurried down from the stage and the people in the endless rows of folding chairs turned and craned their necks, as Death disentangled his rickety limbs from Edith Frederick and rattled down the aisle to embrace old Dennis Partridge, and dig bony fingers into his sleeve.

PENTECOST

✦ ✦ ✦ ✦ ✦

"Des heiligen Geistes reiche Gnad"
Chorale harmonized by J. S. Bach

The Holy Spirit's plenteous grace,
Dropped down from heaven upon this place,
The gift of tongues did freely fall
On the Apostles, one and all.

CHAPTER 77

Give thanks to God, who from the jaws
Of death saved you and me.
Now like a flock of birds we rise,
From clutching snare set free.
            Hymn by Martin Luther

Dear Alan Starr,
There's so much to say, I don't know where to start. But
first I must thank you for being so kind to Charley! We're
coming home as soon as I'm through at the university. I'll
write again. Gratefully,

                                        Rosalind Hall

Dear Rosalind Hall,
It was easy to be kind to Charley. He's such a great little
kid. How is he? Yours,

                                        Alan Starr

Dear Alan,
Charley's fine. He's really big! We take walks around the old
city, and I'm the one who gets tired, not Charley. My organ
teacher taught him to say Herr Professor! Thank you for
telling me about Pip's death. I don't know what to say. I'm
so sorry about the church, and I'm sorry about Pip too.
Once upon a time he and I were close friends. Especially after my husband's death, because Pip was so kind and sympathetic. There was something about him that made it easy
to talk—you know, about private, painful things. He told
me about his frustration over not having a good job, and
about living at home with his mother, and breaking his
heart over his sister Helen. And I told him about the things
that tormented me, terrible things! My husband's death was
the worst, because it was partly my fault that Ted died in
the crash of that helicopter. He'd borrowed my Seconal, because we were both having trouble sleeping, but I think he

took too much, and fell asleep at the controls while he was in the air. When I looked at the bottle afterward, a lot of the capsules were gone. Pip said of course it wasn't my fault, and he was so comforting, I began to feel better. So I told him about the other things. I said I was sure I was responsible for the fire in the balcony of the church and the death of the sexton. I'd been smoking in the balcony that night, sitting there at the organ, and, not only that, there had been a lot of candles at the wedding, and some of them may still have been burning. So when I heard the sirens and the fire engines and went out and saw the church on fire, I thought it was my fault. And then they brought out the body of the sexton, and he was like someone burned at the stake, and I was the one who had touched a match to the straw. And then I told Pip I'd had accidents with church candles before, not once, but twice. I just went on and on, weeping and sobbing, and told him everything. I even told him I'd tried cocaine in high school, and got caught. And Pip said forget it, just forget it. But I couldn't, because Mr. Kraeger was taking the blame for the fire in the church, and I knew it wasn't his doing, it was mine. I wanted to confess. I wanted to let everybody know he was innocent. But Pip kept saying, no, I shouldn't, because everybody had forgiven Martin Kraeger, and his back was broad enough to carry the blame, whereas it would ruin my career, my whole life. Just shut up, he said, so I did, but I felt awful about it.

I've got to stop now. I'll tell you more in my next letter. Here's a picture of Charley at the castle on the rock above the city, with the River Neckar in the background. Do you have one of yourself you could send me? Cordially,

Rosie

Dear Rosie,
That's a great picture of Charley. Here I am. Actually I don't really look this good. I've got an uglier picture, but I'd rather have you think I look like this. Yours,

Alan

Rosie was coming back. Alan looked around his sloppy room on Russell Street and imagined what she would think of it. The place had to be cleaned up. He began sorting his books and papers and picking up his clothes. Only then did he rediscover, in the pocket of his padded vest, the box in which sound had been locked up.

It was Rosie's copy of her own performance of "Wachet Auf." Pip Tower had wanted to steal it, he had torn apart Rosie's apartment in a failed attempt to find it, he had set fire to the apartment in order to destroy it, he had come to the church in the middle of the night and fired a shot at Alan and killed Harold Oates, and then he had been crushed himself under tons of falling rock, all for the sake of this little strip of tape.

It didn't matter now whether the voices at the end of the cassette could be disentangled from the music. It was obvious that the male voice would be Pip's. But just out of curiosity Alan found an audio technician in the phone book and went to him and handed the tape over and told him what he wanted.

"Well, I'll try," said the technician. "The trouble is, a lot of the music will be in the same range as the human voice, so I can only erase the high and low frequencies. But it should help some. As for the crying baby, Jesus! Well, some of it's probably high frequency, and we can get rid of that much. I don't promise anything. I'll call you."

A few days later Alan came back, and the technician played for him the brutalized tape.

"Awful," said Alan, grinning at him. "God, it's awful." The music was tinny and thin. When the voices began they were scratchy and flat, but the words were audible, and there was no question about the identity of the man who said, *You're not just in trouble. You're in prison.* "Good," said Alan. "Thank you, it's what I thought. The dissonance has been resolved."

"Dissonance? What dissonance? Was it a question of dissonance?"

"No, no, not on the tape. It's J. S. Bach. It's the way he uses dissonant harmony sometimes and then resolves it. You know what I mean."

"Could be. I'm not into classical music myself. Jazz. Bluegrass. Country music." The technician turned on a machine, blasting Alan with a nasal whine from Nashville. Swiftly he paid his bill and headed for 115 Commonwealth Avenue.

Cleaning up his own place had been simple. Doing something about Rosie's was a different matter. Alan spent the last of his savings on a couple of new rugs as much like the ruined ones as he could find. He hired a crew of upholstery cleaners. He painted the walls and ceilings and washed the woodwork, with Mrs. Garboyle popping in now and then to exclaim with rapture, "She's coming home! I can't believe it! Darling Rosie! That adorable boy!"

Alan was excited himself, although he tried to temper his anticipation with Homer's warning, "You know, kid, she may not be what you expect. You pick some random girl out of a sack, it's like a pig in a poke. She may be pretty ghastly."

Rosie wrote another letter.

Dear Alan,

It's too bad you're not as good-looking as your picture. I really like it. You look like your sister Betsy. I'll bet I'd like the ugly picture too. I wish you'd send it.

Where was I? I think I was telling you how Pip kept urging me to say nothing about the night of the fire, to just keep quiet about it and it would be all right.

But then suddenly he changed. He came in all upset, about a week or ten days before Christmas, and he'd just come from the hospital where he works, and he'd heard some people talking. He was scrubbing down a bed with Lysol or something, and he couldn't help hearing this police detective in the next bed, who was recovering from an appendectomy, and he was talking to some visitors, a couple of other policemen, about the case of some woman, and pretty soon Pip knew they were talking about me. They knew my whole history, he said, they knew about the cocaine and the earlier fires and they knew everything about my involvement in the fire in the Church of the Commonwealth, and they said I was about to be arrested. Worst of all, they'd been investigating my husband's death all this time, and they were ready to indict me for murder. They had the bottle of Seconal! And the label had my name on it, not Ted's, and my fingerprints were all over it. When Pip told me that, I ran to the medicine cabinet, and it was true, the bottle was gone. So there were two things, two terrible things. The death of the sexton was only manslaughter, Pip said, but Ted's was murder in the first degree. They'd be coming for me any minute, he said, any minute! They might be coming to the door right now. So of course I ran to the window to look, and they weren't there, but I knew they were coming soon, very soon. Pip said I had to decide right now. I couldn't waste time. I had to pack up and run away with Charley.

Well, of course I was shocked and scared, and I didn't want to go, but he kept harping on Charley. If I were put in prison, what would happen to Charley? So at last I said, all right, I'd go to Heidelberg and study at the university and take master classes with Hans Holder on the organ in the Jesuiten Kirche, because I'd always wanted to do that. It was a reasonable solution. I could already speak German, because I'd spent a couple of years in Cologne with my parents as a child. Then Pip said I'd have to use a false name, and he'd fix up a passport and order our plane tickets. Oh, I didn't want to go, but he kept saying, what about Charley? So I packed and got all ready, but then a couple of days later, it was a Sunday, I felt so tearful and sentimental, I went to church, and they have childcare, so I dropped off Charley and went to the service and heard Martin Kraeger's sermon. And afterwards I heard some of his parishioners whispering to each other about what he had done to the church, and how a lot of people were dissatisfied—you know the way there are always people who want to stab their minister in the back. Anyway, I changed my mind. When Pip came, I wouldn't go. I couldn't let Martin Kraeger take the blame any longer. And then Pip tried to drag me out—well, you know the rest. Affectionately,

Rosie

P.S. Do you know if Helen's all right?

Dear Rosie,
I hope you got the flowers. I've never sent flowers to anybody before, especially across the sea. You're probably tired of roses, because probably that's what everybody gives you.

Of course you know it was Pip who took the bottle of Seconal, not the police. And he was lying about what happened in the hospital. The day he got so excited and told you to leave must have been the day he discovered Castle had stomach cancer. Instantly he had a powerful ambition to get Castle's job, and that meant getting the other candidates out of the way by one means or another, especially you. So he made up that story about the police detective in the next bed and came rushing to tell you to leave the country.

I don't know how Helen is. Living with her mother must be horrible. Give Charley a kiss for me.

Love,
Alan

Dearest Alan,
The flowers are beautiful. I've always loved roses best. I kissed Charley for you. Could you send my love to Helen? And take some for yourself! I'm tired of being just a messenger!

Rosie

On the tenth of June Alan waited at the international terminal, watching travellers emerge from customs one at a time—a Japanese family, an elderly couple, a knot of teenagers with backpacks. He recognized Rosie at once, the woman with the small child. Charley was walking by himself, a big two-year-old. Rosie's hair was longer and darker than he had expected, and she was thinner than the girl in the picture.

Her luggage cart wobbled toward him. She tugged Charley forward.

He hadn't meant to embrace her at once, but neither of them could help it. Then Alan swept up Charley and held him over his head and looked at him. "Oh, Charley, it's really you."

"Daddy," said Charley.

"I'm sorry," said Alan to Rosie. "It's my fault. I taught him to say that."

"It's all right," said Rosie. "I'm glad you did. I'm so glad."

They had built up a great thirst. In Rosie's apartment Alan showed her all that was new, and together they put an exhausted Charley to bed in his crib. Then they went at once into the bedroom and helped each other out of dress and trousers and shirt and underwear, fumbling with zippers and buttons, kissing lips, shoulders, breasts, elbows, thighs.

"Oh, Rosie, Rosie, I was afraid we would never—I mean, there's a story by Henry James."

"It's all right," murmured Rosie. "It's all right now."

◆ ◆ ◆ ◆

CHAPTER 78

We must read, sing, preach, write, and compose verse, and whenever it was helpful and beneficial I would let all the bells peal, all the organs thunder, and everything sound that could sound.
                                                            Martin Luther

"Mary, dear, that's a stunning outfit. What do you call it?"

"It's my new persona. I made it. I'm going to make a lot of them. I've solved my wardrobe problem at last."

"Well, it's just great. Really majestic and African or maybe Greek. This is who you really are, is it? You reached down deep within yourself and fumbled around and decided this is what you're all about?"

"Oh, no. I was just lazy. I took a huge piece of fabric and cut a hole in the middle and left openings for my arms in the side seams. That's all. It's not a big statement, or anything like that. But I'm never going back to being ladylike. Never in all this world."

It had been a year since the collapse of the vaulting. The cycle of church life went on, even while the rubble was cleared away and new concrete pilings were driven down with the tremendous earsplitting noise of the pile driver ramming them into the ground. As the new walls went up within the shell of the old, the school auditorium continued to house the ceremonials of the Church of the Commonwealth. There were weddings and funerals and the welcoming of new parishioners.

Helen Tower was one of the new members. Alan and Rosie introduced her to the church, they took her to concerts and museums and the zoo, she played with Charley, she gossiped with Rosie. Then Mary Kelly found a cooperative residence for people with miscellaneous nerve disorders, and at last Helen was able to move out of her mother's house.

It wasn't easy. Mrs. Tower needed someone to be indebted day and night to her bitter sense of sacrifice, and she was reluctant to let Helen go. It took the assistance of Mrs. Barker in the Department of Social Services to pry Helen free.

"My God," she said to Mary, "how long has this been going on?" And she signed her name to the document with a sweep of her hand.

For Mrs. Barker the rescue of Helen Tower was one of her small successes. There were so many failures! That same afternoon she experienced another disappointment while preparing to inspect a foster home on lower Washington Street. A young woman with a familiar face was leaning in a doorway, and Mrs. Barker recognized Deborah Buffington, although her childish features were almost obscured by thick eye makeup and lipstick, her thin fair hair was frizzed into a giant aureole, and her skinny midriff was bare above a shiny tight skirt.

"Why, Debbie, hello," said Mrs. Barker. "Do you live in this neighborhood now?" But she knew with a sinking heart that this wasn't where Debbie lived, it was where she worked.

Debbie glanced at her ferociously, and walked away on tottering heels.

Mrs. Barker rolled her eyes to the sky above lower Washington Street, which was a washed-out blue, empty of clouds, sun, moon, and God. "Just another botchup by the Department of Social Services," murmured Mrs. Barker to herself, and then she began wondering what was happening to Debbie's daughter Wanda. Oh, God, she'd have to find out about little Wanda.

The new Church of the Commonwealth was dedicated on a Sunday morning in May, only two years after the collapse of the old building. James Castle played a tremendous prelude, Martin preached, Barbara's choir sang at the tops of their lungs, and the congregation stared around at the plain white walls and the broad windows of clear glass. Some people were pleased, others were disappointed.

"It's so cold," said Bill Foose. "No stained glass, no carving, no decoration."

"I miss the way it used to be so spiritual and medieval," complained Melanie Chick. "Now it's so *modern*."

Ken Possett was irritated. "Well, at least," he said, "it won't fall down."

After the service Martin and Barbara Kraeger invited the Kellys over for a drink. It was their first wedding anniversary. "And we want to show you something," said Martin.

Mary was curious to see their place on Dartmouth Street. She had visited it once with Homer during Martin's bachelor days, when it had been bleak and shabbily comfortable. Now she was amused to find it just the same. Barbara too seemed to have little interest in interior decoration. But she was a good cook. There were tasty hot things to go with their drinks.

"Delicious," said Homer, gobbling half a dozen. "You know I have to confess, Reverend Kraeger, your church services leave me in a condition of mortal starvation. You provide food for the soul, I suppose, not for the body, is that it? Why don't the ushers pass around trays of snacks every time you make a point, up there in the pulpit? Now, tell us, what are we here to see?"

Martin grinned at him. "Walter Wigglesworth's book. They found it in the cornerstone of the old building when they cleared out the last of the rubble."

"Behold!" said Barbara. She heaved a large box onto the table and lifted the lid.

"Good heavens," said Mary. "There it is, *Divine Inspiration,* just like the book in the painting."

"Yes," said Martin. He stroked the cover. "The painting's torn to shreds, but at least we've got the book."

"Well, what do you think?" said Homer eagerly. "Is it really inspiring? Is it full of spiritual secrets, you know, from one clergyman to another?"

"Oh, it's inspiring, all right." Barbara laughed. "See for yourself." She lifted the heavy book and dumped it carefully in Mary's lap.

Mary turned the pages slowly. "Oh, dear, I'm afraid it's mostly Ella Wheeler Wilcox and James Gates Percival and Edith Matilda Thomas. How disappointing." She shook her head, and dropped the book onto Homer's knees.

Homer too was stunned. "*Seated one day at the organ, I was weary and ill at ease, and my fingers wandered idly over the noisy keys—* My God, I'd forgotten all about 'The Lost Chord.'

You know, Martin, somehow I don't think this stuff is quite right for you."

"Well, apparently it was just right for Walter Wigglesworth. One glance at his precious book and glory descended."

"I guess the moral is," said Barbara, "one person's inspiration is another person's—"

"Hogwash," suggested Homer.

"Crap," offered Mary.

Martin laughed. "So what am I going to do for inspiration now? I'll have to go right back to the Bible and all my old standbys."

"Henry Thoreau might come in handy now and then," suggested Homer primly.

"Oh, sure, and Jim Castle's music, naturally, but the trouble with music is, you can't take out a tidy quotation and repeat it in the middle of a sermon."

"No, that's right," said Homer. "Music just gives you a sort of general unspecified, amorphous, inchoate jolt of something sort of shapeless and unorganized and vague and—"

"But sometimes," objected Barbara, "it can be ecstatic and organized at the same time. I mean—"

"Right," said Martin, "it's the language of the soul, sort of. It's not something you can put into words. It's really kind of—"

"Wonderful," said Mary, "and of course you *can* put words to it, and then sometimes even the dumbest words are transformed into something that's really—"

They gave up trying to define the inspirational nature of music. It didn't matter. Whatever it was, the organ from Marblehead provided it in the rebuilt Church of the Commonwealth, Sunday after Sunday, with its two thousand seven hundred and sixty pipes of wood and metal.

Castle called it glory, and perhaps it was. At any rate the Contra Bombarde bawled and bellowed, the Rohrpipe hooted, the Cymbal squealed, the Trumpets blared their fanfares, the eight-foot Diapason did the solid work of holding it all together in a harmony, perhaps, of the spheres, and the DIV INSP stop knob continued to be connected to nothing, to nothing on earth at all.

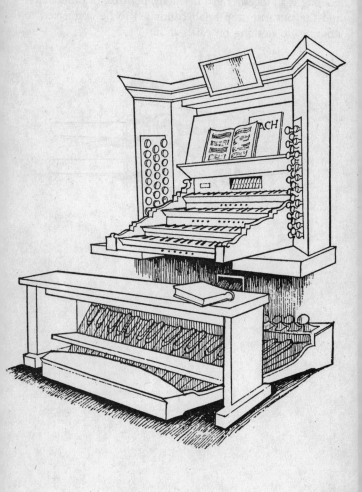

✦ ✦ ✦ ✦

AFTERWORD

T he Church of the Commonwealth does not exist. The site I have given it, the northwest corner of Commonwealth Avenue and Clarendon Street, was once occupied by the Hotel Hamilton. The hotel was demolished in this century, and there is now a playground where it stood.

I apologize for tearing down a perfectly good apartment house on the northeast side of the same corner, in order to dig the excavation for a new hotel. The Church of the Annunciation is another fiction.

The rest of the Back Bay as it appears in this book is real enough: the streets paralleling the river, each with its own character—Boylston, Newbury, Commonwealth, Marlborough and Beacon; the alphabetical cross streets—Arlington, Berkeley, Clarendon, Dartmouth; the churches—Trinity, Emmanuel, Advent (all Episcopal), Old South and the Church of the Covenant (United Church of Christ), First and Second Church (Unitarian Universalist), First Lutheran and First Baptist. The Church of the Advent and St. John the Evangelist (both Episcopal) are at opposite ends of Beacon Hill; King's Chapel (Unitarian Universalist) is near Boston Common on Tremont Street. The physical plant of the Church of the Commonwealth is modelled on that of Old South Church in Copley Square, but some of the illustrations are adaptations of Harvard Epworth Methodist Church on Massachusetts Avenue in Cambridge. The stone vaults are a figment of my imagination.

The registration of the new tracker organ in the Church

of the Commonwealth is very much like that of the Fisk or-
gan in Harvard's Memorial Church, with the addition of a
Bärpfeiffe stop, Trumpets en Chamade, and a Glockenspiel.
The Contrabassoon has been replaced by a Contra Bom-
barde. The drawings are sketches of this organ and of the
Rieger organ in Wellesley's Village Church.

Perhaps I should point out that storm drains and sewers
in the Back Bay and the pilings supporting churches and
houses, the Boston Public Library, and all the businesses and
shops are in satisfactory condition, as far as I know. The water table rises and falls, as always, in whimsical patterns of its
own.

In dir ist Freude, from *The Little Organ Book* of Johann Sebastian Bach

FOR THE BEST IN PAPERBACKS, LOOK FOR THE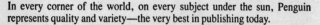

In every corner of the world, on every subject under the sun, Penguin represents quality and variety—the very best in publishing today.

For complete information about books available from Penguin—including Pelicans, Puffins, Peregrines, and Penguin Classics—and how to order them, write to us at the appropriate address below. Please note that for copyright reasons the selection of books varies from country to country.

In the United Kingdom: For a complete list of books available from Penguin in the U.K., please write to *Dept E.P., Penguin Books Ltd, Harmondsworth, Middlesex, UB7 0DA.*

In the United States: For a complete list of books available from Penguin in the U.S., please write to *Consumer Sales, Penguin USA, P.O. Box 999—Dept. 17109, Bergenfield, New Jersey 07621-0120.* VISA and MasterCard holders call 1-800-253-6476 to order all Penguin titles.

In Canada: For a complete list of books available from Penguin in Canada, please write to *Penguin Books Canada Ltd, 10 Alcorn Avenue, Suite 300, Toronto, Ontario, Canada M4V 3B2.*

In Australia: For a complete list of books available from Penguin in Australia, please write to the *Marketing Department, Penguin Books Ltd, P.O. Box 257, Ringwood, Victoria 3134.*

In New Zealand: For a complete list of books available from Penguin in New Zealand, please write to the *Marketing Department, Penguin Books (NZ) Ltd, Private Bag, Takapuna, Auckland 9.*

In India: For a complete list of books available from Penguin, please write to *Penguin Overseas Ltd, 706 Eros Apartments, 56 Nehru Place, New Delhi. 110019.*

In Holland: For a complete list of books available from Penguin in Holland, please write to *Penguin Books Nederland B.V., Postbus 195, NL-1380AD Weesp, Netherlands.*

In Germany: For a complete list of books available from Penguin, please write to *Penguin Books Ltd, Friedrichstrasse 10-12, D-6000 Frankfurt Main 1, Federal Republic of Germany.*

In Spain: For a complete list of books available from Penguin in Spain, please write to *Longman, Penguin España, Calle San Nicolas 15, E-28013 Madrid, Spain.*

In Japan: For a complete list of books available from Penguin in Japan, please write to *Longman Penguin Japan Co Ltd, Yamaguchi Building, 2-12-9 Kanda Jimbocho, Chiyoda-Ku, Tokyo 101, Japan.*